Praise for *Mirror Image*

"Dennis Palumbo establishes himself as a master storyteller with his first crime novel, *Mirror Image*. Using his background as a licensed psychotherapist to good advantage, Palumbo infuses his fast-moving, suspenseful story with fascinating texture, interesting characters, and the twists, turns, and surprises of a mind-bending mystery. Very impressive."
—Stephen J. Cannell
writer/creator of *The Rockford Files*;
New York Times best-selling mystery author

"*Mirror Image* is a deviously plotted thriller with lots of shocks and surprises you won't see coming, and a smart, sympathetic hero-narrator who takes you along as he peels back layers of lies and wrong guesses to get closer to the truth."
—Thomas Perry
Edgar-winning, *New York Times* best-selling author

"Dennis Palumbo's experience as a psychotherapist hasn't just helped him make his hero, therapist Dr. Daniel Rinaldi, authentic, human and a man in full, it's endowed him with the insight to craft a debut thriller filled with action, deduction, and romance, expertly paced for maximum mind-bending suspense."
—Dick Lochte, award-winning author and critic

"Dennis Palumbo's novel is stark and disturbing but there's a humanity running through the core of it that makes this book special. Maybe it's Palumbo's dual training—as a writer and as a psychotherapist—that allows him to plumb the depths and bring up not only darkness but those occasional diamonds of light that sparkle and illuminate and make a book worth reading."
—T. Jefferson Parker
Edgar-winning, *New York Times* bestselling author

"*Mirror Image* is a standout mind-bender! A wonderfully constructed novel that has you seeing double—and all through the eyes of an intriguingly fresh character: a psychologist. Dennis Palumbo knows his craft. This guy can write."
—Ridley Pearson
New York Times best-selling crime author

Mirror Image

Mirror Image

A Daniel Rinaldi Mystery

Dennis Palumbo

Poisoned Pen Press

Poisoned Pen Press
6962 E. First Ave., Ste. 103
Scottsdale, AZ 85251
www.poisonedpenpress.com
info@poisonedpenpress.com

Printed in the United States of America

To
Lynne and Daniel
with love

"All pasts are like poems; you can derive a thousand things, but you can't live in them."
—John Fowles

Acknowledgments

The author would like to thank the following people for their generous help and support:

First and foremost, Ken Atchity, whose enthusiasm for this project never wavered;

I'm also grateful to Annette Rogers, my editor at Poisoned Pen Press, whose astute guidance has been both welcome and extremely valuable;

Robert Rosenwald and Barbara Peters, founders of Poisoned Pen Press, which really does, as their slogan says, promote Publishing Excellence in Mystery;

Jessica Tribble, associate publisher and all-around go-to person—thanks for walking me through this;

My friends and colleagues, for their support of my work over the years—with special appreciation to Hoyt Hilsman, Bobby Moresco, Richard Stayton, Rick Setlowe, Bob Masello, Garry Shandling, Jim Denova, Michael Harbadin, Claudia Sloan, Dave Congalton, Charlotte Alexander, Mark Evanier, Bob Corn-Revere, Lolita Sapriel, Mark Baker, Andrew Gulli, Mark Schorr, Bill Shick, Fred Golan and Dick Lochte;

Jeffrey Trop, MD, for his wise counsel and unflagging encouragement;

And, lastly, Dr. Robert Stolorow, for his profound insights into both the causes and treatment of trauma.

Chapter One

Shame is a deep well.

Face tightened in anguish, a young man named Kevin Merrick was sitting in my office, telling me about the first time he'd slept with his sister.

"I musta been eight or nine," he said. Kevin was in his early twenties, but thinning hair and pained, sunken eyes made him seem older, faded somehow. The three-week-old growth of beard didn't help.

"I'm sorry, Dr. Rinaldi. I didn't think...I mean, shit, it was all so long ago..."

"Take your time," I said.

I let a silence fill the space between us. But inwardly, I was thrilled. After months of intensive work, of building trust and rapport, he was finally opening up, risking connection with another human being.

Not an easy task for him, considering what he'd been through. Life had battered him, left invisible bruises no less real than the old needle tracks on his forearms, the self-inflicted scissor-cuts emblazoned on his wrists.

His eyes flitted to the window overlooking Forbes Avenue five floors below. The steady drumming of the rain masked the usual hum of afternoon traffic snaking out of the Pitt campus.

Beyond, through the grey-black webbing of the storm, you could just make out Heinz Hall and Carnegie Museum, venerable Pittsburgh landmarks, hunched beneath the regal spire of the Cathedral of Learning.

Kevin stirred, hands massaging the arms of his chair. This calmed him. It had taken time, but my office had finally become a sanctuary for him, a refuge. Once, he'd jokingly referred to it as the Womb with a View.

He *did* seem to derive solace from the place: the tan leather sofa, the twin brass table lamps, the marble-topped antique desk. My worn Tumi briefcase leaned against it.

Then there was the stuff my patients *didn't* see—the photo of Barbara taken on our honeymoon, tucked away on a book shelf; a copy of *Ringsider* magazine, autographed by Sugar Ray Leonard, sharing cabinet space with patient files and a pewter hip flask—a gift from my old man after the Allentown fight, twenty years ago. Consolation prize, I guess. I'd gone down in the seventh.

Kevin's eyes had been slowly sweeping the room, as though searching a crowd for a familiar face. His gaze rested finally on some psych journals stacked on the floor.

"Karen was four years older than me," he said at last. "We were in her room…it was late. I knew I was supposed to be in bed, but Dad hadn't tucked me in…"

"Did he usually do that?"

"Every night, since the year before, when Mom died…I remember people saying what a burden he had now. That he had to be both mother *and* father to me and Karen…" He blinked up at me. "What was I saying?…"

"That your father wasn't in Karen's room that night."

"Yeah. Anyway—" His voice caught. "All of a sudden, we were in her bed…just foolin' around…Laughing. I remember how *girlie* I thought the sheets smelled…"

"Girlie?"

"You know what I mean." A crooked smile. "I remember thinking, Yuck, how could she sleep in here?…Those pink, frilly sheets with the girlie smell…Yuck!"

His smile faded.

"Then..." He dropped his head. "Then she *touched* me... and I was so confused. It felt so strange. Not bad, but not good either...I mean, I knew what was happening...I was already pretty good at jerkin' off, ya know?..."

He tried to laugh, a dry rasp that held no mirth.

"And I loved Karen so much...I mean, I *hated* her, too, 'cause she was my older sister and a bitch and everything, but I also loved her...and ever since Mom died, she was—"

He looked away again, at the window.

"And then she had her pajamas off," he said slowly, "and I could see—it was dark, but I could sorta see everything, and *feel* everything...and it felt so..."

Suddenly, a sheet of shame reddened his face. His hands shot up, palms pressing against his eyes, like a child trying to push the tears back in. He cried out.

I leaned closer, on the edge of my leather chair. I could almost see a shudder move through his body, like a powerful wave. I also saw how thin and bony his shoulders were under his light blue shirt.

Finally, he turned, eyes searching for mine. His face was bleached of color, lifeless.

"I...I felt her hand on the back of my neck...I was shocked, surprised...The hand was so strong, pressing my face down... forcing my mouth between her legs...forcing me to...making me...*taste* her..."

Great sobs wracked his whole body. Without a thought, I reached across and held him, felt his body slump in my embrace. His tears were wet on my cheeks.

We stayed that way for an endless minute, the blood pounding in my ears. My own feelings shot through me. Anger. Pity. Some vague sense of anguish...

Finally, I released him, gently guiding him back against his chair. He seemed to be swallowed by it, legs half-drawn up in a fetal position. He closed his eyes.

I took a breath. Kevin and I would have to explore the meaning of my embracing him at some future date. For now, it was enough for me to know that I'd had the impulse to hold him, to cradle him, and so I did.

Fuck it, somebody should've done it a long time ago.

As I watched him settle down, I thought again about the clinical risks I often found myself taking with him. After all my years as a psychologist, it was always new; each patient a new beginning, a chance to teach myself how to do therapy all over again.

I recalled, too, something that Jung had told one of his students. "It's not what you know that heals," he said. "It's who you are." A sentiment I agree with. It's also a notion that conveniently flatters the narcissism woven into every therapist's personality.

Kevin's body had relaxed, and he was reaching for the Kleenex on the side table. As he dried his eyes, I managed a smile, which he managed to return.

Some deep chasm, some important gulf between us had been crossed, and we both knew it. Despite the potential for significant pain ahead, he'd made another crucial step on his personal journey. And at the end, I believed—I *had* to believe—there would come a healing.

I'd never find out.

Within an hour, Kevin Merrick would be dead.

Chapter Two

Kevin had been referred to me six months earlier, following confinement in the West Penn County Psych Ward. He'd been found wandering the aisles of a *7-11* store, bruised and bleeding at three in the morning. Barefoot, wearing only torn pajamas.

He led the police back to his place, an apartment just off-campus, where the trashed room backed up his story: he'd been awakened around midnight by an intruder in a ski mask rifling his bureau drawers. They struggled, then Kevin managed to get free and out through the window. He told the cops he could only remember running like hell, into the night...

And then his memory went blank, until he found himself in the convenience store hours later, being rousted by two uniformed patrolmen.

After his discharge from the ward—where a computer check revealed he was no stranger to local mental health facilities—Kevin was questioned again by the police and a sympathetic Assistant DA, but he could offer no new information about the crime. All he could remember about the man was that he was big, and reeked of sweat.

"Probably a hype, needin' cash," the investigating officer said. "Fuckers don't use ATM's."

The police got a break two days later, when another local resident called 911. Same scenario: sweaty guy in a ski mask helping himself to cash and jewelry in the bedroom. Only this time the apartment's occupant—a retired steel-worker named Hanrahan—grabbed a baseball bat from under his bed and knocked the guy senseless. He was still groggy when the cops arrived.

With his mask off, the burglar was just another junkie, a scared black kid from the Hill District. His name was James Stickey, aka "Big Stick." Nineteen, with two prior convictions. They gave him eight years upstate.

Meanwhile, Kevin just wanted to forget about the whole thing and get back to class. It was springtime, and a week from finals. But his blackout the night of the crime, along with reports of nightmares and frequent disorientation, had worried the Assistant DA enough to call the Department's Chief Community Liaison Officer.

Who was worried enough to call me.

People like Kevin are my specialty. Victims of violent crime. Those who've survived the assault, the kidnapping, the crime itself—but who still lived with the trauma, the fear. The daily, gut-wrenching dread.

Or, perhaps even harder, lived with the guilt of having survived at all when a loved one didn't.

My job is to help them remember what they need to remember, so that they can forget. Or at least achieve a *kind* of forgetting that lets them move on with what's left of their lives.

Though the Pittsburgh Police have a number of shrinks on the payroll, they sometimes make use of outside consultants. Which is how I got into this in the first place.

‹›‹›‹›

It was about five years ago, during the public panic and media firestorm caused by Troy David Dowd, the monster they dubbed "the Handyman." A serial killer who tortured his victims with screwdrivers, pliers, and other tools, he'd murdered and dismembered twelve people before his eventual capture.

Dowd would snatch people outside of roadside diners or highway rest stops in isolated rural areas throughout the state.

Only two of his intended victims managed to escape. One of these, a single mother of three, was sent to me.

Her name was Sylvia. Bound with duct tape, she'd been kept for two days in a stifling, stench-filled canvas tent, buried under a pile of twisted, decaying body parts from his earlier victims. Somehow, during one of Dowd's frequent absences, she was able to cut through a section of tape using the sharp edge of a metallic watch band still strapped to the wrist of a severed forearm.

For weeks after her escape, she'd wake up screaming, clawing the air at the imagined bloody, blackened stumps encasing her. Recurrent flashbacks of her ordeal with Dowd continued long after his arrest and conviction.

In fact, it wasn't until almost a year later—by which time Dowd was on Death Row, where he still sits pending his latest appeal—that Sylvia was willing to even leave the house. She'd walk around the block once with her oldest daughter and go back inside.

I considered this a victory.

My work with her caught the attention of the city fathers as well as the press, and soon the cops were using me on a regular basis whenever they feared for a crime victim's mental health. Or when the DA worried that the victim's emotional stability might be in question when it came time to testify.

Why me? Because of my background in Post-Traumatic Stress, working with Gulf and Iraqi War vets. Because I'd treated numerous victims of trauma and abuse at two state hospitals.

And probably because of something else, something personal, that inextricably bonds me to my patients, and always will. Something *very* personal.

Kevin was stirring.

I smiled at him again, absently pushing my hand back through my hair. Then I instinctively—an instinct reborn a thousand times—felt near the top of my head for the old scar, the familiar ridged surgical scar, where the bullet had gone in...

Chapter Three

Kevin couldn't look at me. Shifting uncomfortably, he finally bolted from his chair. He stood, trembling. Staring out at the black October rain.

I turned to the small table beside my chair for a pen. The monogrammed one from my alma mater. It was gone.

I sighed. I knew where it was. With his body half-turned away from me at the window, I couldn't tell which pocket it was in. But I knew Kevin had it. He'd taken it.

As he'd taken other items from my office over the past months. A stapler. A letter-opener. A silver card case.

In the byzantine mesh of our relationship, Kevin was aware that I knew he'd taken these items, and that I probably wouldn't mention it. And felt both shame at his deeds and elation that he was getting away with it. Then shame at feeling the elation.

What Kevin had been doing, these last few months of treatment, was becoming me.

Hesitantly at first, and then quite blatantly, he'd begun dressing like me. Gone were the Pitt sweatshirt and jeans. He now wore therapeutically-neutral dress shirts and Dockers. Not to mention dark-framed glasses. His beard, without my telltale sprigs of gray, was coming in nicely.

Then today, when I opened the connecting door to the waiting room for our regularly scheduled appointment, I found Kevin hanging up a dripping jacket next to mine on the standing coat rack.

"Can you believe this weather?" he'd said. "Cold as hell, too. I shoulda worn a sweater or somethin'."

I must have been staring at the coat rack, for his glance nervously followed mine. His jacket was light brown, very similar to my own new Eddie Bauer. I'd only worn it a couple times to the office. But enough for Kevin to have registered it and found a similar one.

As I sat here now, watching him stand with his back to me at the window, I thought about those two jackets hanging on the rack in the next room, and wondered if I knew what the hell I was doing.

In our first few sessions, he'd appeared to have some classic "borderline" symptoms—poor self-image, a history of drug use and failed, half-hearted suicide attempts. He was suspicious of my attempts to help him, especially when I prodded him to relive the experience of finding an intruder in his room. These memories only reinforced his sense of violation, of vulnerability.

Then, below these feelings of dread and panic, the predictable litany of self-criticism emerged: he should have locked his windows. Fought back harder against the guy. Hell, maybe he *deserved* what happened to him…

I'd seen it a hundred times. The victim blaming himself as a way to make sense of what's happened, to gain at least the fantasy of control over events that threatened to overwhelm him.

These feelings faded over time, and with them the nightmares, the panic attacks. We began to concentrate less on Kevin's symptoms and more on him.

It was then, as our bond deepened, that Kevin started to mirror me in dress and appearance. I didn't do anything to stop it. Given the shattering loss of his mother at a young age—and now with confirmation of my hunch that he'd been sexually abused as well—it was no surprise he'd be yearning for an identity. Even one that was borrowed.

"If I'm like you," some part of him was saying to me, "I'll be okay. So I'll *become* you."

And I'd been letting him do it. Part clinical judgment, part gut feeling. He'd come into my practice so lost, so fragmented, he needed a platform on which to stand. I was willing to *be* that platform. For how long, I didn't know. I'd hoped that same gut feeling would tell me when it was long enough.

A position I got all kinds of grief for. Recently, I'd presented Kevin's case at one of our peer review conferences at Ten Oaks, a clinic in suburban Penn Hills where I'd been on staff before going into private practice. Predictably, some of my colleagues there were outraged at what I was doing with Kevin. Or allowing to happen.

"It's just an extreme variation of Kohut's twinship longing," I'd argued.

Brooks Riley, the new shrink down from Harvard Med, disagreed. "No, it's a pathological accommodation. The poor bastard's willing to disappear, to allow himself to be literally *usurped*, and replaced by you."

He shook his head. "Christ, Rinaldi, I knew you were nuts. I didn't know you were arrogant as well."

Riley was a prick, but maybe he was right. I knew I was taking a big risk—sure as hell not the first I'd taken in my work. But I was convinced it was paying off. Kevin's bond with me was stronger now. He'd just trusted me enough to reveal the details of his incest with his sister.

A painful, anguished revelation. In the strange, hallowed vocabulary of my world, a breakthrough...

<> <> <>

I cleared my throat, which made Kevin tilt his head slightly. When at last he spoke, still gazing out the window, his words seemed faint as ghosts.

"One day, it all came out. I mean, about me and Karen...I got sick at school and was sent to the nurse's office. Then, all of a sudden—I don't know why—I start talkin' about my sister foolin' around with me..." He turned at last. "I ratted her out, Doc."

"You were just a kid, Kevin," I said gently. "In turmoil. No way you could deal with what was going on inside you. Hell, it was brave of you to—"

"Brave?" He gave me a fierce look, as though I were an idiot. "I screwed everything up, man. It was *me!*"

"What do you mean?"

"I mean, the shit hit the fan. The County sent social workers to our house—my sister just…she just *freaked.* And my poor Dad…Banford's a small town, with small, angry minds. They blamed *him.* He worked at the one goddam bank in town. People deserted him, said he was a bad father—"

"Wasn't he? He sure didn't protect you—"

"His wife had *died* the year before!" Kevin's eyes filled with tears. "And, yeah, he drank…Who the hell wouldn't? Two kids to raise alone, and then *this* shit—"

"Kevin, you can't blame yourself."

"I coulda kept my mouth shut. I coulda dealt with it."

"At eight years old? Come on…"

He looked away from me again. "Big deal. It had already been going on practically every night for months, maybe a year. Why didn't I just—"

I hesitated. Waited for whatever it was he needed to say to work its way out.

"Karen and me…what she did…what *we* did…" He let out a breath. "It's not like I didn't *like* it, ya know?…"

He turned to me at last, a deep angry blush burning his cheeks. This was his secret shame, his sin, and he wanted me to see it.

"I *hated* it…and I *loved* it…Okay?"

I nodded.

Another long pause, as though time had frozen. Then, hand trembling, he reached to touch the back of his chair.

"Later on, after I was placed in County Services, and Karen was sent to counseling…Right in the middle of all this, my Dad takes off…"

"Takes off?"

"Leaves town. Gone. The social worker has to tell me about it herself, one day out in the playground. Dad's skipped town, nobody knows where. No note, nothin'."

"I'm sorry, Kevin."

"So…me and Karen are placed in separate foster homes, and life goes on in Mayberry." A shrug. "Wasn't too bad. My foster father only beat me when he needed a fix, or his old lady wouldn't fuck him, or he lost money on a ball game…" His pale eyes found mine. "Coulda been worse."

"Jesus, I don't see how."

I tried to collect my thoughts. In our first sessions, Kevin had told me only that his mother had died, and that he'd spent his adolescence in foster care. He'd always been vague about the details concerning his father. I figured they'd come in time. Well, they were coming now…

"Did your own father ever contact you after that?" I asked. "Have you talked at all with him since then?"

His silence gave me the answer.

He looked down, his breathing shallow. There was only the sound of the rain clattering against the windows, the ticking of the thermostat as the heat kicked on.

"Where's Karen now?" I asked.

"She left town soon after Dad did. Ran away from her foster home. I never saw *her* again, either. I just found out a couple years ago from some third cousin or somethin' that Karen was out west. Married, with a kid. Anyway, that's the rumor. I had a P.O. box address for her in Tucson. Wrote a few times. She never wrote back." His eyes narrowed. "Hell, that's fine with me."

"Is it?"

"I guess it has to be, right?"

Another long silence. Then, abruptly, he came around and sat down again. He pushed his glasses up on his thin nose. Glasses he didn't need, I reminded myself.

I phrased my next words carefully. "I appreciate the fact that you told me about all this. I know it was hard."

He sat back. "Well, as long as *you're* happy…"

As I'd expected, after such a painful revelation, Kevin's defenses were up. With feigned casualness, he slowly crossed his legs, hands clasped at the knees.

Though there were still ten minutes left on the clock, I knew today's session was over.

‹›‹›‹›

Outside, the storm had subsided, the rain now a misty curtain drawn against the blackness.

Kevin stood up, stretched. "So, Doc, what's the diagnosis? Bi-polar? Psychotic?"

"Beats me. I haven't read that chapter yet."

"Very funny. It's just that I wonder what all this shit has to do with why I came here in the first place."

I took a long pause before answering.

"The way I see it, there are some things you've needed to talk about for a long time. Regardless of what brought you here, some part of you wants to talk about them now."

He considered this. "But I feel a lot better," he said. "I mean, about that night. No more nightmares and stuff. No more guys in ski masks."

"That's good news," I said, walking him to the door. "If anybody deserves a good night's sleep, you do."

"Tell me about it."

I opened the door to the waiting room. It was empty. Kevin was my last patient of the day. As he started for the coat rack, I stopped him.

"Kevin, I meant what I said in there. It took guts to reveal such an old, painful secret…"

He gave me an odd look, a mixture of intensity and ruefulness that I'd never quite seen on his face before.

"Hell, man, I got *lots* of secrets…"

And with that, he turned away. I shut the door behind him.

Chapter Four

I went over to my desk and jotted down some notes about the session while it was still fresh in my mind. I'd need ammo if I was going to present Kevin's case again next week at Ten Oaks.

Though I was still smarting from Riley's criticism, I usually got valuable insight and support from most of the others there, and I felt I needed it. Especially now, in the wake of these latest revelations. The road ahead was going to be tricky.

I glanced at my desk clock. I had plans for dinner, having promised to meet my cousin (and accountant) Johnny Manella at a restaurant in nearby Shadyside. Figuring dinner traffic and rain, parking in the newly gentrified district would be hell. I knew I better get going.

I got up and locked Kevin's case folder in the filing cabinet. Then I checked my voicemail. Three calls, nothing urgent. One even announced good news. A former patient, who'd been raped four years ago, had since married, and had now delivered a baby. In a happy, astonished voice, she promised to send me a photo of mother-and-child, doing fine.

I couldn't help smiling. Nice message to get, especially at the end of a long, hard day. Grabbing my briefcase, I locked the waiting room door behind me and padded down the narrow, carpeted hallway.

Ahead of me, Lenny Wilcox, building maintenance, was backing out of the storage room, balancing an armload of boxes.

He was in his fifties, with smooth black skin and the build of an SUV.

"Hey, Lenny," I said, holding open the door with my foot. "How ya doing?"

"Not bad." An eyebrow went up. "By the way, Doc, I saw you on CNN the other night. A show about that kidnapping in Miami. You ain't gettin' famous, are ya?"

"Hardly. They just needed some talking heads for a panel on trauma. The after-effects on the victims. Since I'd been consulted on the Florida case—"

He shook his head. "Man, I don't know how ya do it. Those poor kids…what they went through…"

"Yeah," was all I said. Lenny didn't know the half of it. And like the rest of the public, hopefully never would.

We exchanged brief good-byes, then I took the stairs down to the parking garage. The stairwell was damp and concrete-cold. My footsteps echoed, a hollow sound that only emphasized the silence as I descended to parking.

Briefcase in one hand, jacket in the other, I shoved the heavy metal exit door open with my shoulder. A blast of cold air hit me as I stepped into the near-vacant garage.

The dim, cavernous structure was criss-crossed with shadows and damp from the rain. Shallow puddles had formed here and there on the uneven concrete.

Then I saw it.

Or thought I did. A flicker of movement, a shadow flitting against the far wall…

I tensed, senses alert. A surge of adrenaline. I peered into the darkness. Nothing.

I glanced over at the attendant's booth near the exit, though I knew he'd be gone for the day. And he was. His little overhead light was out.

I looked around. Not a thing. Probably never was. I'd had a long day, my brain was fried. And yet…

Ignoring my every instinct, I started walking. Most of the other tenants kept banker's hours, so it wasn't unusual for me to be the last one out. I was used to walking across the deserted parking structure, past no more than a dozen remaining parked cars, to get to my assigned space.

So why this prickling at the back of my neck? This sense of foreboding?

"Jesus," I said to myself, aloud. "Get a grip."

My voice echoed off the slab pillars and the scalloped ceiling, absorbed by the deep shadows. I headed toward my car that was parked around the corner, hidden from view by a double column. As I approached the turn, walking briskly, I heard—something.

Some*one*. Crying out. Choked, guttural, in agony.

I dropped the briefcase and coat, took another step—

And heard something else. Behind me. A staccato beating of footsteps, running fast to my left.

I whirled in time to see another access door, at the far wall, closing. It clanged noisily.

I turned back in the direction of the cry. At first I saw only my car, a green reconditioned '69 Mustang, half in shadow, parked in its usual spot. In the space next to it was a beat-up looking Nissan.

As I approached the vehicles, I heard the sound again. I broke into a run, looking wildly about.

Where the hell—?

He was in the darkened space between the two cars. Body crumpled on the cold asphalt. Covered in blood.

It was Kevin Merrick.

Panic tore through me in a fluid rush, as though my heart was pumping ice water. For a moment I couldn't move. Or breathe.

Forcing myself, willing each step, I came toward him, crouching beside him. I reached down and lifted his head, cradling him...for the second time that day.

His eyes were wide, white with horror. His mouth moved, lips trembling, trying to form words. Only a scarlet foam trickled out.

I looked down at his chest, at the spreading rivulets of blood. My mind raced blindly, trying to make sense of what I was seeing.

He'd been stabbed. Repeatedly. Savagely. The blood was... everywhere. Seeping, lava-like, wet and dark. Pooling beneath us.

Finally, as if tearing myself from a dream, I laid him back down on the asphalt and rummaged in my pockets for my cell phone. I found it and dialed 911.

After leaving the address and confirming that an ambulance had been dispatched, I turned back to Kevin.

But it was too late.

Crouching again, I peered down into sad, lifeless eyes. Only his blood, forming an ever-widening circle on his chest, was moving.

I sat back on my heels, stunned. I couldn't swallow. Couldn't think. I just sat there in the awful concrete silence, staring down at him.

Then, through a fog of pain and shock, I became aware of something. Noticed something for the first time.

Kevin was wearing my jacket.

Chapter Five

Sergeant Harry Polk, a beer keg in a wrinkled blue suit, stared at me as I sipped strong, hot coffee. He had the opaque eyes and dour expression of your basic middle-aged civil servant, a man who'd long accepted that most things in his life weren't going to get much better.

I met his gaze through a cloud of steam rising up from the mug. He then glanced at my hands, now washed clean. Only an hour before, amid the chaos of the parking garage, I'd stood in a taped-off corner, numb as a stone, while a Crime Scene tech wiped Kevin Merrick's blood off my hands and deposited the swabs in a plastic evidence bag.

The memory flickered in my mind. Patrol units with flashing lights. A crime lab van with blackened windows. CSU techs in jump suits. An ME wagon, whose bored driver leaned against the hood, listening to blaring hip-hop music. His partner, equally bored, zipping Kevin's body into a large plastic bag.

Polk was openly staring at my hands, with a cop's interest. I'd wondered when he'd notice the purple marks, the discoloration around the knuckles.

"You box?" Surprise etched his florid, drinker's face.

"Golden Gloves. Pan Am Games. A million years ago."

"You any good?"

"Coulda been a contender." My voice had an edge. Not a conversation I wanted to be having right then.

"Why'd ya quit?"

I shrugged. "Marriage. Grad school. Life…Now I just fool around a little in the gym."

He digested this in silence. I guess the picture didn't quite fit the frame. I get that a lot.

Polk nodded at the cassette recorder on the table between us. "Ya mind?" he asked.

"I know the drill."

"Nothin' to worry about. You're a witness, not a suspect. Got a consultant's contract with the brass." An insincere smile. "Hell, you're practically family."

It was going to be a long night. I rubbed my neck, feeling the tight knots like lug nuts under the skin.

Polk and I sat across from each other in a cramped, windowless interrogation room. There were four such rooms sharing the top floor of the old precinct house. A century of brutal Pittsburgh winters had etched huge worry lines in the face it showed the world.

I thought of the rooms below us, the pallid faces of the uniforms on night-shift, the morgue-like ambiance. Old coffee, leftover sandwiches, fading careers.

"Sorry you caught this one," I said to Polk.

A shrug. "Luck of the draw." He looked at his watch. "Where the hell's Lowrey?" His partner, I assumed.

The closeness of the room was stifling. The pea-green walls, water-stained ceiling tiles, linoleum floors. The smell of sweat, cigarettes, and fear.

I glanced at the thick mirror to my left. One-way observation window. Were we being observed? Hard to imagine the precinct captain and some Assistant DA coming down here in the middle of the night. Kevin Merrick was a poor college student with a psychiatric history and no family of consequence in the area. Nobody but a homicide detective on night shift, like Polk, would get out of bed for that. If the victim hadn't been white, I doubted whether even Polk would've shown.

"Fuck Lowrey," Polk said. He turned on the recorder. "This is a preliminary interview with Dr. Daniel Rinaldi regarding the murder of Kevin Merrick, Case File Number 772-33. The time is 12:30 AM, Tuesday, October 12th."

His voice had become oddly stilted, formal. Being on tape made Polk nervous, I noted. After all his years on the force.

"The victim was in treatment with you, Dr. Rinaldi?"

"Yes, he'd been referred to me by Angela Villanova."

"The Chief Community Liaison Officer."

"That's right. She refers crime victims to me when there's concern about the person's mental well-being."

"And what were you and Kevin Merrick working on? I mean, what was the problem?"

"Sorry. Villanova referred him, so that's already in the record. Beyond that, I can't talk about it."

"Patient confidentiality, eh?"

"In a situation like this, it's called privilege."

His voice hardened. "Yeah? Well, in a situation like this, a trial judge can revoke that privilege."

"Fine. Let me know when one does."

He swore under his breath and stopped the tape. "What the fuck's up? This is a goddamn murder investigation."

"I know." I narrowed my eyes at him. "Look, I want to nail the bastard who did this more than you do. And there *are* things I can tell you that might help. But most of the content of Kevin's work with me has no bearing here. Not that I can see. Family stuff, childhood stuff."

"The usual therapy bullshit, eh? No offense."

"None taken. But—"

"Look, Doc." Polk's face flushed with anger. "I know a judge who's a real night-owl. How 'bout I call him and get a phone authorization to revoke privilege? How 'bout I do that before I bust a blood vessel or some fuckin' thing?"

Before I could respond, the door swung open and a tall, well-built black woman in a gray suit entered. She was very pretty, with close-cropped hair and violet eyes. Without a glance in my direction, she slid into the empty seat next to Polk and handed him a file folder.

As Polk flipped through the pages, the woman extended her hand across the table. Her handshake had a lot of muscle behind it.

"I'm Detective Eleanor Lowrey," she said, with a quick, business-like smile. Her lips and nails were painted the same shade of burnt red. "Sergeant Polk's partner."

"Where you been?" Polk said to her, eyes scanning the folder's contents. Papers, plastic pouches, clippings.

"Forensics. The ME's. Lieutenant Biegler's office. Ya know, just screwin' around." She regarded him coolly. "It's a slow night, murder-wise, so we caught a break. Fast turnover in the lab."

"Yeah, some break." But Polk's face had tightened. Slowly he closed the file and lay it next to the legal pad.

"You've been holdin' out on us, Doc." He was smiling.

"No shit. I think I told you why." I was tired, and Polk's attitude was wearing a little thin.

He tapped the file. "Says here the victim was wearing eye-glasses, but the lenses were just clear glass. Crime scene photos show his beard looks kinda like yours. Same with his jacket. Funny, too, about the jacket. About three sizes too big. Lab also found *this* in his pocket—"

He tossed a thin plastic envelope on the table between us. Inside was a monogrammed pen. The initials *DR*, in gilt-edged gold, were visible through the plastic.

"Yours, I assume." Polk was enjoying himself.

"Yes. Kevin took it. During the session. He often…took things like that. Personal things of mine."

"Like the jacket?"

"Maybe. His was hanging next to mine on the coat rack. Though he may have taken it by accident. I didn't realize till I saw his body that the one I was carrying was *his*. In my rush to get out of the office, I just grabbed the jacket hanging on the rack and left. I assumed it was mine."

"Jesus," Lowrey said, with such quiet intensity that Polk and I both turned to her. "You know what this means?"

I knew only too well.

"*I* was the killer's target, not Kevin Merrick."

Polk shrugged. "The kid's about your height, with a beard and glasses, wearin' your jacket. He's walking through a dark parking garage toward his car—"

"Which is parked next to mine. So it looks as though Kevin is in fact me..."

Lowrey cleared her throat. "The ME reports multiple stab wounds with a long, thin blade. Knife, ice pick, no way to tell. Brutal, vicious."

She looked at me.

"What pathologists call a 'pattern of rage,'" I said.

"It's just the preliminary autopsy report," she went on. "Gonna take another couple days to get a drug panel, hair and fiber, the works."

Polk angled back in his chair. "So the killer jumps Merrick, starts slicin' and dicin'. Even if he realizes by then that he's got the wrong guy—"

"He has to finish the job," Lowrey said quietly.

No one spoke for a full minute. Meanwhile, Polk began spreading the crime scene photos before us. I forced myself to look. Kevin's dead, sad eyes stared up at me from the blood-soaked asphalt.

The two detectives seemed to fade from my field of vision. I picked up one of the photos, staring now myself, as though to burn the image of Kevin Merrick into my brain.

"Arrogant..." Riley's words echoed in my ears. There had been a real psychological risk in allowing Kevin to identify so intensely with me. He'd so hungered for a model, a paternal image to relate to. I'd reasoned that we'd work through the identification, give him the confidence to let go of needing to be like me. In time, he'd be able to claim a more authentic sense of himself.

In time. Except that he'd run out of time. By becoming me, he'd intersected with a part of my life neither one of us knew about. By becoming me, he'd died the horrible death that was meant for me.

Lowrey sensed my thoughts. Her hand touched my forearm. "Whoa, you can't blame yourself for this."

I met her gaze. Then I pulled myself out of my chair, looked down at the two detectives.

"Where you think you're goin'?" Polk said.

"Out. I need some air."

Chapter Six

I stood in the precinct parking lot, unmindful of the cold and the continuing drizzle. Headlights twinkled in the night. A few pedestrians hurried by, heads ducked low in their coats or under umbrellas, hands jammed into pockets.

A sudden smell of tobacco hit my nostrils. When I turned, I found Polk and Lowrey standing beside me. Polk's unfiltered Camel glowed dully in the wet gloom.

"Lieutenant says we can cut you loose for the night," Lowrey announced. "But if you remember anything more—"

"I wish I did. All I heard were footsteps running away. All I saw was a door closing."

The three of us stood there, listening to the sounds of the Steel City at night. Car horns, the splash of a rain puddle. A distant chorus of drunken laughter. Students, probably, coming out of a bar. Kids who couldn't imagine that they wouldn't live forever.

"So this Merrick kid," Polk said off-handedly. "He wanted to turn into you, or somethin'? *Be* like you?"

"Not exactly." I thought about saying more, somehow explaining myself. But no words came.

Polk grunted. "Shrinks. Christ."

"Look," I said, "why the hell are we just standing here, wasting time? Kevin's killer is out there somewhere."

He bristled. "You tellin' us how to do our jobs now?"

"Yeah, if that's what it takes."

Polk showed me a lot of teeth. "Geez, Doc, ain't you done enough already?"

I felt anger boil up in my throat.

"Hey," Lowrey said sharply, taking a step between us. Polk and I still glared at each other.

Lowrey glanced at me. "Look, there's not much we can do before we get the forensics, anyway. Maybe run a back-ground check on Kevin Merrick, his family, friends…"

"You won't find much," I said.

"I had that feeling," she replied. "We're havin' a helluva time just finding any next-of-kin to notify."

"He's got a father who could be anywhere. And a sister in Tucson. But I don't know her married name."

"Poor kid." Lowrey shivered in her coat. "Sounds like the proverbial little boy lost."

"Yeah," said Polk, "only now he's little boy dead."

‹›‹›‹›

I sat in the passenger seat as Harry Polk drove his blue Ford sedan up the winding streets toward Mount Washington, just south of the city. I had a trim two-story house near the Duquesne Incline, overlooking the Point. Sergeant Polk was driving me home.

We'd sat in an awkward silence for five minutes, the only sound the slap-and-swish of the windshield wipers. The wet, gloomy streets were nearly deserted.

"Must be nice havin' all that juice downtown," he said absently, lighting another cigarette from the butt of his last one. Acrid smoke drifted in the air between us.

"What do you mean?" I watched the row of World War II-era brownstones and duplexes, gabled and weather-beaten, caravan past my window, against a backdrop of deep Pennsylvania woods.

"Angela Villanova," Polk said. "Community Liaison. I hear you and her are pretty tight. *Paisans,* eh?"

I shrugged. "She knew me from years back, sent some people to me for help. Just started from there."

"I remember. I read about you in the *Post-Gazette*. 'Shrink Turns Personal Tragedy Into Personal Mission.' Somethin' like that, right?"

"You know reporters." I said nothing more.

"Fuckin'-A," he replied. I thought he was going to lower his window and spit.

I wanted to change the subject. "By the way, I'm not a psychiatrist. I'm a clinical psychologist."

"Who gives a shit?"

"The AMA, for one. State licensing boards."

"Uh-huh. That's real interesting. Listen, those people Villanova sent you...that was about the Handyman, right?"

"Yeah. A couple people he grabbed got away. But even so, you're looking at major trauma. Nightmares. Flashbacks. I worked with one of those survivors."

"Yeah, well *I* worked with the victims." His voice grew bitter. "What was left of 'em."

"You were on the Task Force?"

"Me and every other cop in town, plus the FBI, the ATF... Man, if it had initials, it was climbin' up our ass, tellin' us how to do our jobs." He looked over at me. "It was a local cop who finally got him, ya know that? Kranksi. Another big dumb Polack, like me. Brought the guy in."

"I remember."

"Christ, what Dowd did to those poor people...Women, kids, he didn't care. One truly sick fuck, that guy..."

His hands tightened on the steering wheel. "Hear who's playin' him in the movie? DeNiro. Can you *believe* they're makin' a *movie* about that piece o' shit..?"

"I heard. Serial killers are big box-office."

"Well, ain't that nice." He shook his head. "Tell that to the vics. And their families."

He gave a hacking cough, a sputtering of rage. Fished in his pocket for another Camel. Came up empty.

I said nothing. If he wanted to say more, he would. I knew he wouldn't. He was a cop. He'd have nightmares, an alcohol problem, a busted marriage, and an early death by colon cancer. But he wouldn't talk.

We made the turn onto my street, whose edge fell away onto a panoramic view of the Three Rivers and the glistening lights of contemporary Pittsburgh. Gone were the steel mills and factories; in their place stood razor-thin buildings of glass and chrome, of software and bond trading.

The city had changed a lot since I was a kid, a shot-and-a-beer town colliding with the Information Age. Though sometimes, like tonight, I missed the Pittsburgh I grew up in. Forged by immigrants. Musty like the smell of damp wool. A mosaic of thick accents and old neighborhoods, clanging trolleys and cobblestone streets. Before mini-malls and decaf lattes. Before spaghetti became pasta.

Polk slowed the car, as I pointed up ahead to my place, freshly painted a quiet yellow a few years back. I'd also added a rear deck that jutted over the edge of the hill. The houses on either side, my neighbors, were coal-dark, except for tiny porch-lights that made them seem somehow more vulnerable, not less.

"Thanks for the ride," I said as he pulled over to the curb. "When can I get my car back?"

"Tomorrow. Oh, and Biegler ordered some surveillance. No big deal. A unit drivin' by your place every twenty minutes, somethin' like that."

"Surveillance?"

"Hell, yeah. Maybe the killer knows he got the wrong guy. Maybe he don't. If not, he'll find out soon enough. This'll be all over the morning news."

"Jesus Christ," was all I could say.

"It's just hittin' you now?" He laughed. "You're so busy feelin' guilty, you forgot to worry about your *real* problem. Namely, some fucker's out there lookin' to kill you."

Chapter Seven

I spent the next thirty minutes working out my frustrations on the heavy bag in the basement, throwing combinations under the cold glare of the track lights. The large, pine-paneled room is lined with boxes and old tools. Like the unconscious itself, a windowless vault below ground level, a hoarder of memory and regret.

Barefoot, stripped to my shorts, I was covered in sweat. I had Chick Corea on the CD. Loud. It was three a.m.

I worked it hard. Muscles aching, eyes stinging with briny sweat; fists going numb, long past pain. At the end, I clung to the bag, face pressed against the slick, damp leather, gasping for breath.

Memory fragments flickered like heat lightning in my mind: nine years old, the house on Winebiddle Street, my old man in pajamas and robe, sparring bare-handed with me, bob and weave, tapping my cheek with his powerful left, reminding me to keep my guard up, always up, another slap on my face, stinging, another life lesson, always harder than it needed to be...

I pulled off my gloves, went upstairs and hit the shower. Standing under the hot water, steam rising, I peeled the cracked, grimy training tape from my hands. Blood-caked skin came away with it.

I ducked my head under the scalding water. I wanted it to burn, to sear off the day's events, to scour me clean.

<><><>

An hour later, in jeans and sweatshirt, I stood at the window in the front room. In the storm's wake, the purple sky looked like a bruise, splotchy and sore, stretching to the horizon.

Then I saw the headlights. The patrol unit doing its regular pass by my house. I found myself nodding to them through the curtains, though I doubt they saw it. Or were even looking.

It was bullshit, and I knew it. Whoever tried to kill me wouldn't be stupid enough to try again. Not in the same night. Not with the cops alerted.

I was wide awake and jangly. Going into the kitchen, I flicked on the overhead, flooding me in light about as warm and consoling as a solar flare.

Christ, I thought, *gotta put in that dimmer switch…*

Funny, the things you think about at four a.m. A brutal murder and household chores. Death and dimmer switches.

I poured myself a Jack Daniels, pulled up a chair. Polk had suggested I come up with a list of enemies, people who might bear a grudge against me. People from my past. Ex-lovers. Colleagues. Even patients.

A list of enemies? Right. God knows, I'd pissed-off my share of people over the years—in *all* the above-mentioned categories—but not enough to warrant homicide. At least, I didn't think so.

Instead, I kept replaying Kevin's last words to me as he left my office. "I've got *lots* of secrets…"

The look I'd seen on his face. Not guarded, or challenging. Something else. In his eyes. A warning?

No, a *promise.*

I sat up. I'd misread that last moment between us. It wasn't the usual patient's yearning to disclose something painful, terrifying, held back by fear or shame.

I must have passed some test today, and Kevin was sending me a message. He wasn't *wanting* to tell me something else, something important. He was *going* to tell me. Soon.

But what?

Chapter Eight

Coffee in hand, I stood against the door to my back porch, watching the sun rise over the famed three rivers. The arteries in the heart of the city.

Even with the sparse river traffic nowadays. Not like years ago, when the riverfront below was flanked by seventeen miles of steel mills. When coal barges and tugboats clogged the Point and black smoke belched from furnaces and foundries, sprinkling the old buildings with soot.

Now, as the sun pulled deep reds and oranges out of the morning sky, the rain-washed city shone like a scale model under glass. And what new steel there was, embedded in freshly-poured concrete, was imported from Japan.

At six on the dot, I went back inside the house, poured another mug of black coffee, and turned on KDKA-TV.

Kevin's murder was the lead story on the news. The anchorman explained that the body had been found "by his therapist, Dr. Daniel Rinaldi, the noted trauma expert, who was later held for questioning by the police."

Jesus. I clicked it off, sat calmly with the mug on my knee, and waited for the phone to start ringing. It did.

The first call was from my cousin Johnny. "Shit, man, *now* I know why you didn't show up at the restaurant last night. You were busy gettin' on the news."

"That's one way of looking at it."

"Screw it. Not for nothin', though, but you coulda called. Aren't they supposed to allow you one phone call?"

"That's if you're a suspect. I'm not."

Johnny laughed on the other end of the line. Ten years younger than me, he always tried to come off as cool and cynical, a player's player. The Sammy Glick of CPAs.

"Listen, Danny, if you think you ain't a suspect, you're nuttier than one of your patients. The cops don't turn up some poor mook for this thing soon, you're it!"

"You're a goddam ray of sunshine, you know that?" I yawned despite the coffee. I could feel the fatigue settling over me now. The bone-weariness of a sleepless night. The long hours of daylight ahead. Shit.

Johnny's voice hardened. "Trust me, man. You gotta move fast. Hang up with me and call a friggin' lawyer."

"Good advice," I said, hanging up. Almost immediately the phone rang again. I let the answering machine take it.

"This is Stan Brody, WWSW News Radio. Can you just—"

I turned down the volume and went upstairs. Stretched out on the bed, I listened to the phone ringing again and again. The remorseless clicks as the machine recorded the silent messages. I knew who'd they'd be from. The press. Worried colleagues and friends. Probably a couple attorneys offering their services.

Finally, I roused myself and reached for the extension phone. I had some calls to make, too.

As I flipped through my patient roster, I realized I was about to repeat the same steps I'd taken, in almost the exact same sequence, six years before...

Calling my patients and canceling their sessions for the next two weeks. Explaining my need for some personal time. Some responded with sympathy; others got angry. As I expected, a few claimed it was fine with them. No big deal. I knew I'd have the hardest time with them when I got back.

Then I called Paul Atwood, another therapist in my office building, to see if he could cover for me. Luckily, he'd seen the morning news and didn't have to ask why.

"Look, Dan, if you need anything…" His voice grew thick. "You know, I had a patient once who—"

"Thanks," I said, cutting him off. "I'm fine."

A pause. "Right."

〈〉〈〉〈〉

The doorbell rang, waking me. I must have lain back on the bed and fallen asleep. Groggily, I turned over, pulled the bedside table clock closer. 3:15 p.m.

The bell rang again. More reporters? Damn.

I clambered out of bed, eyes adjusting to the afternoon light slanting into the room, and looked out the window. There was a patrol unit parked at the curb. My own green Mustang was parked behind it.

I went downstairs and opened the door. Two uniforms stood there, both young and wearing mustaches. One of them dangled my car keys in his hand. The other had a clipboard.

"Brought your car back, sir," the latter said, offering me the clipboard and a pen. "You have to sign for it."

"No problem." So I did.

As I pocketed my keys, the other cop said, "Sergeant Polk said to tell you to meet him downtown at nine tonight. The Old County Building. They need you there."

"Okay." What the hell was going on?

"He says to just stay put till then. We gotta pull the surveillance on your place. Manpower's short."

"Tell Sergeant Polk I'll sit tight."

"Great. You have a nice day."

Given the circumstances, a strange comment. I stood in the open doorway and watched them drive off. As soon as the patrol car rounded the corner, I went back inside, dressed, locked up the house, and got in my car.

I was not going to sit tight.

Driving down the narrow, twisting roads, I opened all the windows to get at some of that storm-sweetened air. It felt good, bracing. I was starting to wake up.

Pennsylvania is a green state, never greener than after a heavy rain. Trees glisten, leaves studded with tears. Puffs of wind push around the big clouds, sun-spackled, intensely white. The old Appalachian Hills, sloping away before spreading urban tendrils, looking as pristine and timeless as when the first settlers came over four hundred years ago.

I turned off Grandview and headed down toward the Fort Pitt bridge. Traffic was forming in clusters, soon to be backed up on the highway all the way to the airport.

I popped a Jimmy Smith CD into the player and cranked up the volume. *Organ Grinder's Swing*. With Kenny Burrell on guitar, Grady Tate holding the sticks. For a lapsed Catholic boy, the only Holy Trinity left to believe in.

I took a deep breath, letting it out slowly. My fingers drummed on the wheel in time to the music. I was awake, all right. The surreal, dream-like quality of the past twenty-four hours was gone.

In its place was an aching clarity about the obscenity of Kevin's death, and my commitment to doing something about it. Somehow making things right. But first—

I felt the rhythmic bumps from the steel plates as I drove over the old bridge spanning the Monongahela River. I saw my exit up ahead, to the right.

I had to smile. Not for the first time, I was driving down to the river to tell my troubles to a crazy man.

Chapter Nine

"So," he said. "You gonna start talkin' or what?"

Noah Frye took another pull from his beer, then went back to noodling at the piano. Built like a bear, he gave equally bear-like grunts as he played, private chortles of delight and encouragement. Like a white Oscar Peterson.

Out here on the deck of the converted barge, the breeze was cool coming up through the oiled boards. The riverfront bar, called Noah's Ark, was moored at a bank below 2nd Avenue. Every afternoon before the bar opened, Noah sat out here at his old Baldwin upright and played.

Occasionally, like today, I joined him.

"Okay," I said finally. "I guess you know about—"

"Yeah, I saw it on the noon news. Never miss it. I got a thing for the weather girl."

"Kevin was my patient, Noah. My responsibility."

"'Cause he was jumped comin' out of your office?"

"Because he was wearing my jacket. He'd been trying to look like me, dress like me…"

His hands paused above the keys. "So you figure the killer was really after *you*?"

"It's a real possibility. Cops think so too."

"So what can *you* do about it?"

"I don't know. *Some*thing. I…owe him."

Noah shrugged. Just then, a shift in the wind lifted his shirt collar, leaving one flap up. He'd never notice it, nor the way his belt had missed a few loops so that his pants bunched at the waist.

Noah Frye was a paranoid schizophrenic. Without his meds, he suffered from delusions of persecution and gruesome death. So every day he swallowed 100 milligrams of Thorazine. Followed by a Cogentin chaser to quell the Parkinsonian-like tremors caused by the Thorazine.

I met Noah eight years ago, when I was working full-time at Ten Oaks. In and out of mental hospitals since his teens, he was a gifted musician who supported himself doing construction work and odd jobs—in between bouts of delusional terror, homelessness, and street violence.

One night, Noah was standing just inside the clinic's rear gate when he saw one of the staff shrinks, Dr. Nancy Mendors, being manhandled in the parking lot. Her estranged husband had Nancy backed against the hood of her car. Noah ran over, spun him around, and gave him an elbow smash to the face. The crack of jawbone sounded like a rifle shot.

After that, Noah assumed a kind of mythic status at the clinic. It was as if he'd become a trustee, instead of just a patient. After a while, you almost forgot who he was. What he was.

Until something happened to remind you.

Once, a new staffer screwed up his meds and Noah just… slipped his knots. He disappeared, causing a mild panic as therapists and patients alike scoured the building and grounds for him.

He turned up later that day in a diner on Grant Street. He'd found a hammer and some old nails at a nearby construction site, and was going from table to table, asking if someone would please crucify him.

Not long after that, Noah's insurance ran out and he was cut loose from the clinic.

I was the one who found him, purely by chance, a few years later. Driving to work one morning, I caught sight of a homeless guy digging in a trash dumpster. His eyes were glazed, hair dirty and unkempt. Then he grinned, and I knew who it was. Whether he knew me, I couldn't be sure.

I contacted Nancy and a couple other colleagues who knew Noah, and we helped find him a job at this run-down coal barge that had just been refitted as a riverfront bar. Ironically the owner, some retired mining executive, took such a liking to Noah that he named the bar after him. While Nancy, still feeling indebted, continued to prescribe and monitor his meds.

Therapeutically, what we did was outrageous. Maybe even illegal. But it was tangible, pragmatic. A nice change for a therapist. And it worked.

Noah stayed Noah, of course. There are no miracles. Just the hope, in the end, of more good days than bad.

Sometimes, that has be to enough.

When the wind turned icy, I helped Noah pull the waterproof tarp over his piano and we went inside.

Despite the polished bar stools and hanging racks of glasses over the long, beveled counter, you never forgot you'd stepped into the interior of a former coal barge. Port-holes opened to the river, black tar paper hung from the ceiling. The faint scent of oil-soaked water. What Noah blithely called its "nautical motif."

Charlene, the bar's only waitress (and Noah's main squeeze), was already lighting the shaded candles at the corner booths. I took a seat at the bar while Noah went behind and started setting things up.

At the other end of the bar, a TV was showing the evening news. Over the anchorman's shoulder was the by-now infamous video of the Handyman's arrest. This was followed by a shot of Dowd's lawyer talking to reporters.

"Wonder how the appeal's going?" I said absently.

"Who gives a shit?" Noah said, stepping over to shut off the TV. His face grew dark.

"I don't mind the crazies," he said quietly. "It's the *evil* fucks I hate."

A silence fell between us.

A few early patrons walked in then, finding a table. Charlene went over, pad in hand, to take their order. She was from out west somewhere. Big, funny, sexy as hell. She helped run the bar and handle the books. Plus she loved Noah, which could be a full-time job in itself.

I turned back to find Noah staring at me. "Look, this Kevin kid gettin' whacked...I mean, I'm sorry and all, but this ain't nothin' like what happened to Barbara. Fuck it, you weren't responsible then, you ain't responsible now."

"I *know* that, all right?" I kept my voice calm. "Believe me, the last thing I'd do is put myself through that hell again."

"Glad to hear it. 'Cause nothin' you can do will bring that kid back."

"I know that, too."

Another long silence. Finally, I stood up, pushing off from the stool. I was vaguely conscious of other customers wandering in, their voices wafting like smoke.

I felt light-headed. I realized I hadn't eaten a thing in over twenty-four hours. Naturally, as soon as I had that thought, my stomach started gnawing.

"You want my advice," Noah was saying, "fly your sorry ass to Barbadoes and hook up with a couple horny divorcees. Think about it, man. I'm talkin' tag-team blow-jobs."

"Jesus, I wish." I glanced at my wrist; forgot my watch. "What time is it, anyway?"

"Why? Are my fifty minutes up?"

"No, I've got a date with the cops. Besides—"

Just then, I saw the color drain from Noah's face. He was staring at something past my shoulder.

"Well, fuck me," he said quietly.

I turned, as the last person in the world I wanted to see that day came through the door.

Chapter Ten

Dr. Brooks Riley, Chief Psychiatrist at Ten Oaks, was drunk. He steadied himself in the doorway, squinting with exaggerated horror into the bar.

"Rinaldi! Are you hiding somewhere in this floating menace to public health?"

I was off my stool and across the room before Riley could take another step. Faces looked up from leather booths. The murmur of voices grew still.

"What the hell are you doing?" I said to him.

Riley was about my height, with the kind of proud, old-money good looks that usually made me think of yacht clubs, not hospitals. At least when he was sober. I'd never seen him drunk before.

"We're celebrating." He raked a hand through rich, dark hair. His tie, clasped to his shirt with a Harvard alumni pin, was undone at the throat. Despite the Armani suit, he looked, to my surprise, like hell.

"We?"

He glanced back in the direction of the door. "The boss and his wife. While we're chatting in here, they're outside, battling hypothermia."

"Shit." I took Riley by the arm and marched us back out the way he'd come in.

Outside on the sidewalk, the night air had dropped a dozen degrees. A clammy chill joined the fog wafting up from the river's edge.

"We were beginning to wonder," Albert Garman said pointedly. A slight, balding man in his late fifties, he looked even less imposing swallowed up in an overcoat and thick scarf. Only his eyes, which managed to be both pale and penetrating—especially when presiding over case presentations—betrayed his intelligence and ambition. In only six years as Clinical Director, he'd turned Ten Oaks into the most successful private psychiatric facility in the state.

His wife Elaine, mid-forties, and a full head taller than her husband, shivered next to him in her fur coat. According to clinic gossip, her rail-thin figure was the result of a diet rich in cocaine.

I shook hands with both of them. "Come on, you two, let's go inside."

Elaine's laugh was raw as sand. "Honey, I've never been *that* desperate for a drink."

"We thought perhaps you'd be here," Garman said. "I wondered if you might like to join us at dinner."

Highly unlikely. This had to be about Kevin Merrick.

"We called your office," Riley sniffed, "*and* your house, looking for you. After hearing on the news—"

"Yes." Garman glanced past me, at the bar. "Then I remembered your having an interest in this place…"

"We're on our way to Schaeffer's for dinner," Riley went on, oblivious. "This way, you'd get to explain yourself over a nice lobster."

"Explain…?" I glared at him.

"Look, Dan," Garman said smoothly, "Elaine and I invited Brooks to join us for drinks and dinner. We've got good news to celebrate. Then, of course, when we learned about the death of your patient—"

"He *was* the poor bastard you presented at our last case conference, right?" Riley brayed. "Pathetically *mirroring* you, with your encouragement…"

Garman gave Riley a sharp look, then turned back to me. "Honestly, Dan, I just felt you could use some support. I've lost patients myself, and I know how—"

"Hey, guys, I'm freezing my tits off." Elaine bundled her coat tighter. "Can we get to the point?"

"Elaine…" Garman gazed helplessly at his wife.

But she'd pivoted on a high heel and was staring at me. "Look. My sister is seeing some hot-shot at the DA's office, and *he* told her, off the record, that the murdered guy was found dressed like you. That the cops think *you* were the one supposed to get killed."

Garman was shaking his head. "Your sister should learn to keep her mouth shut."

Elaine bristled. "Don't blame Kathy. Blame the married prick she's sleeping with. *He* told her."

Ignoring them, Riley took a step toward me. "You know what *that* means, don't you? I objected to your treatment of Kevin from the start. 'Twinship yearning,' my ass! Try clinical incompetence!"

He raised a finger, stabbing at me with liquor-fueled conviction. "I was right, I *knew* I was right, and now the kid's dead!"

Garman looked up. "Brooks, for God's sake—"

But Riley was on a roll. "His family ought to sue, you know that? Even if they don't, *I'm* going to see to it you get your license revoked!"

He took another step toward me, glowering with anger.

"Back off, Riley." I placed my palm against his chest. "You don't give a damn about Kevin. You've had a hard-on for me since you showed up at Ten Oaks, and now you're seeing your chance to burn me. So fuck you."

"Oh, this is priceless," Elaine said. "Three of our city's finest mental health professionals—"

"Look," Garman said hoarsely. "Elaine's right…"

His wife turned and stepped off the sidewalk. "Hell, I'm going to wait in the car. Have fun, boys." With that, she hurried away across the dark, rain-slicked parking lot.

Riley made a little side step, more like a lurch, then righted himself. No question, an amateur drunk.

I turned to Garman. "Get him out of here, will you, Bert? For his own good."

But Riley swung his head up, eyes red and angry. "You don't *get* it, do you, Danny boy? You blew it! The famous specialist screwed up!"

Again, finger poking me. Hard, jabbing. Eyes sheened with bleary indignation. And something else. The thrill of liquor-fueled bravado, carelessness. Unused to the alcohol coursing through that blue blood.

I saw all this. I should have known. And yet I still said it: "You poke me one more time with that finger, I'm gonna *feed* it to you." Then I batted his finger away.

That's when Riley and I each made a stupid mistake: He took a swing at me, and I did something about it.

I didn't mean to hit him so hard, but suddenly he was sitting on the wet pavement, hand covering his mouth, blood dribbling through his fingers. On the sidewalk next to him, like a pair of thrown dice, were two of his teeth.

"Oh my God!" Garman stared, wide-eyed in disbelief, first at me, and then down at his chief psychiatrist.

"Shit," I said, more or less under my breath. My right fist stung from the blow. I hadn't struck anyone, or any*thing*, without a glove since I was twelve years old.

"You lunatic." Riley's thickening lips found it hard to form words. "You *hit* me! Now *I'm* gonna sue you!"

"Go ahead. But Bert here's a witness. It was self-defense. You swung at me first."

"A witness?" Garman could barely form words himself. "What are you talking about? We're *doctors*, for Christ's sake. We don't brawl on the street."

"Right outside of a riverfront bar, don't forget," I added. "Ought to make a nice picture for the evening news."

"Go to hell!" Riley was struggling to get up, angrily waving away Garman's offer of assistance.

"You're *both* insane," Garman barked at me over his shoulder. "I don't believe this!"

Just then, behind us, the door opened and Noah stood on the sidewalk. In his hand was a Louisville slugger.

"Do I gotta start bustin' skulls or what?" he said, raising the baseball bat over his head. I realized with a start that he wasn't kidding around.

"Sorry, Noah," I said.

"I run a nice place here. If you shrinks can't behave yourselves..."

"I mean it, we're outta here."

Garman looked as though he were about to explode, but Noah had already turned and shuffled back inside.

I glanced over at Riley, leaning against the wall. The lower half of his face sagged, and the handkerchief he held against his mouth was soaked with blood.

"Look, Riley, I'm sorry. We both acted like jerks. And then I—hell, I should've known better. Okay?"

"*Not* okay." He was breathing heavily but evenly. It wasn't the alcohol talking any longer. "You're *toast*, Rinaldi. I'll have your license. I'll sue you for assault. Then I'll figure out some ways to *really* fuck you up."

He pushed himself off from the wall, legs unsteady beneath him. He squinted hard at Garman.

"You and Elaine go celebrate without me." His voice was thick with grievance. "I'll grab a cab home. I couldn't chew that lobster now anyway. Thanks to Muhammad Ali here, I'll be drinking through a goddam straw for a week."

Garman and I stood in silence, watching Riley head toward the parking lot. Behind, from somewhere downriver, you could hear the sound of a tugboat churning the black waters on its way past the Point.

"By the way," I said finally, without turning, "what are you celebrating?"

Garman gave me a sidelong look, equal parts amusement and exasperation. "Not that it matters much at the moment, but I just closed a deal with UniHealth. They're acquiring Ten Oaks and plan on making it the flagship for a franchise of private clinics."

"Franchise? Sounds like McDonald's."

"Not now, okay, Dan? I'm getting enough grief about it from the staff. Nancy and the others."

"My sympathies." I held out my hand. "Thanks for your concern though. Before."

His look at me was frank. "Kevin Merrick was *your* responsibilty, not ours. Our weekly peer reviews are merely a courtesy, extended to therapists who used to work at the clinic. Ten Oaks is in no way directly connected with, nor liable for, Kevin's treatment." He smiled, and only then shook my hand.

"Thanks for clearing that up. For a moment there, I almost forgot who you were."

"That would be a big mistake." Still smiling, he turned toward the parking lot. "I better join Elaine and get going, or we'll lose our reservation. Corner table."

"Look, about Riley…"

He shrugged. "Truth is, something about you has always pissed him off. I guess he sees you as some kind of maverick. You know his type. Philly mainline, marinated for eight years at Harvard. Hidebound, judgmental. Knows everything."

His pale eyes narrowed. "I'd say you've made yourself a real enemy, Dan."

With that, Albert Garman tightened the knot of his scarf and walked off into the night.

Chapter Eleven

The gray walls of the Old County Building loomed ahead in the darkness, ablaze with unaccustomed lights at this hour. Above, the full moon floated like a pearl in oil, clouds threading its glow. I pulled into the lot.

It was nine p.m. Time for my meeting with the cops.

I found an empty space, parked, and went into the main lobby. Then I took the elevator up to the Police Bureau's Central Office on the third floor.

The first person I met there was Angela Villanova. A short, stocky woman in her mid-fifties, she had shrewd but kind eyes, a lacquered cloud of gray hair, and the walk of someone who'd just gotten off a horse.

Though she'd probably never even *seen* one. City girl, to the core. Born and raised in East Liberty, she'd plowed up the ranks to make lieutenant, before accepting the new post of Chief Community Liaison Officer five years ago.

"Danny," she said, spreading her hands. Her voice was breathy, conspiratorial. Something was definitely up.

Angie gave me a quick hug. I smelled her perfume. *My Sin.* She'd been wearing it since she was twenty, when my dad paid her ten bucks an hour to tutor me in math.

We were related, evidently; her father's sister had married my third cousin. Or something. That's the trouble with Italian family trees. There're so many branches, you can get lost trying to trace your way through the foliage.

As we headed down to the main office, I asked the obvious question. "Angie, why—?"

"Why am *I* here? I guess the suits figure having a friendly face in the room will make you more cooperative."

"I sure as hell hate the sound of that."

She shrugged. "First off, I'm really sorry about your patient. I mean, for *you*. Finding him that way…"

"Thanks. But I'm okay."

"Bullshit, but we'll let that pass." A brief smile. "Anyway, the thing is, this murder has heated up all of a sudden. We're in total siege mode."

"What the hell for?"

I was confused. Sure, cops always want to clear murders fast. Mostly for pragmatic reasons. The trail turns cold after the first 72 hours. Plus, high clearance rates make department heads happy, which is always good news for homicide cops. Usually the only kind they ever get.

"Listen, Angie. I don't know how much they told you, but the detectives on this case figure the killer was after *me*, and got Kevin Merrick by mistake."

She waved a hand impatiently. "Christ, that's *old* news. Homicide's working a whole new scenario now."

"Since when?"

"Since we found out the victim's name *isn't* Kevin Merrick."

Chapter Twelve

District Attorney Leland Sinclair pointed to a chair across from his at the conference table.

"Take a seat, Dr. Rinaldi. This thing's rolling downhill, and we don't have much time to get you up to speed."

Unlike most public figures, the DA looked the same in person as he did on the evening news—like a senior tennis pro. Well-connected and ambitious, everyone knew he wanted to be governor one day. And probably would be.

Sinclair turned and introduced me to Lt. Stu Biegler, from Robbery/Homicide. He was probably in his forties, but looked ten years younger. Pale. Male-model thin. His glance at me was narrow-eyed and suspicious.

Polk stepped in behind Angie and me, nodded once to Biegler, his boss, and moved down along the large oval table to where his partner Eleanor Lowrey sat making notes.

We were in the main conference room, sequestered from the maze of cubicles and offices beyond its paneled walls by reinforced double-doors. The mood had seemed pretty tense from the moment I came in, and was ratcheting up fast as we all awkwardly found seats. The pockmarked table was littered with papers, folders, and Styrofoam cups.

Then, before anyone could say a word, the door opened again behind us. The latecomer was tall, blond, wearing a silk blouse and a short, tight-fitting skirt, and was easily one of the most beautiful women I'd ever seen.

She had a dancer's body, with firm breasts and long, very smooth legs. I must have gaped, because I could sense Angie's gaze on me. Felt the chill of her disapproval.

"Sorry I'm late," the woman said to Sinclair, pushing a strand of hair from her forehead.

Sinclair and I got back to our feet. Nobody else did.

"No problem. We're just getting started." He turned to me. "Dr. Daniel Rinaldi, this is Casey Walters, one of our rising Assistant District Attorneys."

"Right. Until the next time I fuck up," she said cheerfully.

I felt her frank appraisal like a searchlight on my face, so I distracted myself by returning the favor. I liked what I saw. High cheekbones. Pale pink lipstick on full lips. The hand that reached to shake mine was strong, sure, with long fingers and short, frosted nails.

Then her glance went to Polk and Lowrey.

"By the way," she said, "I'm late because of the Paula Stark case. Thanks to you two, I just got beat up by her public defender, which does great things for my image."

Polk glared at her. "Are you shittin' me? We got enough to put Paula upstate for a deuce, easy. What about the phone calls to her brother, and the witness?"

"Oh, yeah. The homeboy who swears he saw Paula club the grocer with a wrench from her purse. Before she empties the cash register and escapes to the South Side on the bus. Guys, I can't make a meal out of that."

"It's what happened," Polk said testily.

"Get me the wrench. Get me the damn bus driver. Get me *something*." She spread her hands.

"That's enough," Sinclair said sharply. "All of you."

Polk folded his arms on the table. Pouting.

Shaking her head, Casey took the seat across from me, giving me a brief, wry smile as she settled in.

"Let's not forget why we're here, people," Sinclair said calmly. Then, turning to me: "Dr. Rinaldi, Sergeant Polk and Detective Lowrey reported the details of their interview with you last night.

Including the conclusion you all came to regarding the killer's intended target."

"Me," I said. "Right?"

"A reasonable assumption, given the evidence. And believe me, we're not ruling that scenario out."

"That's right," Biegler said. He rubbed his thin nose. "But there's also a *second* possibility, which I think we ought to keep on the table."

"Let me guess," I said. "That's the one where *I'm* the killer."

Sinclair smiled patiently. "We have to look at everyone, Doctor. That's how it works."

"Then maybe I ought to shut up and call a lawyer," I said evenly. "That's part of how it works, too."

Sinclair and I exchanged cool looks. I got the feeling he figured there was room for only one alpha male in this particular patch of jungle, and he was it.

Angie reached over and tapped my arm. "Cool it, Danny. Nobody here seriously thinks you did it."

"Not *too* seriously, anyway," Polk grumbled. He sat glumly under a "No Smoking" sign, meticulously tearing an empty Camel pack into tiny pieces.

Lt. Biegler shifted nervously in his seat. "Listen, we're getting off the friggin' track here. Right now, the *killer* isn't the problem. It's the victim."

I looked from Biegler to Sinclair. "Speaking of which, I hear my patient's name is *not* Kevin Merrick…?"

Casey Walters spoke for the first time since sitting down. She aimed her blue eyes at me.

"His name may very well *be* Merrick. At least, that's what he's called himself for years."

She checked the file folder she'd just drawn from her slender briefcase. "It's the name on his driver's license, credit cards, everything. Maybe he even had his name legally changed to Merrick. But if so, it wasn't in this state. We're on that already, though it'll take some time. The point is, Merrick wasn't the name he had at birth, or when he was growing up in Banford."

"So what *was* his name?"

"Wingfield. Same as his father's."

I started, letting the name sink in. "Now you're going to tell me—"

"That's right. Kevin's father is Miles Wingfield, founder and CEO of Wingfield BioTech. Cutting-edge genetic research, facilities worldwide. Real media magnet, too. Covers of *Time, Newsweek,* you name it. CNN devoted a whole hour to him. Personal worth conservatively estimated at six to seven billion."

"Jesus," Polk said, though it was more like a moan.

"Yeah," Lowrey said wryly, "but is he really happy?"

Biegler snorted. "I'd say goddam ecstatic. Guy's sixty-five years old, he goes through supermodels like Kleenex. Throw in the dozen houses, fleet of jets, and his very own island, and I'd say, yeah, definitely feeling pretty damn good about life when he gets up in the morning."

"All right, children." Sinclair shook his head. "Now that we've genuflected before Wingfield's wealth and celebrity, let's not lose sight of the real issue. Namely, the cost of having him as an adversary."

I could guess what was coming next.

"He's putting the pressure on to find Kevin's killer."

"Pressure?" Biegler grimaced. "Like Def-Com Four. Wingfield hears about it on the news, realizes it's his kid, and starts making phone calls—"

"Which is how we found out who your patient really was," Casey explained to me.

"Wingfield called the White House, for God's sake," Angie said. "Then the Governor's mansion. He woke the mayor up at five this morning."

"Who called *me* at 5:15," Sinclair said. "More hungover than usual, but lucid enough to realize his ass is on the line. As are *all* our asses, I might add."

"Give the guy a break. It *was* his son," Lowrey said, looking at the white men around the table as though we were all clueless bastards. Maybe she wasn't far wrong.

"Bullshit," Biegler said. "They were estranged. Hadn't seen each other in years, since before the old man got rich. Nobody close to Wingfield even knew he *had* a kid."

"Except for the people in this room," Sinclair said, "and the people he called last night, nobody still knows."

"You want to bet how long *that* lasts?" Casey shook her head. "Christ, the media will be all over this…"

I said nothing. It seemed…unbelievable. The Kevin *I* knew was barely making it, emotionally *or* financially. He lived on student loans, and delivery jobs after classes. Yet all along he was the estranged heir to billions?…

I had another thought. If his father left their town in disgrace when Kevin was a kid, how did he change his life so radically, grow into some *Fortune 500* heavyweight, the Bill Gates of the biotech world?

And had Kevin really had no contact with his father all these years? What about Wingfield's other child, his daughter Karen? Had *she*?

A final, darker notion rose in my mind.

If Kevin's murder *did* have something to do with who his father was, did that mean Karen—wherever she was—might be next?

Unless this whole investigation had begun too late, and she was already dead…

Chapter Thirteen

"Hey, Doc!" Polk was staring at me from his end of the table. He wasn't alone. "You with us or what?"

"Sorry. Just thinking."

Sinclair smiled. "I understand what a shock this is, Doctor. You knew your patient as one person, and now it turns out he was someone else." He paused, aware of its effect. "Assuming, of course, it *is* a shock…"

"Meaning what?"

"Meaning, we need to know as much about Kevin as we can. What *was* his current relationship with Wingfield, if any? Who were Kevin's friends, employers? Did *they* know who his father was?"

Sinclair's gaze at me was unwavering. "In other words, was Kevin's murder a kidnap-for-ransom gone wrong? It's a real possibility, in light of who his father is."

"And I'm supposed to just *tell* you all this?"

Angela Villanova turned to me. "Danny, it's not a violation of Kevin's memory. Or his rights. Not if it helps to find his killer. You know that as well as I."

I waved a hand in surrender. "Yeah, I know. It just goes against the grain."

I noticed Casey Walters staring intently at me. In sympathy? Concern? I couldn't be sure.

"Besides," I went on, "the truth is, all this stuff about Wingfield is news to me. You can trash my office, read my files.

Stick electrodes in my brain, if you want. But Kevin never mentioned Wingfield. I just knew his father as a small-town banker who deserted his family and never looked back. Kevin never saw him again. He spent the rest of his adolescence in foster care."

"*And* in and out of mental hospitals," Casey said, referring again to her file folder. "Tough life for the kid. Mother dead, abandoned by his father, battling mental illness. Living on the edge…" Her voice trailed off.

"I'll want a copy of that file," Biegler announced.

"Copy everyone in this room," Sinclair ordered. "And *nobody* outside of it. But we have to coordinate all this. I spoke to the chief just before I got here, and we've decided to run the whole show from here."

"Hey, it's *our* case," Polk blurted out. I could see from his face he'd just as quickly regretted it.

Sinclair's voice was like ice. "Haven't you been paying attention, Sergeant? Your petty jurisdictional concerns are irrelevant."

"I'm just sayin'—"

Biegler glared at Polk, seething. "You heard the man, Sergeant. They want to run things from downtown, if that's okay with you. This way, if we screw up, and Harrisburg decides to drop a bomb on us, we'll all be conveniently located in the same place. You fucking shit," he added.

Polk sat down, face a livid red. Eleanor Lowrey, her own brow creased with anxiety, touched his arm.

Sinclair sighed. "Look, we better wrap this up. The chief and I have to confer with the mayor in an hour. He wants to figure out a game plan for tomorrow."

"What happens tomorrow?" I was getting tired of playing catch-up. Or maybe I was just getting tired.

"Wingfield happens tomorrow," Sinclair replied. "He's flying in at six a.m. Breakfast with me and the Mayor. And His Honor is not, shall we say, a morning person."

He nodded in my direction. "So. With all due respect to Dr. Rinaldi, and whatever skeletons he may have in his closet, I think we should keep the mistaken-identity theory on the back-burner. Let's work on the assumption the killer knew who Kevin really was—or, more to the point, who his *father* was. The motive must lie there."

"Besides," Casey added, her gaze seeming to challenge him, "Wingfield will be more supportive of a line of investigation going in that direction. Don't you think?"

Sinclair didn't answer. Just gave her a look. Not so much in anger as betrayal. But something else, too.

"One more thing," Biegler said suddenly. He flipped open a file folder on his lap. "What about James Stickey?"

"Who?" Sinclair asked.

"Our vic was robbed and assaulted by Stickey six months ago. He's doing hard time now up in Cloverbrook."

Sinclair's face darkened. "Jesus Christ."

"Can't be a connection," Polk said. "Stickey's just some hype. Broke into Kevin's place for some quick cash. Two nights later, we nailed his sorry ass."

"But there's no indication he knew who Kevin was? That the break-in was a cover for something else?"

Polk shook his head. "Pure coincidence, I'm tellin' ya. Besides, Stickey was in the can when Kevin got killed."

"Maybe," Sinclair said. "But I don't like this. Kevin Wingfield gets assaulted six months ago, and now murdered? And these events are *not* related?"

"On the face of things, sir," Casey said evenly, "it doesn't look like it."

Biegler was sulking. "I still think it's worth putting Stickey on the grill. Just to cover our asses with Wingfield. I'd hate for him to find out about it, and—"

"Okay, okay," Sinclair said briskly. "Send your people up there. Just so we can cross it off the list."

He glanced at his watch, then started straightening his jacket. Seemed like we were about to be dismissed.

Eleanor Lowrey was looking in my direction. "Want Harry and me to accompany Dr. Rinaldi back to his office for those patient files?"

Biegler rose to his feet. "We can send some uniforms to do that," he said irritably. "You two got enough work ahead of you tonight."

"*I* don't mind doing it," Casey Walters said.

This caught me—and everybody else—by surprise. I turned to her. She was leaning back in her chair, stretching. Her breasts were taut against the thin silk of her blouse. You could just make out the beige outline of her wispy bra beneath.

It was strange. I hadn't been with a woman in a long time, hadn't even thought about them much lately. And yet suddenly I felt a long-buried, distant shiver of anticipation. The dryness in my mouth, the tightness in my gut. Forget the past twenty-four hours, the death and the guilt, the shock and the pain.

Now, I thought. *Now* I'm in trouble.

Chapter Fourteen

"You're pretty comfortable around cops," Casey said, spearing a cherry tomato with her fork. "That's rare."

"Let's say I'm used to them."

"Your father was a beat cop on the North Side, right?" Her eyes crinkled at the edges. "I read your file."

"Oh boy."

We were sitting at a corner booth in Tambellini's, splitting a Bordeaux. She'd told me when we sat down that she liked both her wine and her steaks blood red.

"But don't read anything into that," she'd said with a laugh.

"You mean, other than that you're a carnivore?"

"Yeah, right. If you're anything like my shrink, you're already making assumptions about me."

"Not me. I'm off-duty."

"Bullshit. You guys are never off-duty. Like my being late for the meeting. He'd have a field day with that."

"Sure. It's Therapy 101. If you show up late, you're resistant. If you're early, you're anxious. On time, you're compulsive." I smiled. "We have all the bases covered."

The meeting at police headquarters had broken up an hour before, with stern warnings from the District Attorney against talking to the press. As Casey and I headed out the door, Angie Villanova had taken us aside.

"Look, Danny, from the moment Miles Wingfield lands tomorrow, this thing is gonna steamroll. Now I know Kevin was your patient..." She cocked an eyebrow.

"*But...*" I smiled down at her. My old math tutor. From the neighborhood. Now she was the voice of the Pittsburgh Police, a bureaucrat selling me the party line.

"*But,*" she repeated, "after you hand over your files, you're out of this. Leave it to the murder dicks, okay? You're just a witness, like any other citizen."

"Or a suspect."

"Biegler wasn't serious," Casey said, smiling. "Even *he* isn't that dense."

Angie gave my shoulder a parting tap. "Just keep your head down and think good thoughts, and maybe we'll all come outta this wearin' diamonds."

She gave Casey a curt nod and started off, sturdy heels clicking on the polished hardwood.

Then, turning: "And, Danny, don't be such a stranger. Come to dinner on Sunday. Sonny'd love to see you."

She strode away toward the elevators. Her husband Sonny was a retired construction worker, living on disability following the loss of his leg at a job site accident. Even before that he was a bitter, small-minded bigot. Predictably, retirement had not mellowed him.

I could feel Casey's gaze on me. I turned.

"Speaking of dinner," she said, "I'm starving."

Which is how we ended up at Tambellini's, over steaks and Caesar salads. Despite the crowded tables, the frenzied hustle of waiters and busboys, Casey focused on me in a way that made me feel we were the only two people in the room.

"What?" I said, off her look.

"Angie told me you were tall and good-looking," she said. "I just figured it was bullshit. You know, unhappily-married older woman with a crush. Something like that."

"What makes you think she's unhappy?"

"Are you kidding? She might as well wear a sign."

"You're pretty good at making assumptions yourself."

"I'm a DA. It's my job to think the worst. And I'm right most of the time." Again that easy smile. That cool self-assurance.

I wished I could say the same. I tried to keep myself in check, but she wasn't making it easy. Her eyes were deep and reflective one moment, quick and challenging the next. Somehow, despite my best efforts, I felt—there's no other word—*caught* by them.

Jesus, I thought. What the hell's going on? She's at least a dozen years younger than me.

Now, pouring her some more wine, I told myself this was an understandable reaction to the stress of the past twenty-four hours, fueled by no sleep, no food, and the undeniable fact of her beauty. I actually told myself this.

"I've been wanting to meet you," she was saying. "Though not exactly under these circumstances."

We had a window table, and outside the night was dark and thick. Beyond our own reflections in the glass, trees bent before a punishing wind. Another storm moving in.

"Word is, you're good at what you do." She looked at me over the rim of her glass. "I like that in a person."

"According to Sinclair, you're not so bad yourself."

"I have my moments. And I work hard. Law review, two years running. Then a lot of paying dues. I put in my time prosecuting drunk drivers in Wilkinsburg, some white-collar stuff up-state, then applied to the DA's office downtown."

She gave me a sharp look. "And, yeah, it didn't hurt that I was young, female, and easy to look at. But believe me, I earned every break I got."

I believed her.

The waiter came by to offer us coffee. We both ordered decaf. She asked me a lot of questions about my work with crime victims and their families. Whenever my answers were too casual or generalized, she pressed me, narrowing the focus. A good trial lawyer, I thought.

"I can't even imagine some of the things these people go through," she said at one point. "Women who've been raped, or kidnapped. Bank tellers terrorized by armed robbers. How do they go on after something like that?"

"Some of them don't. I mean, they go through the motions. Go to work, pay their bills. But the trauma stays with them, as if they don't still live in the same world as people who've never gone through that kind of experience."

"What do you mean?"

"Well, take the classic symptoms of Post-Traumatic Stress. Flashbacks, nightmares, intrusive images of the horrible event that keep flooding back. Plus a constant anxiety, a kind of hyper-vigilance about danger that can persist for months, even years."

I stirred some cream into my coffee. "And it isn't just in their heads. Exposure to gunfire can alter brain chemistry. Central nervous system pathways are disrupted. This can play hell with REM sleep, causing nightmares, anxiety, inability to concentrate."

I frowned. "Great, this is turning into a lecture."

"Not at all. I'm fascinated. I work the legal end of a crime. Testimony, forensics. Stuff you can sink your teeth into. But what *you* do…"

She hesitated. "Like with Kevin Wingfield. Did *he* have symptoms like that after he was robbed and assaulted?"

"Yes. Especially with his background, a childhood history of physical and sexual abuse. That break-in at his apartment might have triggered old memories of personal violation. Reinforced his anxiety about potential danger, the inevitability of violence. Studies suggest that crime victims exposed to prior domestic violence are at a greater risk for real psychological damage."

"Like the straw that breaks the camel's back?"

"Something like that."

She considered this. "And this doesn't just apply to the victims themselves, right? I mean, I saw a report on the survivors of the World Trade Center. Families of the victims feeling tremendous guilt for having survived."

"It went deeper than that. A couple rescue workers on the scene later committed suicide, convinced they should've done more. Rescued more people. A tragedy of that scope, you're looking at long-term effects on the survivors. Depression, divorce, addictions. God knows what we're going to see when all the research comes in on Hurricane Katrina. The psychological fall-out."

"They call it survivor guilt, don't they?"

"Yeah, but that's too pretty a phrase. Like battle fatigue. It doesn't get to the core, where the pain lives."

I tapped my fingers against the tablecloth. I felt awkward, suddenly. Exposed.

Then her hand reached across the table, rested on mine. "Please," she said. "Tell me about Barbara."

I gave her a quizzical look.

"I told you, I read your file. Please, Danny."

I delayed a moment, and then, inexplicably, I found my voice. It had been so long since I'd told the story, even to myself, that my words tasted strangely new.

"She was a professor of ancient languages. Brilliant. Dedicated. She could also be a major pain in the ass."

"You really loved her, didn't you?"

"Marriage had been my idea," I said. "Me, the scourge of the Pitt psych department...and I'd pushed for marriage, maybe even children someday. The whole traditional thing."

"And Barbara...?"

I shrugged. "For some reason, she went along with it. But we were both workaholics. Driven. There were a lot of conflicts. But somehow..."

Casey nodded.

"Anyway," I said at last, "one night six years ago, we got mugged outside this restaurant near the Point. The guy was young, built like a bull, in a hooded parka. A big 9 millimeter in his hand. He was agitated, muttering...I figured he was probably coked out of his mind."

"Jesus..."

"He told us to turn over our wallets, jewelry. When Barbara fumbled with her purse, he shoved her with his shoulder. Hard. It was like he was coming unglued. Then I saw the gun come up, and I lunged for it. It all happened so fast. I remember our struggling, him backing away, cursing, wresting the gun back... then I heard the shots, bang—bang—bang—and then everything went black."

I let out a long breath. Watched her watching me.

"When I woke up," I went on, "I was in ICU, given a fifty-fifty chance to live. I lived."

I sat back in the chair. "Barbara hadn't been so lucky. I learned later she'd died instantly, at the scene, from two bullet wounds to the head."

Casey dropped her eyes, seemingly at a loss. A strand of hair fell over her eyes, but she didn't push it back.

I ran a finger around the rim of my coffee cup. "You asked about survivor guilt. Well, I had it in spades...I believed Barbara's death was somehow my fault."

"It wasn't."

"I know that now. But I went through the classic stages... blaming myself for allowing us to be caught off guard by the guy. Plus, I had done some boxing when I was younger, so some part of me thought I should've been able to take him. That I'd failed her..."

Casey let a silence fill the space between us.

"What happened after you got out of the hospital?"

"I guess my life fell apart. I couldn't imagine doing therapy again, treating patients. Hell, *I* was the patient now. So I quit my job at the clinic. Totally dropped out. I needed the time to work things out, get a handle on it."

"And did you?"

"Finally, yeah. With some help. It took two years of therapy to realize that *I* didn't kill Barbara, some prick with a gun did."

I paused. "Anyway, soon after, I knew I was ready to work again. More than that, I knew *why* I wanted to work. Maybe for the first time in my career. I got my chance when Angie

Villanova called me out of the blue one day. If you remember, two of the Handyman's victims had gotten away. Angie referred one of them to me."

Casey's eyes darkened. "That reminds me, I guess you heard about the movie—?"

"Yeah. Don't get me started."

Just then, the waiter came over with the check. Before I could make a move, Casey scooped it up.

"I invited *you*, remember?" She took out a credit card. "So that's how you started working with crime victims?"

"Only a few people at first. Then my work-load started to build. In a year or so, I went into private practice full-time. I also signed on as a consultant to the cops."

I smiled. "Funny. My old man hated being on the job, used to get pissed when I even *kidded* him about joining the force myself someday. Strange how things turn out..."

"Is he still alive?"

I shook my head. "Drank himself to death a long time ago..."

Chapter Fifteen

Casey signed the credit card slip and we got up from our seats. We walked outside under a cold, cloudless sky, our coats bundled against the wind.

She followed me in her Lexus to my office building on Forbes. Thick tree branches that canopied my street shook in the wind, sawing against each other like old bones.

I pulled up at the curb. The parking garage was still cordoned off with yellow tape. In the wake of the news about Kevin's father, my guess was that a fresh team of CSU techs was scouring the place even now.

Casey confirmed this, as she locked her car in the space behind mine. She pointed up at bright white lights fanning out from openings in the garage's upper level.

"Poor bastards are in for straight double-shifts," she said as I walked up to her on the sidewalk.

I opened the double front doors and let us into the lobby. Pulled by the wind, the door shut behind us with a whoosh, as though vacuum-sealed. We took the elevator up to the fifth floor.

I unlocked the outer office door, then the connecting door into my consulting room. I flipped on the overhead and led us over to my file cabinets. I'd already signed the subpoena for Kevin's records, so I slid open the file drawer and started looking for his folder.

Casey stood beside me, taking in the décor.

"Nice office," she said. "Kind of like—"

Her voice caught. I turned, and saw that her face had gone ashen. I whirled around, following her gaze.

There on my desk, stark against the whiteness of the blotter, lay a blood-covered knife. The blade was long and thin, the blood dried, caked, black like soot.

I took a step toward my desk, heart pounding.

"Don't," she said, her voice a gasp. "Don't touch it."

"I know."

I stared down at the knife. I'd never seen one like it before. But I knew what it was.

Just as I knew whose blood was on it. It was the knife that had killed Kevin Merrick.

It was also a message.

Next time, it said, the killer would get it right.

Next time, the blood would be mine.

Chapter Sixteen

Casey and I backed out of my office, careful not to touch anything more, and I locked the door.

We went down the elevator without saying a word, then both got into my car. I handed her my cell phone.

I laid my head back against the seat cushion, listening as she called her boss. The conversation lasted less than a minute. When she hung up and rested the phone in her lap, she just sort of slumped in her seat.

"Nobody's going to be sleeping tonight," she said. "Including you and me."

"That's what I figured. What'd Sinclair say?"

"Not much. He's probably trying to figure out how to spin this for the mayor. Sort of a practice run for when they have to spin it for Wingfield in the morning."

"You mean, because it looks like *I'm* the killer's target again?"

She handed me back the phone. "If Kevin *was* killed by mistake, and it's certainly starting to look that way, it means the focus of the investigation has to shift to you. *Your* life, friends, possible motives. The Wingfield connection becomes...well, less relevant."

"But not to *him*," I said. "I mean, if I were Wingfield, I'd *still* want to nail the bastard that killed my son. No matter who the intended target had been."

The cell phone beeped in my hand. I had seven messages in my voicemail, one marked "Urgent." I shrugged at Casey, and punched in my code. The message was from Dr. Phillip Camden. I let out a breath.

"Important?" Casey searched my face with weary eyes.

"Yes and no. I figured I'd hear from Phil sooner or later, after the news hit. It's just lousy timing."

"Want my advice? Unless it's the killer, don't return any calls. You've got enough on your mind..."

"You mean, like staying alive...?"

She gave my arm a reassuring squeeze, leaving her hand there as we waited for the cops. The part of me that was still in the car with her was grateful. But some other part of me had already drifted away...

◇◇◇

Phillip Camden, M.D., Ph.D., professor of behavioral sciences at the University of Pittsburgh, author of three definitive textbooks in the field, was something of a legend in the graduate psych department. Primarily a researcher, not a therapist, he took pride in never having actually *treated* a patient.

Instead, he "evaluated" them—in controlled studies, cranial autopsies, and by virtue of his nationally-known expertise in interpreting psychological tests. "Patients are subjects," he'd announce from the podium. "And the most effective tool for examining them is dispassion."

Dr. Camden's students feared and revered him, but rarely liked him. Which was fine with him. An imposing-looking man in his seventies, he'd sit with his legs crossed in the faculty lounge, brandy in hand, and gaze forlornly across the room at the stack of papers to be graded.

"You know who we attract in the field of psychology, don't you? They come in two categories: Those who can't pass the bar, or lack the critical thinking skills for medicine and the natural sciences; or, even worse, those whose psyches are so fragmented that their only sense of cohesion comes from the idea of 'helping others,' whatever in God's name that means. A narcissistic grandiosity masquerading as altruism."

I was used to these pronouncements. As his teaching assistant—and the one who would end up having to *grade* those papers—I'd been on the receiving end of countless rebukes and insults myself.

Camden was my mentor in the department. He was also my exact opposite in temperament and beliefs. He despised my interest in Kohut, Stolorow, or in any other relational theories of human development. "Postmodernist horseshit," he'd say. "A flight from objective reality."

Phillip Camden was easily the most arrogant, self-satisfied son-of-a-bitch I've ever known. I also learned more from him than any other person in the field.

So it was only natural, if not deeply ironic, that *his* should be the first face looming down at mine—after ten hours of surgery, following the shooting—when I finally came to in the hospital.

"*You* should have died," he said. And that was all he said, before turning and walking out.

Even if he'd stayed, I couldn't have argued with him. Given the head trauma, I *should* have died. Everyone said so, including the specialist flown in from Dallas. I lay in a hospital bed over the next three months, tubes going in and out, and didn't—for some reason—die. After a while, I began to feel I was letting everybody down.

Especially Phillip Camden. On his second—and last— visit to see me, when I was fully conscious and able to sit up, he just stood in a corner of the room, arms folded across his chest, and scowled at me.

"Phil…" My voice was a croak.

"Not a word. *I* will speak to *you* when I must. The occasional professional, and therefore unavoidable, consultation. Am I clear?"

I swallowed hard, at a loss.

Without another look in my direction, he walked out of the room. I haven't seen him since.

I couldn't blame him for his rage, his hatred. I'd been his assistant in the psych department, his favorite student, however contrary and opinionated.

Then, not long after graduation, I'd become his son-in-law. Was it any wonder he felt this way now?

After all, I thought, in the yawning silence of the hospital room, as far as he's concerned, I'd killed his only child. *Gotten* her killed. His daughter, Barbara.

It's taken me a long time since then to believe otherwise. Phil Camden never has.

Chapter Seventeen

A fist rapped impatiently on the driver's side window. I was pulled from my reverie by the sight of Sgt. Harry Polk, craggy face framed in flickering red light from a nearby patrol car, peering through the glass.

"Hey, Doc, ya wanna join the party?"

I looked over to find that Casey was already climbing out of her side of the car. I got out, too, and stood in a street now filled with patrol units, a lab van, and a scattering of semi-interested onlookers.

Polk motioned for me to follow him across the street, where Lt. Biegler and Det. Lowrey stood by an unmarked sedan. The lieutenant looked unhappy.

"The DA wants me to supervise this personally," he explained. We all stood with our hands in our pockets, shoulders hunched against the icy wind.

"CSU guys are doing the office now." Lowrey's mouth was hidden behind the fur lining of her jacket collar.

"Just make sure they bring me the knife first, before it goes to forensics," Biegler said.

Casey joined us from the sidewalk, carrying her own cell phone. She handed it to Biegler. "Sinclair, for you."

The lieutenant spoke into the phone. Once. "Biegler."

For the next two minutes, Biegler just nodded, phone at his ear, not even managing an "uh-huh" or "okay." He shifted his weight from one foot to the other, impatient, embarrassed, suddenly a low link in the chain of command.

Polk gave me a sidelong glance, through the plume of smoke from the cigarette he was lighting. The wind took the smoke and fanned it away like a flag unfurling.

Finally, Biegler got another word in. "Right." Then he hung up and handed the phone back to Casey.

"Okay, here's the deal." He squared his shoulders with importance. "The knife is probably the murder weapon, which pretty much clinches it that the Doc here is the target. Also, looks like the killer is totally confident that he will succeed next time. And wants us to know it."

"Or, at least, wants *me* to," I offered.

Ignoring me, he turned to Lowrey. "Detective, I want you to coordinate the CSU data, keeping me informed at all times. I want everything they find—prints, whatever—funneled through me first."

Only then, a quick look at me. "Dr. Rinaldi, we'll need a list of everything that should be in your office. Files, books, personal items. ASAP."

Finally, he turned and pointed at Polk. "And, Harry, you get the cakewalk. Baby-sitting the Doc."

"No fuckin' way." Polk flicked ash from his Camel. "I'm supposed to be Primary on this investigation."

"Sinclair wants it this way. At least for the next day or two. If the killer makes a move, we've got to have somebody with the stones and experience to block it."

Lowrey punched Polk's arm. "And since we don't got anybody like *that*, you're the next best thing."

"Don't I get a vote?" I asked.

"No." Casey's quick answer surprised me.

She took a step toward me, subtly putting her back between us and the others. Her look was warm and strangely intimate. Again, as if there were nobody else here but us.

"We have a safe house on Fifth," she said. "Just till morning, at least. No way we can let you go home."

Just then, a CSU tech in a blue jumpsuit and gloves came out of the office building, holding a plastic evidence bag in both hands. Lowrey waved him over.

Biegler peered at the long, thin knife through the plastic. Some dried blood from the blade dotted the inside of the bag.

"All right," he said. "Tag it and take it down."

The CSU guy hurried off. Biegler turned to Lowrey. "I want the whole building sealed. Then grab some uniforms and start canvassing the area. Again." He pulled his overcoat collar up to his ears. "That's it. Call me at home if anything pops."

We all watched Biegler walk quickly toward his car, parked a few spaces down the street. Something about the petulant stamp of his footsteps managed to convey the lieutenant's overall disappointment with his life. Conferring with social inferiors at a crime scene, huddling in the frigid wind at one in the morning, having to look at blood-stained murder weapons in plastic bags. He probably figured that wherever Leland Sinclair was right now, barking orders on the phone all over the city, he was indoors and warm, and nursing a drink.

"God, what a pussy," Lowrey said in a low voice.

"Look." I turned to Casey. "I can't do any good stuck in some roach motel, playing cards with Sergeant Polk."

"You've seen too many movies. Besides, this is police business. You're out of it."

"More important," Polk said, "you sure as hell ain't gonna get your ass killed on *my* watch."

"I'm touched."

"Point is," Casey went on, "finding that knife in your office made a believer out of Sinclair. *And* me. This guy's determined, Danny. So let's play it safe, okay?"

"Okay. But let me ask *you* a question. I had to unlock the outer door, and the connecting door, to let us into my office. So how did the killer get in before us, to plant the knife? Shouldn't you guys be trying to learn who else has a key to my office besides me?"

"Give us some credit, will ya?" Lowrey flipped open a small spiral notebook. "We already contacted the owners of the building. They have a master key to all the suites. So does the building manager, a Stephanie Moss, and the maintenance guy."

"Lenny Wilcox?" I frowned. "Forget about him. I've known him for years. And Stephanie's a sixty-three-year-old grandmother of two. Believe me, we're up way past her bedtime."

"How 'bout your friends and family?" Lowrey persisted. "Colleagues. Anybody else who might have a key?"

"Nope. No one."

I was lying, of course. I'd just remembered the one other person who had a key to my office, as well as to my house. In case of emergency. In case he ever got lost or disoriented or needed a place to crash.

But I wanted to talk with him privately first, before saying anything to the cops. Or even to Casey.

I figured I owed Noah that. If not a lot more.

Chapter Eighteen

I couldn't see the killer's face, only the neon flash of the long, silvery blade as it plunged down toward me.

I knew I was going to die.

The stiletto blade punctured my chest, with a sound like ice cracking. Great plumes of blood spurted from the wound. Bits of flesh and bone.

Blood splattered everywhere, spraying the killer. It peppered his dark shirt. Dotted the blur where his face should have been.

Then something in my brain exploded, and a fierce blackness swallowed me whole.

‹›‹›‹›

I bolted awake, upright in the armchair. Papers spilled off my lap onto the carpet. Files, flying open.

Where the hell was I? *Who* the hell was I?…

Memory flooded back. Awareness crashed in around my ears. The cops. The bloody knife. Kevin's murder.

I took a couple of deep breaths, blinking my eyes in the dimness. The table lamp beside me had long since burned out. The one I'd turned on hours before.

Slowly, I got my bearings. I looked around the room, taking it all in as if for the first time.

The hotel the cops had put us in wasn't bad. Quiet, carpeted suite, flanked by two identical rooms that are always "booked," but never occupied.

Dawn light was gleaming in thin lines off the closed window shutters. I'd spent the whole night in the stuffed armchair, head throbbing, listening to the muffled sounds from the street below. Sleepless in Pittsburgh.

Until at some point, I'd nodded off. And dreamed.

Shit, I thought, *some dream*. I rubbed my eyes. Maybe awake was better.

I bent over and started gathering up the scattered files. I'd been poring over them, re-reading case notes from every patient I'd seen since going into practice.

Earlier, I'd made a deal with Polk and Lowrey that I got to review everything first on my own, and only then pass along the name of anyone who seemed in the slightest way capable of murder, or who'd exhibited enough antagonism toward me in therapy to warrant a second look. It was the best way I could think of to assist the cops, and still maintain my patients' confidentiality.

And, as I'd expected, I'd come up with nothing. If one of my patients *did* want to kill me, he'd done a great job hiding it from me during our sessions. He or she, I guess.

I put aside the pile of folders and stretched, feeling fatigue tug at my shoulder muscles.

Across the room, sprawled on one of the twin beds, lay Sgt. Polk, snoring. He was fully dressed, including his shoulder holster and scuffed brown Florsheims. His gun sat in the ashtray on the nightstand, along with an empty Camel pack and two sticks of Wrigley's gum.

He stirred now, a low grumble coming from his throat.

Dreaming, too, I guessed. God knew what. His face was pinched, contorted.

Hours before, as I was climbing into his car to come here, Eleanor Lowrey had put a hand on my shoulder.

"Go easy on Polk, okay?" she whispered. "His wife left him last month. After fifteen years."

What took her so long? I'd thought, as Polk gave us a disgruntled look from behind the wheel. "Ya wanna wrap it up, girls? It's fuckin' freezin' out."

Now, watching his restless sleep, I reminded myself that Harry Polk was just another slob with a story, like the rest of us. Nursing memories of joy and loss, triumphs and failures. Maybe I *could* cut the guy some slack.

Suddenly, Polk opened one rheumy eye, staring at me. "Instead o' just sittin' there on your ass, why don'tcha order us up some breakfast?"

Then again, maybe not.

An hour later, as I downed an unaccustomed third cup of coffee, the phone rang. Polk snatched it up, grunted a few times, and hung up.

"That was Biegler." He popped a last slice of bacon into his mouth. "Wants the background check to go all the way back to the patients you saw when you were an intern."

"That's a lot of people," I said. "And another waste of time. I told you guys, the killer isn't some crazed patient out of my past. That's just Hollywood bullshit."

Polk shrugged. "Not my call." He got to his feet, wiping his mouth with a napkin. "I'm outta here."

I stood up, too. "I'm going with you. I want the same deal we had before. I get first look."

"Forget it. You're stayin' put. Besides, I thought you said it was a waste of time."

"I still think so." I smiled. "But every once in a while I'm wrong."

He failed to see the humor. "What *is* it with you, anyway? Christ."

"Look," I said, "there's no way I'm hanging around here all day. I'm a consultant, right? Let me consult."

Polk rubbed his chin. "Well, one thing's for sure. I let you outta my sight, and you get whacked, I'm screwed."

"Not to mention the paperwork."

He waved a hand in surrender and went off to the bathroom. When the door closed, I called Noah. I had to ask him about my office key, but I still wanted to keep the cops out of it. If they knew he had one, and started hassling him about it, Noah could unravel like a ball of string.

I got his answering machine.

"This is Noah. Our quote for today comes from my main man, the Marquis de Sade. 'Freedom is born in constraint, and dies in liberty.' Roll *that* one around your brain pans, children." BEEP.

Jesus. I left him a message to call me as soon as possible. As though that would do any good.

Chapter Nineteen

Later that morning, under a patchwork sky heavy with the threat of more rain, Sgt. Polk and I drove through the wrought-iron front gates and up the curving driveway to the entrance of Ten Oaks.

Nestled in the bank of trees that inspired its name, surrounded by ten acres of landscaped lawns and gardens, the gable-roofed building looked more like a private boarding school than a psychiatric clinic.

Which, in fact, it had been, until some thirty years ago. Prior to that, it had been the home of one of the city's lesser robber barons, who'd made his millions out of what little industry was left after the Scaifes, Mellons, and Carnegies took their sizeable cuts.

His fortunes declined somewhat after he was found guilty of strangling his mistress with one of her own panties and burying her body under the gardener's shed. In the ensuing years, the family lost most of its wealth and holdings, including this house, to legal fees.

We drove past the massive, gilt-framed double front doors, and into a small lot on the side of the building. Getting out of Polk's car, I could see through the sculpted hedges onto the muddy recreation field, where some patients and staff—indistinguishable in assorted t-shirts, jeans, and sweat shirts—were tossing a football around.

Polk followed my gaze, mumbled something, and shook his head. I knew better than to ask.

Our feet crunched on damp gravel as we made our way back to the entrance. As we approached the doors, whose brass fittings gleamed, a glance at Polk confirmed my hunch that Ten Oaks was not exactly what he'd expected.

I paused at the doors, noting a change in the plaque set discreetly in the rich red brick. It read: "Ten Oaks. A Private Psychiatric Facility." Under these familiar words, new gold-plated lettering added "Part of the UniHealth Family."

Funny how much things can change in just one week.

Polk and I pushed through the doors and entered the egg-shell white reception area, an expensively-decorated room whose high walls always drew my eye up to the circular skylight. Varnished oak beams crisscrossed the ceiling.

In the middle of the room stood a massive oak desk, behind which sat the receptionist, a college-aged Asian girl I didn't recognize. Her name tag read "Amy."

"I'm Dr. Rinaldi," I said, smiling. "You're new?"

"Just two days. Are you on staff, Doctor?"

"Not anymore. But I have visiting privileges." I took out my hospital ID badge and clipped it to my jacket. "Can you tell me if Dr. Garman is free?"

Polk flashed *his* badge. "And if he ain't, tell him to get out here anyway."

Amy's face paled. "Just let me buzz him."

I noticed a new clinic brochure and flipped through it. Nice full-color photos. Smiling patients, concerned doctors. On the back, the tasteful UniHealth logo.

Polk lit up a Camel and squinted around at the walls, covered with drawings done by the patients. Some were colorful, spirited, bravely assertive; most were not.

"I'm sorry, sir," Amy said, an ashtray suddenly appearing in her hand. "Smoking is not permitted."

Her implacable smile was probably an attempt to regain some authority, and he knew it. Polk dutifully took a long last drag of his Camel, then stubbed it out.

The door to our left opened and Garman came out, in a tan shirt and dark blazer. His smile had too many teeth.

"Dan," he said, shaking my hand. "What a shame, you just missed Elaine. Sometimes she pops in to check up on me. Wives, eh?" The smile stayed intact.

"Bert, this is Sergeant Polk, my new dancing partner."

"Nice place ya got here," Polk said dryly.

Garman's watery eyes blinked a couple times. "I understand you need Dr. Rinaldi's old patient files."

"It's just standard procedure, Bert," I said. "Cop-think. I can't believe it's someone I ever treated."

His face was unreadable for a long moment. Then he gave a shrug. "Better safe than sorry, right?"

He led Polk and me back through the door he'd entered, into the main corridor on the first floor. I had to smile, as I often did back when I was on the payroll, at the difference between the cheery reception area out front and the sober reality of the rest of the facility.

Reception was where the family visited, assured by the rich décor and subdued ambiance that their guilt was unjustified. That what they were doing for their children or parents was an act of kindness. That, if anything, choosing a fine facility like Ten Oaks was proof of this.

But back here in the main building, in place of Tiffany-style lamps and hardwood floors, was the track lighting and linoleum of a typical psychiatric clinic. Where, regardless of the fresh paint and cheerful Muzak, the walls were still reinforced to muffle the screaming, and all the doors had locks.

I gave Polk a sidelong glance as we threaded our way through the place. The detective had the stiff walk and feigned attentiveness to detail that most people have in a hospital, particularly a "mental" hospital.

Until we rounded a corner and almost collided with a thin, flaccid man in hospital flannels. He wore blue eye shadow and hoop earrings.

"I'm such a faggot," he said, clutching Polk's forearm. "A stench in the nostrils of God."

"Whatever you say, pal." Polk pulled his arm away, and watched as the patient drifted on down the corridor, sliding along the wall. Quietly sobbing.

"You remember Tina," Garman said to me, nodding toward the fragile-looking woman in her forties coming out of the ladies room. She wore a plain cotton dress and held her hand protectively over her belly.

"Little guy's really kicking today," she said, smiling shyly at us as she disappeared into the kitchen.

I turned to Polk. "Tina. She's been pregnant with Bruce Springsteen's baby for the past fifteen years."

Polk just gave me a sour squint, then fell into step behind Garman again. The sergeant was wearing his palpable discomfort like a badge of honor.

But for me, since grad school Ten Oaks had been pretty much a second home. Even now, I felt a nostalgic tug, the remembrance of a youthful idealism that lingered in these pale green halls, the rows of doors leading to the various day rooms. Dining hall, arts and crafts. One door, marked "GROUP," had a little sign that read "In Session."

Years before, I'd begun my clinical training by leading similar groups, many labeled with such hopeful, poignant names as "Dating and Relating" and "Winning Friends on the Job."

The painful reality, as I came to learn, was that most of Ten Oaks' patients were never going to have much opportunity to date, let alone relate, or to hold down any but the most menial of jobs.

But then, as I also learned, sometimes you'd reach a patient. Or, more accurately, the patient would reach you. Through the fog of medication and delusion would come an amazing insight, a dead-on joke. And you'd connect with the person he or she was *behind* the illness, behind the barriers that separated your disparate views of reality.

As an intern, and then as a clinical member on staff, I gradually understood the wisdom of letting my patients teach me how to be their therapist.

"You with us, Dan?" I heard Garman say. He and Polk stood in the doorway to another, smaller corridor. This led to the offices. Staff lounge. Conference room.

"Right behind you."

I noticed that the conference room door was ajar. One of the staff therapists was alone at the table, filling out some forms. It was where we held our peer reviews, and she was sitting in the corner chair I often used. Where I'd sat the last time I was here, presenting Kevin's case.

Only a month ago. Seemed like a million years.

Garman ushered Polk and me into his office. We each found seats in the stuffed leather chairs facing an ornate lacquered desk. On the walls behind where Garman sat were framed photos of the clinical director shaking hands with the mayor, the governor, and some young corporate type in a Hugo Boss suit that I didn't recognize.

Suddenly, before anyone could say anything, a heavy tread of footsteps halted outside the door.

I looked up to find Dr. Brooks Riley standing there, arms folded. The lower half of his face still sagged, but looked a bit less swollen. His dark eyes found mine.

"You fuck." He squinted in pain.

Garman sat forward in his chair. Voice sharp. "If you're looking for a rematch, Brooks, you're out of luck. We have police on the premises."

Riley barely acknowledged Polk's existence. His angry gaze was trained only on me.

"I meant what I said last night, Danny boy. I'm gonna have your *license* because of Kevin Merrick, and your ass because of *this*." He pointed to his jaw.

Polk looked over at me. "*You* did that?" The trace of a smile. "Son of a bitch."

I waved him off. "Look, Riley—" I began.

Riley turned to Garman, chuckling. "Shit, I didn't even know they *let* white guys box anymore..."

Garman sighed. "That'll be enough, Brooks. Jesus."

I stood up then and glared at Riley.

"You want to do something, *do* it, okay? Get all the lawyers you can buy and come after me. Till then, better stay out of my face."

"Is that a threat?" His eyes narrowed. "Right in front of a police officer, you're *threatening* me?"

Riley's glance went from Polk to Garman, then back to me. I didn't budge. His face got two shades darker.

Finally, he pushed off from the doorframe and walked briskly down the hall. As he turned a corner, his fist slammed against the wall. A vase of cut flowers teetered on its spindly stand and fell over with a crash.

Garman, hands running through his thinning hair, looked helplessly at Polk.

"Sorry, Sergeant. Sometimes you can't tell the patients from the doctors around here."

Polk shrugged. "Not my problem. All I want is those files. *Now* would be good."

"I'll just need a minute."

He disappeared through a side door, leaving Polk and me to sit in a strained silence. A *long* sixty seconds. Then Garman shuffled back in, carrying a thick stack of folders.

"Sorry about the dust, but we haven't gotten around to downloading all these old records yet," he said.

As Polk gathered up the stacks, Garman looked at me.

"Most of these cases go back to before I took over as director," he explained. "Our patient base has changed a great deal since then. Frankly, many of the people in those files couldn't afford to come to Ten Oaks now."

Polk snorted. "So I guess I can forget about sendin' my ex-wife here for a brain overhaul?"

Garman looked pained. "I didn't mean to sound patronizing. We *do* have a number of patients from typical middleclass families. But they have adequate private insurance, or other assets."

"Which buys 'em what, exactly? Gucci straightjackets? Perrier water with their little yellow pills?"

Garman let out a long, slow breath. "You have to understand, Sergeant, it takes considerable resources to run a total-care facility like Ten Oaks. Our patients *and* their loved ones have the right to expect state-of-the-art treatment. The best in custodial and clinical care."

"Jesus, Bert," I said, "you're starting to sound like the brochure."

A sheepish smile. "Yeah, I know. Sometimes I just—"

Suddenly, an alarm bell clanged, echoing down the halls. Garman glanced at a console on his desk. One of the lights was blinking.

"Rec yard," he said, voice tight. He bolted out of his chair, heading for the door.

Polk turned to me. "What is it?"

"Nothing good." I was right on Garman's heels.

Chapter Twenty

"Fucking bitch!!"

The girls looked to be in their late teens. The bigger of the two had the smaller, black one pinned against the chain link fence with a thick, fleshy shoulder. Face bloated with rage, she was screaming obscenities as she clumsily flailed at the other girl with her fists.

Polk and I had bolted into the rec yard, following behind Garman. A throng of patients, mostly male, immediately blocked us while they laughed and shouted encouragement to the girls. Misting rain shrouded the whole yard, making the grass slick as ice beneath our feet.

In a far corner, an older patient with a full beard stood on a bench, yelling, "Chick fight! Chick fight!"

"My God," Garman gasped, trying vainly to get past the human barrier. "Break it up! Stop!"

I glanced at Polk. "Little help?"

Then I waded in.

Following my lead, Polk plunged headlong into the thick knot of patients, jabbing hard with his elbows.

I tried circling the crowd from the other direction, pushing against a growing wave of bodies. Patients were pouring out of the main building now, voices adding to the din, a rising crescendo of pent-up rage and unfettered panic.

This set off a chain reaction, people twisting and slamming against each other, others shrinking back in horror. Everywhere I turned, haunted faces jutted toward mine in the misty rain.

Suddenly I saw an opening and slipped through. I whirled, getting my bearings.

A tight semi-circle of patients had formed around the two fighting girls. The black girl had wriggled free of her tormentor, and was viciously slamming her head into the chain link. Her audience cheered.

By now, I could see burly staffers and a few clinic docs threading their way toward us. They too were shouting and waving their arms, trying to separate the crowd. But I'd lost all track of Polk in the sea of faces.

From somewhere behind me, Garman's voice rose above the din. "Lucy, no!"

The black girl, Lucy, had the bigger girl on the ground now. The white girl was screaming and crying at the same time. Her blouse had torn open, exposing a pendulous breast. Lucy was bent over her, fingers cruelly twisting the big girl's swollen nipple.

"*This* is comin' off, slut," Lucy taunted, bearing down. "Comin' the fuck *off!*"

Over the heads of the crowd, I could see the bearded guy still up on the bench. He had his hand jammed in his jeans, furiously masturbating.

"Lucy!" Garman cried out again.

Suddenly, somebody's swinging fist clubbed me behind the ear, and I staggered a few feet in the mud. Struggling to stay upright, arms outstretched, I collided with another cluster of patients. We collapsed to the ground in a heap.

A rage of my own boiled up inside me. I clawed my way out from under the tangle of arms and legs. Peeling grasping hands off me, ignoring the yelps of outrage and protest, I clambered toward the chain link just beyond.

I'd almost reached the girls, shouldering past a heavy-set patient in overalls, when a familiar guy in thick eyeglasses leapt in front of me and made a lunge for Lucy.

It was Richie Ellner, a patient in his twenties who'd been at Ten Oaks since before I'd first arrived. Gasping from the effort, he was trying to pull Lucy off the other girl when she deftly pivoted and punched him right in the face.

"Richie!" I yelled, catching him as he fell backwards. He collapsed in my arms, blubbering.

The crowd roared its approval, even as more clinic personnel swarmed into the yard. This seemed to turn the tide. As I helped Richie to his feet, I could feel the chaos around us diminishing. It took another five or ten minutes, but some semblance of order was finally restored.

By then, I'd spotted Polk. He and a couple male staffers had reached the two girls and separated them. The bigger girl was hysterical, frantically covering her breasts, tears and blood streaking her face.

Meanwhile, Lucy struggled, screaming and cursing, in the huge arms of a veteran orderly. But since he outweighed her by about 150 pounds, she wasn't getting anywhere.

Richie shook himself out of my own arms and faced me, glowering. "Look, man! Look what she did to my glasses!"

He held them up, showing me the broken frames.

Before I could respond, a stocky, gray-haired nurse came up to us and peered at Richie's face. An ugly bruise had already sprouted on his cheek.

"We better get you inside and take a look at that," she said brusquely, taking his elbow.

Richie frowned at me, crestfallen. "Hey, Doc, we didn't even get a chance to catch up, ya know? Long time, no see." Like nothing had happened. Like we were two old buddies who'd bumped into each other at a ball game.

I smiled. "Go on in, Richie. I'll be there in a sec."

Richie gave me the "thumb's up" sign and went off with the nurse, affording me the chance to look around and survey the damage.

With military precision, the practiced staff had begun herding the patients toward the rear doors, back to their rooms. Bert Garman was standing in the middle of the yard, barking orders to his people. Some of the staff therapists—including the young woman I'd seen making notes in the conference room—were talking individually to the more agitated patients, trying to calm them.

The rain had worsened, fat drops pelting the yard, churning the dirt pathways into mud. I saw Harry Polk slogging toward me. He didn't look too happy.

"Great little clinic you got here," he said. "Weren't you the guy who told me these wackos aren't violent?"

"They're *not*. Trust me, this kind of thing almost never happens. Few patients ever do any physical harm, except maybe to themselves."

"So this must be my lucky day, right?"

I pulled him away from the others. "Harry, just think about it. They're confined, bored, agitated…with pretty much nothing to do between getting pumped full of meds. You don't think they're going to boil over, get into fights?"

"Maybe. But, still, any of these crazies got a grudge against you?"

"Not that kind of grudge. Besides, if you think the killer could be someone from my professional life, why just consider patients? I've got colleagues, former teachers—"

"Don't worry. We'll get to 'em all, sooner or later."

Polk looked down at his muddy shoes, growled something unintelligible and stomped off toward the building.

I held back a moment as Bert Garman came over, hand over his face to shield it from the rain.

He bristled with anger. "Jesus Christ, what happened?" He craned his neck around. "And where's Dr. Riley?"

"Knowing Brooks, he's probably having tea in the staff lounge," I said. "He sure as hell isn't going to get his designer threads dirty wrestling with patients."

He managed a smile. "You're probably right."

I saw him visibly trying to calm himself. "By the way, is this your first encounter with Lucy?"

"Is she a new patient? She looks familiar, somehow."

"Only been here two weeks."

As we walked through the building's double doors, he told me her last name, and I realized why she'd looked so familiar. Her older sister was a major pop singer, an MTV diva with two Grammys to her credit and a steady stream of gangsta boyfriends.

"Lucy's got to be handled carefully, as you can well imagine," Garman was saying as we headed down the hall. "The other one—Helen Frazier—she's been here over a year. Never had any trouble from her before. I mean, I just don't understand this."

I could only nod. Because despite what I'd told Polk, neither did I.

Within a few minutes, staffers were going into patient rooms, carrying little paper cups. After a major incident like this one, there'd be Thorazine cocktails all around.

Just then, a clatter of heels on the linoleum made me turn my head. Dr. Nancy Mendors, small and dark-haired, was hurrying in our direction.

A year or so older than me, her body was still trim and compact. But her face was drawn, eyes red-rimmed with exhaustion. Her worn white coat and faded ID badge were testimony to the many years she'd been on staff.

"Nancy," Garman said tersely, raking his wet hair down with a slender hand. "You missed all the excitement."

"Sorry, Bert," she said, catching her breath. "I was in the ladies' room when the alarm went off."

She touched my arm. "Hey, Danny."

"Hey."

Garman gave us a guarded look, then smiled grimly. "I better go check up on Lucy. We don't want some over-eager intern putting our newest VIP in restraints."

Nancy and I watched him walk away, our shoulders just touching as we stood together.

A thick silence hung between us.

Finally, I made a gesture that took in all the hurried activity in the hall. "Another day at the office, eh?"

She spoke without turning. "Let's hope it doesn't start a trend. By the way, how's Noah?"

"Okay, I think."

"Good. I adjusted his meds a couple weeks back. Put him on Adnorfex. Did he tell you?"

"Nope." Adnorfex was a promising new anti-psychotic.

"Oh."

We always handled these first awkward moments by talking about Noah, his meds, the bar.

"So." She finally faced me. Those dark eyes. Always so frank, so solemn. "How're you handling everything?"

"I guess you've heard, eh?"

"Who hasn't? Hell, you're all over the news." She lowered her eyes. "Sorry about your patient."

"Thanks. Me, too."

"Speaking of which, I want to check up on Richie. I'm his case manager now."

We started down the hall toward the patient quarters.

Nancy and I had known each other since my days as an intern at Ten Oaks. Barbara's death had come just a few months after Nancy's bitter divorce, and we were kind of thrown into each other's arms by loss and regret. As lovers, we'd spent countless nights desperately clinging to one another, between bouts of equally desperate sex.

When it ended as quickly and unexpectedly as it had begun, we were like drunks after a three-day binge, gazing bleary-eyed at each other, each hoping the other would make some sense out of what had happened.

Since then, unless we run into each other when I'm visiting the clinic, or when she's shown up at the bar to check on Noah, we didn't have much contact. But I'd always be grateful to her for being there when I needed someone.

I hoped she felt the same way toward me.

Chapter Twenty-one

We found Richie Ellner sitting on a bench in the A-V room next to a rack of vending machines. His clothes were still wet, spattered with mud. He clutched his broken glasses in thin fingers pock-marked with cigarette burns.

"Richie," I said. "Are you all right?"

Nancy and I flanked him as he rocked back and forth on the bench. Indoors, out of the rain, I got a better look at him.

Twenty-eight going on sixty. Deeply delusional. Eyes bright with fear, clouded with madness, tinged with grief. His father was a senior state senator.

Richie was making an effort to sit still, wrapping himself in his arms, planting his feet firmly to stop the rocking. But he kept shivering, as though having just been pulled from the sea.

"What happened?" Nancy asked him.

"Your standard chick fight. Probably over some guy. Or maybe another chick. Around here, doesn't make much difference what you got goin' on between your legs."

"Who started it?" she asked.

He smiled. "Let me see…I think it was the crazy one."

"Dammit, Richie." Nancy squatted and faced him. "Give me a break here, will you?"

"Hey, I was just screwin' with you." He glanced up at me knowingly. "Not too many laughs around here since you went over the wall, Doc."

"Not too many on the outside, either," I said.

Nancy got to her feet. "Look, we can talk about all this later. Anything I can do for you in the meantime?"

"Depends. We talkin' blow-jobs?"

"In your dreams. I was thinking more along the lines of asking staff to clean you up, bring you a hot drink."

"Nah. I don't wanna miss anything."

"I think the show's pretty much over for today," I said. I reached down and gently took his broken glasses.

He moaned. "Man, those are two bad-ass chicks."

Nancy took the glasses from me. "Why don't I see about getting these fixed?" She looked at me. "Take care, okay?"

I nodded. She patted Richie's shoulder, then headed out of the room.

"Hey," Richie called after her, "*this* time, see that they leave out the micro-transmitter, okay?"

"Right," she called back from the hallway.

Richie gave me a look. "Nice lady. Too bad she's CIA."

His shivers had subsided. Only his eyes, rapidly blinking back tears, betrayed his level of anxiety.

"How've you been, Rich?"

"Fine, man. No complaints."

"Great." I paused. "Now, how've you been?"

"*Oh.* Life sucks, man. It sucks dry tittie and shits green down my face. I tell you my old man finally croaked?"

"No, you didn't."

"Well, that's probably 'cause he's still alive. But it was a swell thought, though."

"He still won't come and see you?"

A dark laugh. "Would you?"

I could have answered in some therapeutic, bullshit way, but I had too much regard for him. He seemed to appreciate my silence.

"By the way," he said, finally. "I wasn't shittin' you before. I mean, Nancy's all right, and she's got some ass on her, but this place just ain't the same without you."

"I'm not sure Dr. Garman would agree with you."

"Garman's a feeb."

"You're wrong there, Rich. Bert Garman is a good doc, and he's done wonders for this place."

"Yeah, right. That's why he sold out to UniHealth."

"Might be a smart move. Who knows?"

He became suddenly animated. "What is this, make nice-nice with the mental patient? These health-care goons are just another cog in the corporate Wheel of Fortune. A cosmic Fuck-You from Vanna White and the wonderful wizards of Wall Street. Pay no attention to the man behind the curtain! It's like Roswell, and Ruby Ridge, and sabotaging our microwaves. It's all connected, man. Oliver Stoned to the max. The World Wide Web. The International House of Panic. Indra's Net and nothin' *but* net!"

His teeth were chattering now, and he'd started rocking back and forth again.

"See, the world ain't goin' out with a bang *or* a whimper. Those Newtonian dichotomies are strictly old-school, horse-and buggy fantasies. Like poets even know what the fuck's up, right? Absinthe-sucking, transgendered freakazoids. No disrespect, but that's not how us *homo sapiens* are checkin' out. No way, Jose. Mankind's gonna be techno-fuckin'-morphed into something even the True Christ wouldn't recognize, and we're all lining up with credit cards to pay for the privilege of goin' first."

Then, as if short-circuiting, he suddenly froze. Body rigid, hands on his lap.

He looked up at me with soft, moist eyes.

Blinking.

"Richie?" I said quietly. "You in there?"

He smiled crookedly. "Hey, did I tell you my old man finally died? Bastard took long enough. I thought he was gonna hang on till the *next* millennium. Man, I'm thirsty. Chick fights always make my mouth dry. That happen to you?"

Before I could say anything, a heavy fist rapping the door-frame behind made me turn in my chair. It was Harry Polk, cell phone in hand, eyes narrowed with purpose.

"C'mon, Doc, gotta go. I just heard from Lowrey."

"What's up?" I said. "And shouldn't we go back to Garman's office for those files?"

"Don't need 'em. We got the killer in a holding cell downtown. They picked him up 'bout twenty minutes ago."

Chapter Twenty-two

Polk was behind the wheel, steering with one hand, trying to light another Camel with the other. He'd practically floored it since we pulled out of the clinic parking lot, and was pushing it even harder as we headed downtown. Under a black sky weeping rain, with traffic coiled like a bag of snakes, he was making turns that had our bodies straining against the seat belts.

"Look," I said, as we bounced over the cobblestones on Grant Avenue, "want me to light that for you?"

"Thanks. Got it." He took a deep drag.

"So, what's going on?"

"It's over, that's what. Second canvas of the area turned up an eyewitness who saw the perp leaving your office building right about the time of the murder."

From the west, thunder rumbled. That new storm was coming in hard.

"Somebody *saw* the guy?"

"Yeah. Witness is named Doolie Stills. Real bottom-feeder. Numbers, that shit. But he picked the killer outta the photo array, and that's good enough for the DA."

Traffic slowed, and we found ourselves behind a line of trucks and SUV's. Polk hit the lights and siren.

"Hold on." He barreled past the line of cars.

"Suspect's a real hard-ass named Arnie Flodine," Polk went on. "Some Oakie from out west, got a sheet as long as my dick.

Assault, armed robbery. Lately, he's been bustin' kneecaps for some local loan sharks."

I considered this. "I don't know. This doesn't seem like the work of a career criminal."

Polk laughed. "No kiddin', Columbo? Like you know what the fuck you're talkin' about."

"Harry, this murder was *personal.* Brutal. There were multiple stab wounds. That sound like a hired job to you?"

"Hey, I knew a collector for the mob, used to motivate deadbeats with a claw hammer. Specialized in facial makeovers." His grin showed nicotine teeth.

"Okay, let's say you're right about Flodine. But don't loan sharks want their muscle to *scare* the guy, not kill him? You can't get your money back that way."

"I already thought of that. The way I figure it, Flodine confronts Kevin in the parking garage, thinkin' he's you, and starts separatin' ribs. Only Flodine realizes he's got the wrong guy, and—"

"Even if you're right, why would he come after *me?*"

Polk stubbed out his Camel. "*You're* the only one who can answer that. What's your thing, Doc? Drugs, gambling?"

"Give me a break."

He snorted. "Once we run your financial records, bet we'll find out you're in debt up to your ass. Whoever you owe money to sent Flodine to put some dents in your piggy bank, only Kevin got killed by mistake."

I looked out the window at the Old County Building shimmering in the rain. "This is nuts, and you know it."

"All I know is, we got the prick." He let out a satisfied sigh. "Funny. Same old story. Sooner or later, somebody just drops a dime on the guy."

Polk swung the car into the parking lot. As he was pulling into a space, my cell phone rang.

For some reason, I took it.

"It's Phil Camden. Again." As usual, my ex-father-in-law wasted little time on pleasantries. His voice sounded even more clipped, more imperious, over the phone.

I spoke quickly. "I got your earlier message, Phil. But this isn't a good time. Maybe tomorrow…"

I glanced at Polk, who was already opening his door. A gust of cold wind, laced with rain, pushed in.

"Don't misunderstand," Phil said sharply. "I don't care whether it's a good time. My calling is a courtesy, one I'm not sure you deserve."

I felt the familiar anger surge in my chest. "Man, you've got a lousy way of showing moral support."

His laugh was a rasp on the tinny cell speaker. "Is *that* what you think this is? Astute as ever, Daniel."

Then he hung up. I sat there, looking at the phone. What the hell—?

I caught sight of Polk through the rain sheeting the windshield. He was side-stepping puddles on his way to the front door. I ran to catch up, and we shouldered through the heavy double doors in unison.

<><><>

Like most government buildings when the weather's bad, the lobby felt airless and over-heated. It was also swarming with uniforms, plainclothes, and a dozen print and broadcast reporters. Everybody knew something was up.

I followed Polk down the lobby and up the stairs. The second floor was even more crowded, and it took us at least a full minute to get to the holding rooms.

Two uniforms stood at the entry door, Polk nodding to them as we went through. Inside, we found District Attorney Sinclair and Lt. Biegler, looking pretty grim.

Polk strode up to his boss. "Where's Flodine?"

"Holding One." Biegler glared at me. "What's *he* doin' here?"

"Doc was with me when I got the call. I figured—"

"You figured wrong," Biegler said.

"That's not a concern at the moment," Sinclair said sharply. His eyes were pinched with worry. Whatever the problem was, he wasn't in control. And it was killing him.

I also remembered that Sinclair had been scheduled to meet with Miles Wingfield and the mayor first thing this morning. Bet *that* hadn't been much fun, either.

"I thought we *had* the guy." Polk frowned.

"He's got an alibi," Biegler replied. "Lowrey's in there with him now, trying to poke a hole in it."

As if on cue, a balding guy in a dark three-piece suit came through the entry door. As soon as I saw his briefcase, I knew who he was. *What* he was.

"That's it," Biegler groaned. "He's lawyered up."

The attorney shook Sinclair's hand, ignoring the rest of us. "Jerome Rossi, representing Arnold Flodine. I'd like to see my client, please."

Without a word, Sinclair and Biegler led Rossi down the hall to Holding One. Polk and I followed behind.

We gathered at the holding room, looking through the one-way glass, as Rossi went in. Inside, sitting across from each other at a formica table, was Det. Lowrey and the suspect. A uniformed cop stood mute in a near corner.

Arnie Flodine was pretty much as Polk described him. Thick, broad-shouldered under a gray overcoat. His face was flat-planed, coarse with stubble. His eyes were dead.

"That's enough, Detective," we could hear Rossi say to Lowrey through the speaker over our heads. "This conversation with Mr. Flodine is over."

"They don't got shit, man." Flodine grinned up at his lawyer. "I was at Vickie's the whole time that night—"

Rossi put a hand on his shoulder. "Shut up, Arnie."

Flodine glared at him, but Rossi kept his eyes on Lowrey. "I understand my client has an air-tight alibi, so there's no way you can detain him."

On our side of the glass, Beigler was shaking his head. "Who's banking-rolling this prick?"

"Probably the loan shark who employs Mr. Flodine," Sinclair said evenly. "I should think that obvious."

The scraping of chairs on linoleum drew our eyes back into the room. Lowrey could only stand there, jaw taut, as Rossi led Flodine out of the room. Frustrated, she drummed her painted nails on the table top.

"Gentlemen." Rossi and his client worked their way past us. Flodine was stiffly buttoning his coat, the wronged citizen indignantly enjoying his freedom.

After they'd left, Sinclair turned to Biegler. "Is Casey still with this Doolie person?"

Biegler nodded miserably. "In the Box."

Lowrey, chagrined, joined us out in the hall. Without a word, we all trudged down to the interrogation room.

Standing guard outside the second holding room was another uniformed cop. As we joined him, I could see why. ADA Casey Walters was in there alone with Doolie Stills.

The witness, bouncing nervously in his seat, was reed-thin, jangly. Like Ichabod Crane on speed.

Casey was standing across from him at the table, arms folded. Eyes cool as blue diamonds.

"Everything okay?" Sinclair asked the cop standing guard. The DA peered into the interrogation room.

The cop shrugged. "So far."

I turned to Sinclair. "Does she always go in the Box?"

"Always." Sinclair spoke with a kind of paternal pride. "I've seen her sweat guys twice the size of Flodine. And she doesn't take any shit from their lawyers, either."

Lowrey said, "Usually she's got a detective in there with her. Want me to go in, Lieutenant?"

Biegler knew enough to glance at Sinclair before answering. The DA gave a subtle shake of his head.

"Let's see what happens," Biegler replied to Lowrey officiously. "The witness seems benign."

Chapter Twenty-three

District Attorney Sinclair flipped on the speaker switch at his elbow. The voices of Casey and Stills crackled from the speaker.

"I don't got nothin' else to tell ya," Stills was saying, watching nervously as Casey moved down the table toward him. He wore a black leather jacket that seemed to swallow his bony frame.

"Then you won't mind telling me again." She stood over him, arms still folded.

His long fingers rolled a pencil back and forth on the tabletop. "Like I said, I was comin' down Fifth that night, after spendin' some time with T-Ball over at the rink. Musta been around seven. Anyway, I turn the corner and I see this guy come tearin' outta this building."

"The office building where the murder took place?"

"Yeah. It was dark, but there's a street light at that corner, and I seen the guy plain as day."

"And you're telling us all this because you're a concerned citizen?"

He chortled. "Yeah, right. Some cops were around, askin' questions. I figgered if I don't come forward, and it gets found out, I'm the one gets jammed up."

"So you were just covering your ass?"

He pointed the pencil tip at her. "Call it anything you want to, lady, I know what I seen. I picked him outta that book of pictures, didn't I? Man, that's one ugly motherfucker." His laugh was high and thin.

"You realize," she said, "that consorting with a known felon like T-Ball violates the terms of your parole?"

"Aw, come on. You ain't gonna bust my balls over that, are ya? I mean, I'm givin' ya Flodine here."

Casey said nothing then, just continued to look at him. This seemed to make Stills even more anxious. He started flicking the pencil between his fingers.

Suddenly, the pencil slipped from his grasp, rolled across the table and fell on the floor.

"Shit," he said.

To my surprise, Casey bent and picked it up. As she rose to her feet, tossing the pencil back on the table, I thought I saw something happen. I couldn't be sure, but it looked as though her lips brushed by Stills' left ear.

As Casey turned away, a change came over Stills. His eyes widened in a fixed stare. Sweat beaded his forehead. The man was suddenly terrified.

Seemingly unmindful of this, Casey casually pulled out the chair on her end of the table and sat down.

"Now, are you sure about what you've just told me?" she asked him, her voice suddenly three degrees warmer.

Stills was having a hard time making his mouth work.

"What was that, Doolie? I didn't quite catch it."

"I said," Doolie stammered, swallowing hard, "I said I'd maybe like to revise my statement."

"What do you mean? Revise it how?"

"Change it, okay? I wanna change my story. I mean, that's all it *is*, anyway. Just a story. None of it's true."

"I'm confused, Doolie," Casey said. "Now you're saying you *didn't* see Arnie Flodine the night of the murder?"

"No, I didn't!" His voice rose, thick with fear. "I didn't see nothin'! I wasn't even *near* Fifth that night. I spent the whole time with T-Ball. I swear it."

For the first time, someone on our side of the viewing glass spoke up.

"What the fuck—?" It was Harry Polk.

Biegler shook his head. "I knew this was too easy."

"Will you all be *quiet*, please?" Sinclair snapped.

Inside, Casey was leaning back in her seat. "You're going to have to explain this to me, Doolie."

He spread his hands. "Can'tcha just forget I ever said anything? Just forget the whole thing?"

"Why would I do that? You've caused the police a lot of trouble. We apprehended a suspect, because of you."

"Look, I admit I fucked up. What do I gotta do, pay a fine?" He tried smiling at her, but it didn't take.

"Why did you lie about Flodine? Unless…" She sat forward. "You *know* him, don't you?"

He nodded, miserable. "Fuck yeah, I know him. We did some time together a year or so back, and he was always pushin' me around, takin' my shit. Look!"

He twisted in his chair, to let his jacket sleeve fall off his shoulder. "See this arm? Fucker broke it in two places. They patched me up, but it still don't work right. Hurts like hell, too."

"So when you heard about the murder—"

"I swore I'd always get back at that prick. I mean, it's all I talked about once I got out. Then last night—I was coked outta my mind and goin' on and on about Flodine, and T-Ball, he says, 'You're always talkin' about fucking over this guy, but you don't got the stones to do it,' and I says, 'Oh, yeah, man? Oh yeah?'"

"So that's when you got the brilliant idea of pinning this unsolved murder on Flodine."

Stills sniffed. "It was all over the news. You were still lookin' for the guy. I figured, now's my chance."

Casey stood up, palms out flat on the table. "Well, you figured wrong. Flodine has a solid alibi for the night of the murder. We'll have to cut him loose."

"Sure, I get that," Stills said, his face the picture of contrition. "There's just one thing."

He reached for the pencil again, started tapping it on the table. "I mean, does Flodine know who fingered him? Like, does he know it was me? That's all I'm askin' here."

"You know how it is, Doolie." Casey walked in our direction, toward the door. "Word gets around."

Stills' face froze. "But…but if he finds out—"

Casey stood at the door and looked at him. "You want my advice? Make yourself scarce." A tight smile. "Oh, and you can keep the pencil, Doolie. We've got lots of them."

Doolie Stills sat stricken, wide-eyed and wordless. A sudden odor told us he'd lost control of his sphincter.

"Aw, hell," Polk said.

As Casey came out of the Box, Biegler nodded to the uniformed cop. "Go on in and process him outta here, before he stinks up the whole place."

The cop wasn't too happy about this assignment, but he nodded and went into the holding room.

Casey joined the rest of us, straightening the collar of her blouse.

"Good work," Sinclair said to her.

"Thanks, but this just puts us back where we started."

Casey's eyes found mine. "Hey, aren't you supposed to be holed up somewhere, playing cards with Sgt. Polk?"

I smiled. "I talked my way out of it."

Polk shot me a look. But before he could say anything, another uniformed cop came through the entry door.

"Sorry to interrupt, sirs," he said. "But Dr. Rinaldi here has a phone call. Guy says it's an emergency."

Instinctively, I touched my jacket pocket. After my conversation with Phil Camden, I'd shut off my cell phone.

"Somebody called you *here?*" Biegler growled.

"Well, it's where I've been spending most of my time lately," I answered. I turned to the cop. "Who is it?"

"Says his name's Art Tatum."

It was Noah.

"Oh, yeah," I said gravely. "Good thing you tracked me down." I turned to Sinclair. "A patient. In crisis."

The DA waved a hand. "I don't care who it is. If you need to talk to this guy, do it. Just don't leave the building without informing either Sergeant Polk or Detective Lowrey. Are we clear, Doctor?"

"Crystal."

After sending a glance in Casey's direction, I followed the cop back out through the door.

Chapter Twenty-four

The desk sergeant punched a blinking light on his phone cradle, then gestured toward the men's room.

"Extension's over there, you want some privacy, Doc."

"Thanks." I went over to the extension phone set on a small table, sequestered away from the main flow of lobby traffic. I picked up the receiver.

"Art Tatum?" I laughed. "Not on your best day."

"Hey, you figured out it was me," Noah said.

"Wasn't too hard."

"I was gonna say Bill Evans, but somehow that didn't sound like me. Ya know what I mean?"

"I'm just glad you got back to me. It's important."

"You're a hard dude to find, man. I called your cell, your office, your house. Then it occurs to me the cops probably got you under wraps, since there's some homicidal maniac out there tryin' to punch your ticket. So I tried there. Glad I reached you while you still got a pulse."

"Great. Listen, Noah, remember that key to my office I gave you a couple years back? In case you ever needed a place to crash?"

"You gave me a key? To your office? Hey, man, thanks."

"Stay with me here, okay? Do you still have it?"

"I'm still tryin' to remember you givin' it to me."

"Look, ask Charlene. Maybe you gave it to her, for safekeeping. Wait, let me ask her. Is she there?"

"No, she's down at the bar. Workaholic, that chick."

"Then where are you calling me from?"

"Let me look around." There was a long pause. "Oh, yeah. Lobby of the Penn Hotel. One of them fancy phone booths, with the cushioned seats and the little overhead lights. I just love makin' calls from in here."

"Noah, the Penn Hotel is miles away from the bar. How'd you get there? You take a bus?"

"I think I walked. I like walkin' in the rain. Me and the Ronnettes." He gave a short, high laugh. "Remember that tune? Just mainstream pop, but at least it spoke from the heart. Not like that soulless shit nowadays…"

"You *walked*?" Something was wrong. Something in his voice was setting off my internal alarm bells.

"By the way," Noah went on, "they got a real loser playin' piano here in the lobby. Sucks on ice, this guy."

I heard his phone booth door open. "Hey, somebody call the Music Police!" he shouted. "Guy in a tux is killin' Duke Ellington."

I could hear an embarrassed murmur of voices, under another shrill laugh. Then the door clicked shut again.

"Jesus, Noah, hotel security's going to toss your ass if you don't chill out."

"What are you, my mother?"

I kept my voice even. "Look, Dr. Mendors told me she adjusted your meds. You're not screwing around with the dosage or anything?"

"Man, I'm surprised at you. Hell, no. Honest."

"Okay, okay. But, listen to me now. I want you to call Charlene and tell her where you are so she can pick you up. And don't forget to ask her about the key, all right?"

"What key?"

"Okay, look, I'll call her myself, right now. Just do me a favor and stay where you are. *Capice?*"

"Okay, but only since you asked nicely."

I hung up, then called Charlene on my cell.

"Noah's Ark," she answered. "Charlene speaking."

I explained why I was calling.

"No, he never gave me a key," she said wearily. "Never mentioned one. But I'm sure glad you found him."

"Well, he sort of found me. But, listen, I got a weird vibe from him over the phone. I think he's in trouble."

"Funny, I thought he was actin' strange myself this morning, but with Noah it's kinda hard to tell—"

"He's not messing with his meds, is he?"

"I don't think so. But I'll grill him when he gets home." Her voice softened. "And thanks, Doc. I'll send a cab over to the Penn for him when we hang up."

"There's a special place in heaven for you, Charlene."

Her laugh was rueful. "If there ain't, there oughtta be." We hung up.

Before I left, I put in a call to Paul Atwood, the therapist covering for me, just to make sure none of my regular patients were in crisis. Thankfully, things were relatively quiet on that front.

I made my way across the lobby again. I was feeling the effects of another sleepless night, so I took a detour to the coffee lounge, two flights down to the basement.

The place was well-lit but empty. Plastic tables and chairs, vending machines. I put some coins in a slot, got black coffee in a Styrofoam cup, and pulled up a chair.

The Metro section of that day's *Post-Gazette* had been left on the table. The lead story was a recap of the Handyman's current Death Row appeal, with numerous quotes from the serial killer's attorney. He seemed quite confident that his client's scheduled execution would be stayed once again. "Troy David Dowd's mental competency, and thus his culpability, remains the cornerstone of our argument," the lawyer told reporters.

There was also a story about the upcoming movie based on Dowd's crimes. In addition to De Niro, Susan Sarandon had just been signed to play Sylvia Lange, the woman who'd managed to escape with her life. And my first patient after going back to work following Barbara's death.

I blew steam off the rim of my cup. Sylvia's recovery from her ordeal had been so slow, so torturous. What the hell was this new film going to do to her? Having the most horrific events of her life replayed as entertainment. Millions of people knowing her story. Or at least the Hollywood version of it.

The anger rose in my chest as I kept reading the article. Making a movie about Dowd was nothing less than a second violation of his victims and their families. Not to mention the real possibility of retraumatization for Sylvia and the other survivor, that 12-year-old boy whose name has thankfully never been revealed.

I made a mental note to phone Sylvia, see how she was doing. I wanted to make sure she had a support system in place—shrinks, family, and friends. She'd need it, now that the publicity surrounding the film was growing. And it was only going to get worse. Interviews with the director and cast on *Entertainment Tonight*. Getting their "take" on the story. Christ!

I folded up the paper and tossed it into a trash can.

"What's the matter, Danny? They spell your name wrong or something?"

The voice caught me off guard. I turned in my seat.

It was Casey, leaning against the open door. She had her jacket thrown over one shoulder, her long silken legs crossed at the ankle. It was a pose, the studied casualness, the confidence with which she held her body.

She gave her audience a long look, then pushed off from the door and walked to my table. I stood up and pulled out a chair for her.

"I was hoping I'd see you again today," I said.

"I know."

"No, that wasn't what I meant. I mean, well, yes, I wanted to see you—but I was talking about something else."

She leaned back, enjoying this. That knowing smile.

I gave her one right back. "Anyway, where do things stand now?" I sipped the hot, black coffee, giving no sign that I'd just scalded my tongue. Mr. Smooth.

"Let me see," she said easily. "There's still somebody out there looking to kill you. Biegler's people haven't got squat, and Leland says the mayor is demanding an arrest in twenty-four hours. Wants every available cop on the case."

"This all come out of that meeting with Wingfield this morning?"

"According to Lee, it wasn't exactly a meeting. More like an audience with the Pope. A really *pissed-off* pope."

"Bad combination: unlimited wealth and a thirst for revenge. The man wants his son's killer."

"Or he wants blood." Her lips tightened. "The mayor's. Yours. Mine. Anybody's."

We grew silent. I watched the coffee cool in my cup. When I felt her eyes on me, I glanced up.

"Look, about you and Sinclair…"

Her gaze didn't waver. "That's…over. Now."

I shook my head. "None of my business, but—"

She shrugged. "He's got a wife and kids. *And* political ambitions. What did I expect?"

Her beautiful face softened, showing faint signs of fatigue under the alabaster skin. Strain at the edge of her eyes.

"You know the worst part?" she went on. "My pride. I hate being reduced to some kind of cultural stereotype. You know, female protégée, older male mentor. So…retro. So damn conventional."

"Conventional? I don't think that's something *you* have to worry about."

A wry smile. "You're just saying that 'cause you want to jump me."

My embarrassed look made her laugh suddenly. Her eyes became animated again.

"Hey," she said, "weren't you going to ask me about something?"

"Yeah. Doolie Stills…"

"Too bad that didn't pan out. We could've used a break."

"But how'd you get the truth out of him? You did *something*, I know it. When you picked up his pencil. I thought I saw you whisper in his ear as you were getting up."

"I did. One word. I said, 'Harpoon.'" She flicked a piece of lint from her sleeve. "Doolie's a smart guy. I knew he'd get the message. I figured he'd tell me the truth after that."

"Harpoon?"

"Yeah. I was letting him know I'd see to it that his parole violation landed him in a cell with Cecil 'Harpoon' Washington, ex-NFL pick, former bouncer with two manslaughter convictions, and legendary prison stud. Harpoon's always looking for a new bitch, and Doolie knows he's just his type: white, skinny, and verbal. He could tell Harpoon lots of street stories during those long prison nights. Between getting ten stiff inches up the ass on an hourly basis. The word is, Harpoon's got a big appetite, and doesn't mind if things get a little rough. His last two pets ended up in surgery."

I must have stared. Casey smiled.

"It worked, didn't it?" But her smile tightened a bit at the corners. First time I'd ever seen her defensive.

"Sinclair's right," I said at last. "You're good."

"Meaning what?" Her voice grew an edge.

"Nothing..." Suddenly, the air between us thickened, coagulated like blood.

"You got a problem with it?"

I stared, at a loss. "Hell, no—"

"You *do*, don't you?"

"I said, no..."

Her eyes narrowed. "I mean, who the fuck are you?"

Something was happening, a sea-change, an eruption of raw feeling. Like I was looking at a different person.

I spread my hands. "Look, I was just—"

But Casey was livid, leaning across the table. Face flushed as though it had been slapped.

"I do what I *have* to do," she said. "And I like it. *Love* it. So go fuck yourself."

"Dammit, I'm not—"

She reached under the table, eyes still holding mine, and brought up her hand, fingertips glistening.

"See? Just talking about it gets me wet."

She stood then, and reached across the table, and streaked the side of my face with her juices.

And bolted out of the room.

Chapter Twenty-five

I never knew my mother when she didn't have to be fed through a tube. She lay in her hospital bed, dying as beautifully as the Irish saint my father thought her to be, unmindful as I squeezed her hand.

I was about four, I think. Maybe three. I just remember being small, feeling small, the child-flesh of my forearm indented by the cool bed railing as it rested there, reaching through for her cold fingers, as though to keep her from heaven, and me from hell.

My father told me she'd been very sad for a long time, and the doctors had tried to help by putting lightning into her brain, a cleansing electrical storm like the kind that used to wash away the smudged, sluggish air of Pittsburgh summers. But it had only made things worse.

By the time I was five, I was motherless, and being raised alternately by my father, between shifts and binges, and my mother's sister. Since her husband Frank worked in the produce yards off Penn Avenue, I ended up spending most of my teenage after-school hours working with him.

Called "the Strip," it was a world I knew well. As a child, I'd played along the railroad tracks that ran behind it. Later, I'd earn spending money unloading crates of lettuce, peppers, and tomatoes from the backs of trucks.

I remember sweaty old men, skin dark and wrinkled as olives soaking in brine, shouting at each other over the static blare of

Pirates games on transistor radios. Two-wheeled carts, piled high with produce, would bounce crazily over unused streetcar tracks imbedded in the cobblestone pavement.

Over the years, nothing much has changed. The streets still smell of men and ham and cheese left to age; of truck exhaust and rotting vegetables; of animal fat and flatcar timber and smoke from thick black cigars.

To this day, there's a triangle of memory in my mind: my mother's death, the yards, and, just beyond Penn, the PAL gym that was old when my dad first took me there thirty years ago.

It was a black-bricked hulk in a forgotten alley of a forgotten street. Fight posters of heavy-jawed Italians and Poles posing menacingly for the camera hung like dry, cracked adhesive tape, shredded and stained by age.

Inside, likewise, nothing much had changed. I stood there now in training sweats they keep here for me, blinking salt water out of my eyes as I worked the ceiling bag. Needing to hit something. Anything. To hear the percussive slap of fist against leather, echoing.

After what happened with Casey, I couldn't go home to an empty house. I felt jangly, upended.

I mean, what the hell *had* happened? And what was I doing about it? What didn't I know about her, and why didn't it bother me more? There were a hundred questions I should be asking myself and I wasn't asking them.

Maybe because I didn't want to know the answers.

Whatever message she was sending, I refused to decode it. To assess or interpret. All the usual therapist's defenses against merely reacting.

I touched the side of my face, still slick from her. Mixed now with my own sweat. Insane, this wanting of her. Against my every instinct. Despite—

To hell with understanding *her*, I thought; I didn't understand *me*.

<>< ><>

Outside, the rain must've been coming in gusts. I was vaguely conscious of its staccato drumming on the roof, like thrown handfuls of pebbles.

The gym was nearly deserted, except for an old-timer playing Solitaire by the door and the bored young cop that Biegler had assigned to me. With the case growing cold, and the pressure from the top mounting, the police figured Polk had better things to do than baby-sit me.

My bodyguard, a guy named Schotz, lounged against the wall. He was young, with steroid-pumped arms that stretched the dark fabric of his uniform. He was typical Pittsburgh: stolid, unambivalent, third generation at the job.

He pretended boredom as he watched me pepper the bag repeatedly with angry right-hand jabs.

"Not bad." A grudging comment. "How's your left?"

"Reliable." Macho bullshit for the benefit of the kid.

He grunted. After leaving the station, it hadn't been hard to talk Schotz into detouring here for a couple hours. Until he saw the place. No state-of-the-art equipment. No music. No babes.

I finished my work-out and nodded toward the locker room.

"Shower, okay?" I said. "Ten minutes."

Schotz shrugged. "Just don't get killed."

A phone rang, and I glanced over at the front desk. But it was Schotz' cell. He answered it, then took a few steps away and held it furtively to his ear.

<>< ><>

I came out of the locker room wearing the same clothes I'd had on all day, now damp from my shower.

Officer Schotz had moved again, this time lounging against the front door. As I neared, he pushed off, sullen.

"Hey." His voice was all cop.

He put a hand on my arm, stopping me. Just then, Harry Polk pushed the door open behind him, his face dark as grain leather. Before I could say a word, his thick hands were on my shoulders, turning me.

"Jesus, Harry!—"

I felt the sharp snap of handcuffs on my wrists.

I craned my neck around. "What the hell—?"

"Daniel Rinaldi, you're under arrest for the murder of Dr. Brooks Riley. You have the right—"

"What? Brooks?.."

Polk pulled me toward him, eyes like marble chips. "They found him in his office at the clinic a couple hours ago. With two nasty slugs in his heart."

Chapter Twenty-six

For the next couple hours, I was the prime suspect in the murder of Brooks Riley.

The facts were these: Earlier that day, after the patients were secured following the incident in the yard, Bert Garman called an emergency meeting of all clinic personnel. Riley never showed up, nor did he answer at his extension.

That's when Nancy Mendors offered to see if he was still in his office. She found the door closed, but unlocked. She knocked twice, got no answer, and went in.

Brooks Riley was sitting in his chair, wearing a look of surprise, or maybe just a final annoyance. Thick blood was congealing on his chest like red sealing wax, darkening at the edges.

Nancy's screams brought a nearby orderly on the run, followed by Garman and the rest of the staff. Investigators reported later that nothing in the office seemed to have been disturbed. The metal cabinet holding patient files, though flecked with blood, was securely locked.

By five o'clock, after a quick review of witness statements from the scene, Lt. Biegler had ordered Harry Polk to arrest me.

I got all of this from Polk himself as we rode back to the Old County Building. We parked under the station. Then he brought me upstairs and into the same interrogation room that had hosted Arnie Flodine only a few hours before. Biegler was waiting for me, arms folded, glowering.

Polk unlocked my handcuffs and pulled out a chair. We sat across from each other like chess opponents, shoulders hunched, wary and hostile. There was no window, but I could sense that beyond these walls another night had fallen.

"Sure you don't wanna call your lawyer?" Polk said.

"Not yet," I said. "Though he could probably use a laugh."

"You think this is funny?" Biegler's brow narrowed.

"No, I think it's bullshit. I didn't kill Brooks Riley. For one thing, I *couldn't* have."

"Like hell," Polk said. "The ME figures Riley got clipped sometime between noon and four this afternoon. I know for a fact that you were on the premises at Ten Oaks, 'cause I was there with you."

"That's right, Harry. *You're* my alibi. Then, after the riot in the yard, I was with Nancy Mendors, until *you* showed up again to tell me they'd arrested the killer. So when the hell did I shoot Riley?"

"*During* the riot," Biegler said. "Sgt. Polk tells me you and he got separated in all the confusion."

Polk's head bobbed. "I lost sight of you for at least ten minutes. Plenty of time for you to slip out of the crowd, shoot Riley in his office, and come back out to the yard."

I stared at him. "By that same logic, *you* could be the killer. I lost sight of you during those same ten minutes."

"Problem with that," Biegler said, "is that *you* got a motive. Dr. Riley threatened to sue you in front of witnesses. Dr. Bert Garman and his wife Elaine. Riley swore he'd destroy you. Ruin your life."

"Plus we got Garman admitting that you punched the guy out the night before," Polk said. "I saw what you did to Riley's jaw, remember? At the clinic."

"So he threatened to sue me. That doesn't mean I killed him." I leaned back. "C'mon, guys, make up your minds. First, you say I'm the intended victim of a murder. Now you say *I'm* a murderer. Which is it?"

Biegler leaned in, bristling. "Don't fuck with me, okay? I *still* like you for the Kevin Wingfield killing."

I pushed down my own anger, focused on Polk. "Come on, Harry, you *know* this is crap."

"Maybe. But look what we got: you and Brooks Riley hated each other, personally and professionally. Then today, another angry exchange between you two. So when the patients go ballistic, you see your chance to sneak away and do Riley. Problem solved."

"Nice story," I said. "But where did I get the gun to shoot him? And where is it now?"

Biegler was smug. "CSU's scouring the clinic and grounds as we speak. We'll find the damn gun, guaranteed."

I took a breath. "Look, *anybody* at Ten Oaks could've used the riot for cover and killed Riley."

"But only you had a motive."

"That you *know* of," I insisted. "Believe me, Riley was not a well-liked guy."

Polk snorted. "Well, he got one hell of an attitude adjustment this afternoon."

"Besides, about this so-called riot. Like I told Polk, that kind of thing is just *not* typical patient behavior. Isn't it strange that such a golden opportunity would suddenly present itself? Unless the fight between the two female patients was staged—"

"No shit?" Polk laughed. "Believe it or not, us dumb cops managed to come up with that same theory ourselves. My partner's over there now, questioning the two broads."

"That's my point. If somebody *did* arrange for those girls to cause a diversion, it would have to be someone on the inside. At Ten Oaks, I mean."

Biegler shrugged. "You go there once a week for professional consults, don't you? You've still got visiting privileges. That's inside enough for me."

Suddenly, the door swung open and Casey Walters strode in, face flushed with anger. In her hand was a cell phone.

"Counselor." Biegler gave her a curt nod. "Just in time to file the papers."

She just glared, pointing the phone at him like a gun. "It's for you."

Biegler blinked in confusion and instinctively back-stepped. Casey moved closer, voice hard as flint.

"As soon as I heard about this shit," she said, "I got a hold of Sinclair."

"Hey, you can't—" But he bit off his words, staring nervously now at the phone as if it were actually loaded.

"Go ahead," she pressed him, "the DA's waiting to hear why you've arrested a guy we've had in protective custody for the past two days. Who, by the way, consults for the department and has a fucking *cop* for an alibi."

Biegler swallowed hard and took the phone from her hand. "Lt. Biegler here." He moved stiffly to a far corner of the room.

Casey swung around and looked at me for the first time. "Hi ya, Danny. I don't know about you, but I've had enough of this place for one day."

I got to my feet. "Works for me."

"Hey—!" Polk protested, rising out of his chair.

"Look, Harry," I said angrily, "either book me now, in which case I'm calling a lawyer, or I'm walking."

Polk looked helplessly at Biegler, who stood with the cell phone glued to his ear. The lieutenant just waved impatiently in our general direction.

Casey touched my elbow. "Let's go."

But I wasn't finished. I moved around the table to face Polk.

"One more thing," I said. "When he gets off the phone, tell your boss I'm refusing police protection, as of now. Truth is, getting busted for Riley's murder has kinda taken all the fun out of it. Besides, if Schotz is the best you can do, I'll take my chances going solo."

Polk growled. "Hell, you can't just—"

"Actually, I can." I turned to Casey. "*Now* we can go."

"You sure about this? I mean, Sinclair's not gonna like—"

"It's *my* life, Casey. It's time I took it back."

Our eyes locked. After a long moment, she nodded.

Biegler was still on the phone as I followed her out of the Box, feeling the heat of Polk's stare on my back.

Chapter Twenty-seven

The night was dark and the skies were finally exhausted of rain. The city stood drenched, dripping from every rooftop and cornice, brooding in the gloom.

"Rain stopped," Casey had said when we first stepped outside. "Maybe it's a good omen."

We were walking toward her car in the lot. The rain-slicked street was deserted, and our footsteps echoed hollowly from the pavement.

"Thanks for coming to my rescue."

Casey frowned. "Biegler's such a shit. He waited till Sinclair had left the building before ordering your arrest. Luckily I caught Lee between meetings at his office. He's probably still tearing Biegler a new one."

"I didn't know Sinclair was such a fan of mine."

"He isn't. He's just not stupid. Biegler's so anxious to make this all go away, he jumped the gun."

"Well, in his defense, Riley's murder *is* pretty damn strange. I mean, there's no reason to assume his death and Kevin's are connected, but if not, it's a helluva coincidence."

She didn't answer. I looked over to see her head tilted down, eyes scanning the pavement.

I waited.

"Look," she said at last, "I'm not going to apologize for my behavior earlier. I'm not proud of it, but I won't apologize, so if that's what you need from me—"

"Let it go, okay?"

She glanced up finally, the doubt in her eyes as stinging as a reproach.

"You shrinks call it 'acting out,' don't you? Or just 'inappropriate.' *There's* one of my favorite bullshit words."

We'd reached the precinct parking lot, ablaze with light from the overhead lamps. Casey showed her ID to the middle-aged cop half-dozing in the entrance kiosk, who waved us in.

We walked in silence to her parked car.

"Do me a favor, will ya?" she said. "Get in."

She slid behind the wheel, then waited as I came around and got in on the passenger side.

Her face was beautiful in the pale light, but somber and still, like a cameo. Her look at me was intense, yet guarded.

I took a guess. "You're wondering if you can tell me something. Whether you can trust me."

"Yes." Her voice was flat.

"Look, I understand. You don't really know me."

"I know enough. We have a lot in common. Loners, I think. Survivors."

She tilted up her chin so that her gaze seemed to soften. A cotton-thick warmth grew inside the car.

"I guess I hope…" Her voice trailed off.

I leaned across the car seat. My hand found hers.

"What?" I said quietly. "You hope…?"

She gently pulled her hand out from under mine. A brief, sad smile lit her face, and then was gone.

"Sorry," she said. "It's been a long day. Longer than most. The garbage I see, the way people live their lives. Like Paula Stark. Remember that case I was arguing with Polk about? We had to cut her loose. Not enough evidence. But, Christ…she's got no job, an alcohol problem, a four-year-old whose father could be anywhere. She's probably in some shit-hole right now, blowing some stranger for rent money, while her kid waits in the next room. I mean it, sometimes I hate this goddam job."

She looked out through her smudged side window. "And I *am* sorry about this afternoon. I felt judged by you and it pissed me off. I guess I wanted to shock you, or—hell, I don't know. Just…don't think anything about it, okay?"

Sure, no problem. I hesitated. Wanting to challenge her, to probe.

Instead, I merely said, "Okay."

We said good-bye with a brief, collegial hug that brought her face near mine. I breathed in the scent that rose from the hollow of her throat where the skin disappeared beneath the sharp V of her blouse. Then I got out of the car and watched her drive off.

She'd said she would offer me a ride home except for the mountain of paperwork that still lay ahead tonight. Plus a promised follow-up call with Sinclair.

I turned and headed back across the lot under a sky black and thick as wet ink.

I earned every break I got, she'd told me that first night. Driven, self-assured. Yet there was something else beneath the surface. Not just the vulnerability routinely disavowed by high-achievers. More shaded, elusive.

I walked back out to the street. The night air was sharp with cold and the damp from recent rains.

The brisk honk of a car horn made me look up. Though the street was empty, I saw what looked like a cab parked at the far intersection. I hailed it.

No more detours tonight, I thought. *Go home. Get some sleep. Besides, something odd had struck me about Kevin's murder, and in the morning I—*

Belching exhaust, the cab had started up and was heading in my direction. As it approached, wheels sluicing water, I saw the cabbie's shadowed face, slowly taking form through the smudged windshield. His stare was strangely intense, yet familiar, as though he recognized me.

No, that wasn't it. Then I felt the truth hum along my spine like an electric shock.

He'd been waiting for me.

The cab rolled to a stop in front of me, the back door swinging open. I backed up a step on the pavement.

Suddenly, I felt a strong pressure on my shoulder, a thick hand pushing me inside, across the seat. I turned, wrenching free of its grip.

He slid in beside me.

I hadn't heard him come up behind me. A big man. Wide-shouldered, thick-limbed. Military-style buzz-cut. Face smooth and implacable as marble.

"Mind if I share the cab? Since we're headin' in the same direction."

I recognized the gun in his hand. A 9 mm Glock. I'd seen one before.

Chapter Twenty-eight

I had to admit, the guy was good.

As we walked across the crowded lobby of the Burgoyne Plaza, his arm around my shoulder, voice slurred as though laced with booze, nobody could have guessed there was a gun in his other hand, pressed hard against my ribs.

I knew where we were going. The Burgoyne was Pittsburgh's newest and most prestigious hotel, the final jewel in the crown of the city's thirty-year Renaissance. Modeled after a French chateau, its classic lines and sparkling cut-glass windows contrasted with the smooth modernity of the "new" Steel City. Inside, salmon-colored marble floors and heavy crystal chandeliers assured its high-profile guests that no expense had been spared.

The Burgoyne was where the President stayed on his last visit, and the Secretary of State. Even Oprah. So it was no surprise that Miles Wingfield would do the same.

I got a sharp poke from the gun barrel as the big man guided us toward a bank of gleaming elevator doors. A nearby placard announced that the top three floors were temporarily closed for remodeling. Regardless, we entered the far elevator and he pressed the button for the top.

On the way up, I thought about my chances with this guy. I'd been thinking of practically nothing else during the cab ride here to the hotel. Except the brief moment spent imagining the look on Polk's face when he learned that—not five minutes after pissing all over police protection—I'd been grabbed off the street. Right outside the station.

I now eyed the guy who'd done it. Something like 280 pounds of hard-packed muscle. Eyes cool as ice chips.

The mirrored, velvet-carpeted elevator shuddered to a stop, and without a word the big man put his free hand on my elbow. At the same time, the door slid silently open onto an ornate hallway, leading to four suites.

Most of the doors were open, and a dozen men and women in power suits hurried in and out of them. Phones rang constantly, and I could make out laptops and fax machines, their clean, digital lines in stark contrast to the *belle époque*-era chairs, sofas and tables arrayed around them.

At the end of the hallway, another set of doors was guarded on either side by security guys who could have been clones of the one still gripping my elbow. Without a word, one of them opened a door for us to enter.

Inside, the suite opened onto a wide, high-ceilinged room halved by a stand of picture windows overlooking the Point. With a final, bone-crushing squeeze of my arm, I was more or less shoved into the middle of the room.

I turned, feeling the anger burnish my face, to see my captor casually walking away. Mission accomplished, he took up a position in a near corner, arms behind his back.

I let out a breath, standing there amid the reflection of the city lights spilling from the windows. The black of night looked blacker still against the splintered glow, but I could just make out the Monongahela below, mirrored surface wrinkled by the wind.

"I do think it's the best view in the city," a female voice said behind me.

I turned to find a pretty, auburn-haired young woman crossing from another door into the room. She walked stiffly toward a long white sofa, before which stood a glass coffee table. Atop it was a silver tray holding two crystal goblets and a bottle of Evian water.

"I always like to be high up," she continued, sitting carefully on the sofa. "Gives you perspective. Takes you out of yourself, if you know what I mean."

I guessed her age at twenty or so, though her poise and subdued manner suggested a maturity beyond her years. Even so, her tailored skirt and blouse failed to disguise the supple, youthful curves of her body. She also wore the placid expression of a veteran employee of the wealthy. *In* the inner circle, and yet not *of* it.

Following on her heels was another man, whose smile showed the whitest teeth I'd ever seen. He was young, too, maybe mid-twenties. Designer clothes. A corporate face that belied the smile. And, somehow, vaguely familiar.

He crossed the room in two brisk strides, and, to my surprise, extended his hand. I looked at it.

"Peter Clarkson," he said, oblivious.

It was then, with his hand outstretched, that I finally placed him.

Because the last time I'd seen him, Clarkson was also shaking hands with someone. Albert Garman. In the photo I'd noticed in Garman's office at Ten Oaks the day before.

Before I could even digest this information, Clarkson was making introductions. Observing the niceties. Like everything was normal. Like I hadn't just been brought here at gun-point.

"I see you've met Sheila." He nodded at the girl sitting with hands folded on the sofa. Her eyes looked right through me, opaque.

Then Clarkson jerked a thumb in the direction of the big man in the corner. "And, of course, Carl Trask. Our Head of Security."

"Thanks," I said. "I hadn't caught his name."

"That's 'cause I hadn't thrown it," Trask said. Hands still behind his back as though welded there.

Clarkson ignored his words and turned back to me. "I'm afraid we can only spare you twenty minutes or so. As you can imagine, there are many painful, personal details to attend to. Then we're off to Singapore. Our merger with Cochran International, as I'm sure you've read about. And then that Senate sub-committee thing."

I heard what I was supposed to. "So Wingfield's gone public. About Kevin, I mean?"

"Not yet. Mr. Wingfield informed his executive staff only this afternoon that the murdered man in the news was in fact his own son. Our people will release a statement to that effect tomorrow morning." A reflective pause. "This is a tragic time for all of us in Mr. Wingfield's employ."

Sheila spoke to the air as though the rest of us weren't here. "It was such a shock. His having a son at all. Then...what happened. So horrible."

"Yes," I said quietly. "Yes, it is."

Now I understood the flurry of activity on the floor.

And it had nothing to do with any mergers. Wingfield's spin doctors were gearing up for the media assault that would inevitably follow this bombshell development in Kevin's murder, which would elevate the story to national status.

I could just picture it. The ratings-grabbing "personal interest" aspect involving a poor, perhaps mentally ill college student whose famous father was worth billions. Made-to-order for the tabloids, cable channels, talk radio, the internet. Kevin's case could end up being another Crime of the Century, right up there with O.J. and Jon-Benet Ramsey. God help us.

Clarkson was eyeing me warily, as though reading my thoughts. "Why don't you sit down, Doctor?"

"I'll stand, thanks." Fuck him.

Suddenly, I felt an iron grip on my shoulders, and a chair being kicked against the back of my knees. Then the barrel of Trask's gun against the base of my skull.

"Unacceptable," Trask said evenly.

I sat. The gun stayed where it was.

I looked up at Clarkson. "I changed my mind."

Clarkson's smile hardened. Then he strode toward a wet-bar that stood near the far window. When he finally turned again, drink in hand, his gaze had grown sour.

"I don't think you understand, Doctor. You just fell down the goddam rabbit hole." He sipped his drink.

"Give me a break," I said. "This John-the-Baptist act closed out of town a long time ago. Just bring in Christ Almighty and let's get this over with."

A hoarse laugh drew my eyes, though I knew what Miles Wingfield looked like. Hell, everybody knew.

"Dr. Rinaldi." He moved with an easy stride into the room and beamed down at me. "You put on a pretty good act yourself, considering your position."

I stirred, rolling my shoulders. Trask pressed the gun harder against my neck.

Wingfield waved a hand. "Please. Don't get up."

He laughed again, forcing it a little this time for effect. The man was in his late-sixties, but looked years younger. Thick, wavy gray hair. Face untroubled as a monk's. Clad in one of his signature, personally-tailored Armani suits, reminding me of the infamous *Forbes* cover shot of him in front of a huge mirrored closet, with literally hundreds of designer suits arrayed behind him.

I'd been thinking a lot about Wingfield, and what I'd remembered seeing or reading about him since first learning he was Kevin's father. His story was movie-perfect. Coming from a small Pennsylvania town, he'd not only built an empire and become a national figure, he'd crafted a new self.

Not just another "self-made" man, but a media-cultivated, PR-enhanced, self-*created* man. Knowing, sophisticated. Eschewing the "aw-shucks" demeanor of other financial giants like Ted Turner and T. Boone Pickens, Wingfield was the embodiment of a deep cultural belief—that sudden wealth confers on someone his true worth. That success controls destiny, and not the other way around.

No wonder the media loved him. Coming late to his fortune, he was a testament to transformation, to molding his own, new reality out of one he'd discarded. Miles Wingfield was a public relations wet-dream. A Gatsby without the angst.

Until you were within five feet of him. Then you saw it. Felt it. *Knew.*

He bent and gripped my shoulders with a surprising, wiry strength. His eyes, locked on mine, held a filmy gaze. His smile was small and ruthless and devoid of humor.

"I'm afraid I've made my attorneys very unhappy," he said. "But I had to meet you in person. See the man whose professional lapses brought about the death of my son."

His hands lingered on my shoulders, fingers relaxed now, their touch light as down.

"You should've listened to your lawyers."

For a moment, he merely watched my face with detached curiosity. Then, silent still, he let his hands drop from my shoulders. As he turned away from me, I thought I saw his tight smile go slack. As though melting.

"Look," I went on, "it's not that I don't understand what you're after. I'd probably want the same thing. But—"

He swiveled his head now toward Clarkson and Sheila. "I'd like some private face-time with Dr. Rinaldi."

Peter Clarkson said nothing, just finished his drink with a long swallow and nodded. Sheila got smoothly to her feet and followed Clarkson toward the door.

Watching her leave, Wingfield smiled. "Great girl, Sheila. Best tits in the building."

Sheila's shoulders stiffened, almost imperceptibly, but she kept walking. I stared at Wingfield.

His brow furrowed. "You don't believe me, Doctor?"

Without a word, Clarkson touched the girl's shoulder. She froze.

"Trust me," I said quickly. "I believe you."

Wingfield sighed as though burdened, and crooked his finger at Clarkson. Again, he touched Sheila's shoulder.

She paled, unmoving. Then, taking a full breath, the girl walked gingerly back into the room.

"Do me a favor, will you, honey?" Wingfield smiled at her. "Show Dr. Rinaldi your tits."

I bucked in the chair. "Christ, Wingfield—!"

Trask tapped the back of my head with the gun barrel. His fingers dug into my shoulder.

Sheila stood transfixed, as though she hadn't quite heard correctly.

Wingfield folded his arms, still smiling. A busy man, unaccustomed to waiting. "*Now*, please…"

She took another breath. Then, hands trembling, Sheila slowly began to unbutton her blouse.

Yet she kept her face immobile, looking straight ahead. Her stare unwavering.

That's when I knew. Sheila was blind.

I glanced around the room. Peter Clarkson was standing off to one side, eyes averted. Looking for something to do with his hands.

By now, Sheila had peeled off her blouse, letting it fall to the floor. Her full, firm breasts somehow more exposed than concealed in the flimsy lace bra. Awkwardly, she reached behind her back to unclasp it. Hesitated.

Wingfield looked over at me, the exasperated host spreading his hands helplessly. Then back to the girl, eyes narrowing to sharp points.

"Sheila, sweetheart, we haven't got all day," he said.

Her face pinched fearfully at something she heard in his voice. Steeling herself, she began unfastening her bra.

"Damn it, Wingfield," I said. "Make this stop."

Trask rapped the side of my head again with the gun butt. I didn't even feel it.

Sheila seemed to be having trouble with the clasp.

Clarkson started snapping his fingers. "Come *on*…"

"Aw, Christ," Wingfield said suddenly, waving his hand at the girl. "Forget about it. Now I'm just bored."

Sheila stared, unblinking. Her bra was undone, but she clutched the straps over her tremulous breasts.

"Go on, you two," Wingfield said. "Leave us."

He pointed to Clarkson, who hurriedly came over and scooped up her blouse from the carpet. Then, brusquely, he took Sheila by the elbow and hustled her out of the room.

Wingfield shrugged. "You'll just have to take my word for it," he said to me. And smiled. "Blind since birth. She makes her eyes follow your voice. Amazing, eh?"

I stared. *Okay, you piece of shit. I got the message.*

It was then that I knew for sure. I'd sensed it before, in my life, in my training. In the few times when my work brought me into contact with someone like him. But I could never prove it. Not before any clinical board, not even with a battery of tests. I had only my gut, my experience, to go on.

And what I saw in that tiny smile. Those milk-white, remorseless eyes.

Miles Wingfield was a true sociopath.

Chapter Twenty-nine

Behind me, Carl Trask cleared his throat. "Anything ya want *me* to do, Mr. Wingfield?"

"What you do best, Carl. Shut up and look lethal." He gestured toward the far corner. "But do it over there, okay?"

The pressure of the gun left my neck; then the heavy pad of footsteps moved off. Without another word, Trask took up position again in the corner.

Wingfield turned and poured himself an Evian water.

"I wasn't sure we'd have the opportunity to meet," he said. "Before things became...well, unpleasant. I'd hoped Mr. Trask here would be able to persuade you to come."

"His gun was very persuasive." I stood up.

Wingfield frowned. "Gun? What are you talking about?" He looked past me. "Carl? What is he talking about?"

Trask grinned. "Beats hell outta me, Mr. Wingfield."

"You see, Dr. Rinaldi," Wingfield said smoothly, "it appears you came here voluntarily."

He leaned forward, his voice amiable. "I promise you, given my considerable resources, nothing I do will be outside the law. There's no need."

"Except kidnapping. Assault with a deadly."

He shrugged. "What was it Sheila said to you? About perspective? I see before me not a victim of anything, but rather a perpetrator of an unspeakable crime. Against me."

He sipped his water. "I see a man who came here full of contrition for his acts against me and my family. Who offers an apology I cannot, and will not, accept."

"I don't remember apologizing to you for anything."

Wingfield considered this, turning the glass in his hand. "That's right, you haven't. Why not?"

I was silent.

"I said, why not?" Something changed in his eyes.

Suddenly, he closed his fist on the glass. It shattered noisily, water and splintered crystal flying.

Wingfield took a full step toward me, bristling. Livid with rage. Unmindful of the deep gash in his palm, oozing freely, welling blood.

"Don't you understand what you've done to me?" he shouted. "The steps I'll take to destroy you?"

There was no grief in his eyes, only white hatred. Narcissistic rage. Kevin's death was no tragedy in itself. What I saw on his face wasn't the horror of a parent's loss of a child. It was the pain of insult.

He stood, glowering. Until the anger etched on his face turned to disdain, and then to disinterest.

Finally, he looked at his cut hand, curled his fingers to pump the blood. A thick, red rivulet, spreading. He seemed fascinated.

"Yes, I have a fleet of lawyers, and the resources to ruin you. I will see you in the gutter. But will that really satisfy me? Will that be enough?" His gaze found mine again. "No, Doctor. No, it will not."

We stood that way for a long moment, our eyes locked. Without turning, he finally spoke.

"I've changed my mind, Carl. Go have a smoke."

Trask hesitated a moment, then padded out of the room.

"Good man," Wingfield said, as the doors to the hall closed softly. "Ex-Navy SEAL. Special Ops. I'm lucky to have him. They wanted him as a consultant on Fox News. That's where all the old soldiers go now. They don't die, and they don't fade away. Instead, they all get agents and trade sound-bites with Bill O'Reilly."

He took a silk handkerchief from his pocket, wrapped it around his hand. Then, to my surprise, he bent over the coffee table and began gingerly picking up shards of glass. Swabbing up water with a napkin. This seemed to calm him.

"Do you have children, Dr. Rinaldi?"

"No."

"Then you couldn't understand what I meant just now. That no matter what I do to you, it won't be enough. It won't bring Kevin back."

Wingfield straightened up. "I know what you're thinking, Doctor. How can I talk this way after abandoning my children years ago? After leaving them in Banford."

"Maybe you could explain that to me."

"It's not complicated. I was presented with a business opportunity that meant I had to leave town, so I took it. There was no life there with my kids anyway. All the gossip, the scandal. I was branded a horrible father because I hadn't known about what was going on under my own roof. Frankly, I didn't have a clue."

He smiled. "You have to understand, I didn't belong in that town to begin with. Its smallness was oppressive, its view of life provincial, constraining. I tried to fit in, for my family's sake. To deny my true self, my...well...my larger perspective on life's possibilities. Especially for a man like me."

He sighed, burdened. "Instead, I worked in a bank whose total assets wouldn't cover my current weekly payroll. I was expected to behave and think as though I were...ordinary. I was suffocating, you understand? Barely aware of anything other than the lack of air."

"You mean, like what might be going on between your own son and daughter...?"

"As I said, Dr. Rinaldi, I hadn't a clue." His head tilted. "Though even now, I find their...behavior... literally unthinkable."

"You had no idea at the time? There *are* signs, things to look for..."

He sat back on the sofa arm. "Not to me. Then again, after my wife's death..." Here he paused. "Perhaps I was just too upset to...I mean, wouldn't any man be?..."

He gave me a strangely careful look, as though he was trying to gauge my reaction to his story.

"Besides," he went on, "in a real sense I didn't desert my children. *They* deserted *me*. Years after I left Banford, I made repeated attempts to contact them, and was rebuffed. This was after I'd founded Wingfield BioTech. I merely wanted to help them. To have them share in my good fortune."

He looked off toward the huge window. "But they each, in their own way, rejected me. Kevin changed his name, lived like a bum. In and out of mental institutions, straggling his way through college. Karen ran away, got married and divorced. There may be a child." He shook his head. "Frankly, they've both been quite a disappointment."

Classic. Nothing's his fault. *He's* the injured party, the aggrieved, the justified.

"Since Kevin's death, I feel I should try to contact my daughter again," he went on distractedly, adjusting the makeshift bandage on his hand. "Carl has his people on it, and assures me he'll have a name and location in two or three more days."

"Whatever he comes up with, you better hand it over to the cops," I said. "They'll be wanting to talk to any of Kevin's immediate family."

"Of course. Anything that will help catch the killer. Not that it matters. I don't care about some sub-human piece of trash. And I don't care if his intended victim was really you. I hold you, and you alone, responsible for what's been done to me."

"That's just it. Nothing's been done to *you*. It happened to your son."

The silence between us was very still. Dead air.

Then, as slowly as if attached to a set of old gears, a smile began to form on his lips. That small, hard smile.

"You know, you'll soon wish it *had* been you killed in that garage after all," he said quietly. "Not Kevin."

Another aching silence, emptied of everything but his hate.

Then, as though nourished by it, he stood up abruptly and put his hands together. As if in prayer.

"Anyway, time to get down to business. As I say, my legal representatives will be taking over from this point on, so it's unlikely I'll be seeing you again. You're not the only project demanding my attention, you know."

"Yeah, I heard. The Cochran merger. The Senate. You're a busy guy."

He ignored this. "I will of course be suing you for malpractice, wrongful death, loss of your license, and financial damages for my emotional pain and suffering. You'll be brought before the appropriate boards, as well as civil court, and, if possible, criminal court. You will, I promise you, be eviscerated to the fullest extent possible by law. Shall I have Peter call you a cab?"

My jaw tightened. "No thanks. I'll get myself home."

He shrugged, uninterested, and turned away.

I watched him cross the room. He was a businessman, on a schedule, and this part of his business had been concluded. I literally felt myself drop, like a downed plane, from his radar screen.

Meanwhile, my mind raced, considering what he'd just laid out. I had all the appropriate insurance, and thus access to lawyers, support from various professional organizations and the like. *I* had resources, too. But not like Wingfield's. Not enough for what I'd be up against.

It was time to see myself out.

Wingfield was flipping idly through a stack of papers as I headed for the door. Without looking up, he spoke again.

"By the way, you might be interested in the expert witness we've retained to present the clinical evidence against you. The foremost man in his field, they tell me."

Only then did Wingfield look up.

"In fact, I believe you two know each other?" He spoke easily, hooded eyes devoid of light. "Dr. Phillip Camden?"

Chapter Thirty

It was midnight by the time I got home, changed my clothes, and poured myself an Iron City. I was in the kitchen, with Coltrane's dusky tenor pouring softly from the CD speakers.

I'd flagged a cab—a legit one—outside the hotel and spent the ride back up to my place with both rear windows down. I let the bracing cold hit me, clearing the cobwebs.

I brooded on the darkness, and the events of the past forty-eight hours. Kevin's death, and then Brooks Riley. The cops. Wingfield. And now Phil Camden.

It was like a black storm rising up out there in the night, gathering strength, heading in my direction. My life's work, everything I'd built. That mattered to me.

As we drove over the lookout, a sliver of moon hung in the sky. Edged like a knife-blade.

He was out there, too, I thought. In that same night. Perhaps gathering strength as well. Watching that same moonlight glint off the length of another long, thin blade.

Watching. And waiting.

That's when something shifted inside me. Fueled by rage, and incomprehension, and a welling grief over the obscenity of Kevin's murder. Those sad, lifeless eyes still looking up at me...

Fuck the cops, I thought. *And* Miles Wingfield. Hell, fuck the killer.

I was through playing defense.

By the time the cab pulled into my driveway, bathing it in lights from the front porch, I already knew what I had to do.

<><><>

Sam Weiss' voice was a hoarse mumble on the phone.

"Jesus, Danny, it's after midnight."

"Yeah, I know, Sam. Sorry. We need to talk."

Bed sheets rustled as Sam turned to his wife and whispered something. Then his voice again, coming more fully awake.

"Okay, just give me a minute to get to a phone downstairs. This better be good."

I waited, taking another pull from my beer.

I'd known Sam Weiss for years, since first coming back to work after Barbara's death. Sam was a feature writer now for the *Pittsburgh Post-Gazette,* but he'd started there on the police beat. He'd been one of the lead reporters on the Handyman story, and had snagged an exclusive interview with Troy David Dowd after his arrest. A year later, Sam wrote the best-selling book on Dowd's crimes that became the basis for the movie now underway in Hollywood.

Naturally, this got him local notoriety, a feature position at the paper, and the veiled envy of his colleagues. It also got him the expensive two-story house in Squirrel Hill where I'd just called him.

I heard the click of a receiver picking up.

"I'm here," Sam said. "I just realized, this is about your patient that got killed, right?"

"Right. Kevin Wingfield."

"Wingfield? I thought his name was Merrick."

"So did I. Watch the morning news. Kevin was Miles Wingfield's son."

"*The* Miles Wingfield? Holy shit. You know what this means? This could be bigger than—Holy shit."

"Tell me. That's why I'm calling you. I need to get the jump on this before the circus comes to town."

Sam's voice dropped an octave. "What do you need?"

"Everything there is on Miles Wingfield. Background, financial stuff. Whatever you can find. Rumor, gossip. The works." I hesitated. "And, Sam, I need it by tomorrow."

He gave a laugh. "Sure. No problem. Anything else?"

"Look, I know what I'm asking. And if you can't do it, that's okay, too. I know you work for a living."

A long pause. "You also know I owe you. Big-time."

I was taken aback by the emotion in his voice.

"That's got nothing to do with this," I murmured. "Believe me, you don't owe me anything."

"Not how I see it, Danny. Never will be. You got her through it, man. It was *you*. So shut the hell up about it."

A few years back, Sam had called me in a panic about his beloved kid sister. A high school junior, she'd been brutally raped by a hitchhiker she picked up. Before leaving her bruised, naked body by the side of the road, he'd taken the trouble to carve swastikas in her face and breasts with an Exacto-knife. Sam used to drive her to my office himself almost daily for eighteen months.

"So," Sam went on, "how 'bout we meet at Primanti's tomorrow, around one? I'll have the goods by then."

"Thanks. Thanks a lot."

I hung up, and immediately began flipping through my address book again. I found Nancy Mendors' home number and dialed. She picked up on the second ring.

"Hello?" Guarded but alert. I knew from experience that she'd be wide awake. Nancy was an insomniac.

"It's me."

"Dan. Thank God. I thought it was another reporter. I almost didn't pick up."

"I'm glad you did." I paused. "How're you holding up?"

"Not great. I-I still can't get the image of Brooks out of my mind. The blood…"

"I'm so sorry you had to find him like that."

She hesitated. "You know, it's funny, about you and me…Do you realize we've each found a dead body in the past two days? I mean, what are the odds?"

That thought had already occurred to me. But I didn't say so. It wasn't the kind of thing you could make sense of by talking about it.

"The cops have been there all day," she went on. "Poor Bert's going crazy. All the press, the bad publicity. Patients destabilizing left and right. Not to mention their families calling, frantic—"

"But what about *you*?" I insisted. "Shouldn't you take some personal time? I'm sure Bert—"

"He's already ordered me to stay home the next few days. Though one of the cops actually told me not to leave town. Can you believe that? Like on TV."

"Don't sweat it. You found the body, and that makes you a prime suspect. I've been there. They'll get over it."

"Elaine *did* say I should get a lawyer."

"Bert's wife?"

"Yeah. I have to admit, I was surprised. I mean, the Lady Garman came right down with *their* lawyer in tow. Like a tigress protecting her mate."

"Why were you surprised?"

She managed a rueful laugh. "Does Elaine strike you as Loving Wife of the Year?"

"I guess I haven't given it much thought. Listen, what about Lucy and Helen? That fight in the yard."

"Yeah, a detective interviewed each one separately. Female cop, I forget her name."

"Detective Lowrey."

"That's her. Anyway, pretty soon Lucy's lawyer showed up— real high-powered type—and that was the end of that. I swear, there were more lawyers than cops on the scene."

"Christ, tell me no other patients were questioned."

"Oh, yes. Another cop set up a makeshift interrogation room, I guess it's called, and trooped them in one by one."

"No way Bert Garman should have allowed that."

"He tried to stop it, Danny. Though you should've seen Richie Ellner. Had to be sedated *and* restrained. All the fear and confusion, uniformed authority figures throwing their weight around…It was all too much for him."

"I can imagine. Poor bastard."

"Anyway," she went on, "according to the grapevine, doesn't sound like anybody saw anything. Practically all the patients were out in the rec yard at the time, undoing years of treatment." A wry whistle over the phone. "Must have been some party."

"You didn't miss a thing."

"Danny?…" Her voice small. Tentative.

"Yeah?"

"Thanks for calling. I…it's good to hear your voice, you know? I mean, after today."

I took a breath. "You just get some rest, okay?"

A beat of silence. "Right. Sure."

She softly hung up.

<><><>

I had one more call to make. Unfortunately, I got Sonny Villanova instead of his wife.

"Who the fuck is this?"

"Sonny, it's Dan Rinaldi. I know it's late, but could you put Angie on the phone? It's important."

"Angie? Angie's asleep. *I* was asleep. The whole goddam world's asleep, except the asshole I'm talkin' to."

"C'mon, Sonny, cut the shit and put her on."

"All right, hold on. Christ."

I opened a second Iron City. Though I'd turned down the volume, I could still make out the honeyed timbre of Sarah Vaughn. A night siren luring me out of myself, my troubles, my own damn stubbornness. Was Sonny right? Was every sane person in the world asleep?

Angie's sharp voice crackled in my ear. "What's up?"

"Angie. Thanks. Listen, I need a favor."

"Are you kiddin' me? I shouldn't even be *talkin'* to you. I heard about you refusing police protection. The DA's spittin' nails.

Biegler wants to pull you in again, charge you with obstruction. Just to get your ass off the street."

"That's bullshit."

"No, sir. 'Cause *this* time I'm inclined to agree with them. We're in the middle of a high-profile case here. Word is, Wingfield's going public tomorrow—"

"I know."

I could tell this threw her, but she did her best not to indicate it.

"Good," she said crisply. "So you know. Then you also know you're a big piece of this puzzle, and the last thing we need is you getting yourself killed."

"Gotcha. Now, about that favor—"

"I'm gonna hang up, I swear it."

"No, you're not. 'Cause we're *paisans*. Family."

She laughed. "Yank my other one. Shit."

"Just make a call to the uniform watching my office. They've still got it under seal. But I want to get in."

"Why?"

"Just a hunch. But I think I know how the killer got in and planted the murder weapon on my desk. Don't you want to find out if I'm right?"

Chapter Thirty-one

Phil Camden's house was on a quiet street off Walnut. Many Pitt faculty lived in the area, a hushed conclave sheltered by trees and stone fences. Close enough for a short commute to campus, far enough away in style and ambience as to be of another world entirely. Where the houses all had libraries and velvet-toned wall clocks, and drinks were served before dinner.

I stood at Phil's front door, framed by the porch light, and leaned on the bell.

In a minute, I heard a heavy shuffling from the other side of the door, then the sound of bolts being unlocked.

Phil Camden opened the door and peered out through sleep-clouded eyes, his glasses at an angle on his nose.

"Who the hell—? At this hour?"

That voice, so sharp, so threaded with authority, still had the size and weight I remembered.

But the man did not. Though it had been only five years since I'd last seen him, he had aged much more. And gotten smaller, shrunk into himself, burdened at last by time and labor. And grief.

"Phil…" I began, though half the anger I'd carried up to his porch had already faded. "Look—"

He adjusted his glasses and drew himself up. The cold fire in his eyes leapt up, as if on command, and steadied.

"*You?*…What in God's name?…How dare you…?"

"We have to talk," I said quickly. "I know you're working for Wingfield. I know what you're trying to do."

"Go to hell!"

He started to close the door, but I blocked it with my foot. He glared at me in disbelief.

"I should call the police," he said hoarsely.

"But you won't. You *want* to talk to me. That's why you called me earlier. On my cell phone."

"That was a courtesy. To notify you that I'd been retained in legal action against you by Miles Wingfield. I thought it the proper thing to do."

"Maybe. But right now, the proper thing is to let me in your house so we can talk about this like men."

He considered this. I guess propriety won out, because he stepped back and let the door swing open.

I let out a long breath as I watched him turn and pad down the carpeted hall toward his study. I closed the door behind me and followed.

The house was just as I remembered it. Formal, tasteful. Antique furniture. Venerable bookshelves laden with classic texts. Dim, hushed. A house born before the era of civil rights, feminism, and pop culture. A house shaped and contained by one man's proud intellect and iron will.

Phillip Camden turned on the lamp over his study desk, then sat heavily in the stuffed leather chair. Sighing, he motioned impatiently for me to take the one just beyond the pool of light.

We'd said not one word since I'd entered the house.

He found a small notebook and consulted it.

"I'll be brief," he said. "Regarding Kevin Merrick, nee Wingfield. I'll assume you're familiar with his case history prior to coming into treatment with you."

"Yes. I got his files from County psych after his confinement there."

"Following a robbery and assault he'd suffered—"

"That's right. It happened six months prior to entering therapy with me. Kevin had surprised a burglar in his apartment. There was a struggle. Kevin managed to escape."

Camden studied a document paper-clipped to a file.

"I further assume you noted Kevin's diagnosis at his three previous psychiatric institutions. As well as the results of the tests administered periodically during the last seven or eight years of his life."

I shrugged. "He pretty much got the whole buffet. TAT. MMPI. Bender-Gestalt. Plus about two dozen mental status exams, over the years. Clumsily administered, I'm sure, by some trainee trying to impress his or her supervisor."

"Is that mere cynicism, or are you trying—fairly clumsily yourself—to make a point?"

I leaned forward in my chair. "People like Kevin get tagged with labels pretty early on, and spend the rest of their lives trying to wriggle out of them. You know what it's like in the mental health system."

"So we should just throw away diagnosis altogether?"

"Of course not. But calling the categories of mental illness objective is total bullshit. Hell, they change every time there's a new edition of the damn manual."

Camden threw down the folder in disgust. "This discussion is over. You are as infuriating now as when I had the misfortune to select you as my graduate assistant."

He was visibly agitated, and took a few deep breaths to calm himself. Beyond the bubble of light cast by the desk lamp, the room faded into a thick darkness.

"I will now return to the facts of the Wingfield case, as they've been presented to me in these documents. I will do so with alacrity, and then I will return to my bed."

"I'll bet you will. And you'll sleep like a baby. I mean, how can you work for a man like Miles Wingfield? Why would you help him?"

His voice was cool and placid as a deep lake. "I should think that obvious. Because his complaint against you affords me the opportunity to injure you, to bring you pain. As you did me."

I sat back, at a loss. It wasn't that anything he said surprised me. It was the purity of intent. As always, Phil Camden's clarity of purpose was breathtaking.

I looked at him. "You're wrong, Phil. I loved Barbara with all my heart, as you did. And this is wrong."

He held my eyes for a long moment, then referred once again to his notebook.

"The facts are plain: you mishandled Kevin Wingfield's case from the start. The patient was found wandering in a convenience store, with no memory of the preceding three hours. A dissociative state triggered by a violent encounter with a burglar. Given these symptoms, his history of voluntary *and* involuntary commitment, and obvious borderline features—"

Here he stopped, fixing me with a stare. "Given these conditions, a course of drug therapy, behavioral protocols and rigid out-patient monitoring is the conventional, prescribed treatment. As I will testify."

"Hell, you just outlined the kind of treatment Kevin had been receiving for years, with little real effect."

He shrugged this off, but I pressed on.

"Look, I honestly think our work together after the robbery attempt was the first genuine incursion into Kevin's inner world. The sexual and physical abuse he'd suffered as a child denied him the healthy development he needed, the affective attunement he yearned for."

"Which *you* provided, by virtue of your superior wisdom and compassion?"

"Which I *hoped* to provide, by giving him a model to emulate. From which he'd hopefully emerge, with enough inner resources to become whole again."

I took a breath. "It was a risk, yes, but a calculated one. Based on our level of trust and intimacy. On Kevin's courage. It was our work together, and I believe in it."

Camden just shook his head. "I always felt you took your cases too personally."

"How should I take them—*im*personally?" My voice hardened. "Christ, you can't even *work* with patients."

"No need. You know my methodology. *Who* Kevin was, as a person, is irrelevant."

"Not to me."

We just stared at each other. Two entrenched, unmoving antagonists. Using professional differences to mask what really lay between us. And always would.

Finally, I stood up. "To hell with this. I'm not going to defend my work with a patient. Not to you."

"Perhaps not. But soon you will have to. In court."

He took off his glasses and rubbed his eyes.

"This is pointless," he said wearily. "You've stormed the barricades, confronted your foe. Now let's both return to our lives and await the inevitable legal conflict."

He shut off the lamp and the room was plunged into darkness, except for a dim light thrown from the hall.

Camden slowly got to his feet.

"I trust you can see your way out?"

Chapter Thirty-two

The uniformed cop stationed outside my office was apparently expecting me, since he gave me a nod as I neared the door. What he wasn't expecting was the cup of coffee I handed him, from the all-night diner around the corner.

He was heavy and florid-faced, and climbed up out of the metal folding chair with some effort. He took the steaming Styrofoam cup in both hands.

"Thanks, Doc. Lt. Villanova told me you was comin'."

Flat Pittsburgh vowels. A working-man's stance, weight shifted to one foot. Pure blue-collar cop. Like my old man.

"Sorry for the late visit," I said. "Couple things I want to check in the office."

"No problem. Besides, it's nice to have company. CSU's been here and gone. Quiet as a tomb since yesterday."

The cop, whose name tag read Johnson, lifted the yellow crime scene tape from across the office door.

"By the way," he said, as he ushered me in, "we put your mail in a pile on the floor. After goin' through it. Ya know, for threats an' stuff."

"Thanks, officer." I crossed the darkened waiting room and unlocked the connecting door to my office.

"Take as long as ya want," he said. "Touch anything ya want. Tech boys have dusted the hell outta the place."

I waited till he went back out into the hall, then I entered my office and flipped on the overhead.

Strange feeling. The last time I was in here, Casey and I had been backing away from the knife that killed Kevin Wingfield.

I glanced at my desk top. The blotter had been taken down to forensics. Everything else remained, but had obviously been moved, examined.

I opened the desk drawer and checked the organizer tray. The little compartments holding paper-clips, pens, stamps. In one, I found what I was looking for. Or, rather, *didn't* find it. Which was what I'd expected.

This compartment was where I kept the spare keys. One to the public rest rooms, down the hall. The other a spare office key that opened both the outer door and the inner, connecting door.

This key, as I'd guessed, was gone.

It was the only thing that made sense. Kevin had often taken various things from my office when I wasn't looking. My pen. A letter-opener. What if one time, when I'd stepped out of the room for some reason, he'd opened the desk drawer to see what he could find?

My office key. Labeled with my suite number. It would have been irresistible. So easy to slip in his pocket, carry it around with him during the day.

Then, the night of his murder, he's stabbed on the way to his car in the garage. During the assault, the key falls from his pocket. The killer apparently hadn't gone through his victim's pockets after the murder, since the cops had Kevin's personal effects. In fact, that same night Polk had shown me my monogrammed pen recovered from the body.

So the key *must* have fallen out, with my pen and the other things Polk showed me. The killer spots it. By now, he knows he's killed the wrong man. But he scoops up the key, sees the label. It's the key to my suite.

Maybe he decides right then to come back later, leave the knife as a warning to me. Maybe he's not thought ahead that far. But he pockets the key anyway, and takes off...

Yes. *Had* to be how the killer got in and planted the knife. Which meant it *hadn't* been with the key I'd given Noah. Which also meant there was no reason to mention that key to the cops, and getting Noah mixed up in all this.

I picked up the pile of mail the cops had left—some journals, invitations to conferences, and the like—and went back out into the hall. Officer Johnson had finished his coffee and was leaning back heavily in his chair.

"Got what you needed, Doc?"

"Thanks, yeah."

I left him there, a tired beat cop on the late shift, rocking back slightly on his heels, guarding an empty room.

I was tossing the stack of mail onto the passenger seat of the Mustang when my cell rang. I sat behind the wheel, glanced at the dashboard clock. Two a.m.

It was Casey. "Hey, you're up."

"More or less. I just left my office. I think I got something the cops'll want."

"Great. I wanted to talk to you, too."

I settled back in the seat. "Shoot."

"Not on the phone. Why don't you come over?"

"Now?"

A long pause.

"Danny. Don't make me ask twice."

I chewed on that. But not for too long.

"Okay, give me your address."

She did, and hung up. I looked at the phone in my hand. Then at my own eyes in the rear view mirror.

Did I know what I was doing? Did I care?

Casey's condo was near Edgewood, her building part of a new, upscale complex set against its sloping hills.

I followed a series of lights atop identical brass poles to the residents' parking lot, and then searched for the visitor spaces she'd told me about.

The night air had dropped another ten degrees. I pulled my coat up around my throat and hurried to the front of her building. I buzzed her number. She buzzed back, and I was in.

I found her door and knocked. Nothing. Knocked again.

"Come in," she called from the other side of the door.

I did. Her place was spacious, yet simply furnished. Almost perfunctory. As though her sense of herself, her measure, lay elsewhere. In paneled offices, hammering out deals with defense lawyers. In courtrooms, examining witnesses and confounding suspects. Alone in a bar at some ungodly hour, going over briefs. No, Casey didn't live *here*. She lived only in those places. *For* those places.

Music played from two Bose speakers set in the ceiling corners at the recommended angle apart. Something a little too high-tech for my tastes. Oh well.

"Casey?" I took a few more steps into the living room.

"In here." I tried to track her voice.

"Where?" This was ludicrous.

Her voice had an edge. "Where do you think?"

I took a breath. Tried to have a coherent thought. Make some kind of argument within myself about what I was doing. What *we* were doing.

Then I went into the bedroom. She wasn't there.

"Hey," she called out from another room. "You gonna give me a hand or what?"

I turned, now better able to gauge the direction of her voice. I crossed the hallway, made a left, and went into the kitchen.

Casey was leaning against a large cooking island that dominated the small kitchen. It had a tiled top, and, for half its width, a thick wooden chopping block.

She was propped against the wood, blowing a wisp of hair out of her eyes, as she struggled to open a bottle of Merlot. She was dressed simply in jeans and an oversized Land's End shirt. Her feet were bare.

Her eyes cut over at mine. "Yo. Feel free to jump right in, Sir Galahad."

I took the bottle from her. The corkscrew was buried up to the hilt. I braced the bottle against my upraised knee, got some leverage, and twisted. In half a minute, I got the cork out.

Only then did I look up, to see Casey smiling at what was probably a look of intense concentration on my face.

"Good man." She scooped up two wine glasses from near the sink and placed them on the tiled counter. I poured us each a glass. She raised hers in a toast.

"To peace in our time," she said.

I laughed, and we drank our wine in silence. Then she put down her glass, took mine from my hand, and began unbuttoning her shirt.

"Okay, so much for the formalities," she said, resting her hand on the chopping block. "Now come over here and fuck me."

Chapter Thirty-three

"Go ahead," Casey said. "Knock yourself out."

Her eyes burned, an ice-blue flame holding pride and challenge. Inviting my hunger, my abandon, my need.

We were in her bedroom now, washed by pale lights. She arched her back against the cool white sheets, her naked body a leonine display of golden skin and taut, gym-toned muscle. My fingers traced the swell of her breasts, curved along the honeyed cavern of her inner thighs.

Her body moved beneath my touch as though snaked with fire. She drew me into her and laughed as I crested up once more, pulled into the vortex, lost, beyond all thought.

Now we were loving again, fucking, hard, sweat slick where our bodies slammed together, her blonde hair splayed against the pillows. Then she was astride me, her knees digging into my ribs, her neck curved like a smooth white sculpture as she reared back.

We found each other again and again the rest of the night, hovering somewhere between sleep and wakefulness, desire slaked and then reborn…

As the hours melted away until dawn.

Her touch, her mouth, her fierceness.

She denied me nothing.

‹›‹›‹›

Casey came out of the shower still dripping wet and rolled onto the bed beside me. After a quick kiss, she turned her head toward the TV.

"Anything new?" she asked, pulling back her wet hair to lay her cheek against my chest.

"No. They all smell blood in the water. CNN ran the press conference with Sinclair and the Chief again."

"Wingfield go on camera yet?"

"No. On *Good Morning, America,* one of his lawyers said he's in seclusion. Unavailable for comment."

She tilted her head up. Eyes narrowed with concern.

"They're going to come after you again, Danny. The press. The cops. Kevin Wingfield is the Dead Celebrity of the Hour, and you were his therapist. And, Christ, if it leaks that he was *dressed* like you, that the killer…"

I said nothing. Her arms encircled my waist.

"I already know the answer to this," she said flatly. "But any way I can talk you into laying low? Going into seclusion yourself till this whole mess burns itself out?"

"No way. I'm in it and I'm getting in deeper. Maybe I can come up with something. Go at it from a different angle than the cops."

"Like with the office key," she said. I'd told her how I thought the killer had gotten in to plant the knife.

Casey sat up on her elbows, watching archived footage of Wingfield shaking hands with the German Chancellor, doing *schtick* with the President at his vacation ranch.

Then pictures of Wingfield BioTech labs and corporate offices around the world. The last image was a college snapshot of Kevin Wingfield, the same one they'd run with the murder story when he was still just Kevin Merrick.

I stirred. "Listen, while we're on the subject…"

Her smile was a tease. "I get it. You just slept with me so I'd keep you in the loop about the investigation."

"You got me, Counselor." I bent and kissed her softly. "But let's face it, I've probably been cut from Sgt. Polk's Christmas card list. And I bet Sinclair's decided against inviting me to his country club." I looked off. "So unless I can work something out with Eleanor Lowrey..."

Casey punched my arm. "Don't push it, Doc." Her eyes darkened. "And don't get cocky. I don't like that."

I met her gaze. "Duly noted."

Then, with the quickness of a summer storm, her face suddenly brightened.

"I *did* hear a couple things, though. Last night. The first was about the murder weapon."

I stared at her. "Okay, you got my attention."

"Forensics finally ID'd the knife. Only it's not a knife. It's kitchenware. A skewer, like for shish-ka-bob. Very upscale. You can get it from Williams-Sonoma."

"Funny. Exotic and mundane at the same time."

"But listen. The skewers are sold as a set of two."

I let out a breath.

"Yeah, I know." Her voice softened. "That's why you gotta be cool, Danny. The bastard's still walking around out there, waiting to use the other one."

"Again, duly noted. The second piece of news?"

"Biegler finally sent Polk up to Cloverbrook to talk to James Stickey. He's meeting him later today."

"I don't know. I think you were right about the break-in at Kevin's apartment being just a coincidence. Besides, Stickey was already in prison when Kevin was killed."

She shrugged. "Biegler's desperate. He knows his job's on the line. His clearance rate sucks lately, and nobody likes the little prick anyway. It'd serve him right to finish up his twenty in Parks and Recreation."

"Sinclair's got to be feeling the heat, too."

"Or basking in it. He knows a conviction on Kevin's murder pretty much lands him in the governor's mansion."

We channel-surfed the news for a few more minutes. The networks had already begun running a colorful graphic under their coverage of the story: "The Hunt for Kevin's Killer."

"Look," I said reluctantly, "I've got some calls to make, and I have to be across town by one."

"And I'm due in court in an hour. So we'll have to make it fast."

"What?"

She grinned. "You didn't think you were getting out of here without feeding me breakfast?"

Then she put her head under the covers.

Chapter Thirty-four

I was feeling all of my forty years as I headed downtown under a bright, cool sun. But despite whatever was happening between me and Casey—not to mention the accumulated effects of sleep deprivation—my mind was buzzing. There was a lot to do.

Traffic slowed as I neared the Fort Pitt Bridge, so I scanned the news stations. Nothing new, though I did learn that the police were releasing Kevin's body to Wingfield tomorrow for a private service. Talk about slicing through red tape. The chief also promised—again—to spare no effort to bring a speedy resolution to the case.

Not surprisingly, Brooks Riley's murder had a much lower profile. At this point there were few leads. However, patients and staff at Ten Oaks were still being questioned, as were the victim's family and friends.

I shut off the radio and made the turn onto my street. Then I hit the brakes.

Quickly, I pulled around behind the Mobil station on the corner. Shielded by a towering maple, I peered at my house a hundred yards down the street.

It had begun. There were at least a dozen news vans parked at or near the house. Reporters paced the curb, lounged in my driveway, perched on my front porch rail.

I looked left at the corner, where a black sedan was parked at the curb. A disgruntled-looking guy with a briefcase leaned against the car, arms folded.

My new life, I thought. *Cameras and subpoenas.*

I got on my cell and checked the messages. The first was from Johnny Manella, who'd called last night.

"Hey, I just heard from Aunt Angie that now the cops are lookin' at you for that *shrink's* murder. Mother of God. Maybe now you'll listen to your favorite cousin and get some legal. Try Ralph Puzzini, best criminal attorney in the biz. He got Manny Salerno off last year, remember? And not for nothin', but you still owe me a dinner."

The next message was from Paul Atwood. After assuring me that my none of my patients were in crisis, he went on to the reason he'd called.

"I just heard on the news about your patient's real name. Damn, talk about deep pockets. But if Wingfield *is* going to sue, forget about those limp-dick APA lawyers. You need a cruise missile. I had a friend who hired some guy named Harvey Blalock. Specializes in clinical malpractice. My friend swears by him. Write down this number."

I did, and immediately dialed Blalock's office. To my surprise, his secretary put me right through.

"Dr. Rinaldi? Harvey Blalock." His voice was rich, deep. Practiced in giving assurance.

"Sounds like you were expecting me."

He chuckled. "Well, let's just say I had a feeling. I saw the news like everybody else this morning."

"So how bad's this going to be?"

"My guess? As bad as it gets. You been home lately?"

"Funny you should ask. I happen to be hiding in my car around the corner. I see reporters. I see process-servers."

"Okay, here's the drill. Talk to no one. Check into a hotel. As soon as we hang up, I'll contact Wingfield's people and get the paperwork flowing in my direction. From now on, the only communication you have with Wingfield or his representatives will be through me. I'll get all the necessary patient files, statute listings and opposition expert testimony from his lawyers. Any idea who they're using to make you look like an incompetent piece of shit?"

"Dr. Phillip Camden."

"Jesus H. We're gonna have our work cut out for us. By the way, I assume you're retaining me."

"Well, you come highly recommended. Plus, as we speak, I'm watching my front lawn turn into a media circus. Given the circumstances, Mr. Blalock, I think I'll go with my gut and sign on with you."

"A wise decision. And call me Harvey. Now give me your cell number and let me go to work."

"Before we hang up, you ever hear of a defense lawyer named Ralph Puzzini?"

Blalock gave another short laugh. "Man, you *are* having a helluva week. But, sure, if you need a criminal attorney, Puzzini's at the top of the food chain. I also know a good forensics accountant, if you're in trouble with the IRS."

"Not yet, but the day's young. Thanks."

I hung up. Through the windshield, I saw one of the Mobil attendants pointing in my direction and talking excitedly to a guy wearing a press badge.

I turned the key in the ignition as the reporter started running toward the car.

"Hey! Dr. Rinaldi! Wait—!"

I almost side-swiped the guy peeling out of there, jumping the curb, and heading back toward the Incline.

Chapter Thirty-five

Sam Weiss pointed to the thick, sloppy sandwich in his other hand. "Now *this* is a cheesesteak. With fries, slaw, and tomatoes. *In* the damn sandwich."

We were crowded into a corner table at Primanti Brothers Deli, on the Strip. Packed as usual at lunchtime, the noise level was off the scale.

Sam had put on a few pounds since I'd last seen him, but still owned that same crooked smile and tousled jet-black hair. Maybe the same jeans. Though my age and the father of two, Sam always looked like he just came from the dorm.

He took a gulp of his Rolling Rock. "Funny I'm seeing you today. I'm doing a big new piece on Leland Sinclair."

"I'm not surprised," I said. "The Wingfield case is a DA's dream. Unless he doesn't nail it down."

"Yeah, but he's a tough interview. Never shows the cracks, know what I mean? Doesn't mix it up."

"He's a WASP, Sam. All they want is Scotch and quiet."

Sam drained his beer and signaled for another, then reached under his chair for his briefcase. I watched him, nursing my Iron City, as he flipped through some folders.

"Thanks again for doing this," I said.

His glance up at me was sober. "Hey," he said. Then he moved our plates aside and laid out some papers.

"Some of this I got from McMahon in Business. Some from an SEC guy who owes me. Plus a couple sources I can't tell you about. How much do you want?"

"For now, just the highlights."

He glanced up to acknowledge our young waitress as she put another beer down in front of him. He watched her saunter away for a long moment, then looked back at me.

"Well, first of all, what do you know about a guy named Terry Mavis?"

"Name sounds familiar. Some kind of scientist?"

Sam rolled his eyes. "Won the Nobel-fucking-Prize, Danny. He was, like, ahead of everybody in gene mapping, or whatever. Real Brainiac, but with no head for business."

"That's important?"

"Hell, yeah. Let's say you're a genius when it comes to cutting-edge genetic technology. Your ideas about creating new, life-saving drugs will revolutionize the pharmaceutical industry. But you're not interested in all that. You just wanna have fun. Do drugs and party on yachts and get laid till Mr. Happy falls off."

He offered me a press photo of Mavis accepting his Nobel award. He was beefy, with a broad face framed by long, darkish blond hair. He looked a lot like Meat Loaf.

"Damn shame, too," Sam went on. "'Cause Mavis was in the same league with Salk. Watson and Crick. Those guys."

"*Was?*"

Sam smiled. "I'm getting to that."

I waited impatiently while he glanced through some color-coded folders. Apparently, he had a system.

"Okay," he said at last. "Here's where we jump ahead in our story. Now this is in the public record. What everybody knows. Miles Wingfield lives in Banford, Pennsylvania, a widower with two kids. Pillar of the community. Vice-president of the Sunshine Savings and Loan. Then, according to his official bio, a business opportunity enables him to quit his job and move to Palo Alto, California."

I held up my hand.

"Wait a minute. That's a pretty big gap there. Any 'official' reference to what happened to his kids?"

"Nope. Not that I could find."

I sipped my beer. There had to be Social Services or family court documents detailing the incest allegations, since they led to mandated separation of Kevin and his sister. However, given the ages of the children, the records had probably been sealed. I did wonder if there were documents regarding their placement in separate foster homes following Wingfield's sudden departure from town.

Sam was studying me intently. "'Course, since Wingfield's son ended up as your patient years later, I guess *you* know more about what happened back there than I do."

"Nice try. Nothing I can talk about."

"But *something* weird happened in Banford, right? All my research keeps turning up rumors that Wingfield *had* to leave. That whatever this 'business opportunity' was, he leaped at the chance to skip town."

I shrugged. He shook his head.

"Anyway, speaking of gaps, when Wingfield *did* show up in Palo Alto, he had over two million million bucks in his pocket. And nobody knows how he got it. His official line is that it came from investments. But my Wall Street buddy says the rumor is, he'd embezzled it from Sunshine Savings and Loan. Nothing was ever proven, but…"

"Wait. Back up a minute. What exactly happened to his wife? I mean, how did she die?"

Sam shuffled some papers, pulled out a Xerox of a faded newspaper article from the *Banford Messenger.*

"I had one of their people fax me the story this morning. Goes back fifteen, sixteen years."

He pointed to the photo accompanying the article. It was a posed shot of a slim, pale woman in a print dress standing next to a younger, sober-faced Miles Wingfield. "That was his wife. The former Dorothy Louise Carlyle."

It looked like they'd been photographed at some sort of Christmas party, perhaps for the bank. Other couples in conservative suits and dresses were arrayed behind them.

But, as I would have guessed, Wingfield stood out. Not only because his suit looked new and tailored. It was the way his eyes looked almost challengingly at the camera. Chin stiff, he'd refused to smile. To be "caught" among these people. Everything about him seemed to proclaim *"I don't belong here..."*

"Miles and Dorothy were married for nearly eighteen years," Sam went on. "Then, about six months after this photo was taken, Wingfield takes the kids to the movies. When they get home, they find Mom lying dead in the bathtub. She's swallowed a bottle of pills."

"Any suspicion of foul play?"

"None. She did leave a note, though. It just said, 'I can't take it anymore.' Whatever the hell that meant."

Maybe Wingfield's wife knew what was going on between her two children and couldn't cope with it. Blamed herself in some way. Or maybe it was something else. Some private torment having nothing to do with any of this.

Sam put the article and some other papers in a manila envelope. "Anyway, here's all the Banford stuff I have. As much local color as I could scare up."

"This is more than I expected, Sam. Thanks. But getting back to Wingfield..."

Sam took a long pull of his beer. "Like I was saying, he shows up in California with serious money and starts looking around for something to do with it. Besides buying clothes and cars. I mean, *really* giving his life a total up-grade. Which is when he hooks up with Terry Mavis."

He grinned. "Maybe they met on one of those yachts I mentioned, 'cause Wingfield turns out to be a real party animal once he hits the West Coast. Anyway, Wingfield starts bank-rolling Terry's genetic research in exchange for the lion's share of the patent ownership."

"Smart move," I said. "Wingfield gets in on the gravy train just as it's leaving the station."

"Classic Horatio Alger story, except with a nice twist." Sam's smile was more crooked than usual. "Just as they're about to go public, Terry Mavis conveniently OD's. Cocaine cocktail. The company's thrown into turmoil, legal battles ensue. But when the smoke clears, Miles Wingfield is sole owner of the patents and launches his new venture, Wingfield BioTech. And the rest, as they say, is history."

Sam spread out some additional folders.

"Check this out. Last couple years, the company diversified like crazy. Hit the Triple Crown of corporate greed—research, production, *and* distribution."

I began flipping through the folders. "With all that diversification," I said, "I'm betting that includes health-related franchises. Insurance groups, hospitals."

Then I found it. UniHealth.

Sam tipped the folder toward him, reading upside-down. "Yeah. Wingfield BioTech is the principal shareholder in UniHealth. They've been buying up high-end mental health facilities and nursing homes. Nowadays, babyboomers with big portfolios need somewhere to stash their crazy kids and elderly parents. UniHealth saw a vacuum in the market and started filling it."

I nodded. "They just bought out Ten Oaks."

Sam whistled. "Where that shrink turned up murdered?"

"Yeah. Brooks Riley."

"Think there might be a connection?"

I gave him a look. "I'm listening."

"Just spit-balling here, but what if this Riley guy objected to Ten Oaks selling out?"

I shook my head. "I know the clinical director, Bert Garman, well enough that if Brooks *was* putting up a stink about it he would've told me. Besides, even if Brooks *did* object, he had no power to stop it. Garman not only runs the place, he heads up the Board of Directors. And from what I've heard, the Board couldn't wait to sell the place to UniHealth. Pretty big pay-day for all concerned."

Sam frowned. "Still…I mean, the guy *did* get shot. You think it has anything to do with Miles Wingfield, too?"

I leaned back in my seat, stretched. "Hell, Sam. I don't know. At this point, I'm just trying to—"

Suddenly, my cell phone rang. It was Casey.

"You need to take that?" Sam asked.

I nodded, and answered the phone. "Hi. What's up?"

"Danny. You're not gonna believe this." Her voice was breathless. "I just talked to Biegler. Remember I told you he sent Polk up to Cloverbrook to talk to Stickey?"

"Yeah. What did Stickey have to say?"

"Not much. They found him this morning in the prison laundry. With a shiv stuck in his throat."

Chapter Thirty-six

An hour later, I was checked into a room at the mid-town Hyatt. On Sam's insistence, I'd borrowed one of his credit cards and registered under his name. He said any seasoned reporter would routinely canvas all the hotels in the area, promising a healthy finder's fee to the desk employee who coughed up my room number.

"You just have to lay low for the next couple news cycles," Sam had said. "They'll lose interest in you as soon as there's a break in the case."

"*If* there's a break." We shook hands. "Thanks again."

"Don't thank me. Just don't get killed. There might be another book in this when it's all over, and I'll need you as a source."

"I'll try not to let you down."

My hotel room was on the top floor, with a view toward the Three Rivers. Cathedrals of clouds rose over the far hills, presaging another storm coming in from the west.

I'd turned on the news as soon as I got in the room, but didn't hear anything about the death of an inmate at Cloverbrook. No surprise. The cops were probably keeping it under wraps. Then I surfed the cable channels, but they were just rehashing the known facts about Kevin's case.

I shut off the TV and began sorting out on the bed all the info Sam had given me. I knew it'd be slow going. Maybe later tonight, after I'd taken care of some other things.

I took fifteen minutes to shave and shower, and then I pulled up a chair at the small varnished desk. I looked at my watch. I had two hours.

<><><>

"Sylvia?"

"Yes? Who—? Is this Dr. Rinaldi?"

"Yes, it's me."

I let a long silence hang in the air, watching the blinking light on the hotel phone console.

Sylvia Lange's voice changed during that silence, came across the line now flooded with feeling. "Oh, Doctor..."

I could hear the tears. Her crying was hushed, choked, as though parceled out in careful patches of breath.

"I was hoping you'd call," she said finally. "I mean, with everything in the news...I was so worried—"

"I know, Sylvia. And I appreciate it." I also knew what she needed to hear. "But I'm fine. Really."

"That's good. I've been praying for you, you know."

"Couldn't hurt either. But I was wondering about *you*. With this latest appeal for Dowd, and now the movie..."

"I don't know which upsets me more, the thought of him getting away with it, or that damned movie." She sniffed. "And I know it's silly, but I don't look anything like Susan Sarandon. Though God knows I wish I did."

"Dowd isn't getting away with anything, Sylvia. His lawyer's just trying to get around the death penalty. But the Handyman's locked up tight. Forever. He won't be able to hurt you or anyone else again."

"Uh-huh."

I paused. "Are you still seeing the psychiatrist?"

"Yes. Dr. Fukanaga. He's upped my Zoloft. What a surprise. Plus I have a new therapist, who's pretty good, even though she's half my age. And I'm in a local trauma survivor's group. So I guess I'm covered, therapy-wise."

"I'm glad you're taking care of yourself."

"Yeah. But I miss you, Dr. Rinaldi. I wish I hadn't moved so far away."

"You said yourself, you needed a change of scenery. Some anonymity. And I hear Bucks County's beautiful."

"Sure. If you like clean air and mountains and lakes."

I smiled, visualizing her round, matronly face. That sturdy, wry humor. She probably owed her sanity to it.

I spoke softly. "Listen, Sylvia. I'm still here. I haven't gone anywhere."

"I…Thanks for saying that. Just knowing you're out there… thinking about me sometimes…it helps."

After we hung up, I stared out the hotel window, at the approaching darkness. In all the ways that matter, Sylvia was still my patient.

It's a lesson they don't teach in school. About what really happens between a therapist and patient. That when the therapy works, something intangible, indelible, is exchanged, so that a felt trace of the other is imprinted, forever, on the soul.

<>◇<>

I figured I'd better check in on Noah, too, so I phoned the bar.

"Noah's Ark, Noah speaking."

"Me. Just wanted to make sure you got home all right."

"Where'd I go?"

I laughed. "Last time we spoke, you were in a phone booth at the Penn Hotel."

"Oh, yeah. No worries, Charlene sent a cab for me. Made the guy's day. I'm a big tipper, as you know."

"Well, try to stay put tonight, okay?"

"Will do. Besides, my band's playin' tonight, and I was gonna invite you to come check it out."

"I don't know…"

"We got a guy sittin' in on sax, some blues freak from Jersey. I think he's bipolar. Anyway, wait'll you hear us. Man, we put the funk in dysfunction."

Before I could answer, my cell phone rang. It was in the pocket of my jacket, which was thrown over a chair.

"Hold on, will ya, Noah? That's my cell."

I reached over and slipped the cell out of my pocket.

"Dr. Rinaldi? Harvey Blalock."

"Hey, I was going to call you. I've gotten a room at the Hyatt."
I gave him the room number.

"Good boy. I just wanted to let you know I spoke to the District Attorney, and he assures me there're no plans to charge you in the Riley murder. At least for now."

"You know Leland Sinclair? How well?"

"We play golf once in a while. Besides, I'm president of the Pittsburgh Black Attorneys Association. He and I both know he'll need our endorsement when he runs for governor. Anyway, unless you like paying lawyer's fees, I wouldn't rush out and retain Ralph Puzzini just yet."

"Okay. Speaking of fees, we never discussed yours."

He laughed. "Why ruin what looks like the beginning of a beautiful friendship?"

I managed a laugh, too. After talking about finding a time to meet in his office in the next day or two, I clicked off and checked back with Noah on the land-line.

"Sorry, Noah, you still there?"

The line was dead.

I called right back, feeling an inexplicable, mounting anxiety as it rang six or seven times.

Finally, Charlene picked up.

"Charlene, it's Dan. I was just talking to Noah."

She sounded harried, distracted. "You were? He was just here...maybe he's—shit, I don't know where he is..."

"Look, if he—"

"Sorry, Doc, another customer's come in. Gotta go."

She hung up.

I stared at the receiver. Then at the wall print of a Turner landscape just above the desk. Then at the scattered papers and files waiting for my attention on the bed.

Strange, this feeling twisting inside my stomach about Noah. That something was about to happen. That something was... wrong.

Chapter Thirty-seven

A blustery wind whipped the flaps of my overcoat as I pushed open the door of the Spent Cartridge. The cop bar was a dark, wood-paneled anachronism wedged between two recent high-rises on Liberty Avenue. As always during shift changes, the place was packed.

A haze of cigarette smoke veiled the room. I made my way through the throng of off-duty plainclothes, past the noisy bar where the evening news played on a wide-screen TV nobody was watching, and reached the booths at the back.

Sgt. Polk and Det. Lowrey sat across from each other, over burgers and beer. Without preamble, I slid in next to Lowrey. I smiled at her.

Her violet eyes narrowed for just a moment, then softened with what seemed like bemusement.

"Dr. Rinaldi. Nice to see you again."

Polk, working over a mouthful of burger, swallowed noisily. "What the hell are *you* doin' here?"

"Just checking in with the team. Casey Walters told me about Stickey. She also said you guys mentioned coming here after work."

"She did, huh?" Polk looked across at his partner. "Can you believe the balls on this guy? *You* wanna toss his ass, or should I?"

"Chill, Harry. Besides, with all the shit goin' on in your life, maybe the Doc here can give you some advice." She turned to me. "He sure as hell doesn't listen to *me*."

"Yeah, right." Polk pointed a ketchup-smudged finger at me. "One thing, man. You better pray that Lt. Biegler don't come waltzin' in here right about now. He wants your goddam head on a pole."

"Don't worry," I said, "Biegler wouldn't set foot in this place. Figures he'd be slumming."

Lowrey laughed. "You got *that* right."

"Look," I said, "just fill me in on what's going on. I'm on the payroll, so I could probably find out through official channels, but I'd rather get it from the people who *don't* have their heads up their asses."

"Gimme a break," Polk said irritably.

"C'mon, just tell me about James Stickey…"

Eleanor Lowrey enjoyed watching the slow burn coloring her partner's face. Finally, Polk shrugged, but he made me wait until he'd finished off his burger.

"Nothin' to tell," he said. "I go up this morning to Cloverbrook—now *there's* a fuckin' garden spot, nothin' but tractors and cow shit and this big, ugly-ass prison. Anyway, turns out Stickey ain't in his cell. They call out the troops, and we find him stuffed in a clothes basket in the laundry room. Been dead at least a couple hours."

"Any suspects?"

"Oh, yeah. About fourteen hundred of 'em."

"Well, what's your gut feeling? You think his death is connected to the Wingfield case?"

"Could be, but I doubt it. Could be anything. Drugs. Turf. Maybe he got tired of bein' somebody's bitch."

"Aren't you investigating?"

"Not our jurisdiction. The local cops are tryin' to pick up some leads. Ain't gonna come up with squat."

Eleanor Lowrey nodded thoughtfully. "Part of me agrees with you, Dr. Rinaldi. Too damn coincidental. But…"

She took a sip of her beer. A black female cop didn't make Detective First Grade by wasting time on dead leads. *Or* pissing off her veteran partner.

I turned to her. "By the way, I was talking to Nancy Mendors, and she told me you interviewed those two girls at the clinic. About the fight."

"You sure get around, Doc. Yeah, I took a run at each of them. But I didn't get much. Lucy's family had a big-time lawyer there in about ten minutes, so that was that. The other one, Helen Frazier, just clamed up, except to call me a nigger cunt on my way out the door. All in all, a real fruitful afternoon."

"Somebody put them up to it," I said. "At least *one* of them. Maybe with money or drugs. Then the killer used the diversion to slip into Riley's office and shoot him."

Polk eyed me caustically. "Yeah. The killer. Whoever *that* might be."

"Give that one a rest, will ya, Harry?" Lowrey said carefully. "Even *you* don't believe it."

Polk and Lowrey exchanged looks, and I saw something pass between them. Like a secret code. The thing that anchored their relationship: Regardless of rank, years on the job, even differences in race and gender, partners don't bullshit each other. Simple as that.

Harry Polk got to his feet and announced, "I'm goin' to the can. Let Freud here get the check."

As he shuffled off, Lowrey shook her head and reached for the bill. But I snatched it up.

"My pleasure," I said, to her surprised face. "Harry seems pretty stressed-out. Even for him."

Her eyes softened. "I feel sorry for him. He just got served the divorce papers an hour ago. So it's official."

I considered this. "Hey, I know it's not your job, but don't let him crawl too far into a bottle tonight. He's not looking so good."

"We're partners, Dr. Rinaldi. So I figure it *is* my job. But don't worry. I'll bring him home with me tonight. Luther won't mind. I've done it before."

"Luther?"

"My Doberman." Again, that bemused smile.

As I flipped some bills onto the table, a chorus of angry voices rose from the bar area. I glanced up to see the bartender using the TV clicker to pump up the volume.

"Screw you guys," he growled, "I wanna hear this."

On the wide-screen, the graphic said "Breaking News," under an image from a helicopter's vantage point of a scarred, fire-blackened building. Obviously long-abandoned, it stood like a ghost amid rubble and scattered debris.

The TV picture was jerky, moving in and out of focus, as the camera swung in a high circle around the site. Surrounding the building were a half dozen police units, lights pluming up against the wintry darkness.

Lowrey and I stood, straining to see over the backs of a dozen heads now clustering at the bar. I just managed to get some of the news announcer's words.

"…apparent hostage situation…police have confirmed the identity of the suspect…a photo has been released…"

A blurred head shot appeared in a corner of the TV screen. Institutional setting. Pale green hospital tunic. It was an old picture, but—

I threaded my way to the bar, getting a closer look at his face.

As I felt the blood drain from my own.

Chapter Thirty-eight

Nancy Mendors aimed her dark eyes up at mine as two cops fitted the Kevlar jacket snugly across my chest.

"Danny, you don't have to do this." Her soft voice dopplered away, lifted by the wind, shredded by the rattle of helicopter blades a hundred feet over our heads.

"Richie knows me," I said. "He trusts me. I think I can get him to come out."

All around us, steaming klieg lights were like blurred suns, making angled silhouettes of the piles of rubble, the fenders of cars, the upraised guns. The whole area was cordoned off, bracketing the tension. Hard faces, backlit against the night, loomed in at me.

Sgt. Chester, the bullet-headed SWAT leader, got in my face long enough to give me a sour, frustrated look, and then stomped off, shouting orders to his men. The decision to let me try to talk Richie Ellner into surrendering had come from upstairs, and Chester was cleanly pissed.

Bert Garman, shivering in his overcoat next to Nancy, wasn't happy about it either.

"Richie's out of control," he said. "He's taken a *hostage*, for Christ's sake. The security guard…"

"They *think* there's a hostage," I said. One of the two cops prepping me slammed a thick black flashlight in my hand. Felt like a length of lead pipe.

When I got here twenty minutes ago, I'd found Bert Garman and Nancy Mendors conferring with the police. I pulled Nancy aside and got the story.

Apparently, Richie had been one of a group of clinic patients being taken by van to Memorial Hospital for observation. Their level of agitation had escalated after Brooks Riley's murder, and Garman had ordered some tests.

According to the other patients, when the van stopped at this intersection, Richie had bolted from his seat, gotten past the orderly in charge, and ran out onto the street. The driver gave chase, but Richie had too big a lead and vanished into the bowels of the building.

"What *is* this place?" I'd said to Nancy, peering up at the dilapidated structure, streaked charcoal-black.

"Some old dry-cleaning plant." Her words were clipped, as though hollowed-out from shock. "Caught fire a couple years ago. Burned out. Abandoned."

She'd held my arm, dark hair buffeted by the wind. "Danny, I can't bear the thought of Richie in there. Alone. Terrified. They're going to kill him."

Even as I tried to comfort her, I'd already begun thinking about running something by the cops. About getting them to let *me* have a chance to talk to Richie.

It took a lot of argument and calls to the brass, but I'd finally gotten the go-ahead. The fact that Richie's father was a prominent senator, and was at that moment flying down from Harrisburg, put the idea over the top.

Now, as I slipped a reflective jacket over the vest, Lieutenant Frank Lucci, in charge at the scene, came over to have the last word. Lucci was former military, tall, solid, with a face tough as a shaving strop.

"Let's get this bullshit over with," he said, avoiding direct eye contact. "Chief says you get five minutes. *Five* fuckin' minutes, okay? Then SWAT goes in and takes the bastard out."

"Got it."

"Remember, there might be a hostage. Building's been abandoned since the fire, but the holding company says they keep a security guard on premises. To run off the crackheads, homeless. If he's down, we gotta assume the perp took his gun. Which means the perp is violent, *and* armed."

"I know all this," I said. "Now let me get in there."

Nancy's eyes narrowed with anger. "He's right, Danny. This *is* bullshit. Some kind of misplaced—"

"Dr. Mendors," Garman said. The sharpness in his voice seemed to surprise her, and Nancy fell silent. Then he put his arm around her. Also uncharacteristic.

As was the fierceness in the look he gave me. "I hope to God you know what you're doing," he said.

Then, with a proprietary grip on Nancy's shoulder, he turned them both away.

⟨⟩⟨⟩⟨⟩

Ten feet into the building, and the reality of a world beyond its crumbling walls was eclipsed. The lights and sounds at my back, proof of men and movement, grew fainter with every step into the burned-out hull.

I swung the flashlight beam in a wide arc to get my bearings. It illuminated a labyrinth of blocked corridors, scattered piles of rubble, the black and twisted remains of machinery. At the far end of this main floor, spiraling up like a DNA helix, stood a fire-scarred metal stairway.

"Richie!" I started walking. High walls of hulking, rusted equipment made a catacomb of the factory floor.

I glanced up, shining my light at the warped, bowed ceiling above. There were four floors stacked above me. He had to be up there somewhere.

"Richie!" I called again. "It's me! Dan Rinaldi!"

I knew I couldn't stop moving. Given Lucci's deadline, every second counted. I headed for the spiral stairway.

It was slow going. The wind was a high shriek. Dust swirled like a live thing, a mix of plaster and ash that burned my throat, choking me with every step.

The flashlight beam bounced ahead of me as I made my way slowly, carefully, through the rubble. Thick darkness hung like a shroud beyond the stroke of the light.

A dull gleam shone off the railings of the metal stairway, just ahead now. I sped up, impatient suddenly, careless. *Come on, come on!* Running now—

Something caught my foot.

An upraised floor plank? Debris? I staggered and pitched forward, hitting the floor hard. The flashlight flew from my hand, skittered away. *Shit!*

I lay there, gasping. A stabbing pain where my elbow had hit. I blinked against the dust, reaching with outstretched fingers for the flashlight.

It had rolled only a few feet, light elongating along the splintered floorboards. *Okay. Okay.*

I took a breath and crawled forward to retrieve it. In the darkness, I felt a sudden whisper of movement across my knuckles, a pinch of claws—

Christ! I lurched upright. I flapped my hand as if the rat still clung there, and, in two quick strides, scooped up the flashlight.

I grasped the rail of the stairwell and stepped up, panning the floor with the light. A dozen pair of moist eyes blinked up at me. Then that familiar scurrying sound.

At the edge of the circle of light were some overturned boxes, each about the size of a brick. Rat poison. Some of the boxes had been nibbled open, their contents spilled like dry riverbeds on the floor.

"You're gonna need more than that," I said aloud to no one in particular.

I climbed the winding metal stairs. Squinting to see up into the swirling opacity of dust and darkness. The stairway trembled, swayed, beneath my weight.

Finally, I reached the top, a charred expanse of mottled flooring and collapsed walls. Only half a ceiling stretched overhead, the rest exposed to the black sky.

Steeling myself, I threaded across the uneven floor. The wind's shriek grew louder, like a cry of pain, of torment, of the damned.

It wasn't the wind.

"Richie?"

I ran quickly forward, my path suddenly blocked by a huge chunk of masonry. Half a chimney stack, collapsed onto itself. I clambered down its jagged length.

I could hear Richie's anguished cries clearly now. The cops would come breaking in any moment, and I was so close, almost there, almost—

On the other side of the barrier was a huge, rain-bloated cardboard box, wet and crumbling with mold. Though empty, it was slick, cumbersome. I put both hands on the box, pushed it aside.

There was something under it. Some*one.* Dead.

I bent down, aimed the light. Found his face, and the spindly black beetle scrambling out of his open mouth.

I got to my knees and quickly swept the light from the contorted, frozen face, down the expanse of blue shirt, pressed pocket, ID badge.

The security guard.

I pressed my fingers against his throat. Nothing. I bent to listen for breath. Again, nothing.

I felt for the holster strapped to his belt. His gun was gone.

"Shit, Richie," I whispered.

Slowly, I got up and moved around the body. A charred leather trunk with brass hasps stood up ahead. I poked it with my light, and saw a fabric of spider webs shivering in the wind.

Then, not ten feet beyond, the walls converged to a deep V. There, latticed in shadow, cowering in the ceaseless push of the wind, was Richie Ellner.

I moved in a crouch to the trunk, then peered over it for a better look at him.

He was an apparition, a nightmare out of Goya. Clothes dirty and ash-covered. Huddled in semi-darkness, trembling violently. Head and torso cloaked in shadow.

On the floor between us, twisted frames secured by tape, lay his thick, cracked eyeglasses. Forlorn, hapless.

"Richie," I called softly, urgently. I moved closer. "It's me. Dan Rinaldi..."

The shadowy head reared up, and again that awful wail of agony. One of his hands waved like a stalk, and I saw metal glinting in the darkness. The security guard's revolver.

"Richie, I know you have a gun..."

I crouched behind a splintered crate.

"I also know you didn't hurt that guard. There's not a mark on him. I think he died of a heart attack. You hear me, Richie? You didn't hurt that man."

His keening stopped abruptly, followed by an even more ominous silence. I took another step. I was only six feet away from him now, though in that empty blackness it felt like a chasm.

"Richie..?"

He began sobbing. Deep, choking sobs.

Then a voice so thin, so strained, it seemed to be coming from somewhere else. The dark side of the moon.

"They're inside, Doc...they're eating me up from the inside. That's been the problem all along."

"Richie, I'm going to come closer." I walked very deliberately toward where he huddled against the wall.

"Stay back! Stay back!" His right hand shot up again, waving the gun.

"For Christ's sake, put down the gun." I kept my tone firm, unequivocal. "You're not gonna hurt me."

"You just stay back, okay? Okay?" His words were strangled. I could hear a gurgling sound.

"I got it all under control now, Doc," he went on, wheezing. "Control, control. Been the damn problem all along. Crowd control. Mind control. *Pest* control."

Slowly, I raised the flashlight.

"I'll stay put, Richie," I said, "but I want to take a look at you. Okay?"

"That's what it's about, see?" A choked spasm. "What it's always been about. Pest control. They're eating me up inside, and I never knew. Nobody did. Not even you."

"I'm just taking a look, okay, Richie?"

I moved the flashlight beam tentatively across the floor, till it touched his shoes. Then, I inched it up his legs to his chest.

"Just a quick look, and then—"

"Not even *you*, Doc..."

Suddenly, the light hit his face, and I saw into the maw of hell. His features were haunted, blasted. His eyes were unnaturally wide, deathly white, rivulets of blood seeping from each eyeball. His mouth hung slack, foaming with a bloody froth.

He screamed at the beam, bringing his left hand up against his eyes. He had something in that hand.

A box, about the size of a brick. Opened.

"Richie, no!"

I lunged for him, but he backed away, swinging his gun hand wildly. Screaming in pain and outrage, he squeezed the trigger. Shots echoed.

I hit the floor and rolled, feeling and hearing the bullets whizzing past my ear. I scrambled across the floor and behind the crate again, gasping.

Forget my five minutes. If the cops heard those shots, they'd come swarming in. *Now.* And they'd cut him down.

"I *get* it now," Richie was saying. "Just pest control. Like Terminix. All those shrinks and doctors and hospitals. Nothin' but pest control..."

"Give me the gun, Richie. The cops—"

He fired another shot in my direction, then leaned back and poured some more of the poison crystals into his mouth. He staggered like a drunk swigging from a bottle, but stayed upright. Then he turned, transfixed, as he chewed and swallowed, blood-streaked drool streaming from the corners of his mouth.

Fuck it. I jumped up and bolted across the floor, even as he raised an unsteady hand to fire the gun.

I didn't make it. Turning too late, diving, the slug slammed into my Kevlar vest.

Richie doubled over in pain. He lurched against the wall, retching violently. The box of rat poison hit the floor. But he still held the gun.

Gasping, spackled with blood and vomit, Richie collided with the wall and scratched his way, crab-like, along its rough, pock-marked surface.

Staggering to my feet, I went after him. I had to. I knew where he was going.

Richie got to the window a scant few seconds before I could reach him. Clutching the scorched frame, Richie waved the gun shakily in my direction.

"Tell him, Doc. Tell my father…"

"Tell him what?"

I took a half-step. He was beyond an arm's length away. I blinked into the gun barrel, held now with both his hands, trembling spasmodically. His body was half-way out of the window.

"Tell him *what*, Richie?"

The police assault had begun. I heard shouts from below, the crack of axes and battering rams against mortar, the pounding of heavy footsteps on the stairwell.

Outside, the roar of the police helicopter. A powerful arc light streamed through the broken walls, painted an incandescent halo around Richie's body in the window.

"It's the police, Richie. You gotta—"

Richie's face screwed up into a grotesque grin. Except, impossibly, his eyes. Weeping tears of blood, they held a final, terrifying lucidity.

"Tell my father I didn't scream. All the way down…I didn't scream…"

"Richie, no!!"

He let himself go and fell backwards. I reached out, hands clutching empty air…

I watched, numb, as he spiraled down, in a deliberate silence, lit by police searchlights. A nightmare in slow motion, tumbling limbs flying, to sprawl hard against the scattered debris below.

Sharp, officious voices filled the air. More lights. Cops converging on Richie from every direction.

I collapsed against the window frame, closed my eyes, gulped acrid air. Blood pounded my earsdrums. Approaching footfalls, anxious voices calling my name.

I didn't answer. They'd find me soon enough.

Chapter Thirty-nine

"Here, this always works for me." Elaine Garman offered me a drink. "Though *your* mileage may vary."

Her smile looked forced in the faint light from the table lamp. But the rest of her—designer clothes, upswept hair, studied haughtiness as she reclined against the sofa back—seemed undiminished by the night's events.

Which was more than I could say for everybody else. Bert Garman was pacing the floor of his living room, more agitated than I'd ever seen him. Meanwhile, curled in a chair behind him, Nancy Mendors followed Garman's movements with heavy, sallow eyes, as if hoping his repetitive rhythm might eventually lull her to sleep.

I'd been trying unsuccessfully to banish the after-image of Richie's falling body from my mind. It had lingered, indelibly, for the past five hours, most of which had been spent giving my statement at the mid-town precinct.

Though that makes me sound a lot more coherent than I was when the cops found me. Apparently I'd blacked out from pain and the shock of Richie' suicide, and the EMT guys had a tough time getting any straight answers out of me about how I was doing.

Finally, satisfied that I wasn't going to lose my value as a witness by inconveniently dying, I was brought up to Lt. Lucci's office.

"Richie never meant to hurt me," I explained to him, as his bloodshot eyes narrowed skeptically. "He just used the gun to keep me back. All he wanted was to die."

"Scarfin' down a box of rat poison, yeah, you could say that." Lucci's scowl held no sympathy. "Meanwhile, his old man's across town right now, raising holy hell about how we handled the whole thing. Like it's *our* fault his kid was a fuckin' whack job."

I waved him off. "I want to see the toxicology report. This wasn't just a psychotic episode. There was something else. I mean, he was like guys I've seen on angel dust."

Just as they were about to release me, reports started coming in from CSU and the ME. Apparently, my guess about the security guard's death had been correct. Heart attack. Probably the shock of encountering a raving intruder.

"Funny about your Richie," Lucci had said as he ushered me out of his office. "I've seen a lot of jumpers. They almost always scream on the way down. But your guy? Not a peep." He scratched his beard stubble. "Funny."

"Yeah." I walked away.

When I stepped out of the elevator in the main lobby, I was met by a crowd of reporters, pressing against a rope barrier manned by some uniforms. A volley of voices rose up at once, peppering me with questions about Richie's death, and my connection to the Wingfield case.

Then, from out of nowhere, another uniformed cop appeared at my side, taking my elbow. "Come on."

He led me down a side corridor to a private door, and then to an unmarked unit idling on the other side. "Brass said to make sure you don't step in shit."

"Little late for that."

He shrugged, uninterested, and got behind the wheel. Ten minutes later, he dropped me where I'd parked my car, a couple blocks from the building site. As I stood at the curb, watching him drive off, I heard a car horn bleat.

A pair of headlights flared, and I squinted as Bert Garman rolled up in his late-model BMW. Nancy Mendors was still with him.

"Get in," she said. "We've waited half the night."

"Thanks, but my car's right here."

"You're coming home with me." Garman's voice was laced with fatigue. "You need a drink, and we need to talk."

"You're half right." But I got in.

After which, we drove in a tense, awkward silence out of the city and across the bridge to Garman's tudor-style house in a well-maintained area of Greentree.

Now, under Elaine Garman's watchful eye, I downed my drink and waited for its miraculous effect. My chest ached from where the bullet had hit the vest, and my ankle throbbed as though wrapped in barbed wire. Everything else just hurt like hell.

I handed Elaine my glass. "I think I need a refill."

As she got up almost gaily, and went to the polished wet-bar, I leaned back and took some deep breaths. When I focused again, I found Bert Garman glaring down at me.

"You know how many messages I got tonight from Uni-Health's lawyers?"

"A lot?"

He frowned. "First Riley's murder, and now a patient commits suicide. UniHealth feels screwed having bought Ten Oaks. They're considering pulling out of the deal, for cause. Which means I'll have the other board members out for my blood. I could lose my job. Hell, they could *sue* me."

I shrugged. "Well, if they do, I know a good lawyer."

Nancy grimaced. "This isn't funny, Dan."

"I agree. Richie's death isn't one bit funny. And *that's* what we should be worrying about. Finding out what the hell happened. Not this other shit."

Garman threw up his hands and sank into an armchair. Unlike his wife, with every passing hour he was looking worse.

Clothes disheveled, creased, limp with sweat. Face pinched, drained of life.

"I wanted you and Nancy here together," he went on wearily, "because I want us all on the same page. For the cops. The insurance company. The press."

"And Richie's father, the senator," I said.

He groaned. "Don't remind me. It's gonna be a goddam feeding frenzy. But I'll handle it. I'll take point. All I need from you two is cooperation."

"Meaning what?" asked Nancy.

"Meaning, we have one, consistent story. One version of events."

"And what would *that* be?" Elaine mixed drinks.

Ignoring her, Bert Garman folded his arms. "Just what actually happened. A suicidal patient escaped from the clinic van. By the time competent mental health personnel and police arrived on the scene, he'd jumped from the top floor of a building, taking his own life."

Nancy laughed bitterly. "You don't think his family's going to sue the clinic? Maybe even me personally?"

"Why you?"

"I was his case manager. I prescribed his medication."

"Did you do anything different? Alter his treatment in some way that can hurt us?"

She took a minute to think. "Six weeks ago, I put him on Adnorfex. Then, after Brooks' murder, I prescribed an Ellavil kicker. He was becoming unglued. We discussed this, Bert. Remember? Changing the protocols for some of the patients having difficulty with Brooks' death."

Garman nodded. "Yes. Yes."

I turned to her. "You have all your case notes, the altered treatment schedule?"

"Of course." Her lips tightened.

"Who administered the meds?"

"An orderly, or intern, I suppose. I'd have to check the shift record."

Garman clapped his hands together, like some kind of coach. "Good. Let's get the paperwork assembled. I have a call in to the clinic attorneys. And the board's meeting first thing in the morning."

Nancy glanced at her watch. "Which won't be long now."

Elaine Garman returned with a drink in either hand, gave one to me. Then she sidled back over to the other end of the sofa. Watching us over the rim of her glass.

The three of us kept on talking for another hour, trying to build a clinical picture to the best of our understanding, reviewing Richie's last seventy-two hours. As we struggled, my glance would occasionally find Elaine Garman still sitting on the sofa arm, smiling at our consternation, casually swinging her slim, gleaming leg.

<>>

"Everything's turning to shit," Nancy said, leaning back against the headrest. "It's been going that way for a long time, really. But I always had work. The clinic. My port in the storm."

"Even if UniHealth pulls out," I said, "Ten Oaks will survive. It has one of the best reputations in the state."

"It *did*. But now, after all this..."

We were sharing a cab, taking her home. Despite Bert Garman's offer to drive each of us where we needed to go, I'd insisted he try to get at least a couple hours' sleep. He had a brutal day ahead of him.

Now, in the pre-dawn darkness, our cab moved through empty streets toward Shadyside, and the modest row of apartments just off the business district. Nancy's building hadn't changed much over the years, a gabled structure made newly-fashionable during the area's gentrification.

At the curb, I helped her out of the cab and put my arm around her. She felt alarmingly thin, frail.

"Give me a minute," I said to the cabbie.

As we walked to the front door, Nancy's head lay against my shoulder. I could feel her sort of slump against me, as though finally allowing herself to deflate.

"I'm gonna miss Richie," she said. "I mean, I really liked him. Cared about him…"

"I know. Me, too."

She paused. "It's funny, but nowadays the only people I see regularly are patients. We're as intimate as friends, and yet not friends. Now just the idea that I won't see him every day…I guess I still can't believe it."

She smiled up at me. "Classic shrink's trap, and I fell right into it: My patients are my social life. I mean, how lame is that?"

"It's not lame. Just common. Don't beat yourself up about it." I squeezed her shoulder.

"Don't worry," she said. "I've got plenty of *other* things to beat myself up about. Like, maybe I screwed up his medication. Or missed some obvious signs that he was deteriorating. Let's face it, Danny, he died on my watch."

We reached the building entrance, and Nancy slipped out of my arm to search her purse for keys. I watched her pale, earnest brow in the faint porch light. I knew she'd never forgive herself for what happened to Richie.

"It wasn't your fault," I said. "It wasn't anything you did, or didn't do. I'm sure of it."

"Maybe you're right. Maybe he was just tired of his life. Tired of being lonely. I can understand that."

I looked at her. "You gonna be okay?"

She nodded, then leaned up and kissed my cheek. Then she turned without another word, unlocked the outer lobby door, and went inside.

The cab pulled around the far corner of the abandoned lot, still choked with lab vans, CSU techs, and uniforms. The building itself seemed even more desolate in the unforgiving dawn light. Some early-rising onlookers milled at the scene, restless behind the crime scene tape, waiting for something new and interesting to happen.

My Mustang was parked where I'd left it, on a deserted side street shadowed by industrial squalor. I paid the cabbie and got out. Here, cloistered by weary, silent buildings that blocked the morning sun, the world seemed suddenly empty, hushed.

I headed for my car. Lost in thought, it wasn't until I'd reached the driver's side door that I noticed that someone was sitting behind the wheel.

I froze, my hand inches from the door latch.

Scratch marks. Paint chipped away. The lock had been forced.

Shadows stretched across the man in the driver's seat. A bearded man. Unmoving. Staring straight ahead.

I forced air into my lungs.

"Hey," I said. I pulled the door open.

It wasn't a man. Or alive. Pink, plastic hands rested at its sides. Belted into place, the manikin sat as stiffly upright as a soldier in church.

It was also smoothly naked, except for the costume beard and wire-rimmed glasses that clumsily framed the serene, staring face.

And the torso streaked with thick, dripping globs of red paint, just below the knife embedded there. Where the heart would be.

Though I knew it wasn't a knife. It was a skewer. Thin, long-bladed. Buried to the hilt in the manikin's chest.

Reeling, I grasped the open door frame to steady myself. Stared hard at the crusting, scarlet blotch. Crude, finger-painted letters spelled out a single word.

"Soon..."

Chapter Forty

"At least we know where the second skewer is," I said to Casey. "Forensics has the pair now. Maybe we'll get lucky and they'll find something."

She eyed me doubtfully. "You mean 'cause we've been so lucky up till now?"

We were in my room at the Hyatt, naked under the bedsheets. According to the table clock, it was two in the afternoon. Casey was taking a long lunch.

"Biegler has a team checking all the up-scale retail outlets," she said, "trying to get a lead on where the killer got the skewers. He might go back for another set. Unless he decides to be creative and switch to butcher knives."

"He won't," I said. "It's part of his communication with me. You don't have to be an FBI profiler to figure that one out. Plus, I think he's proud of the uniqueness of the murder weapon. That's part of the message, too."

Casey shivered involuntarily. "Jesus, it's like you're starting to know the guy."

"Something tells me I already do."

After finding the manikin in my car, I'd called Harry Polk and waited for him and the forensics team to show up. By this time, I knew the drill only too well. CSU towed my car back to impound to start the work-up, while I went with Polk back to the station.

"We got a pool goin' at the office," Polk said as we drove into the police lot. "Smart money says you're gonna be dead by the weekend."

"My tax dollars at work."

He grinned. "At least you gotta hand it to the perp. That beard-and-glasses thing. Nice touch."

We found Detective Lowrey waiting impatiently for us in Polk's cramped cubicle. We filled her in on the details.

After which, I said, "I assume even Biegler's smart enough to keep this second death threat from the media."

Polk shrugged. "Long as we can, yeah."

I got up to leave, and Lowrey got up with me. "Listen, I'm sorry about the jumper. Senator Ellner's kid. From what I hear, you did everything you could."

I had no answer to that. "By the way, anything new on the Brooks Riley murder?"

Polk smiled. "Funny you should ask. 'Course, you bein' pals, you probably know this already. About Nancy Mendors."

"What about her?"

"She and Riley were more than just colleagues. Turns out, they've been doin' the nasty on the sly for months. Till loverboy broke it off a week ago."

He turned to Lowrey. "What do ya think, partner? Sound like a motive to you?"

<><><>

I got back to my room at the Hyatt and tried to call Nancy at the clinic. Nobody knew where she was. When I tried her place, I got her machine. And her cell was off.

I'd learned from Polk and Lowrey that they expected to bring her in for questioning soon. But Biegler wanted more artillery first: phone records, a warrant to search her place. All they had right now was clinic gossip that had emerged early on in the investigation of Riley's death.

Nancy and Brooks Riley. I hadn't seen that one coming.

Now, in retrospect, it made a kind of sense. Nancy was lonely, vulnerable. I could see her swept up into an affair with the clinic's brash new head of psychiatry. Devastated when he ended it. But driven to murder…?

I began running the details through my head. The patient fight in the rec yard, which Nancy missed, claiming to have been in the rest room. The fact that she offered to go look for Riley later that day, when he didn't show up for a meeting. Which was when *she* found the body.

I could see from the cops' perspective how it all laid out. But did I believe it?

I had an image of Nancy's drawn, sad face. Vivid memories of my own brief time with her. How we'd clung to each other, sustained each other.

Nancy deserved more than the law's presumption of innocence. She deserved my support. And she'd get it.

I checked my messages. Sam Weiss. Angie. Harvey Blalock. Concerned, well-meaning calls. How was I holding up? Richie Ellner's dramatic suicide had led the news.

I answered none of them. Instead, I stood under a scalding shower for fifteen minutes and fell, still wet, onto the bed.

Exhaustion. Escape. Who knows? But I slipped into a deep, dreamless sleep.

<><><>

Until a pounding at my hotel room door woke me, and I got groggily to my feet. The table clock said noon.

"Danny, it's me! Open up." It was Casey.

I pulled on a robe and opened the door.

Before I could say a word, she'd thrown herself into my arms. Then her lips found mine, pressing into a deep, urgent kiss. I sank into it with my whole being.

Her lips moved to my ear. "Thank God," she whispered. "Thank God you're all right."

Her tongue flicked my lobe. Though still half-asleep, I felt my erection. I let the robe fall open…

When, abruptly, she took a step back. Eyes brimming with anger, she stabbed my chest with her finger.

"What the hell's *wrong* with you, Danny? It's not enough somebody's trying to kill you, you have to be a big hero and try to rescue some jumper. Christ!"

Then she turned on her heel and marched to the phone. With her back to me, she called out, "I'm going to order you up a decent meal, which I know you haven't had sense enough to do for yourself, and then we're gonna talk."

"Casey—"

Only now did she turn back to me, eyes falling to my open robe. She smiled.

"And don't worry, I'll take care of that other thing, too. My motto: Feed 'em first, fuck 'em for dessert."

Which she did.

Chapter Forty-one

It was now two-twenty, so when Casey stirred in my arms I figured she needed to get back to the office.

"Danny," she said, "I want to run something by you."

I nodded. Her voice held a rare hesitancy.

"Listen," she said. "You know that by now we've run every background check in the world on you."

"Don't remind me."

"So, we know about your family, friends. That riverfront bar you hang out at. And about Noah Frye."

I leaned up now, so that we were both propped up on an elbow, facing each other. The hotel room seemed cooler.

"Casey, where's this going?"

She frowned. "Hey, I know he's your friend—maybe your best friend. He's also schizophrenic. With a sheet. Vagrancy, drug busts, drunk and disorderly."

"That was a long time ago. Besides…"

"Look at Kevin's death. Brutal, savage. Like somebody out of his head. And damn personal."

I kept my voice light. "You're straying out of your field, counselor."

"Yeah? What about the murder weapon turning up in your office…? That first warning."

"I told you, Kevin had probably taken the key."

"But what if you're wrong? I got to thinking, maybe your friend Noah has a key. Does he?"

I debated answering. Finally: "I gave him one, some time back. But he lost it. Hell, he says he doesn't even remember my giving it to him."

"Unless he's lying."

"He's not."

"Then what about this second warning?…A fucking *manikin?* Finger-painted death threats? Sure looks like nutso behavior to me. Psychotic. Whatever."

"Maybe that's what it's *supposed* to look like."

She sighed heavily. "Danny, I'm worried about you. And I just don't think we should rule anything out."

"It isn't Noah. He'd have no reason."

"We're not talking about *reason.* We're talking about *crazy,* which your friend officially is."

"I can't believe you're serious about this."

"Okay, then. So where is he?"

"What do you mean?"

"I mean, Noah isn't at work, or at home. His girlfriend hasn't seen him since early last night."

"How would you know that?"

"I asked her. I called her at the bar this morning, and again right before I got here. She told me Noah's been acting pretty weird lately, and she's worried."

"Well, one thing's for sure," I said firmly. "We've gotta find him. For *his* sake."

I started climbing out of the bed, but Casey stopped me. She drew herself closer, face softening.

"I hate it when I piss you off." She kissed my shoulder, my upper arm. Lips warm, insistent.

I smiled down at her. "I'll get over it."

She leaned up then, full breasts grazing my chest. "Don't. I'm counting on some make-up sex."

Before I could say anything, my cell phone rang. I gave her a quick look. She nodded. I picked it up.

"Dr. Rinaldi? This is Leland Sinclair."

Casey was close enough to hear his voice on the phone. Her eyes widened in surprise, and she quickly sat up.

"I guess I shouldn't be surprised you have my private cell number," I said to Sinclair.

"I guess you shouldn't," he said. "I'll be brief. I need you to come here to my office in one hour. And please tell Ms. Walters I'll want her here, too."

I saw the color drain from Casey's face. Then she crossed her arms across her breasts as though angry. But I could tell this had shaken her.

Sinclair must have read something in my long pause, because he went on, dryly, "Yes, I know where she is, Danny. I assume it's okay if I call you that? You can call me Lee. No need for the three of us to stand on ceremony."

My own voice tightened. "What do you want?"

"We just received a message from a woman who claimed she was calling from a phone booth out of state, and would call back in exactly one hour. She says she has information about the Kevin Wingfield case, but will only talk to you. I want you down here, where we can monitor the call. And try to trace it."

"Who is she?"

A pause. "Karen Wingfield. Kevin's sister."

Chapter Forty-two

From my seat in the District Attorney's ornate corner office, I could see the profile of a grinning gargoyle just outside the window. Still dripping from the recent rains.

I was on a headset, next to a plainclothes tech operating some sleek digital equipment. The call from Karen Wingfield was due any moment, and was going to be patched from the main switchboard to Sinclair's office, as well as to a police communications lab three blocks away.

"Remember," said Lt. Biegler, sitting across the room between Sinclair and Casey, "we'll need some time to make the trace. So mostly just listen and keep her talking."

"Sure. I think I have some experience with that."

Biegler scowled and folded his arms.

Meanwhile, I couldn't help noticing Casey's discomfort. She'd been avoiding Sinclair's eyes since we got here. Despite her obvious distaste for Biegler, she seemed glad to have him seated between her and Sinclair.

For his part, the DA was as reserved as ever, with only his clipped voice betraying any subterranean tension. Whether it was anxiety about the possibility of a break in the case, or suppressed anger about Casey and me, I didn't know. And at the moment, didn't care.

The tech glanced up from his watch. "She's late."

Instinctively, we all looked at the phone.

Two minutes went by. Three.

Biegler stirred. "Look, maybe she—"

Suddenly the phone rang and everybody jumped. The tech gave me a silent two-second count, then nodded.

I picked up the phone. "Hello."

"Dr. Rinaldi?"

The voice on the other end was thick, harsh. Made more so as it echoed in the room from a small speaker at the tech's console. "This better be you," she said.

"It is. The police told me you wanted to talk to me."

Sinclair, Biegler, and Casey were all leaning forward in their seats, the lieutenant's smooth hands gripping his knees so tightly the knuckles were whitening.

"Where are you calling from, Ms. Wingfield?"

"Like I'm gonna tell you. And you can cut the 'Ms. Wingfield' shit. I hate that name. I don't use that name."

Her voice was slurred, though she was attempting to keep it clipped, under control. So it came out belligerent. No question she'd been drinking or was stoned. Probably to get her courage up for the call.

"What name are you using nowadays? Your husband's?"

"My *ex*-husband, the prick. And I wouldn't use *Billy's* name if you paid me. And don't try to keep me talkin' so you can trace the call. I'm smarter than that."

I made a judgment call, and sharpened my tone. To get through the substance fog and the fear.

"You called *me*, Karen. If you have something to tell me about Kevin, then tell me. If not, stop wasting my time. All we want is to find his killer. What do *you* want?"

"Shee-it." Her laugh was raspy, turning into a cough.

I could hear every year of the hard life she'd led since running away from Banford as a teenager.

"I'll tell you somethin', Doc, you sure don't sound like the shrinks I seen on *Oprah*. I thought you guys were supposed to be nice. To care about people."

"I cared about Kevin. A lot."

A long pause on the line.

"You still there, Karen?" I ventured.

"Yeah. The thing is, seein' my father's lawyers on TV, sayin' how he's all devastated and everything. I just—I couldn't fuckin' stand it. It's all bullshit."

She sniffed, coughed again. "And I only wanted to talk to *you* 'cause I figured you'd understand. You probably knew Kevin better than anyone else in his life, and sure as hell care more about what happened to him than the fuckin' cops. *Or* the sick bastard that raised us." Another pause. "You know about all that, right? All that abuse shit?"

I answered carefully. "Kevin told me about you and him. But there's no blame. Even though you were the older, you were both minors. Given the—"

Her laugh popped from my earpiece and the room speaker like the snap of static. Casey sat back, blinking.

"No blame?" Karen's voice was reproachful. "Didn't Kevin tell you what happened? What our father *did?*"

I hesitated. "I guess I don't know it all. We hadn't gotten that far into—"

"It was my *father. He* was the abuser."

Again a long pause, as though gathering strength. Voice raw. "Fuck, I'm not gonna get through this…"

Casey sat up then, looking concerned. Biegler made a big show of rolling his eyes. I ignored them both.

"Take your time, Karen," I said. I glanced at the tech. He shook his head. No trace yet.

Karen took a breath, then launched into her speech. "I'm only gonna tell you this once. You can use it any way you want. Kevin and me…we were like the actors in a play, and our father was the director. I mean, we were all part of it together. Kevin would be in bed with me…"

"How did he get in bed with you?"

"Don't interrupt, goddam it! I can't—" Voice choked, thick with tears, or booze. "I was gettin' to that…"

Another long pause. "Sometimes Daddy would carry Kevin into my room. He'd be asleep, and wake up to find himself under the covers with me. Daddy used to make me take off my clothes and be waitin' naked for him and Kev. Then, he'd put us together...See, Daddy liked to be there with us, putting my mouth on Kevin's thing, or pushing Kev's mouth down on my—you know, down there—and takin' our hands and placin' 'em where he wanted. I would be cryin' and feelin' like shit, like a whore from hell 'cause Daddy said this was what I always wanted to do with Kevin, and that he was only tryin' to make me happy, and that if me and Kev were happy then he didn't miss Momma so much. That filthy pervert bastard used to make us hump till we came, or else make me give my sweet little Kevin head till he popped, and sometimes I'd look over and see Daddy's big hairy cock hard as a flagpole, pokin' through the sheets, and him sayin', "You're makin' your Daddy so happy, your Daddy that misses Momma so much." And then he'd come all over us, and I remember how sticky and wet and hot it was, and how it made me want to throw up, which I did sometimes. But mostly I remember Kevin's face—how white, how blank, like his soul was gone already, up in heaven with Momma..."

Then, abruptly, silence.

I glanced up, to find the other people in the room frozen in their seats. Casey's hand was over her mouth.

Then I felt the tech tapping my arm. They had the trace. He glanced back at Biegler.

"Karen...?" I said quietly.

"Yeah." Distracted. Spent. "You know the funny thing? After he got rich and famous, Daddy tried to contact me."

"How?"

"One day some private eye finds me—I was livin' in some shit-hole in Utah, and pregnant—anyway, he says my father wants to see me again, make everything okay between us. Promised me tons of money..."

A sharp, bitter laugh. "So I kicked the guy out and moved away the next day. Never even told my husband about it. Just told him the law was after me and we hadda disappear. Billy had a good job for once, so he was kinda pissed off. He beat me up pretty bad—I mean, worse than usual, I almost lost the baby—but we ended up leavin'."

Another hacking cough. "I know what you're thinkin'. Why not cash in, after what my father done to me? I sure coulda used the dough. Well, I say fuck him, *and* fuck his money. That'd just make me his whore again."

"What about Kevin?" I said softly. "Have you seen him at all since you were kids?"

"Nope. And I knew I wouldn't. In fact, the PI told me Daddy was lookin' for Kevin, too. But I knew Kev would spit in his eye, like me. I guess he did, eh? On the news, they said he was poor and livin' under a fake name..."

Her voice trailed off. "Fuck, I need a drink..."

"Karen." I sharpened my tone again. "Why did you call us? Why tell us this now, after all these years?"

"'Cause Kevin's dead," she answered coolly. "And I'm gettin' out. For good."

Biegler and Sinclair exchanged looks.

"Wait." I hurried. "Tell me where you are. If you're in some kind of trouble, we can help you."

"Trouble? You mean, 'cause my crazy scum-bag ex is after me, tryin' to get my little boy..."

"Your child is with you?"

"Asleep in the flatbed, next to me. I gotta skip town fast. Billy's right on my ass. And I can't let him have Davey. Not after he—shit, I sure can *pick* 'em..."

"Karen, listen..."

I looked up to see Biegler and the tech guy huddled in a far corner, whispering urgently. Then the tech guy raced out of the office.

"Anyway," Karen went on, "I figure you fucks got this phone number by now, so I gotta blow. Hell, I won't even be in the country in another twelve hours. So *you* listen. Find out who killed Kevin, if that's what you want. But it don't matter. Daddy killed him a long time ago. Me, too."

"There's got to be something we can do for you."

"You can arrest my bigshot Daddy for bein' a fucking child-molesting perv, is what you can do."

What I said next made Sinclair and Casey stare at me in alarm, but I had to tell this poor woman the truth.

"Karen, there's nothing I'd like better than to make your father pay for what he did, but the law can't touch him. It happened too long ago. The statute of limitations on sexual abuse ran out already, at least in your case."

A long, withering silence. "Shit, I shoulda known he'd get away with it. And the pisser is, he's still doin' it."

"What do you mean?" I asked.

"People he got workin' for him. You can get their bios off the Internet..." Again, that bitter, slurred laugh. "Yeah, Doc, even here in trailer-trash central, we know how to get online..."

"People who work for him...?"

"The execs, the people close to him. You don't think they got to make him happy? Play his little puppet-master games? Go ask—what's their names? I wrote 'em down..."

I heard a flutter of paper on the other end of the line.

"Here," she said. "Peter and Sheila Clarkson. Bet *they* got a story."

It took me a moment to register the names. The young man and woman I'd met in Wingfield's hotel suite.

"You mean—"

"Get a clue, will ya, Doc? They're brother and sister."

Then she hung up.

Chapter Forty-three

Not five minutes after I got off the phone with Karen Wingfield, the tech returned to Sinclair's office to report that she'd vanished. By the time the local cops in Tempe, Arizona, pulled up at the truckstop phone booth from which the call originated, it was empty, the receiver dangling from its cord. Like in the movies.

"Poor girl," Casey said. "What a life she's led."

"Yes," Sinclair said stiffly. "Tragic."

Adjusting his tie, the DA crossed the room in two long strides and sat behind his massive desk. He looked unhappy.

"Nevertheless, we didn't get much from her call. Other than allegations against Miles Wingfield, none of which, even if true, are actionable. More importantly, she told us nothing that sheds new light on Kevin's murder."

"So what are we going to do?" Casey asked.

"About what? About Wingfield? Nothing we *can* do. Assuming you believe the girl's story."

"Don't you?" I asked.

"After twenty years in this job, I've seen pretty much everything people can do to each other. So do I think what Karen described is possible? Hell, yes. Every day we hear of another public figure whose private life sounds like some porn movie. Or horror movie. Or both."

"This isn't a press conference," I said evenly. "What's your point?"

Casey glanced nervously at her boss. But he just smiled.

"My point, Doctor, is that whatever Miles Wingfield did or didn't do, *he* isn't the issue here."

"Bullshit." I put my hands on the desk, facing him. "Wingfield's a suspected molester. If Peter and Sheila Clarkson *are* siblings, it would indicate a repetitive pattern in his behavior. I happened to have met them, and they're not minors, but maybe they *were* when they first encountered Wingfield. Which means, it's likely they've been replaced by another pair. A younger brother and sister, who even now—"

Biegler shouldered up to me, frowning. "How do you know all this? About these Clarksons—?"

"I met with Wingfield the other day. At his hotel." I gave him a thin smile. "Kind of an impromptu thing."

His eyes narrowed. "And you didn't *tell* us about it?"

"I've been busy." I turned back to Sinclair. "You've got an obligation to check this out and you know it. Reasonable suspicion of current sexual abuse with minors. You can start by questioning the Clarksons."

"You're *serious*," Sinclair said. "Do you have any idea what you're suggesting? How this would play in the press? While reeling from the tragic loss of his son, Wingfield learns that the police—instead of catching the killer—are looking into allegations that he sexually abused him. *And* his daughter! The mayor would have our skins."

"But based on what Karen said—"

"What *she* said? You heard her. She sounds like some low-life slut. Wingfield's people would have a field day. Karen's an estranged child. A spiteful loser striking back at her father during his time of greatest pain."

"Maybe," Casey said quietly but firmly. "But we have a duty to at least look into it."

"Fine. Do what you think best." Sinclair's smile was cool. "Bringing down a man like Wingfield *would* be quite a feather in your cap."

Casey bristled, and took a step toward the desk. "I resent that! Besides, coming from *you*—face it, you care more about Wingfield's campaign support than—"

Sinclair's smile froze, a strangely unnerving effect on such a patrician face. If he ever did run for governor one day, I thought, this was what his campaign photo will probably look like.

Lt. Biegler cleared his throat uncomfortably. Casey, meanwhile, was looking down at the carpet.

"Would you like to finish that thought, Ms. Walters?" Sinclair sat forward, hands clasped on his desk blotter.

Without looking up, Casey shook her head.

Sinclair then turned to me. "Doctor, thanks for your help. I'm sorry Karen Wingfield's call didn't offer more insight into the case. But make no mistake, the prime goal here is catching Kevin's killer."

A deliberate pause. "And, of course, stopping him before he kills again. Which seems his intention. I understand the manikin he left bore quite a resemblance to you."

"After a bad night, maybe."

His eyes narrowed. "Even so, perhaps you should reconsider accepting police protection. Dan."

"Thanks but no thanks. Lee."

We stared at each other for what seemed like forever. Then Sinclair waved his hand in mock surrender, and reached for the phone.

"Okay, people. I need the use of the hall."

As Biegler, Casey and I started to file out of the room, Sinclair called from his desk.

"Not you, Casey. I'd like a word. In private."

She caught my wary look, but instantly glanced away. Then, without another word, she went back into Sinclair's office and shut the door.

An hour later, at least one mystery was solved.

Noah had been missing for quite a while now, and ever since Casey told me her suspicions about him I figured I'd better get hold of him before the cops started thinking along those same lines. Playing dress-up with a manikin and sticking a kitchen skewer in its chest had "crazy" written all over it. Dangerously crazy.

So I grabbed a cab outside the Federal building and went down to the waterfront bar, where I found a pissed-off Charlene scrubbing pigeon droppings off the outside deck. The chill from the river frosted the air.

"You wasted a trip, Doc."

She was down on all fours, revealing a wide expanse of back as she wrestled with a large wash bucket. Turns out she'd finally heard from Noah, who'd crashed the night before at an old girlfriend's place and needed a ride back.

"Can you *believe* that asshole?" she said, face red and tear-streaked. Her hands were covered with soap foam, and every time she slapped the scrub brush on the wood slats the deck shook. "Says he slept on the couch, but..."

I crouched next to her. "Well, at least he's alive."

"For now." She sniffed loudly, before attacking the gray-white stains again with the brush. The muscles on her beefy forearms bulged like ropes. "But not for long."

"Look, Noah screwed up. Everybody does. Maybe you—"

Charlene stopped and pointed the dripping brush in my direction. "You want some of what he's gonna get? Huh? Then shut the hell up."

She went back to work, cursing under her breath. "Men! You all stick together. Like sink hair."

I knew enough to get out of there, but not before promising I'd call later to make sure Noah was all right.

I thought I heard her laugh in disbelief as I headed out of the bar.

⟨⟩⟨⟩⟨⟩

By the time I got back to my room at the Hyatt, a brilliant sunset was painting the low-slung clouds over the Point. Cold light glazed the silver and glass skyline.

I ordered up a steak and an Iron City and spent the next several hours poring over the material Sam Weiss had provided me about Wingfield's life in Banford, and the rise of his biotech company.

Plus, I'd finally managed to get a duplicate package of Kevin's medical records since first entering the system years before as Kevin Merrick. This included three public psychiatric facilities, as well as a board-and-care home run by the Sisters of Charity.

Also, the police had returned my own files to me, and I spent some time trying to organize these. I paid particular attention to my notes of the peer review meeting at Ten Oaks at which I'd first presented Kevin's case.

At the top of my notes was the roster of participants: Bert Garman, of course, running the meeting; Brooks Riley; Nancy Mendors; an older, semi-retired psychologist who sometimes nodded off right in the middle of discussions; two young interns who were there accumulating educational hours toward licensure, and me.

I stared at my own hastily-scribbled notes, sipping my beer in the lonely ambiance of the hotel room.

Was there something there, between the lines? Something I'd missed? Or nothing at all?…

Just after eleven, I got a call from Noah. I could hear the raucous sounds of a bar crowd in the background.

"Charlene said I hadda check in with you. What are you, my parole officer?"

I laughed. "Noah, you shiftless bastard. You know what you're doing to that poor woman?"

"Hey, Danny. News flash: *I'm crazy*. I've been known to shoot the breeze with Satan and his minions. On the plus side, I eat pussy like a champ. She's gotta take the good with the bad."

"Okay, but listen. I got enough on my mind without worrying about you wigging out on me. Just stay cool."

"No problem. Like the man says, I don't want the cheese, I just want out of the trap. Later, amigo."

As he hung up, the phone rang again. Casey.

"I was just going to call you," I said. "What happened with Sinclair?"

"Nothing. He's got his dick in a twist because I'm seeing you. He'll get over it. But I'll be in the dog-house for a while, filing motions and cataloguing old cases. Paralegal shit-work to take me down a peg."

"Damn, I'm sorry about that."

I could almost see her shrug on her end of the line. "Hey, that's life in the big city. But I've got *real* news. I wanted to tell you before it came out. They just arrested your shrink friend Nancy for Brooks Riley's murder."

I'd guessed this was coming, but still it took me by surprise. "That's just crazy, and you know it."

"Maybe not. She had an affair with Riley, which she never told us about, and which he suddenly ended. She has no alibi for the time of the shooting, except for claiming to be in the ladies room— alone—during the patient riot. A 'riot' she could easily arrange. As a staff clinician, she had daily contact with both patients. That's two out of three right there: motive and opportunity."

"I've got a feeling I'm gonna hear number three."

"Right. The means. When the cops tossed her place, they found a gun. Smith & Wesson 22. Classic chick weapon."

"She's a single woman, living alone. Keeping a gun for protection. The city's full of them. Besides, wasn't Riley killed with a .38?"

"Yes, but it's the kind of evidence that sways a jury. Any decent prosecutor could make the case that she had a familiarity with firearms. So she gets hold of a .38 and shoots the bastard who broke her heart. *I* could sell that."

I bet she could.

"Listen," I said, "thanks for letting me know. I'll try to get in touch with her again. Speaking of which, Noah Frye's turned up. He's down at his club right now."

"So what? I *still* like him for Kevin's murder. Schizo with history of violence turns on therapist-buddy, kills wrong guy by mistake. I could sell *that* one, too."

"Maybe. But you'd be wrong."

"There's always a first time."

The assurance in her voice made me smile.

"Now, go," she said. "Call your old girlfriend. See if I care." Her laugh had just the right edge.

We said good-bye, and I tried Nancy Mendors, at home and at the clinic. I left messages at both, including the phone number of Ralph Puzzini, the criminal attorney.

I couldn't sleep, so I just lay there looking up at the ceiling. For some reason, I kept re-playing that phone call with Karen Wingfield in my head.

Something about that call...

Then, abruptly, I found myself sitting up, staring out the hotel window blackened by the remorseless night.

There was only one thing to do.

Chapter Forty-four

Clouds of mist rose from the trees lining the Pennsylvania turnpike, serrated by shafts of sunlight. The chill frosted the windows of my rental car. It was just after dawn, and I was heading southeast into Somerset County. On my way to Banford.

I'd called Angie Villanova late the night before, to start the bureaucratic process going that would get me access to Somerset County records. She'd made all the expected noises, but within an hour she came through.

I made a few other calls, the last to a rental car agency, and got on the road before the sun came up.

Now, just outside town, I found a drive-through and got two cups of coffee. I downed one, then sipped the other as I drove with one hand over a sloping hill, at whose apex was a sign indicating the Banford city limits.

A patchwork of farms, open fields and truck stops lay under a chiaroscuro sky, narrowing into what appeared to be the main business district. Faded, gray-bricked buildings, trimmed with paint-flecked wood, shared real estate with new chain stores, mini-malls, and a sprawling Chevy dealership that seemed to be the backbone of the economy.

The Banford Civic Center was a small cluster of low-roofed buildings fronted by a weathered statue of some Greek goddess holding a scroll. I parked in the lot beside the only two other cars, both Chevy's.

I made my way past the shuttered windows of the mayor's office and the city council, and followed the wall signs to a door marked "Records." It looked closed, but was unlocked, and I went in. I was expected.

A tall, gangly kid in his early twenties glanced up sourly from behind a counter.

"You the guy from Pittsburgh PD?" He peered at me over the top of rimless glasses.

I nodded, and showed him some ID. He sniffed a few times while scanning it, then handed it back.

"I'm here early, ya know," he said, irritably. "As a favor, one jurisdiction to another. My boss called it professional courtesy. I call it a pain in the ass."

"Well, I appreciate it." I smiled. "I hope you had time for some breakfast."

"Not even." He grimaced. "Just forced down some Sanka and hauled ass over here."

"So you're here alone?"

He gave me a suspicious glance. "Why you askin'?"

"Just curious. I saw two cars in the lot."

"Oh. The old Impala belongs to the cleaning lady." He craned his neck, called into the rooms behind him. "Hey, Claire! You in there?"

"No, I'm out dancin' with Fred Astaire," came a throaty voice, followed a moment later by a dour, red-faced woman in her late fifties, pushing a soggy mop through the open door. She wore men's overalls and a Steelers cap.

The clerk frowned. "Don't come bringin' that thing in here now. I got business with this guy. Official business."

Claire looked us both over with a blood-shot eye. "Like I give a shit. *You* called *me*, remember, Eddie?"

The clerk, Eddie, turned his back to Claire and made a big show of knotting his tie. Over his shoulder, Claire gave him the finger and shuffled back inside, dragging the mop behind her.

Eddie indicated the stacks of files and ledgers on the counter between us. "Boss said I hadda pull some old files for you. Man, I ate dust for an hour." He gave a cough.

I nodded. "The child abuse allegations against Miles Wingfield. Police reports, court records. I'll take anything you have."

"That's just it, mister. We don't got nothin'."

I frowned. "You mean the records are sealed?"

"I mean, they don't exist," he said. "I pulled everything we had for the years you wanted. Every police report, every family court case. There ain't nothin'."

"That's impossible."

"'Fraid not. Seems there was a fire about five years back in the old Records room, just two blocks over behind the VFW Hall. Lost nearly half the stuff stored there. I mean, sure, *now* they're transferrin' what's left into the computer, but what's gone is gone, right?"

I barely hid my frustration. He shrugged.

"Sorry you made the trip all the way down here for nothin'." He didn't seem that sorry.

"Listen," I said, "any chance some related material might be here? The Wingfield children were ultimately sent to foster homes. Is *that* information here?"

"Oh, man, you're shittin' me." He looked crestfallen. "That stuff's in a whole different section. I mean, I didn't know I was supposed to pull *those* files..."

"That's okay." I smiled. "I'll wait."

Eddie glared at me a long moment, then, sniffing noisily again, he turned and disappeared into the back.

I figured he'd need a while, so I went back outside for some air. The morning sun shone bright and cool, but already the mists were evaporating from the surrounding hills. I saw a few cars pulling into spaces. Merchants unlocking their doors, pulling up their window blinds.

I heard a noise and turned to find Claire backing out of a door into the alley behind me. She was twisting dirty water from the mop into an old bucket. Then, as if sensing my presence, she looked up. I walked over to her.

"You know, Eddie's got shit for brains," she said without preamble. "Plus, he's only been in Banford a couple o' years. Family moved here from Virginia or somewheres."

"Meaning what?"

"Meanin', he don't even *remember* the Wingfield mess. But I do. It was a helluva scandal, him bein' a big-shot at the bank and all."

"He's an even bigger shot now," I prompted her.

"Yeah, I seen him on TV once or twice. Got himself rich and famous." Claire spat into the wash bucket. "That don't mean he gives a damn about Banford. He ain't done nothin' for *us* with all that money. Bastard just left and never looked back."

"Well, things got pretty hot for him here."

Claire leaned against the mop handle and looked off.

"Yeah, I remember all the rumors. Hard to believe he didn't know what his kids were doin' after the lights went out. But in the end, the County took the kids away from him anyway. Just to be on the safe side, I guess."

We exchanged frank looks. A helluva world.

I thanked her for her time, and made my way back to Eddie's office. He was back standing behind the counter.

"I found what you wanted," he said. "But you're not gonna be happy about it."

He showed me two thin files, from the Foster Parent Division of Somerset County Social Services. I looked at the names neatly typed on the tabs of each folder.

Kevin Alexander Wingfield.

Karen Carlyle Wingfield.

Kevin's middle name didn't mean anything to me, but I recognized Karen's immediately. Carlyle was her mother's maiden name. It was still common practice in these small towns to use a maiden name as a middle one.

I flipped open both files on the counter. It took only moments to discover the meaning of Eddie's cryptic comment.

"Kevin's foster parents are both dead," I said, not raising my eyes from the files.

"Yep." Eddie leaned over, so that our heads almost touched. "And the other ones—Karen's—see, they got divorced and the husband moved away. Left no forwarding address. The wife's still here, though. At Rolling Hills."

He said the words very deliberately, as though I'd understand their meaning. I glanced up at him.

"Nursing home," he said, with an unpleasant smile. "You want the number?"

Chapter Forty-five

I went outside to make the call. After some prodding, I got the receptionist to put me through to the room where Mary Lees, Karen's foster mother, was confined.

"Hello?" A youngish, weary female voice.

"Hello. My name's Dr. Daniel Rinaldi. Is it possible for me to speak with Mary Lees?"

Her tone sharpened. "I'm her daughter Joan. Are you from the insurance company? Because I already told that other man who called—"

"No, I'm not with any insurance company. I'm working with the Pittsburgh Police, and we're looking into—"

"Oh, right. On the news. Kevin Wingfield."

"Yes. We got a call from his sister Karen. I know she'd been put under foster care with your parents some years back..."

Suddenly, her words erupted into an angry torrent. "Look, who the hell do you think you are, bothering my mother about this? I was a kid myself when my parents took Karen in, and if they hadn't needed the money—I mean, that little slut never gave Mother one moment's peace. *Or* gratitude."

"I'm sorry, Ms. Lees, but—"

"You know Karen even came on to my *father*? Not that *he* was any prize, after what he put Mother through the whole time they were married. Drinking, gambling..."

"I understand, and I—"

"The best day of my life was the day she ran away from home. The *second* best was the day *he* moved out. Figures he'd bail on Mother the moment she got sick and couldn't take care of him anymore. Now there's just me…"

Her voice was a hoarse mixture of tears and rage. The bitter, parentified child, doomed to the role of caretaker. Faithful chronicler of her family's woes. The one adult left standing.

"Look, Ms. Lees," I began carefully, "I don't pretend to know about what your family's gone through. And I don't want to further burden you *or* your mother, but I did want to ask a few questions about—"

"Questions? You mean you want to *talk* to Mother?"

"If I could, yes…"

"Well, you *can't*. She can't talk to you. She can't talk to *me*. Or anyone. She's got severe Alzheimer's. Like a zombie. I sit here all day, holding her hand, and she just stares at me. With no idea who I am. None. God's little booby-prize for me after all I've been through, everything I've done. So to hell with you, and to hell with your questions!"

The line went dead.

Chapter Forty-six

Sam Weiss was unhappy.

"You hear who they just signed to play *me* in the Handyman movie?" He stabbed angrily at his scrambled eggs. "Vincent Schuler."

"Sorry," I said. "Never heard of him."

"*Nobody's* ever heard of him! The director thought it'd be 'interesting' to go with an unknown in the part. Some *schmuck* they found doing dinner theater in Chicago."

"Might be a good idea." I smiled behind my coffee cup. "Does he at least *look* like you?"

"Who gives a shit what he looks like? Dowd gets Robert DeNiro, and I get what's-his-name! I mean, Christ!"

Sam went on like this for another few minutes, and I just let him. It was noon, and we were in a small café in Shadyside. I'd asked to meet him here, since my house was still staked out with media types. Though not as many as that first day. As Sam had predicted, I was losing my celebrity with each passing news cycle. Fine with me.

Now, our table cleared of dishes, I told him about my trip to Banford the day before. After which, he sat back, arms folded across his Pink Floyd sweatshirt.

"Pretty damn convenient, those files lost in a fire."

I shrugged. "It doesn't get me any closer to Kevin's killer. But it's part of a package on Wingfield I'd love to dump in Sinclair's lap." I drained my cup. "Speaking of which, how's your profile of my favorite DA coming?"

"Great. Two interviews with him, and I've got nothing I couldn't get from his press kit. Armor-plated, that guy."

"Oh yeah." I got up, tossed some bills on the table. "Look, I've gotta go. I heard on the news this morning they've arraigned Nancy Mendors for Brooks Riley's murder."

Sam rose too, zipping up his windbreaker. "I also heard she's out already. Somebody just posted her bail."

‹›‹›‹›

Nancy sat on the edge of her sofa, swallowed up in a thick ter-rycloth bathrobe. Her dark hair was wet from the shower, and slicked back behind her ears.

She'd answered the door that way, and led me into the living room, unmindful of the wet prints left by her bare feet on the carpet. Her slow, deliberate gait made me wonder if she'd tranked herself a little.

The afternoon sun slanted wide and soft through the drawn curtains. I came in now from the kitchen, holding a mug of hot tea. Without a word I put it in her hand.

"Thanks." She inhaled the aroma of orange pekoe. "I mean, for everything. Referring me to Frank Puzzini. He's a great lawyer. But then, making my bail…" She glanced down. "Jesus, Danny, I don't know what to say."

I sat opposite her. "Don't worry about it."

No need to mention the equity line of credit I'd taken out of my house to get the funds.

"When the judge set the amount," she went on, "I almost lost it. Puzzini argued that I didn't have that kind of money, but I guess since it's a homicide…"

"The DA's crazy if he thinks you killed Brooks."

"Maybe not. I *wanted* to kill him. The two-timing prick. Truth is, I was really mad at myself. For being so stupid. So needy."

"Whoa…"

"I mean, I can't believe it. I've actually turned into one of those…those *women*. Forty-ish and desperate. Just grateful for a date on Saturday night. So what if he's got two kids, alimony payments and a beer gut? He's male. Available. Maybe it'll turn into something. Maybe..."

She put down the mug on an end table.

"With Brooks, it wasn't like that. It was fresh, and exciting. Then there's his position as chief of psychiatry, so all my father issues get covered..."

I took her hand. "Stop it, Nancy. Don't try to be so smart about it. If he made you happy..."

Her shoulders fell, bathrobe bunching like wings.

"Naturally, after I'd pretty much fallen for him, I find out he's sleeping around. When I confront him about it, he acts as if our relationship had always been casual. That I'd made it into something it wasn't. He was right, of course, the lying bastard. But I still hated him for it."

Her hand slipped out of mine. "Anyway, I have to get ready in a few minutes. I'm meeting with Puzzini. To plan my defense." Again, that rueful smile. "Any ideas?"

"Sure. You didn't do it. That's your defense."

She looked as though she wanted to say something, then stopped herself. Slowly, she got to her feet. So did I.

I touched her shoulder. "If you need anything..."

Nancy shook her head. "I'll be fine. Thanks...for being my friend."

I put my arms around her and felt her melt against my body. The smallness of her.

As I went out the door, I saw her sit down again, staring with empty eyes at the tea cooling on the table.

By three o'clock, the sun had warmed things up enough for me to open the rental car's windows. Though flags snapping from poles by the river gave evidence of a still-brisk wind. Pure East Coast, football-town weather.

Stuck in traffic near the Fort Pitt Bridge, I used the time to make calls. First, I checked with police impound, and learned they planned to release my car by five tonight.

Then I tried Casey at work. To my surprise, she picked up. And tore into me.

"Where the hell have you been? You think you can just disappear for a day without *telling* me—? Or *anyone?*"

"You're right. I'm sorry if you were worried."

"Why would I be worried? I mean, sure, you might be stuffed in a hole somewhere with an ice-pick in your chest, but why the hell should that concern *me?!* Besides, I can always get forensics to loan me that manikin, for old times' sake. Shit, if it were anatomically correct, I'd have the whole damned show—!"

I hated to interrupt when she was on such a roll, but there were things I needed to know.

"Speaking of forensics, did they find anything?"

"Yeah, I think we can safely say it was a death threat. Not that I give a damn."

I heard her let out a breath. Calming herself.

"Other than that, nothing. They're trying to match the paint used in the message. The usual pissing in the wind. Like with the murder weapon."

"The killer's damn good at covering his tracks," I said. "I wonder if he's done it before."

"Who knows? But he's bound to screw up eventually."

"Or not. Meanwhile, any leads on Karen Wingfield's whereabouts?"

"None. If she was telling the truth, she's out of the country by now. I can't say I blame her."

I maneuvered the interchange and headed downtown. I'd scheduled a meeting with Harvey Blalock in his office at three. I figured I'd just make it.

"Speaking of which, how are *you?*" I said.

"Still in the shitter with Lee, doing grunt work. I won't get out of here till midnight."

"Midnight works for me. I'll bring the Merlot."

Her voice grew tentative. "Uh, I don't think so…"

"You don't want company?"

"No, I don't want Merlot. Bring champagne. And a bucket of ice."

"You don't have ice cubes in the fridge?"

"Yeah, but I'll be using *those* on you. Guess how?"

Then she hung up.

‹›‹›‹›

Harvey Blalock was a thick-waisted, balding black man with an iron handshake and an easy smile. He moved adroitly in his tailored, three-piece suit through the corridors of his law firm, leading me back to the corner office. This high up, the windows on one wall looked out on the sloping streets of the North Side, and the rows of tenement houses.

"So I never forget where I came from," he explained, as he offered me a chair opposite his massive desk. Family photos were arrayed along the top, along with a Duquesne University mug holding pencils and pens.

"It's a pleasure to finally meet you," I said.

"No, it isn't." His look was frank. "Nobody sitting in that chair ever wants to be there. I imagine that's true for many of your patients as well."

"At first, yes. Much of the time." I glanced at some files on his desk blotter. "Is that me?"

"So far. I have two of my best people researching the relevant case law. And I'll need some names from you, too. Colleagues in the field—preferably not of your personal acquaintance—who can explain and support your treatment methods with Kevin Wingfield."

"I can get started on that."

"But I have to tell you, not ten minutes ago I learned something that may delay things for a while."

I sat forward. "What do you mean?"

"I just heard from Wingfield's attorneys that their chief expert witness will be unable to give his deposition at this time. Maybe not for the foreseeable future."

"Phil Camden? What happened?"

"It seems Dr. Camden's in the hospital. He's had a heart attack."

Chapter Forty-seven

The irony wasn't lost on either of us. As he had done years ago, following the shooting that killed his daughter, now I was the one standing over a hospital bed.

Swathed in blankets, hooked up to monitors displaying his vitals, Phil Camden looked cadaverous. His eyes, though still burning with life, were small, bitter.

"The poets, as usual, are wrong." Voice slurred by the sedative. "There's nothing ennobling about suffering."

I leaned across the bed rails. "The nurse said I can only stay a minute. I just wanted to see how you are."

"Recuperating, you'll be sorry to learn." He cleared his throat. "And soon to be well enough to give testimony. So if you assumed your visit here was a death watch, I'm afraid you're in for a disappointment."

"Damn, and I came all this way."

I poured water from the bedside carafe into a paper cup and put it to his lips. He glanced warily at me, then took a few sips.

"So, Phil," I said. "What *is* it exactly that keeps you going? It can't just be your hatred of me."

"You'd be surprised. It's a tonic."

We regarded each other for a long moment.

Finally, I buttoned my coat. "Okay. For the record, I hope you live. But I sure as hell don't know why."

"It's obvious. Your self-ideal requires that you maintain empathy for me in my illness, even as I remain your enemy." He took a breath. "A sorry humanism which will inevitably be your downfall."

With that, he turned his head away on the pillow.

I just stood there, looking at my father-in-law's back as he lay under the sheets. Until the silence grew oppressive, a communication in itself. A door closing.

"Good-bye, Phil," I said at last, and walked out of the room.

On my way to pick up my car, I stopped at the 23rd precinct and went up to Lt. Frank Lucci's office. He was just going off duty, so he wasn't exactly thrilled when I asked to see the lab's toxicology report on Richie Ellman.

"Just came in," he said, tossing me the file.

He sat back in his chair. "Take your time, Doc. Why should *I* have a life?"

"I appreciate it, Lieutenant. Just need a minute."

Lucci grunted something, then made a point of cleaning his nails with a penknife blade while I scanned the report.

Pretty much what I expected. Fatal levels of industrial rat poison—much of it still undigested at the time of death. Evidence of psychotropic medication. Apparently Richie took his morning dose of Adnorfex, plus the Ellavil Nancy had recently prescribed.

"Mind if I make a copy of this?" I asked Lucci.

"Suit yourself. Copy room's down on three. But don't rush—I *like* missin' beer call every once in a while."

As I went out the door, I heard Lucci mutter, in a voice I was supposed to hear, "Consultant, my ass..."

Always nice to make new friends.

By six o'clock, I was pulling out of the police garage in my green Mustang. The interior smelled of chemicals, and had all the unmistakable signs of a thorough going-over. Seats in the wrong position, rear view mirror out of line. And not a single speck of dust.

Above, the moon's crescent had grown fat and yellow, looking like a Halloween decoration hanging against a black-patterned curtain of sky. Pittsburgh's array of lights shone against the gloom of an ever-deepening fall.

I maneuvered my way through dinner-time traffic and found a spot half a block from the Spent Cartridge.

As I hoped, Polk was inside, sitting alone at the bar and knocking back what looked like his second boiler-maker.

"Easy, big fella," I said, as I took the stool next to him. Ignoring me, he very deliberately licked his lips before slamming the shot-glass down on the counter.

"If you ain't buyin', get lost," he said.

I signaled to the bartender. "Line him up again," I said. "And I'll take whatever you got on draft."

Polk eyed me warily. "You gotta want something, Doc. What is it?"

"Just the latest on your case against Nancy Mendors. I can't believe the DA's serious."

"Sure he is. We're nowhere on the Wingfield murder, and Sinclair's lookin' like shit. He needs a quick win."

"That's the way I read it, too."

"Besides," Polk said, "I think she looks good for it. Her affair with Riley. Piss-poor alibi. Gun."

"Wrong caliber."

"What do juries know about caliber? She has knowledge of guns. Plus motive: a woman scorned. End of story."

The bartender brought his beer and whiskey, and placed a tall, cool one in front of me. "Bud," he said, by way of explanation, and moved off.

Polk contemplated the drinks in front of him. "Fifteen years, I never cheated on my wife. Not once. All that time, workin' the streets, bustin' whores and hypes who'd do anything for a fix. Okay, maybe a blow-job once in a while from some runaway, just so I don't drag her ass back home. But that's it. No strange pussy. Pussy's sacred, I figure, between husband and wife. It's like my code, or somethin'. But now, all of a sudden, she divorces me. Well, fuck her. And fuck me." He lifted the beer glass. "Cheers."

We drank in silence, the sergeant draining his beer in two gulps and reaching for the shot glass. He threw it back, eyes glazing between heavy lids.

"Listen, Harry," I said. "You want the number of somebody I know? He's good with this kind of stuff. Been through a divorce himself. Real no-bullshit guy."

"Ya mean, a shrink or somethin'?" Polk laughed, wiping his mouth with his sleeve. "Like *you*? Gimme a break. I was just shootin' my mouth off. Forget about it, okay?"

"Okay."

He pulled his head down between his shoulders, like a bear going into hiding. I knew better than to push it.

"Look," I said. "Maybe I was outta line. You just want to drink alone, I'm gone. You want some company, I'll hang around. Up to you."

Polk took a slow breath. Tapped the shot glass against the bar, like a Morse code key.

"You can hang around if you want," he said finally. "I don't give a shit."

I nodded, sipped my beer. "Then let me ask you one more question. About Nancy, and her alibi. You questioned everybody at Ten Oaks, right? Patients, staff?"

"*Everybody*. I mean, run the numbers: Everybody was seen by at least one other person the whole time. Except Nancy Mendors." He grinned. "Next to you, she's my favorite suspect..."

I smiled back. "But what about the patients' family members? Other visitors who might've been there during the outbreak, or just before?"

"We thought of that, too." Polk rubbed his temples. "All visitors have to sign in and out. There were only a few relatives visiting patients that morning, and we got their names, their visiting times. All had alibis, too."

I let this sink in. Then I remembered.

Polk was gesturing toward the bartender again when I grabbed his forearm.

"Wait a minute, Harry."

He blinked at me, confused, as the bartender shuffled over. "Bring us two large coffees," I told him. "To go."

The bartender glanced doubtfully at Polk, then nodded and headed off to fill the order. Polk glared at me.

"Can't I even get shit-faced in peace?" he said.

"Not right now." I leaned in closer. "Listen, you have to get a hold of Detective Lowrey. You and she have to question those two girls from the clinic one more time. Separately. Tell each one you *know* who paid her to start the fight in the rec yard. Tell her she's facing accessory charges unless she rolls over on Riley's killer."

Polk laughed sourly. "That kinda bluff only works on TV, Doc."

"Unless you really *have* the name of the killer. And I think we do."

Polk just stared, as the bartender brought over two large Styrofoam cups of coffee.

"They're both for you, Harry," I said.

I stood up, and threw some bills on the bar. "You coming or not?"

Chapter Forty-eight

Only a few lights were on in the house, muted behind closed drapes. Hard voices, rising in argument. The sound of shattering glass.

As the three of us approached the front porch, Polk smiled at Lowrey. "Geez, ya think we're comin' at a bad time?" His service weapon was in his right hand.

Det. Lowrey reached the door first and knocked loudly. Polk was right behind her, and I stood off to one side.

The sounds from within grew still. Then, footsteps.

Albert Garman, face flushed, opened his door. What looked like a fresh wine stain blotched his shirt.

"Yes?" He peered out at us. "Dan? What is this?"

"Pittsburgh Police," Polk said. "I'm Sergeant Polk, this is Detective Lowrey."

Garman's eyes flickered as awareness dawned. "Yes, of course. I remember you. But what—?"

From behind him, a shrill, slurred voice. "Who the hell is it? Send them away!"

Polk held his gun hand behind his back. "We'd like to come in, Dr. Garman. We have an arrest warrant."

"A warrant?" Quickly, Garman managed to collect himself. "There must be some mistake."

"May we come in, sir?" Lowrey said. "Now?"

"Dammit, Bert!" Another hoarse shout from inside the house. Garman winced visibly.

Embarrassed, he finally nodded and stepped back from the door. As we filed past him inside, his eyes found mine.

"Elaine and I...we've been fighting...money problems. But she's been drinking and—Jesus, can't this wait?"

I spread my hands. "I'm sorry, Bert."

Polk and Lowrey had gone on ahead, into the living room. I nodded to Garman, and we followed.

We found Elaine Garman in silk pajamas, swaying unsteadily on bare feet. Her eyes blazed with a mixture of incomprehension and rage. She was very drunk.

"What is this, a surprise party?" she said, coming towards us. Trying awkwardly to avoid the spray of broken glass on the carpet. The remains of a wine bottle.

Bert took his wife's arm. "Let me help you, honey."

Elaine batted his hand away. "Like I can't find a drink without my seeing-eye dog..." She took another halting step toward the well-stocked wet-bar.

She never made it. Eleanor Lowrey moved adroitly in front of her and blocked her path. "Show me where your bedroom is, Mrs. Garman, and I'll help you get dressed."

"Like hell. What the fuck is this?"

"An arrest, Mrs. Garman." Lowrey gripped her shoulder. "You're under arrest for the murder of Dr. Brooks Riley."

"*What?*" Elaine squirmed in the detective's grasp.

Bert whirled, facing Polk and me. "Elaine couldn't possibly— You can't really think *she* killed Brooks—?!"

"Take it easy, Doc," Polk said smoothly.

"This is total bullshit," Elaine said, trying hard to steady herself. Regain some control.

"'Fraid not," Polk said. "We got your new best friend Lucy downtown. She told us how you kept her supplied with coke in exchange for starting that fight in the rec yard. Said you told her the exact day and time to do it."

"She's lying," Elaine said. But some of the bluster had gone out of her voice.

"I don't think so, Elaine," I said quietly. "When Sgt. Polk told me Nancy Mendors was the only one at the scene without an alibi, I thought back to when he and I showed up that day to pick up my patient files."

I turned to Garman. "Remember, Bert? When you came out to meet us in the lobby, you said Elaine had just left. As the wife of the Clinical Director, it occurred to me she probably didn't have to sign in or out. So what if, instead of leaving, Elaine had simply gone to some empty room near Riley's office—and waited?"

Garman shook his head. "I don't believe it."

"It lays out," I insisted. "Brooks barges into your office when Polk and I are there. He and I exchange words, then he returns to his office. Suddenly Elaine steps inside the door, shoots him twice, and—as previously planned with Lucy—calmly goes out to her car just as the fight breaks out. The alarm sounds, the rec yard's swarming with people. So naturally the cops figure the riot was a cover for the shooting. But instead, it had happened just before."

"But why?" A kind of anguish was building in his eyes. "Why would Elaine want to kill Brooks?"

"Because they were having an affair," I said. "And when he broke it off, she—"

"*No!*" A sudden, plaintive cry, as though torn out of him. "That's not possible—"

He swiveled where he stood, staring at his wife.

"Elaine?" His voice aching.

His wife managed to twist herself from Lowrey's grasp, and stood back, face darkening. Her eyes were glazed.

She threw the words at him. "You stupid shit…"

Polk gave her a warning look. "You got somethin' you wanna say, Mrs. Garman, I gotta read you your rights."

"Fuck you," Elaine said.

Polk shrugged, and Mirandized her anyway. She didn't seem to register it.

I caught Polk's eye. He nodded, and I took a step toward Elaine. She had a hand against the wall, steadying herself. She glared at me, cornered, wary.

"I talked with Nancy Mendors," I said. "She admitted having an affair with Brooks, until he suddenly ended it. She told me she suspected he was seeing other women. When I started thinking about the possibility that you could've killed him, I wondered if—"

"I'll bet you did," Elaine said coolly. Behind the belligerence, a dull pain shone in her eyes. "Brooks was a busy man—and proud of it. He told me about Nancy himself. Right before he said it was over between *us*, too."

She blinked once, slowly. "I asked him if there was someone else. You know what that bastard said? He gave me that shark smile and said, 'Honey, there's *always* someone else.' Then he said he was surprised that a woman as skinny as me could have saggy tits. Must be my age. He hadn't minded at first, but now—"

"Who *cares* what he said?" Garman staggered toward his wife, eyes wide. "How could you *do* this? How could you—?"

"Puh-leese." She laughed bitterly. "Don't you dare. You think I've forgotten *your* affairs over the years? What you put me through—"

"But that was a long time ago. You said you still—"

Elaine gave him a boozy smile. "I lied."

Polk held up a hand. "All right, folks, it's time we took this show downtown."

Elaine took another step back, stumbled. "I'm not goin' anywhere..." She struggled to right herself.

Garman turned to Polk. "For God's sake, Sergeant, you can see she's in no condition to—"

Polk smiled. "Don't worry. I'll drive."

"To hell with all of you!" Elaine suddenly shouted, voice laced with contempt. "You think I'm stupid? All I did was sleep with the bastard. That doesn't mean I killed him. You can't prove anything. It's Lucy's word against mine. A mental patient with a coke habit. Christ!"

I knew she was right. Other than Lucy's testimony, the case against Elaine Garman was as circumstantial as the one against Nancy Mendors. Even if Lucy *was* telling the truth about the drugs she got for causing the diversion at Ten Oaks, any evidence of it had long since gone up her nose.

There had been just enough for me to convince Polk, and for Biegler to get a warrant. But without more...

Nobody said anything for a long moment. Then, forcefully, Lowrey walked over and took hold of Elaine's wrist. "Come on, Mrs. Garman. Let's get you dressed."

Elaine Garman looked at Lowrey as though seeing her for the first time. "I love your lip shade. What is it?"

Lowrey just shook her head and started guiding their suspect out of the room, toward the rear hall. Meanwhile, Polk sat wearily on the arm of the sofa.

"Don't take all night," he called after them.

I watched Bert Garman sink into a chair in the corner. He looked like he'd aged a year in a half hour.

Polk cleared his throat. "We got a search warrant, too, Dr. Garman. Team's gonna be here any minute."

"I suppose you're looking for the weapon," Garman said quietly. "You won't find anything. We don't keep a gun in this house."

"Never know what a search will turn up," Polk said.

I gave him a look. "Give us a minute, will ya?"

Polk shrugged, and lumbered to his feet. Then, without a word, he stepped out onto the front porch.

I took his place on the sofa arm. "Listen, Bert, I'm sorry about all this."

"Me, too. Sorry, but not surprised." Garman sighed. "I mean, the police thinking Elaine killed Brooks—that's just ludicrous. But their affair...I *knew* she was seeing someone. I could feel it. I even accused her a few times, but she always denied it."

"Did you suspect Brooks?"

"I'd heard a rumor he was sleeping with Nancy, but—hell, if I believed every rumor at Ten Oaks...Funny, but Elaine always seemed so dismissive of Brooks. Disdainful. I remember one time, after a faculty function, all she could talk about was how arrogant he was…"

Bert looked down at his hands. "I've been a real idiot, eh? So blind. So wrapped up in clinic business…" He paused. "You know, if Elaine *did* kill Brooks, it must mean she really loved him. That it wasn't just some sleazy affair. He'd hurt her so badly she…"

He stood up then. "Dan, despite everything, I've still got to help her."

Muffled footsteps made us look up in tandem. Lowrey was leading Elaine back into the room. Garman's wife had changed into a stylish pants suit and low heels.

"I'll need a coat," she ordered.

Lowrey looked at Garman, who went quickly to the hall closet and returned with a sable coat. Elaine took it from him before he could help her put it on.

Polk came in then from the front door. I heard the sounds of a vehicle pulling up to the curb outside.

"That's CSU," he said, handing Garman the search warrant. Bert didn't even look at it.

"Any damages to my house, I'll sue the whole damn city," Elaine Garman said. "Bert, for once in your life, be a man and keep an eye on these pricks. Pretend you give a shit about anything other than yourself."

Bert just stood there, face drained of life.

"Any time, folks," Polk said sharply.

Lowrey gripped Elaine's elbow more tightly than was probably necessary and led her out the door.

‹›‹›‹›

It was a good forty minutes after midnight when I finally arrived at Casey's place. I'd waited with Bert until the search was finished at his house, and he'd left to be with his wife at the police station. Then I'd headed up the Parkway to Casey's condo, remembering to stop for some champagne.

I also remembered the bucket of ice.

Chapter Forty-nine

It was 4 a.m., and Casey had made scrambled eggs. As she brought over a pitcher of juice, light from the kitchen lamp highlighted the fullness of her naked breasts.

We sat across from each other at the small breakfast table. Hair wild from bed, skin burnished, she looked so fresh, so beautiful. I told her so.

"That's just your cock talking," she said. Something shaded her brief smile.

I looked at her. "Don't…"

"No. Don't *you*…" Her eyes were cool. "I'm happy just being the best fuck you ever had…or ever will. Let's not get stupid about it."

"Yeah?" I held her gaze, insistent. "What happened to the woman who took my head off because I didn't tell her I was going to Banford?"

She laughed easily. "You want consistent, get yourself another girl."

She leaned up and gave me a quick kiss, then sat back and began pouring honey from a little plastic bear onto some toast. End of discussion.

"In other news," she said wryly, "Leland called me earlier tonight about Elaine Garman. Though it'll be a miracle if it gets to trial. Not without the gun."

"It's a stronger case than they have against Nancy. Polk said they were dropping the charges against her."

"Thanks to you." She took a sip of coffee. "You make a stand-up ex-lover, Danny boy. Good to know."

I let that one go. "Any follow-up on the Clarksons?"

"Oh, yeah. Poor Karen was telling the truth. They're siblings, all right. Peter went to work for Miles Wingfield while still in junior high. Some kind of intern program in business. Kid sister Sheila came along, too, though details about their job descriptions are pretty sketchy."

"Any family?"

"Their parents died when they were just kids. They were raised by an aunt."

"Where?"

"Palo Alto, California. You figure Wingfield latched onto them when he moved there?"

"Fits the pattern," I said. "Abusers tend to like their victims to be of a certain age. Once they grow up, the abuser loses interest."

"You don't think he's having sex with them now?"

"I can't know for sure. People change. Even abusers. But I'd guess not."

"Then why keep these two around? In his employ?"

"Maybe just because he can. He still exercises powerful control over them. I saw it myself in his hotel room."

I stirred. I still ached from my struggle with Richie Ellner, and going a couple rounds with Casey tonight hadn't helped. Though it was a small price to pay.

She saw me wince, and smiled. "You okay, tiger?"

"I'll live." I decided to change the subject. "I hear Wingfield's due back in town this morning. Then it's more hearings on that Cochran merger. Busy man."

"Not busy enough. Lee and the mayor have been summoned to another papal audience at nine. Wingfield's turning up the heat."

I had a thought. "Maybe we should turn it up on *him.*"

She glanced up. "How?"

"Let me work on it."

Casey nodded, and took a big bite of toast. A drop of honey fell between her breasts. She and I both watched its slow, glistening slide toward her belly.

"Hey, Doc." She looked up. "You wanna get that?"

◇◇◇

I left Casey's place an hour after sunrise, but already the day was bright as a new dime. This early on a Sunday, the Parkway was practically empty, so in less than twenty minutes I was heading up Mt. Washington, toward home. And, I promised myself, about a gallon of fresh coffee.

I'd just made the turn onto Grandview when my cell rang. It was Harvey Blalock.

"Hi," he said carefully. "I just heard again from Wingfield's people. About Phillip Camden. Seems he's not improving."

"Yeah, I know. I saw him yesterday."

"For what it's worth, I'm sorry about him. But, shitty as it is to say so, at least it's some good news as regards your case."

"I guess that's one way to look at it."

Blalock paused. "If you want, we can talk tomorrow, Dan. It can wait."

"No, I'm listening." I pulled over to the curb and put the car in park. I needed to concentrate on Harvey, not driving. "Go ahead."

"Well, I just got off the phone with Wingfield's lead attorney, and they're gearing up for war. Ya gotta love these Harvard Law types. They always do the gentlemanly thing and alert opposing counsel before cutting your balls off."

"Glad you're entertained. What are we talking about here?"

"For starters, expert depositions on current, approved clinical practices, as opposed to your treatment of Kevin. Character witnesses attesting to your maverick nature, your flouting of convention, and other traits deemed romantic and courageous in popular culture, but which in fact are the hallmarks of a disaffected and grandiose rebel."

"Thanks a lot."

"Hey, that isn't *my* opinion. I'm just reading what's in front of me. There's more, but—"

"Harvey, do me a favor. Just tell me what you think. Gut check."

"Gut check? I think we're in deep shit. For instance, I understand from Mr. Harvard Law that they're going to take a hammer to your credibility, your general judgment. Like your involvement in Richie Ellner's suicide. They're even talking about getting Senator Ellner involved…"

"But he barely *saw* his son these past few years," I said. "Richie was an embarrassment, a political liability."

"Maybe at one time. Now he's fodder for the Senator's grief and righteous indignation. Face it, the voters love suffering. They think it builds character. Or something."

He cleared his throat. "Anyway, the frontal assault remains focused on Kevin Wingfield. And as soon as they find another heavyweight to replace Dr. Camden—"

"I get the picture." I let out a breath.

"Didn't mean to hit you with all that at once," he said at last. "But you're a tough man to get hold of."

"Sorry about that. And Harvey—thanks. I appreciate everything you're doing."

He gave a throaty laugh. "Hell, I'm just getting warmed up. You hang in there, okay?"

◇◇◇

At last I pulled into my driveway. I'd circled the block twice, checking for news crews, but hadn't seen anyone. It appeared the siege had ended. At least for now.

The Sunday *Post-Gazette* lay on the front porch. A photo of Troy David Dowd accompanied another story about his latest appeal.

Poor Sylvia, I thought. Just what she needs to read with her morning coffee. The nightmare that won't go away. Wait'll it's playing down the street at the Cineplex.

I slipped the paper under my arm and put the key in the lock.

That's when I noticed the broken pane of the front window, a few feet to my left. Shielded from the street by a thick hedge, the bottom half of the glass was gone. Tiny shards dotted the sill.

Someone was in the house.

Chapter Fifty

I wasn't thinking. Later, I realized I should've immediately called the police.

Instead, I swung open the front door and stepped inside. The house was as dim as a cave. Shapes stood in shadow as I crept in, carefully laying the newspaper and my ring of keys down on the floor.

I decided against turning on the lights, moving instead by feel and memory through the living room, then into the hall. The open door to the kitchen was just ahead. No lights on in there, either.

Then I heard it. The music.

A throbbing, muffled sound. As though very loud, but coming from far away.

No. *Beneath* me. The basement.

Slowly, guiding myself along the wall, I moved down toward the kitchen. Paused, straining to hear. Nothing but the insistent pounding of the music. Louder now.

I took another step. Something made me glance into the kitchen. Curtains drawn against the bay window, the room was criss-crossed with shadows.

But I could just make out something. There, on the floor. The silverware drawer, upended, pulled all the way out of the cabinet. Contents scattered on the cold tile. Forks. Spoons. But no knives.

All the knives were missing.

I kept moving toward the two doors at the end of the hall. One led to the garage. The other to the basement.

That was the one I was supposed to open. The one with the butcher knife sticking out of the wood, just above the door knob.

I gripped the knife by its handle and pulled it out.

Heart pounding, I reached with my free hand for the knob and pulled open the door—

Ear-splitting music flooded from the basement below. Discordant, pulsating sounds, all reverb and bass. Some kind of electronic music, dialed up to maximum distortion.

Knife at the ready, I started down the stairs. The noise level rose with each descending step. Piercing. Maddening.

The room below me was pitch black, a concrete hell of deafening sound and windowless darkness. At the bottom step, I could make out my free weights stacked in a corner. The heavy bag, like a hanging man, swayed black against a deeper blackness.

Then, at the far end of the room, a sliver of light.

The door of the furnace room. Closed. Light on inside. He was there.

I stretched out my hand, feeling for the light switch. The overheads. Somewhere about—

Here! I flipped it on, flooding the basement with light. I blinked in the sudden brightness, then whirled toward the torturous sounds.

A large boom-box sat on the floor near the wall. Twin insect-eyed speakers vibrated from the din. I kicked the plug from the wall outlet.

The sudden silence was like a sharp blow. Shaking it off, I rushed to the furnace door.

It was locked. Its broad, wood-paneled front was impaled by a dozen different knives. Long, serrated blades. Short, wide ones. All stabbed into the door with tremendous strength. A long vertical line of knives, intersected a third of the way from the top by a horizontal one. A cross.

Then I knew.

"No!" I shouted, throwing down my knife.

I kicked hard, twice, at the door. The hinges buckled. I stepped back, hurled myself at the wood. It flew open.

Noah Frye, wild-eyed, was backed against the upright furnace in the cramped, airless room. A large carving knife filled both hands, its deadly tip pressed against the base of his own throat.

"My God, my God, why hast Thou forsaken me?" he cried, sinking the point of the knife into his neck.

"Noah!"

I lunged and grabbed his huge fists where they were molded to the knife handle. With all my strength, I dragged the knife away from his throat, now oozing blood.

Noah fought like a man possessed. We struggled furiously, hands locked, in the small, heat-baked room, banging against the cinder block walls. His blood smearing my face.

Finally, I hooked one of my legs behind him, and, shifting my weight, sent us both tumbling to the floor. I landed on top, knocking the wind out of him.

It was all I needed. I drove our clasped hands against the side of the furnace, knocking his knife free.

With a howl of rage, Noah tried to push me off, but I'd anchored myself between the furnace and the near wall. In such close quarters, a big man is at a disadvantage. He was pinned. It was over.

Faces inches apart, he stared up at me with frantic, livid eyes. His hair was matted with sweat, a tangled thatch.

I saw the blood bubbling from his throat. Quickly, I pulled out a handkerchief and pressed it, still folded, against the oozing wound.

We stayed that way for a couple minutes, until I felt the tension slacken in his body, and saw a weary softness tinge his features. Tears filled in his eyes.

"I've got to get to a phone, Noah." I took one of his hands, placed it on the handkerchief, then covered it with mine. "Keep pressing it here, okay?"

He gazed up, uncomprehending.

"You're not going to die, man," I growled.

The tears rolled down his coarse-stubbled cheeks.

"Dammit, Noah, I'm *not* going to let you bleed to death in my basement. So wipe that stupid, zombie-ass look off your face and get with the program here. Understand?"

I searched his ravaged, stricken face.

Then I felt the slightest movement in his hand beneath mine…as he began pressing the blood-soaked handkerchief down on his wound.

Chapter Fifty-one

The ER doc looked younger than the ones on *Grey's Anatomy* as he came out of the surgical unit, his face a mixture of fatigue and petulance. That's the downside of needing urgent care on a Sunday morning. You get first-year residents who feel sorry for themselves. Inexperience and attitude. A bad combo.

I got up from the waiting area couch and joined him near the reception desk, where Harry Polk had lounged for the past hour making eyes at the young nurse's aide.

"Guy gonna make it?" Polk asked the doctor absently.

The resident, whose name tag read "Dr. Olsen," nodded. "Mr. Frye will be fine. We just have to repair his self-administered tracheotomy, and patch up some defensive bruises." Olsen looked askance at me. "You guys must've really mixed it up, since you don't look so good yourself. I can only assume you felt it necessary."

"You had to be there," I said. "What about the blood-and-urine work I wanted? And the stomach contents."

"I have the lab on it," Olsen replied. "And we pumped his stomach. Mr. Frye's psychiatric history certainly warrants these measures. But I'll feel better once I've talked to his attending psychopharmacologist."

"I called Dr. Mendors," I said. "She's on her way."

"No rush. Mr. Frye will be out for a few hours. My guess is, the guy's a walking medicine cabinet. Sooner or later, the system breaks down."

I frowned. "Any other thoughts?"

"Well…" He drew me away from reception. Over my shoulder, I saw Polk shrug and look at his shoes.

"You know," Olsen said importantly, "I did six months' psych rotation, and I know that sometimes a suicide attempt is a gesture of defiance, or even hostility."

"No kidding?"

"Look at the facts. Mr. Frye came to *your* house to kill himself. Waiting for you to show up, so that he could do the act right in front of you. The ultimate 'fuck you' to the one witnessing the death. It's in the literature."

I folded my arms and glared at him. I wanted to say something about MD's and their pathetic "six months' pysch rotations," after which they routinely feel qualified to render psychological diagnoses for the rest of their careers. I also resented Olsen's patronizing tone, and the fact that he didn't look old enough to shave.

But I didn't say anything. Because he was right. At least on paper. I'd been thinking along those same lines myself during the drive down here to Pittsburgh Memorial, following behind the ambulance.

"Just food for thought," Olsen added, before heading back over to reception. He and Polk passed each other in the hall as the sergeant strolled up to me.

"What was that all about?" Polk said, sucking on a toothpick. "Or were you docs using the *big* words?"

"Sorry, Harry. Look, I'm going to wait here for Nancy Mendors. You need anything more from me?"

"The usual paperwork. You oughtta be an old hand at filling out incident reports by now." Polk sniffed loudly. "Speakin' of which, anybody try to kill you lately?"

"Not lately. But, thanks. I'd forgotten to worry about it for a while."

"Just thought I'd ask." He walked off.

‹›‹›‹›

"Danny?"

It wasn't Nancy's voice, calling from the end of the hall. Instead, Angie Villanova walked briskly toward me. Within moments, I was wrapped in the familiar—and always slightly insistent—warmth of her embrace.

"Soon as I heard," she said in her clipped, brassy voice, "I had to come down to offer moral support."

She led us back to the couch. "Jesus, what you've gone through..." A thin-lipped smile. "'Course, it hasn't been *all* bad for you. Not from what I hear."

"Casey?"

"City Hall's a tight little circle, Danny. People talk. In her defense, I'd say she's trading up. I mean, sure, Sinclair's a prize fish, but he's a cold one."

"Hey, what *is* it with you and Casey? You seem to frost over yourself every time you see her."

Angie tapped her chin dramatically. "Now let me see. She's young and beautiful. Will probably be DA herself one day. And feels entitled to all of it." She gave me a look. "Have I left anything out?"

"Come on, you've done pretty well yourself, Angie."

"I guess. Sure." She lowered her eyes. "But she's..."

"This isn't about her."

"I know. Maybe I just need to see her as an ambitious bitch so I'll feel better. Still, she *was* the ADA who referred Kevin to me, after he'd been questioned that night he was robbed. That's why I called you in. So she must have a heart somewhere under that firstclass rack."

Angie flashed me a semi-lewd grin, but it didn't stick. She aimed her eyes at the floor again. I waited.

"It's just...I mean, with Sonny and me—It's not so great, ya know? And now, with the kids gone..."

She stopped suddenly and climbed to her feet, clutching her jacket around her as if it were a blanket.

"Aw, the hell with it. But sometimes..." A rueful look. "Sometimes, it's hard to watch the Caseys of this world. Now just forget I said anything. Okay?"

"Will do. Thanks for coming by, Angie."

"Hey, we're family. It's in the rules."

A clattering of heels announced another visitor. Nancy Mendors wore jeans under a voluminous sweater, and black boots that shone in the corridor lights. As we hugged, I smelled a subtle perfume.

I smiled to myself. No longer being thought a murder suspect does a lot for a person's mood.

Chapter Fifty-two

"She seems nice." Nancy opened the window on her side of the car. We were driving out of town, toward Penn Hills. And Ten Oaks.

"Angie?" I smiled. "She's something. Part Old World Italian, part feminist. Depends on when you catch her."

Angie had hung around at the hospital another hour, while Nancy visited Noah and consulted with Dr. Olsen about their mutual patient. As we said good-bye, Angie repeated her objections to my refusing police protection. As I'd expected. As *she* expected, I wouldn't budge.

Back in the ER, I learned that Noah had been moved to Intensive Care. He was still sedated when I joined Nancy at his bedside. Bandages circled his neck like a collar.

"We got lucky," was all she'd said.

Now, as a blustery wind hurried the clouds overhead, Nancy leaned back against the headrest.

"My lawyer says the DA had to drop the charges," she said wearily. "With the evidence against Elaine Garman, Puzzini could argue that there are *two* credible suspects, thus guaranteeing reasonable doubt."

She reached over to touch my forearm as I drove. "I owe you a lot, Danny. I know that."

"Wait'll you get my bill."

"Tough guy." She took her hand away.

I changed the subject. "How'd it go with Dr. Olsen?"

"You mean, the annoyingly *young* Dr. Olsen? Okay, I guess. He's competent enough."

"Did he share his theory about Noah's suicide attempt? I've been wondering about it myself."

"I knew you had. But he's wrong. The way I see it, no matter what was going on in Noah's mind, some part of him reached out to you. Saw you as his friend, his protector."

"Maybe..."

"Think about it. In the grip of a chaotic, delusional state, he managed to get himself to your house. To guide you to the basement with the music. To signal his suicidal intent by displaying his crucifixion obsession with the knives, outside the furnace room door. Then he *waited* in there, knife in his hands, until you broke the door down."

Her voice rose. "Jesus, Danny, he didn't want you to *witness* his suicide. He wanted you to *stop* it!"

We drove in silence for a minute. "I guess I like your version better. Thanks."

"Don't thank me. I happen to be right about this. I've known Noah as long as you have, and almost as well."

True enough. "Olsen say anything else?"

"Just that when Noah comes to, he won't be talking for a few days. Not with his throat injury."

"Charlene will probably appreciate the quiet."

Nancy peered out the window at the rush of rolling greenery. We were driving through residential Penn Hills, with its cluster of tree-shrouded cul-de-sacs.

"God, I'm so worried about all this," she said. "First Richie Ellner, now Noah...I mean, what's going on?"

"I'm not sure. I'm hoping we'll find some answers at the clinic." I made the turn onto the exit ramp.

"Bullshit." We exchanged looks. "I know what you're thinking, Danny. Why we're going to Ten Oaks. Richie and Noah had similar atypical psychotic episodes. And there's only one thing

linking the two of them. One person they have in common."
She took a breath. "Me."

Things were pretty quiet at the clinic. Sundays were when most of the patients were picked up by family members and taken out for brunch, or a walk. The few remaining patients were usually too depressed to leave their rooms, or else were on special watch. So other than a case manager and some orderlies, staff was at less than half-strength.

Which was why, as Nancy and I headed down the main corridor, most of the office doors on either side of us were closed. Including Brooks Riley's, still striped with crime scene tape.

One door stood open. Bert Garman sat behind his desk, face in his hands, eyes looking out between his fingers as if from behind bars. He was wearing the same clothes as the night before.

"Jesus," I said. "Didn't you go home last night?"

Garman closed his fingers, rubbed his forehead. "Only long enough to help Elaine pack after the cops released her. She wanted to move into a hotel."

"I'm so sorry," Nancy said.

He shrugged. "Our marriage has been over for a long time. With enough blame on both sides, believe me."

I looked at the piles of papers and files scattered atop his desk. His computer was on, displaying multi-colored graphs. "You need anything?" I asked.

"Other than a miracle? With all the bad press, our acquisition by UniHealth is on life support. Luckily, those greedy bastards know a cash cow when they see one. As long as I can keep the patients' families happy."

Garman fished around the loose papers, raised one up to show us. A form letter. "I'm sending this out to all the families. We're having a big meeting next week to allay any fears about the clinic. I'm also pulling every string I can to pressure the media to back off. I mean, there's got to be *other* stories to cover."

"Except Ten Oaks keeps giving them a new one every other day," I said. "Murder, suicide..."

Garman's voice grew sharp. "That reminds me. I heard about Noah Frye, and I'm sorry. But I'd appreciate it if you both could keep it quiet that he used to be a patient here. Even though that was before my time, when I was still at Clearview Hospital, *any* connection, even tangential, with Ten Oaks just adds more fuel to the fire."

I folded my arms. "There *will* be an investigation. Noah's medical history will be part of it."

"I *know* that, Dan. But you don't have the board of directors up your ass every day."

"No," I admitted. "I guess I don't."

"That's right. *You* get to be the stalwart idealist, and I'm Ebenezer Scrooge. Well, to hell with you."

He looked over at Nancy. "And *you*, too. This used to be a nice, cushy little profession till you liberals showed up."

His attempt at banter was undone by the flecks of pain in his pale eyes. Even he seemed to be aware of this.

"Don't worry, I'll be all right." He waved us away. "I'll just wallow in paperwork till the bars open."

Nancy winced. "Great. That's a load off my mind."

As she and I turned to leave, Garman stirred. "Hey, what are you guys doing here, anyway?"

"We came by for Nancy's briefcase," I said. "She thinks she might have left it in her office."

Another lie. I was getting good at them.

On my instructions, Nancy opened the door to the medical dispensary, then locked it behind us. The small room gleamed a greenish-white under the fluorescents.

With a second key, she unlocked the sturdy metal cabinet where the clinic meds were stored, in innocuous little white boxes.

Nancy took down one of these and opened it. I took the safety-sealed pill bottle from her hand and read the label. Then I poured some pills into my hand.

Adnorfex. Fifty milligram tablets. I dropped a few into my jacket pocket and closed the bottle again.

She gave me a look. "There's nothing here, Danny. Adnorfex's been on the market over a year. The clinical trials were stringent. I saw the data myself. Besides—"

"Can I take a look at your book?"

I picked up a thick ledger from its shelf, flipping through pages of her small, careful handwriting until I found October of this year.

"Here it is," I said. "The Adnorfex you prescribed for Richie Ellner. And that you procure for Noah."

She nodded. "I designate him as an uncooperative outpatient whose care is maintained by a private benefactor. I still have to keep track of where the pills go."

I was staring at the row of boxes on the shelf.

"What is it?" Nancy craned her neck to follow my gaze.

I took down two boxes and showed her the fine print under the drug company's logo and the interminable list of directions and contra-indications.

"These two boxes are different from the others," I explained. "The drug company switched distributors."

"So? What does that mean?"

"I'm not sure. But I'm starting to get an idea."

I handed her one of the boxes. She had to tilt it up to the light to read.

"Speedway Distributors. A Division of Cochran International." She looked at me. "Again, so…?"

I smiled. "You've got to start reading the financial news, Doctor."

Chapter Fifty-three

Peter Clarkson had a pretty nice swing. Even before the ball vanished into the darkness, you could tell it would cover a lot of distance before falling into the tree-shrouded valley below.

The driving range was on the crest of a hill that overlooked the faded business district of Verona. Even from this height you could see the steel-gray surface of the Allegheny River, implacably flowing beside the rust-pitted railroad tracks that ran alongside it. Only the mournful hum of a late-night bus idling at a corner rose up from the lonely streets.

Clarkson stepped back from the tee. Powerful arc lamps overhead created a bright pool of light a dozen feet in any direction, beyond which the night was black and cold. Except for Clarkson, the small driving range was deserted.

"Nice shot," I said, stepping into the circle of light. "But I think it was starting to slice."

My feet sank into the worn green felt, its permanent tees spaced like buttons along the thin strip.

Clarkson pivoted, startled. "Jesus! What the hell are *you* doing up here?"

"I wanted to talk to you." I took another step closer. "I knew you and Wingfield were back in town. Your secretary said you planned to come by here after a business dinner."

"Yeah? First thing in the morning, I fire her ass."

He found his grip on the club and took a practice swing. "Piece of shit club. The kid behind the counter said it was the best they had."

"Well, you'll have to take it up with him later. I just gave him a fifty to go get himself a pizza."

"Now why the hell would you do that?" he said. Eyes cold and green as brackish water.

"I thought it'd be better if we spoke in private."

He pointed his club at me. "Maybe that wasn't so smart. For you."

"Easy, Peter. Don't make me take that thing away from you."

"Look, what the fuck do you want? I don't have all night. Sheila's waiting in the car for me. In the lot."

"I know. I saw her. She doesn't mind just sitting there, alone, while you work on your game?"

"I guess not. She's in her own world half the time, anyway."

He swung the club around like a pointer, its arc taking in the sloping valley, and the glittering lights from the river.

"Guy at the Burgoyne recommended this place," he said easily. "Oakmont's just down there. Beyond those trees."

"I know. They've played the U.S. Open there twice. Arnold Palmer used to hit practice drives from exactly where you're standing. Only without the slice."

He stared at me for a moment, then started to walk away. "Look, this is bullshit. I'm not gonna—"

Without thinking, I reached and caught hold of his shoulder, spun him around. He was too off-balance to connect with the club, and his swing just fanned the air as I ducked beneath it. I managed to grab his wrist, then hook my thumb around his and pull it back.

He gasped, stunned. The golf club clattered to the ground. I picked it up.

Clarkson back-stepped in a crouch, holding his thumb with his other hand. "You son-of-a-bitch."

"Not compared to you. Co-conspirator in a murder. Then there's the sex with your sister. Your *blind* sister. Maybe we should start there."

Flexing his injured hand, Clarkson stood straighter. Gave me a thin smile. "Listen, you don't know who you're dealing with."

"Like hell. I know what kind of man Miles Wingfield is. I learned in Banford about the fire that conveniently destroyed the court records concerning his children. And I'm damn sure that a genetic scientist named Terry Mavis didn't die of an accidental drug overdose." I paused. "Of course, *you'd* know more about that than I would."

"You're bluffing. You don't have shit." But Clarkson's face had turned wary. Eyes like a cornered animal's.

I had to do this just right. He was a dozen years my junior. If he decided to make a run for it, I was screwed.

"We know you started working for Wingfield after he moved to California," I went on carefully. "Some kind of school intern program."

"So?"

"I mean, I thought *Wingfield* was a sick bastard. But you're right up there. That's why you two made such a good match. Especially when you found out about his...special needs. Tell me, how much did he pay you to let him join the sex between you and Sheila?"

Clarkson's lips barely moved. "More than you'll ever see in your life, asshole."

Something had shifted in him. His eyes were resolute points. He'd made a decision.

I saw it too late. The moist night air pricked my throat as I took a sharp breath. He'd taken a small handgun out of his jacket pocket.

I knew what I was supposed to say. The code word. But I said something else instead.

"When did it start between you and Sheila? Was it when your parents were killed?"

He raised the gun and pointed it at my chest. "Go on. Let's talk. Doesn't much matter now. And lose the club."

I dropped the club to the ground. Kept my voice level.

"Poor Sheila. Blind since birth, then losing her parents... Desperate, she turned to the only family she had left, her big brother..." I raised my eyebrows. "How old was she? Nine, ten?"

"Eleven." He held the gun easily now. In control. "But she developed early. Hell, I used to get boners just watching her take a shower..." A brief, salacious smile.

"Then Wingfield brings you into his world," I said. "The money. The parties. All in exchange for letting him orchestrate the sex between you and Sheila."

Clarkson's eyes shone. A strange, narcissistic pride emanated from him. The trickster, revealed. Boastful.

"And Sheila," I continued. "She went along with all of it, because of you. She loves you. You're her whole world. The only real world she knows."

"Blah, blah, blah...Now you're boring me, Doc." His forefinger stroked the gun's trigger.

"Until you and she got too old for Wingfield," I quickly went on. "And his interest started to wane. What were you by then, seventeen, eighteen...?"

"Yeah. Something like that. I knew he was looking around for somebody else...other sibs. Younger. But he had bigger problems at the time..."

"Terry Mavis?"

I risked a glance at the gun. No chance for a grab at it. He stood just out of reach, not letting anything we were saying distract him. Not yet, anyway.

"Young Dr. Mavis...Man, for a science geek, that guy could *party.* But everybody said he was brilliant. And Wingfield was his biggest fan. Spent millions on Mavis' research for a drug with milder side effects than Thorazine or Haldol. The new 'magic bullet' for psychotic patients. It was called Adnorfex. Only one problem..."

"It didn't work."

"Nope. The doc tried to explain it to me once. The genetic material he'd worked with had developed a mutated nucleus or some shit. He said it trip-wired the brain's receptor caps, making them even *more* receptive to...what the hell was it?—"

"Neurotransmitters," I said flatly. "From what you're describing, it'd be like punching *more* holes in a sieve, so that the neurotransmitters flooded the patient's brain. Similar to an LSD flashback, activating regions most sensitive to delusions. Sudden, terrifying delusions."

"Yeah, that's it. Terry said it was like giving LSD to a psychotic."

Now I understood what had happened to Richie Ellner. *And* to Noah. And God knew how many others throughout the country.

"No wonder Wingfield was freaking out," I said. "After all that time and money, Terry Mavis had handed him a big load of nothing."

Clarkson laughed. "Oh, yeah. But the buzz had grown too huge around Adnorfex. Investors were beating down the doors to get in on it. Wingfield had sunk almost everything he had into its development. Things were coming to a head."

"And all your data was shit."

"Grade-A shit. And when it comes to FDA approval for a new drug, clinical trials make or break you. So Wingfield pulled every string he had to put Adnorfex on the fast-track for FDA approval. But to do that—"

"He had to rig the clinical data," I said.

"He pressured Mavis big-time. And the boy genius was so strung out and in debt, he had no choice. So he went along with it. Until he was about to testify before the FDA Review Board. Suddenly he got an attack of conscience. He said he was going to reveal that the clinical trials had been rigged. That we'd seen severe negative reactions in test subjects using the new drug."

"So Terry Mavis had to go."

He grew sullen, uneasy. Tightened his grip on the gun.

I took a guess. "Now I understand why you're still working for Wingfield. He forced you to help him kill Terry Mavis. Made you an accomplice in staging the overdose."

"Don't be so smug." Clarkson roused himself with anger. "Look what bein' such a smart-ass got you. Alone on a hill looking down the barrel of a gun..."

He sniffed loudly. "Besides, I was already in too deep. I knew about the rigged data. If Mavis *did* testify before the Board, *I'd* be fucked too."

"But not as fucked as you were by helping kill Mavis. Because then Wingfield had a lock on you forever."

I paused. "As for Sheila...I guess she stayed because she loves you. Because she has nowhere else to go. Maybe because, after all that's happened, she still thinks her safety lies with you."

"*Shut up!* I don't wanna talk about Sheila, okay?" Clarkson stepped forward, thrust the gun barrel at my face. "*Okay?*"

I felt the gun pressed against my brow, and willed myself to breathe. Too late for code words now.

"No more talk. Instead, I think I'll just blow you away. Right now. How about that? *Right now.*"

He cocked the hammer.

I closed my eyes and thought about Barbara. Her last moment on earth. Had it felt like this?

Chapter Fifty-four

Clarkson's gun-hand began to tremble. He blinked, forehead beaded with sweat.

"But that wouldn't be smart." He lowered the gun and stepped back. "And I've gotta be smart."

I felt a long breath leave my body. Struggled against a rising panic, my heart pounding like a hammer.

"It's gotta look like an accident," he was saying. "I did it before, with Terry Mavis. I can do it with you."

"Maybe." Keep him talking. Just a bit more. I just needed a little more.

"But you haven't finished the story." I forced myself to stay focused. "Mavis is dead. Adnorfex gets okayed, distributed. Wingfield gets rich. Everything's great. Until…"

"Until what, Doc?" Clarkson scratched his cheek with the gun barrel. "You're so fucking smart, you tell me."

"My guess is, a few months after Adnorfex's release, abnormal side effects start getting reported by hospitals and clinics."

"Right again. But you gotta admire Wingfield's balls. Through UniHealth, one of his companies, he starts buying up the hospitals and clinics where these cases were being reported. He even pays off the patients' families—Not that this is anything new. Hell, Warner-Lambert did the same thing when diabetics started croaking from using Rezulin."

"Is that why UniHealth bought up Ten Oaks? I saw the picture of you shaking hands with Bert Garman."

"Yeah, that was taken when we closed the deal. Funny thing is, we hadn't heard any negative reports from Ten Oaks. Not yet, anyway. Still, it's the most profitable clinic in the state, and Wingfield wanted it under the UniHealth roof." He winked. "Business *is* business."

I had to ask. "Did Bert Garman know about the problems with Adnorfex?"

"Hell, no. All he cared about was getting rich. Stock options for the clinic's board of directors was part of the deal, and he had the biggest share." He laughed. "But talk about pussy-whipped... I met the wife. A cast-iron bitch with a worse habit than Terry Mavis. Poor bastard."

I considered all this as Clarkson rocked on his heels, brandishing the gun.

"But even Wingfield must have realized he couldn't keep buying off trouble," I said carefully. "Not with reports about the drug's side effects growing. He loses everything if the news gets out."

"That's right." Clarkson made a beckoning motion with his free hand, as though to a slow student. "So...?"

I took a breath. "So he comes up with a plan. By merging with Cochran International, Wingfield can use them to distribute Adnorfex world-wide. In markets far less rigidly monitored and regulated. If he moves fast enough, he can still make a fortune before having to halt production of the drug."

But Clarkson didn't seem to be listening anymore. His look at me had become bored, disengaged.

"Sorry. Wasn't paying much attention there at the end."

I watched as the glimmer of an idea rose in his eyes.

"You know," he said, "I was just thinking. Helluva drop from up here, eh?"

He feigned a horrified look at the edge of the green felt. And the dark sweep of nothingness beyond.

"I mean, way up here. In the dark. A guy loses his balance. Falls. It could happen, right?" He shrugged. "What do you think, Doc? Feel like taking the plunge?"

"Not without a fight," I said evenly. "Besides, what are you going to tell Sheila after I'm found dead? That you had nothing to do with *that*, either?"

"Fuck Sheila!" Vehement. Bitter. "I *told* you, I don't wanna talk about her."

I held his gaze. "I forgot."

He closed his eyes. "God, I'm so sick of it...Sick of *her*. She's so—man, she was born blind in more ways than one, if ya know what I mean."

Then he gave a thick, violent laugh, and strode toward me again. Something more than rage burned on his cheeks. Something deeper. Inchoate.

Then it came. Loud, harsh, a torrent of words.

"You wanna know the God's truth? *I'm sick of fucking her!* I've been sick of it for a long time. Christ, I've cheated on her for years. Right under her fucking nose. Stupid blind bitch..."

"Yeah, you're some man," I said coolly.

He steadied the gun. "And you're a *dead* one."

Clarkson nodded toward the lip of the green. Beyond was a six-inch strip of gravel, then a bottomless drop to the valley below.

"Move," he said.

"Peter! No!!"

A choked female voice echoed, making us both turn.

There, stepping awkwardly out from under the foliage of some young oaks, was Sheila. With her hesitant gait rippling the folds of her simple cotton dress, she seemed like a ghost emerging from the edge of the woods.

"Sheila!" Clarkson stepped back, almost stumbling, but clutching tight to the gun. He pointed it surely in my direction.

Haltingly, hands groping to feel along stems and shoots, she made her way onto the driving range, not a half-dozen feet from her brother.

"I was worried when you didn't come back to the car," she said, eyes staring at the space between Clarkson and me. "I thought I heard your voice...and someone else's...so I just followed them."

She seemed waif-like, fragile. But more than that. It was as though something within her was...unraveling.

"You *heard* us...?" Clarkson swallowed hard, glancing from Sheila to me, then back again. "How much—?"

It was then that I really saw Sheila for the first time, and cursed my own blindness. Her trembling hands. The anxiety pinching the edges of her blank eyes. The supreme effort it was taking merely to keep herself intact.

I understood suddenly the psychic cost of the smooth demeanor she displayed that night in Wingfield's hotel suite. The feigned self-assurance. The porcelain-like facade masking an unbearable agitation, anguish.

"Dr. Rinaldi is here with you, isn't he?" She lowered her eyes, veiled by her rich auburn hair. "I recognized his voice. You're planning to *kill* him..."

Her own voice a wisp. Disturbingly child-like.

"Listen, Sheila, you don't know what's going on. This prick can hurt me...hurt *us*..."

"Oh, Peter. Please. There has to be another way..."

She drew toward him and clutched his arms. Desperate. Confused. Clarkson moaned, an intimate sound, and embraced her with his free arm, kissing her neck. The gun, in his other hand, was pressed between them.

"Oh baby," he said smoothly, in a voice I'd never heard from him before. Lover. Protector.

"I love you, Peter," she whispered, the shine of tears in her eyes. "I'm so sorry..."

Then, before I could move a muscle, the gun went off, the sound echoing off the trees. Clarkson's arm fell from her shoulder as he staggered back, clutching his chest. Blood spread through his splayed fingers.

Sheila, openly sobbing now, held the gun in her small white hand. With a final gasp, Clarkson sprawled onto his back on the cold ground. His legs twitched spasmodically.

She sank to her knees next to her dying brother.

As I moved toward her, Sheila's face came up, stern with purpose. She held the gun tight against her temple.

"No, Doctor!" She knelt stiffly, as a postulant might, unseeing eyes focused on the horizon.

I froze, as the night around us filled with the sounds of slamming car doors, heavy footsteps and harsh voices. Bobbing flashlights flickering against the shadowed trees.

I turned, shooting a warning look to Polk, Lowrey and the uniformed cops converging on the scene.

"Tell them to stay back," Sheila said. "Please."

As Polk motioned to the others to keep their distance, I looked past the circle of uniforms to see Casey just coming up, bundling a heavy parka around her shoulders.

We exchanged looks. This would not end well.

"Sheila." I risked a step.

Her face shone under the lights. "I lied to Peter. I'm afraid I heard more than I let on. Much more. You both have such strong voices. So male. So sure."

Grazing her ear with the gun barrel.

"Sheila, please," I said. "Let me take the gun."

She smiled. "When I'm done with it." She drew in a breath. "The air's sweet up here. I imagine there's a wonderful view, too. I always appreciate a nice view."

She pulled the trigger.

Chapter Fifty-five

Detective Lowrey had stayed behind to supervise the crime scene, so I only had the faces of Lt. Biegler, Sgt. Polk, and Casey glaring down at me. We were all crammed into Biegler's office, a chair short. The yellowed plastic wall clock read three-thirty. a.m.

"You're one lucky bastard." Polk sagged against the near corner like a six-foot sack of grain.

Casey, sitting opposite me, grabbed my chair arms.

"Dammit, why didn't you give the code word when Clarkson pulled a gun? What were you trying to prove?"

"Nothing," I said. "I wanted to hear what he had to say. If you guys had come crashing in right then, we'd never have learned what we did."

"Meanwhile, you could've ended up at the bottom of a hill, in a hundred pieces," Casey insisted.

Biegler shook his head. "I *never* liked the idea of him wearing a wire," he said bitterly. "Civilians always screw things up in the end."

"Consultant," I corrected him.

Polk laughed. "Ya don't know when to quit, do ya?"

Casey whirled to face Biegler. "Listen, if it wasn't for Dr. Rinaldi, we'd have nothing to give the Feds. Now we do. Evidence of federal crimes against Miles Wingfield, unearthed in the course of our homicide investigation. My guess is, a lot of what's on the tape is inadmissible—especially with the key witness, Peter Clarkson, dead—but it lays a foundation for a full investigation. Points them in the right direction."

"So what?" Polk said. "The idea was to get enough on Clarkson to force him to roll on Wingfield. Right?"

Casey nodded. "Especially now that Sinclair thinks there's more political capital in going after Wingfield than in putting all our focus on the murder inquiry."

"Really?" I asked. "Why the change?"

"Well, for one thing, we're nowhere on finding Kevin's killer. And Fox News just did a poll that shows public opinion's all over the map: There's sympathy for Wingfield's loss, versus an image of him as a ruthless tycoon who let his kid live a semi-marginal life, versus anger at *Kevin*, believe it or not, for being an ungrateful child."

"Gotta love those polls," Polk said. "To the press, it's all just one big soap opera."

"Meanwhile," Biegler said, "we let a murder-suicide go down while we're parked in the trees ten yards away. We're going to look like shit."

"C'mon, Lieutenant," said Polk. "Okay, maybe we shoulda had a man watchin' the blind girl in the car. But even so, we'd probably have let her go up to Clarkson, see what she had to say. Who figures she's gonna whack him?"

"It wasn't what she had to say," I offered. "It's what she *heard*. Finding out her brother's real feelings about her. That he'd been cheating on her for years. She must've decided right then and there to kill him. Yet with Peter gone, her whole world was gone, too. So...she left it."

Polk's face was grim. "Her own brother...Jesus..."

"Forget *him*," I said. "We've got enough to prove that Wingfield's a real threat to any minor children with whom he's in contact..."

Just then, the phone rang on Biegler's desk. "That'll be Sinclair," he said, sighing as he picked it up.

‹›‹›‹›

"Listen," I said to Casey, back in her office. "Thanks again for believing me when I said I wanted to go after Clarkson.

Especially since all I had was a prescription bottle and a couple of hunches."

She yawned. "Don't thank me. I guess something about you makes me go all soft in the head."

"Right." I smiled. We both sipped vending machine coffee, watching the dawn light gleam hazily on her window blinds. The offices beyond her walls were silent, empty.

"Still," I went on, "how'd you get Judge Cahill to grant the warrant for me to wear a wire?"

"I knew Sandra Cahill before she went on the bench. When we were just a couple of legal hotties trolling the bars."

I smiled at the image in my mind. "So you know where the bodies are buried."

"Better than that, I know what she's done with *hers*—and with whom. But you want to know the real reason? Judge Sandy has a ton of Wingfield BioTech stock, and wants the inside scoop on whether to dump it. Believe me, she'll want first crack at listening to the tape, admissible or not."

She drained her coffee and tossed the cup in the trash. I could see her deep fatigue in the pallor of her skin, the tightness at the corners of her mouth.

"A helluva night, eh?" She kicked off her shoes and pulled her knees up to her chin, settling back against the small leather couch. Giving me a sad smile.

I sat next to her. Threaded my hand through her silken hair. "You're still thinking about Sheila, aren't you?"

Casey nodded, eyes moist. I knew I was seeing a secret part of her. Not the vulnerability a therapist sees, but what lives in that hidden chamber of the heart to which only a lover is granted access. Knowledge of the body revealing more than can be named, spoken. Pointing to where the real mystery lies.

To my surprise, Casey reached over and unbuttoned my shirt, gently spread it open. Then she huddled close, laying her head against my skin. I drew my arms up, holding her tight. We barely breathed.

Time was lost to me. A few minutes, maybe more.

"How long do I get you like this?" I whispered.

She kissed my chest. "You don't. This isn't happening. This is a dream."

I felt her hand move down my side, toward my crotch. Felt her sure fingers find me through the fabric, stroke me. Grow me in her hand.

"*This,*" she whispered, face still buried in my chest, "this is real. Only this."

She shifted position, astride me now. She freed me, put me inside her. It was wordless. Almost without sound or breath. With glances averted.

As though the empty offices on either side were filled with the ears of the curious, the prurient. As though we were vandals of the heart, getting away with something.

Chapter Fifty-six

It was nine a.m, and, over her protests, I joined Casey in the elevator up to Sinclair's office.

"Do you just *like* pissing him off, or what?"

After locking her office door, we'd grabbed a few hours' sleep in each other's arms, until a phone call from Sinclair's secretary woke us with the news that Casey was needed at once. She balked when I said I'd accompany her.

"Look," I'd said, "if Sinclair's going to rake you over the coals because of last night, I want to be there."

I sat up, rolling the kinks out of my shoulders. I was getting too old to sleep on office sofas. "You went out on a limb for me, Casey. I don't want you on it alone."

She'd made some more noises about it, but could tell I wasn't going to budge. Then she turned away from me to straighten the collar on her jacket.

We'd been strangely awkward since making love. Almost distant. Maybe we'd gotten too close. Or at least one of us had. I just wasn't sure which one.

Now, as Sinclair's secretary ushered us into the DA's office, the cold morning light splashing the paneled walls pulled me back into the sober present.

Rising from the chair behind his desk, Sinclair looked wan and sallow-eyed, despite the square-shouldered posture and patrician manner he couldn't shed.

"Dr. Rinaldi," he said. "It seems you can't stay out of the news. I should get the name of your publicist."

"Wrong place at the wrong time. It happens."

"Apparently more than once, in your case." He turned to Casey. "Look, this is official business. Unless there's a reason you've invited Dr. Rinaldi to join us…"

Before she could reply, I leaned across his desk and planted my hands on the blotter, on either side of the framed photo of his wife and kids. My eyes met his.

"Cut the shit, okay? If you want to burn somebody for last night's fiasco, I'm the guy. I threw out the play-book and didn't give the code word when a weapon was displayed. Don't blame the cops *or* Casey."

"Believe it or not, I'm not really interested in your opinion."

Casey touched my elbow. "I can defend myself, okay?"

She turned to her boss. "C'mon, Lee. We *got* a lot more than we lost last night. I'm guessing City Hall thinks so, too."

"That's because you haven't been on the phone with them." Sinclair was curt. "*Excuse* us, Doctor? Or would you rather be forceably removed? In cuffs?"

"Been there, done that. You want to kick me out, go ahead. I'll just go see a friend down at the *Post-Gazette*, give him a real scoop. About Wingfield and Adnorfex, and the murder of Terry Mavis. Hell, the brother and sister sex stuff *alone* will—"

There was a long pause. Then Sinclair shook his head.

"Doctor, your role in this investigation, such as it's been, is over. I'm going to order Lt. Biegler to put you under house arrest, for your own protection."

"Do what you have to. But that's not the point."

"Really? And what, exactly, is?"

I sat on the edge of Sinclair's desk. Nudged some kind of antique table clock. "The point is, I'm *in* this thing. And I'm sticking, all the way to the end. For Kevin."

He reached for his phone. "I've had enough of this…"

I came off the desk to face him, planting my feet. Crowding his space. His hand, unmoving, on the phone. We must have looked pretty pathetic staring each other down.

I was right. Casey gave a short laugh.

"Christ, no matter what, it always turns into a dick contest. I'm sorry now I fucked either one of you."

She sat down, arms folded, and looked out the window.

I shrugged at Sinclair. "I don't know about you, but I don't have a snappy come-back to that."

He waved his hand angrily and sat down again behind his desk, carefully returning the antique clock to its exact former position on the blotter. Anal prick.

Not that I was thrilled with my own behavior. He and I were like two flints striking off each other, and probably always would be. But I had no real reason to assume he was a bad guy. At least, no worse than every other political animal with big ambitions.

"Okay, look," Sinclair said at last. "The fall-out on this Clarkson business has already started. I got a call from Judge Weitzel in DC. Sandra Cahill faxed him a transcript of the wire-tape, and all hell's broken loose."

Casey chuckled. "I can imagine."

"Yeah, those pricks at Justice are just drooling at the thought of embarrassing the FDA on their fast-track procedures. Meanwhile, there'll be an injunction against further manufacture of Adnorfex."

"What about a recall?" I asked.

"Already in motion," Sinclair said. "Justice and FDA lawyers have to agree on the wording. But we're already notifying hospitals and clinics. The faster we can get the damned drug off the dispensary shelves, the better."

"For everyone," Casey said. "You can bet the Feds are in full damage-control mode."

Sinclair agreed. "This could be a PR nightmare, so everybody wants to look head's-up on this thing. Including the SEC. Maybe even the Surgeon General's committee on sex abuse. They haven't had any press for a while. This is like hitting the jackpot."

"I was just about to ask," I said. "What about County Child Protective Services?"

"They've been alerted about Wingfield, but it won't be easy. A full-scale investigation of his personal life and habits could take months. He's got a firewall of lawyers, and all the money he'd need to cover his tracks."

Sinclair took a breath. "Speaking of which...as of right now, we don't know where he is."

Casey jerked forward. "What do you mean?"

"I mean, we just learned that Wingfield checked out of the Burgoyne Plaza at four this morning. That's why I needed you up here. His departure took his entire staff by surprise. Nobody knows where he went."

"How could something leak so fast?"

"Wingfield's got plenty of friends in high places. Wouldn't be surprised if one or two were on the pad. Anyway, we've got a joint police-Justice team at the hotel right now, interrogating Wingfield's top people."

"With his resources, he could be anywhere," I said.

"Doesn't matter. He hasn't offically been charged with anything. And won't be, until the Feds can gather enough tangible evidence. Assuming they can. For now, Wingfield's free to go wherever he wants."

"If I were him," Casey mused, "I'd head for some country that doesn't have an extradiction treaty with us."

"Let's cross that river when we get to it." Sinclair glanced at his desk clock. "Time to get it in gear, Casey. We've got a ball-buster of a day in front of us."

Casey stood up, punched my arm. "You heard the man, Danny. Now beat it." Playful, but not.

I gave Sinclair a sidelong look. "You weren't serious about that house-arrest stuff, right? I mean, now that we're all best buddies again?"

"Just stay out of the papers, okay, Doctor? *And* out of the morgue."

Chapter Fifty-seven

Outside Sinclair's office, I remembered that I owed Harvey Blalock a call. But the lawyer beat me to it. I'd no sooner gotten behind the wheel and pulled out of the Federal Building garage when my cell rang.

"Dan?" His tone sounded urgent.

"Harvey," I said. "I was just about to call you. Tell me you've got good news."

He hesitated only a moment. "I guess that depends. I just heard from Wingfield's people about Dr. Camden. The hospital called them. Seems he's taken a turn for the worse."

"What do you mean?"

"They don't think he's gonna make it through the day."

I let his words sink in, even as I changed lanes to make the left onto Liberty Avenue, toward Pittsburgh Memorial. The midday sun flashed sharply across my windshield, like the path of a searchlight, as I turned into the logjam of downtown traffic.

"Thanks, Harvey," I said at last. "I'll get back to you."

I got there in half an hour.

Once again, I found myself in my father-in-law's hospital room, standing at his bedside. Once again, I studied the blinking lights of the machinery keeping him alive, the tubes and wires.

His eyes were closed. His proud face sunken, wrinkled like a flattened rubber mask. He was barely drawing breath.

The attending nurse, a smooth-skinned Korean woman of indeterminate age, had told me he'd been drifting in and out of consciousness for the past few hours.

"I don't think he even registers that you're here," she murmured. "But you can try holding his hand. It's what I do sometimes when a patient's ready to let go. I always hope it comforts them." A sad smile. "At least, I know it comforts me."

After she'd left the room, I stood looking down at him. Working through the cascade of conflicting feelings I had toward him. All the hatred and bitterness that we'd exchanged like gunfire. All the shared though unacknowledged grief that had carved the chasm between us since Barbara's death.

And now this. Sure as hell not the end he would have wished for. Christ, how insulting, how ignominious he'd find his own dying. Alone in a cold hospital bed, tubes going in and out. Being pitied by the likes of me.

It was then that I reached through the bed rails and, to my own surprise, took his hand. And squeezed.

Another surprise. Phil squeezed back. An involuntary response? Or only acknowledgement of my presence. Letting me know he was still in there.

I listened for a few moments to the wheeze of the machines, the clicking of the monitors.

"I'm sorry, Phil," I said. "I'm truly sorry."

I was about to turn away when I felt the barest, almost imperceptible closing of his bone-thin fingers, still encircled by mine. I stared down, rooted, as his hand slowly tightened in my own. And held fast.

"Phil...?"

Then, just as suddenly, his fingers relaxed again. His hand felt limp, like an empty glove, in mine.

I looked down at his motionless face. What had just happened? What did it mean?

Suddenly, a warning bell sounded from one of the bedside monitors. Instinctively, I touched his skin, dry and thin as rice paper. I felt for his pulse. Nothing.

I turned, my own heart pounding, eyes glued to the monitor screen. Flat lines marched in a row across its dull face...

Before I could react, two ICU nurses and a resident were rushing into the room, pushing a crash cart. I barely got out of the way as they huddled above the bed, the resident barking orders, the nurses moving in a kind of choreographed blur of activity.

Then, less then a minute later, the resident was calling the time of death for one of the nurses, and another staff physician—older, haggard—had arrived to survey the scene. He and the resident conferred briefly, in flat, unnecessary whispers, and then he turned to me.

"I'm sorry for your loss," he said, not unkindly.

I don't remember if I even answered him. I just stared, numb, at Phil Camden's body on the bed. That huge presence, that iron will, suddenly no more.

Had he been reaching out to me when he squeezed my hand? Had the chasm finally been crossed? Or had it been nothing more than reflex, the body's last involuntary exchange between muscle tissue and nerve endings?

I'd never know. Phil Camden was gone.

Leaving only a final, implacable silence.

Chapter Fifty-eight

As I headed up the hill toward Mount Washington and home, I glanced again in my rear-view mirror.

There it was, a blue-black sedan without front plates. Snaking in and out of traffic, keeping just the right distance back. Never accelerating or slowing in a way that would draw attention to himself. But always there.

He'd been following me since I drove out of the hospital parking lot, and then across town to the Fort Pitt Bridge. Maybe before that.

The only thing I know about being tailed I picked up from the movies. And a story my old man told me once about when a manpower shortage got him pulled off the beat and assigned for one night to a detail that was following a suspected low-level gangster. There'd been a rash of bank jobs, and the cops were so desperate for leads they'd begun shadowing every Capone wannabe in town.

"I was the wheel-man that night," my father boasted. "The detective sittin' next to me was some rookie kid who couldn't even fill out his suit. Didn't know the streets, the shortcuts. Didn't know shit. If it wasn't for me, we woulda lost the SOB in Murraysville."

He never got around to telling me what happened that night. If anything. Over the years, I've wondered whether the story was even true.

Then, as always, I'd feel like shit for doubting him. Maybe I should've given him more of a break. Maybe—

I glanced up at my rear-view again as I turned onto Grandview. Traffic had thinned. He'd be easier to spot.

But he was gone. Turned off a few blocks back, I figured. *If* anyone had really been following me at all.

I pulled into my driveway and looked at my quiet, empty house. Sitting behind the wheel, the engine still running, I knew what I should've been thinking about: *Had* I been followed? Was it *him*? The killer?

But I was thinking about my old man. How, like a good wheel-man, he still shadowed *me*. Knew the streets, the short-cuts. Knew, no matter how much I protested, me.

I grew up wanting so much not to be like him, only to find out how much I was. Prickly. Stubborn. Despite a couple degrees and a clinical license, just another hardass Italian kid from Pittsburgh.

I imagined him sitting in that shuttered house right now, nursing a Rolling Rock, waiting for me. With those weary, blood-shot eyes. Skeptical. Unimpressed.

And he'd be right. At least about one thing. This had all started with the brutal murder of one of my patients, a lost and troubled kid named Kevin. It didn't matter what his real name was, who his father was. None of it did.

Only one thing mattered. I'd promised myself I'd help find out who killed him, and I hadn't.

I shut off the engine and stepped out into a cool, blustery day overhung by thick white clouds. The break in the storm front had held since yesterday, and might hold another day still.

I breathed in the sharp, wintry air. My father wasn't in that house, waiting. He didn't have to be.

I'd told Sinclair that I was in this all the way, till the end. And I was. Which meant, I realized now, I had to do something I should've done before.

Go back to the beginning.

Chapter Fifty-nine

At the end of our last session, Kevin had said to me, "Hell, man, I've got *lots* of secrets."

During the past two weeks, I believed I'd learned what he meant. That his real name was Wingfield. That his father had been a participant in his sexual abuse as a child. And that not only was his mother's death a suicide, he'd experienced the horror of finding her body.

But what if I was wrong? What if the "secrets" he referred to were about something else?

I thought about this now, as I spread all the files relating to his case, and his prior treatment history, on my kitchen table.

I'd made some scrambled eggs, which I ate without tasting, and was on my second cup of black coffee. Sonny Rollins' throaty sounds from the CD player filled the kitchen, as did a somber afternoon sun.

I pulled the phone closer. I'd already listened to my messages, checked in with Paul Atwood, and called the hospital asking after Noah. Dr. Olsen was unavailable, but the duty nurse assured me Noah was recovering nicely.

"The perfect patient," she added. I'd smiled at the receiver. That's because he wasn't able to talk yet.

Finally, I turned my attention to the papers and files arrayed in front of me. It would take a while, but I'd have to go through it all. Again.

<>< >

It was nearing four in the afternoon when I got off the phone with Admissions at the Sisters of Mercy board-and-care home. Unfortunately, as a religious charity, their records of Kevin's treatment there were far less documented than would be required at state hospitals or private facilities. Moreover, Kevin's stay had been brief.

The nun I spoke with tried to be helpful. What few records they'd retained listed his name as Kevin Merrick. A good Samaritan had brought him to the home after finding him stoned out of his head and bleeding from superficial, self-inflicted cuts from a Swiss Army knife. He had twenty-eight dollars in his wallet and a Pitt student ID card.

"According to our files," the nun had explained, "he checked himself out about six weeks later. One of our counselors referred him for out-patient drug treatment, but there's no way to know if Kevin followed up."

Now, as I sorted through my files, I realized there was just one more call to make.

I glanced at the reports from Clearview Hospital. A sprawling, underfunded public institution on the North Side, it was the last known facility that Kevin had been admitted to, before seeing me.

I called and got the Assistant to the Head of Records, a Mrs. Vivian Boone. I'd just begun to identify myself when she cut me off.

"Oh, I know who you are, Doctor," she said, in a breathless voice. "You've been on the news."

"So everyone keeps telling me. Anyway, I *would* like to ask you some questions…"

"Of course." I heard some clicks from her computer keyboard. "However, according to our files, you've already been sent a complete copy of Mr. Merrick's records from his stay here at Clearview…Oh, dear, I suppose I should call him Mr. Wingfield now, shouldn't I?"

"Let's just refer to him as Kevin," I said. "It'll be easier. And, yes, Mrs. Boone, I have all the hard copy here with me. But I was looking for something that might *not* be in the record. I wonder, is there someone I could speak to who happened to be at Clearview during Kevin's stay?"

"You're speaking to her," she said proudly. "I worked in Admissions. This was a few years back, when I first began here. But I do remember Kevin quite vividly."

"You do?" This took me by surprise. Clearview was a huge facility. "I'm amazed you can remember one patient out of so many you've admitted over the years."

"Well..." She paused. "After what happened to Loretta Pruitt...I mean, nothing was ever *proven*. But a place like this, you can't help but hear the rumors."

"I don't know a Loretta Pruitt. What happened?"

"Oh, Loretta was a lovely girl, just lovely. But in terrible shape when she came to us. Drug use. Trouble with the law. Bipolar, I think the doctors said." Another pause. "Do you need me to pull up her records?"

"Not yet. You seem to have a good memory."

The flattery found its target. "Well, I *am* good with details. Have to be, in this job. Anyway, here's the thing: poor Loretta was murdered. Strangled."

"Murdered? When?"

"That's the whole point, isn't it? I mean, about Kevin and everything. See, Loretta was found one morning, on the lawn outside the east wall, wearing only her nightgown. The police said she'd been strangled during the night, up on the roof, and then thrown off. Like an old bag of garbage. Just broke all our hearts."

"My God, I'm sorry. It must have shaken everyone. But what does this have to do with Kevin?"

Her voice fell to a conspiratorial low. "Doctor, most people around here think *he* did it."

Chapter Sixty

"Here's where they found her." Vivian Boone, a matronly woman in a yellow rain slicker and hood, pointed at the coarse earth at our feet. "Poor thing."

We stood in the damp night air, breath frosting like exhaled smoke, on the east lawn at Clearview Hospital. Though it was obvious no grass had grown here in a long time. Nothing but a broad expanse of hard ground and rain-etched rivulets.

Now Mrs. Boone was pointing to the edge of the roof, five floors above.

"The police said she must've been thrown from up there. Already dead. Dear God."

I squinted up against the gloom, as though there was anything to see after three long years. The roof eave was a stark silouette against the black, pouting sky. Torn shingles dangled from the edge, turning in the wind.

It was nearly nine o'clock. We stood alone in the blustery yard beneath the massive building, one of a quartet of grimy cinder-block structures covering almost a square mile of the city's squalid North Side.

Just then, a powerful klaxon horn bleated out a series of short, biting notes.

"Lockdown," Mrs. Boone said.

I followed her hurried steps toward the barred side door. Waited as she fumbled for the right key.

Like some kind of Dickensian throw-back, Clearview was a heavily-secured public facility for the clinically insane, the indigent, and the socially inconvenient. Just twenty miles from Ten Oaks, it seemed light-years removed in space and time. The cold, looming walls were streaked with graffiti, and worse. The grounds a moonscape of broken concrete and debris.

Outside, just beyond high barbed wire, crack houses and rusted-out cars and broken men sleeping in boxes.

Mrs. Boone was tugging my sleeve. Her face was pink from the cold. I smiled and pulled the heavy door open, ushering her inside.

After our initial conversation, it had taken a few hours—*and* another round of calls—to get permission to visit, as well as to cajole Vivian Boone into staying late and showing me where Loretta Pruitt had been found. It hadn't been hard; the tragic events seemed to thrill her.

"Like I said, Kevin was never officially a suspect," she said now, leading me through the labyrinth of narrow, unpainted corridors. With lock-down, the lights had all been dimmed. "But there were rumors that he'd had a special relationship with Loretta. The kind we don't encourage, as you can imagine."

Our route took us past rows of small, recessed rooms, from which came guttural cries and the occasional, wrenching sob that trailed after us like a reproach. I tried to imagine someone as fragile as Kevin in such a place.

She seemed to sense my thoughts. Her face turned under the hood. "I know, things could be better around here. But there's nothing we can *do*. Our budget's been slashed. Place is held together by string and paper clips."

Mrs. Boone stopped abruptly, eyes narrowing. "But we *do* help these poor people. As much as anyone can."

I nodded, but she wasn't buying.

"Anyway," she said briskly, fishing in her raincoat pocket. "I dug out a photo of Loretta, from her file."

I glanced quickly at the yellowing picture. She'd been right about one thing: Loretta Pruitt was pretty. Early 20's, maybe. But thin, wan. Haunted eyes.

I handed back the photo. "You said there were rumors about Loretta and Kevin?"

She nodded, as we continued down the corridor.

"They'd been seen together a lot before that night. Eating together. In the rec room. Just talking, apparently. But keeping to themselves."

"That doesn't prove anything. Certainly not that he had anything to do with her death."

"No." Her voice cooled considerably. "But he checked himself out of Clearview the day after Loretta died. *The very next day.* As soon as the police were finished interviewing him, he just... vanished. A lot of people around here felt the police should have dragged him back for more questioning, but they said they had no cause."

We'd reached a set of paneled double-doors, leading to the staff offices. She pulled the hood back from her head.

"Besides," she said, "Kevin threatened to ask for a lawyer, a public defender, if they tried to hold him."

I said nothing, trying to picture the Kevin I knew demanding legal counsel. Demanding *anything.*

Mrs. Boone clucked her tongue impatiently.

"Sorry," I said. "Just thinking."

"I know. A terrible thing. Loretta's murder cast a real pall around here. Some of the top staff even quit. As for that Kevin— well, you'll never explain to *me* why he was in such a hurry to leave the scene of the crime."

As I was thanking her for her time, the doors opened and a tall, slender man with a shock of white hair stepped out. Mid-sixties. A sour face behind bifocals.

"You must be Dr. Rinaldi," he said. "I'm Dr. Calvin. Mrs. Boone here said you're interested in Kevin Merrick. Or whatever they say his real name is."

"Did you know him? Were you on staff at the time?"

He frowned, adjusting his glasses. "I've been on staff since the Ice Age, Doctor. And yes, I treated Mr. Merrick for a short time. It's in the file," he added.

"Of course." *Christ.* "Tell me, what kind of patient was Kevin?"

"Difficult." Dr. Calvin gave me a weary smile. "Now, if you'll excuse me…"

He turned toward the door, Mrs. Boone following right behind. Then, hand on the doorknob, he glanced back at me.

"One thing you *won't* find in the file. Curious thing. Toward the end of our work together, Mr. Merrick started wearing glasses like mine. Even seemed to be combing his hair as I did."

My eyes widened. "Yes. What did you do?"

His gaze was incredulous. "I put a stop to it, of course. Good-night, Doctor."

‹›‹›‹›

I was still roiling with anger as I strode across the deserted parking lot outside the main building.

Goddam it! Even three years ago—even *here*—Kevin had reached out for some kind of connection. For a mirror to hold his shifting, incomplete sense of himself. Only to have it stamped out by some hide-bound relic who should've long since just taken his gold watch and gone fishing.

I reached my car, and gave myself a moment to cool down.

Whenever I get self-righteous, I'm usually trying to turn my own guilt into anger. The plain fact is, the mental health profession had a number of chances over the years not to fail Kevin, and we blew every one.

I took a breath. If I wasn't going to blow *this* one, I had to stay focused.

Was the murder of Loretta Pruett the secret Kevin had alluded to? And if he'd lived to stay in treatment, would he have ever told me about it?

I was still thinking about it as I turned my key in the car door. Then my hand froze.

A hundred yards to my left, a broad shadow seemed to separate from the larger darkness and move toward me.

A car, picking up speed. That same blue-black sedan, engines roaring. No lights on, bearing down.

He'd followed me here. Been waiting for me. And now—

Before I could move, the sedan suddenly flashed its brights and made a U-turn in the lot, wheels spinning.

Spewing dust and gravel, he raced back the way he'd come and headed for the exit.

Like hell. I climbed into the Mustang and peeled out after him. Our engines sounded like staccato gunshots in the dark, desolate night.

He sped up and barreled through the opened exit gate, fishtailing onto Harris Avenue. By the time I got out of the lot, he'd already raced up the street and disappeared.

Engine idling, I stared through my windshield at the end of the street, where tendrils of exhaust drifted like firecracker smoke.

Chapter Sixty-one

New storm clouds spread like ink blots outside the dirty precinct windows, as I made my way across the detectives' floor. But I wasn't here to see Polk or Lowrey. I was here to see Detective Second Grade Ed Hingis.

He wasn't at his desk. A uniform told me Hingis was downstairs in the target range, practicing for his upcoming placement test. So I went down there.

Ed Hingis was tall, black, and an excellent shot. He'd just finished a round. We stood there in silence, watching the familiar silhouette target being wheeled along its guide wire into Hingis' hands. The bullet holes were pretty evenly divided between the head and the chest.

He led me out a side door into an alley fronting the motor pool. The night was dark, cold, and moonless.

Hingis lit up a slim cigar. "Brass don't mind the cigs, but they'd prefer you smoke these babies outside."

"So," I said, to a cloud of acrid smoke, "tell me about that night. About Kevin Merrick."

"Not much you don't know, I'd guess. Couple uniforms found him wandering around a store in his pajamas. They brought him in and I happened to catch it. Slow night."

"You interviewed him in the Box, right?"

"At first, I didn't know what we were lookin' at. Maybe the kid was a vic, maybe a perp. Ya never know."

"What did he tell you?"

Hingis sighed, and flicked ash against the side of the brick building. His cigar end flared in the darkness.

"Look, Doc, I know you're sorta on the job, and I guess you feel guilty about the kid. But you're wastin' your time. I grilled him for an hour. Says he surprises this guy goin' through his stuff, they fight, he escapes and starts runnin'. Then he blacks out. Don't remember nothin' else, till the uniforms pick him up. But like I said, you *know* all this, right?"

I nodded. By now, I was starting to feel like I was foraging in a barren field, looking for crumbs.

"So then you called Angie Villanova," I said, "and she called me. Something about Kevin's manner worried you."

"Not *me*, Doc. The Assistant DA. *I* ain't no social worker. She watched the interview from outside the Box." He shrugged. "Didn't seem that interested. Guess it wasn't high-profile enough for her. If ya know what I mean."

The detective fell silent. I shook his hand. "Look, thanks for your time. And good luck on your test."

"Luck is for losers," Hingis said. The tip of his cigar burned hot, eating oxygen.

❬❭❬❭❬❭

I stood in the doorway, arms folded.

"Bert, I need your help."

I'd found Bert Garman in his office at Ten Oaks, head bent over thick account ledgers. Some opened Chinese take-out was placed strategically atop the desk.

"You're starting to worry me, Bert," I said, stepping inside. "Don't you ever leave this place?"

"And go where? Home to an empty house? Empty bed?"

I sat on the edge of his desk.

"Besides," he went on, "I doubt you'd want any help from me. Not given the way my life's going at present."

"Sorry. I know." A pause. "Marital status?"

He managed a feeble smile. "Last I heard, Elaine was talking to lawyers—and *not* about her defense in Brooks Riley's murder. She knows they'll never even get an indictment. Not without the gun."

I spoke carefully. "Look, Bert. I know *I* was the one who steered the cops to Elaine. But maybe I'm wrong. Maybe I let my feelings for Nancy Mendors cloud my thinking."

Garman sat back in his swivel chair, hands behind his head. "No, you're not wrong. Elaine killed Brooks."

"How can you be so sure?"

"She told me. After getting assurances from her attorney that communications between husband and wife are privileged, she confessed to killing him. Though it wasn't exactly a confession. More like... I don't know, but she sure enjoyed telling me about it."

"Jesus Christ."

"She's hated me for a long time, Danny. *Really* hated me. I mean, it's actually sort of breathtaking."

We were silent for a long moment.

"I still love her, by the way." He grimaced. "Yes, I still love the coke-snorting, murdering bitch-on-ice. Kind of makes me a tragic figure, don't you think?"

I'd never pictured Bert Garman as a disillusioned romantic, but lately a lot of people were turning out to be full of surprises.

Right now, on the other hand, he wasn't looking too good. He'd started drinking long before ordering in dinner, maybe even from a bottle hidden in a desk drawer. He wouldn't be the first therapist I knew who did.

"Look, I ought to call you a cab," I said. "You look beat, and you're in no condition to drive."

He made a point of focusing his gaze. "You should have seen me an hour ago. But you're right, I've got to get out of here. Besides, didn't you say you needed my help with something?"

"Yes. About Kevin Wingfield. But—"

Garman fished in his jacket pocket and came up with a set of keys. He tossed them to me.

"We'll take my car, but *you* drive. How's that?"

Chapter Sixty-two

A hard, stinging rain had begun pounding the city. I squinted through the sweep of clicking windshield wipers, steering Garman's BMW through the winding streets. I was headed to a Starbucks I knew, by way of Edgewood, passing rows of venerable houses with mansard roofs, Republican lawns.

I glanced over at Garman, whose head lolled against the neck-rest, eyes riveted on the storm.

"Look, we can talk about Kevin tomorrow," I offered.

"No, I'm okay," he replied. "Funny, though, 'cause I've been thinking a lot about Wingfield. The father, I mean. I think *he* was the one who killed Kevin. *Had* him killed, anyway."

"Wingfield had his own son murdered?"

I heard the smile in Garman's voice. "Hey, you're not the only one who can play detective."

A boom of thunder almost drowned out his words. His head swiveled toward me at last.

"Okay," I said. "Why Wingfield?"

"Because somehow he found out that Kevin was in therapy with you. Maybe he was afraid you'd learn about his incest with his children and cause a scandal—not to mention possible ruin. Makes a helluva motive."

"I don't know. Wingfield's probably a sociopath, but even *they* usually value their children. If only as extensions of themselves."

"I'm not saying he wanted *Kevin* dead. He wanted to silence *you*. Once you knew what he'd done to his kids, you were a threat. The cops have been right all along—you *were* the target. Except that because Kevin had begun to dress like you, Wingfield's hit-man got the wrong guy. He accidentally killed Wingfield's own son."

A web of lightning flashed against the clouds roiling overhead. Rain lashed against the car windows.

But I barely noticed. I was thinking about Carl Trask, Wingfield's Head of Security. If Garman's theory was right, Trask might be the likely hit-man. Wingfield would have to choose someone very close to him and totally reliable.

There was just one problem.

"Wait a minute, Bert. If you're right, doesn't that mean Wingfield would need to kill *anyone* who'd treated Kevin—or knew *Karen*, for that matter. And that's not possible. If he were really afraid of exposure, it *would* be simpler to kill his kids."

I thought some more about it. "But since that's unlikely, he'd instead try to *buy* their silence. Maybe that's what he was doing when he hired detectives to track them down and offer them a big piece of the Wingfield fortune."

"Unless he'd never *had* to worry about any of this before now." Garman shrugged. "Maybe Kevin kept the incest to himself all these years. I remember from our peer supervision sessions, you reported that Kevin said he'd never told anyone before telling you."

"That's right. But how would Wingfield know what Kevin was revealing to me in treatment?"

"Your session notes," Garman said. "In your office."

Two cars ahead of me, an SUV was fish-tailing at the flooded intersection to a chorus of bleating horns. I threw another look at Garman, then made a sudden right onto a side street and parked at the curb.

I turned in my seat. "Let me just talk this out. Maybe Wingfield's been keeping tabs on his kids all along. At least on Kevin. Especially since the robbery attempt. Someone following Kevin to his sessions with me twice a week. A pro who would know how to get into my office and pick the lock on the filing cabinet."

Garman's voice rose. "So the guy makes photos of your treatment notes and shows them to Wingfield…"

"Who sees that Kevin is spilling everything to me. Wingfield can't take the chance on trusting my professional ethics when it comes to confidentiality. He had to worry that, sooner or later, Kevin would tell me his real name. Moreover, Wingfield knows I'd have a duty to warn about any current contact he might be having with minors. Abusers know all the rules. So he sends a goon to kill me."

"Only Kevin dies instead," Garman said.

"Which explains all those death threats against me. The knife in my office. The manikin. Wingfield wants me to know that the killer's still out there, waiting to try again."

Garman looked puzzled. "What manikin?"

I smiled. "Oh, yeah. The cops kept the second threat under wraps. Probably the only thing so far that hasn't been leaked."

Garman tugged at his lower lip. "Well, what do you think? Should we tell all this to the cops?"

"It's *your* theory, Bert." I drummed my fingers against the steering wheel. "I don't know, though. Something about it feels wrong…"

My cell phone rang. I snatched it out of my pocket. It was Casey. She was breathless.

"Danny, I thought you'd want to know as soon as I did. We found Wingfield. Or at least, we know where he is. One of his execs at the Burgoyne admitted that he'd helped arrange Wingfield's departure."

I sat up straighter, at the same time turning the key in the ignition.

"Where is he?" I said into the phone.

"Pittsburgh International. There's a small, private outfit on the satellite strip called SkyLark Aviation. Very exclusive. Runs jets for corporate clients, VIP's. Turns out, SkyLark's owned by Wingfield BioTech."

I laughed. "Of course it is."

Garman tapped my shoulder. "Hey, what's going on?"

I ignored him. "You sending in the troops to pick him up?" I said to her.

"I was afraid you'd ask. Sinclair's on a conference call with three federal agencies figuring out how to approach Wingfield. With no credible evidence..."

"And meanwhile, Wingfield flies off to Pago Pago—"

Her tone sharpened. "Look, I don't like this any more than you do. My guess is, we're going to at least have his plane held. Maybe use the weather as an excuse..."

Again, I felt the gnawing sense that something was wrong. And that if Wingfield was allowed to escape, it'd never be put right...

"Okay," I said into the phone. "I hope when the vote comes down, it's in favor of sending a platoon of cops to the airport. Because I'd hate to crash the party alone."

"Danny, no—!"

I clicked off and turned to Bert Garman.

"Okay, Bert, get out of the car."

"What? This is *my* goddam car!"

"I promise you'll get it back. Now scram."

"No. If you're going after him, I'm going with you."

"Like hell. Get the fuck out of the car."

"*No*, Danny. Wingfield's screwed with *my* life, too. When the shit hits the fan, he's going to lose everything. The Feds'll freeze his assets. His purchase of Ten Oaks will be tied up with accountants for years. And I—"

His jaw tightened. As though to stop the words.

"And you were going to be so rich," I said quietly.

He drew a long breath. "You have no idea..."

I rubbed my eyes. I didn't have time for this. Not when every minute counted.

"Look, I don't know exactly what I'm going to do when we get there. But I *do* know you're keeping your ass in the car. Try to come with me, I'll lay you out. I mean it."

He spread his hands. "Hey, man, you're the only hero type in this car. I just want to see the bastard hauled away in cuffs."

I pulled out onto the street.

With the rain rattling the windows, visibility a joke, and two lanes of bumper-to-bumper traffic between me and the nearest on-ramp, I was concentrating so hard on driving that I guess I didn't notice it.

The blue-black sedan with no front plates.

Following.

Chapter Sixty-three

Skylark Aviation was a beetle-shaped, four-story structure, nestled behind security gates at the far edge of the airport. The top floor, aglow with lights blurred by the driving rain, was a circular bulb of bowed glass and curved struts, affording an expansive view of the runways stretching to the hills.

I'd taken the first airport exit and then swung around the two-lane outer rim, almost skidding on the sluicing water, until I spotted SkyLark. Other than a few cars in the lot, fronted by chain link and a well-lit guard kiosk, there weren't any signs of activity.

"That guard's gonna stop us," Garman said nervously.

"I know."

I glanced over at the small hangar attached to the west side of the building. Through its mural-sized windows, I could make out the shapes of three large corporate jets with the SkyLark logo emblazoned on their tails.

I was still debating what I was going to say to the guard when I opened my window and pulled to a stop at the kiosk. The lights on within revealed a trio of monitor screens, ledger book and phone. But no guard.

"What the hell?" Garman peered past me into the guard box. "Think we can just go in?"

"I wouldn't, if I were you," came a harsh voice just beyond and behind my window.

Before I could react, my door was jerked open by a smiling, narrow-eyed Carl Trask. Holding a machine pistol in his free hand.

"C'mon out." He stepped back, unmindful of the rain dousing his uncovered head. His gun——maybe an Uzi, I didn't know—was pointed at my chest. "You first, Doc, then your friend."

I got out of the car, hands away from my body. Garman scrambled out behind me. Trembling, he had to grip the door frame to steady himself.

Ignoring him, Trask stared at me. "Okay, let's get out of the rain. Mr. Wingfield wants to have a little talk with you. After that, he said you an' me could have the next dance. I'm really lookin' forward to it."

He leaned in, face inches from mine. Then he rammed the point of his gun in my ribs. Pain exploded in my gut, and I doubled over, gasping. It took everything I had to stay on my feet.

"Oh, Christ." Garman sagged against the car, voice cracking.

Trask laughed and silenced Garman with a look. I straightened up, gulping air. Trask nodded at the building, and Garman and I walked stiffly ahead of him toward the entrance.

‹ › ‹ › ‹ ›

Miles Wingfield stood at one of the bowed windows, looking out at the lights.

He didn't bother to turn as Garman and I were brought at gun-point into the spacious lounge. Typical *Fortune 500* mileu: crystal fixtures, shining wet-bar, polished Japanese wood cabinets. Money likes to see money.

The only other person in the carpeted room was a steward of some kind, a slender man in his fifties in a crisp black suit. His breast-pocket handkerchief formed a neat triangle of white. He was pouring Dom Perignon into a fluted glass and studiously avoiding looking at the Uzi glued to my back.

"Thank you, Stevens," Wingfield said, staring at his own reflection in the glass. The steward looked up. "I'll be the only one drinking."

The steward replaced the bottle in its standing ice bucket and padded out of the room.

After the door closed behind him, Wingfield turned and gave me that small, tight smile. Another tailored Italian suit, black silk shirt, and tie. Hands in his pockets.

"Time is short, Dr. Rinaldi. For all of us. So say your piece and let's bring things to an end, okay?"

As before, his voice smooth, amiable. Eyes veiled with a milk-white film.

"It's over." I feigned a bravado I didn't feel. "The cops are on their way. The Feds. Hell, with any luck, CNN."

"Yes, I know." Wingfield was unperturbed. "Though not quickly, I assure you. One of my friends in Justice is slowing things down as best he can."

"I'm not surprised." And I wasn't.

"Before they get here, with their lawyers and their warrants, I'll be long gone. And you'll be dead."

Wingfield glanced past me at his head of security.

"Stand over by the doorway, will you, Carl? If that gun goes off in your hand, you're liable to spray the whole damn room."

I heard Trask snort behind me, then felt the pressure of the gun ease off my spine. Out of the corner of my eye, I watched the big security man lumber over to the door.

Wingfield sighed, and swiveled back to me. "I had so wanted to see you destroyed, Doctor. To deliver the public humiliation and ruin you deserve. Your death would have come eventually, of course, when it suited me. But now it looks like that'll have to happen sooner rather than later. Though Carl promises me it *will* be a long, agonizing process. Right, Carl?"

"You got my word on that, sir."

"And the photos?"

"I'll Fed Ex 'em to you. Pre- and post-mortem. You won't be disappointed."

Standing next to me, Bert Garman looked kind of queasy. I jerked my thumb toward him.

"You mind if he sits down?" I said to Wingfield. "He's not as used to this kind of thing as I'm getting to be."

Wingfield motioned to a chair. Garman collapsed into it, taking what was probably his first breath since we'd driven up to the guard shack.

Just then, a phone on the table near Wingfield rang. He picked it up, listened a moment, and hung up.

He walked toward me. "That was my pilot. Seems we have clearance to depart. He's rolling our jet out of the hangar as we speak."

"Where are you headed?" I asked.

"Does it really matter, especially to you?"

"I'm a therapist. I like closure."

Wingfield gave a short laugh. "You know, Doctor, in a way I'm glad you were foolish enough to come here. I can console myself that I was able to look you in the eye one last time before you died."

"Too bad you can't say that about James Stickey."

"Who?"

"Stickey. The guy who broke into Kevin's apartment to rob him. The guy you had killed in prison."

"Oh, yes. The piece of ghetto trash who dared assault a member of my family." He shrugged. "That was nothing. Just a loose end. In memory of my late son."

"Who *you* had killed," Bert Garman gasped. They were the first words he'd spoken in ten minutes.

Garman's face blanched to a whiteness matching that of his eyes. Sweat beaded his hairline.

"Dr. Garman." Wingfield turned to him. "I recognize you from Peter Clarkson's description. He said you were a fool, though I've always thought otherwise. Not after the fine job you've done with Ten Oaks. I've seen the numbers. Very impressive. I was happy to acquire it."

He stood over Garman, who shrank back in his chair. Wingfield lifted his hands out of his pockets and put them firmly on Garman's shoulders.

"But for a man of your clinical experience, your grasp of my character is pathetic. I *loved* my children, both of them. In ways you could never possibly imagine. We shared intimacies beyond your feeble dreams. I could no more kill Kevin than kill myself."

Wingfield straightened then, tapping the tips of his fingers together as though in deep reflection.

"So maybe poor Peter was right, and you *are* a fool. Doesn't really matter. I *was* going to keep you on as clinical director, but I suspect UniHealth is about to undergo a drastic restructuring. The government will freeze everything during the inevitable investigations to come. So, frankly, I'm not going to need you around."

He smiled over at Trask. "You mind taking care of Dr. Garman here, along with Rinaldi?"

"No!!" Garman tried to wriggle out of his seat, but Wingfield shoved him down with surprising strength.

Leaning against the door, Trask nodded soberly. "No problem, Mr. Wingfield."

As Wingfield gave Garman's shoulder an almost paternal pat, I scanned the room, figuring the odds.

On the one hand, I had nothing to lose. On the other, I didn't see a move. Trask and his gun were a dozen feet away from where I stood. And though I assumed Wingfield wasn't armed, I had to take the possibility into account.

My brow was wet with sweat, my breathing shallow. I tried to think. Focus.

Miles Wingfield sniffed noisily. "Okay, Carl. Time, as they say, is money."

I saw that same shift in his body language, the thing I'd sensed before at the Burgoyne. His transaction with Garman and me was over. Old business.

Meanwhile, Trask was motioning to Garman and me with the Uzi. "Okay, assholes. Move."

My mind raced as we walked slowly toward the door. Maybe outside, in the stairwell. He'd skipped the elevator bringing us here to the top floor, so probably he'd do the same going down. Maybe I had a shot at something there.

I heard Bert Garman's quiet, almost resigned breathing beside me as we reached the door. Mentally drifting, going away somewhere in his head. Dissociating...

Already dead. Already gone.

Chapter Sixty-four

Trask tapped my shoulder blade with the gun. "C'mon, open the goddam door."

I took a breath and reached for the door handle.

Suddenly, the handle turned itself.

Trask sputtered. "What th—?"

The door flung open. I turned fast, my shoulders pushing Trask's gun hand aside. He staggered back as I pivoted and grabbed the gun barrel.

Everything happened at once. I grappled with Trask for the Uzi, our bodies slamming against the near wall. Suddenly the gun went off, shooting a stream of bullets across the room. Bert hit the floor, hands over his head.

Shots pierced the huge windows, the shattered glass exploding into glittering shards. Wingfield crouched behind the table, unharmed. Trask and I still wrestled for the gun, his face a mask of rage. Then—

"Danny?..."

Casey's voice. Shrill, panicked. How? Where?

Trask drove me back against the wall again, knocking the wind out of me. The room tilted...

Had I even *heard* Casey's voice?

Or was it her voice screaming in my mind as I struggled furiously with Trask, the lethal gun caught between us. I pulled his fingers from the trigger, but now he used the gun as a club, ramming its barrel into my side.

We careened through the opened door onto the floor of the narrow hall, arms locked, gasping, straining, cursing.

Then, a shadow of movement. Someone running out of the lounge. Legs moving past us. Bert Garman, heading down the hall, toward the stairs.

Trask buried his elbow in my throat, bearing down with all his weight, eyes glazed with murderous fury. The will to fight began draining from me.

A sound I didn't recognize boiled up from my throat. I reared and butted his head with my own. He reeled back, sputtering. I managed to lock my hands around the gun and swung with all my might at his face.

Blood spurted in a wide gush as he howled in agony. His nose was split, cheeks caved in like craters. His eyes rolled up. Then he fell backwards, and stopped moving.

Gasping, spitting blood, I scrambled to my feet. Disoriented. Maybe in shock. I almost fell against the wall, but righted myself at the sounds of a fight coming from inside the lounge.

Voices. Screams.

I scooped up the gun and veered back through the door.

Casey and Wingfield struggled beside a shattered window, rain sheeting through its gaping hole.

He held a heavy bronze paperweight in his hands, and she was fighting him for control of it. An ugly red gash smeared her forehead.

"Casey!"

Her eyes blazing, Casey slammed Wingfield against the jagged glass shards, forcing him back onto its sharp teeth. He yelled, writhing in pain, and dropped the bronze to strike with his hands. Blood ran in thin rivulets from his neck and shoulders.

I ran towards them, gun raised. Wingfield snarled, slapping at Casey, snatching her hair, trying to keep his balance. With a fierce cry, Casey planted her feet and shoved him with all her strength.

Wingfield toppled back through the yawning opening in the glass, legs kicking at empty air.

And then he was gone.

His screams were a torrent of rage thrown up against the night. I got to the shattered window just in time to see him hit the rain-slicked pavement below with a sickening thud. His twisted body lay sprawled on the tarmac, pummeled by the storm.

Just as Richie Ellner's had lain broken against the rubble outside an abandoned factory a week before. From another fall. From another window.

The sputtering whine of twin engines drew my eyes away from the body below and toward the SkyLark jet taxiing out of the adjacent hangar.

At the same time, the phone rang behind me on the table. I didn't bother to pick up.

Miles Wingfield was going to miss his flight.

Casey came to stand beside me, her body trembling. I put my arm around her shoulders as she forced herself to peer out the window, rain pelting her face. She stared down at the pavement for a long time.

I spoke to her profile.

"Even after all he's done, it's still hard to see him dead. Isn't it?…Karen."

Chapter Sixty-five

"Bert probably went to call the police," I said, as Karen Wingfield and I slumped on the floor, backs against a broad wood cabinet. "So we don't have much time."

She merely sat there staring out at the storm. I dabbed the gash on her forehead with my handkerchief.

She found her voice. Soft. Tentative.

"How did you know?"

"I didn't," I said. "Not for sure. Until I spoke with Ed Hingis about the night Kevin was brought in. Hingis questioned him in the Box, but he told me you stayed outside, watching through the one-way. Yet Sinclair said you never did that. You liked to be *inside*, with the witness, the suspect. It occurred to me that you didn't go in the Box because you were afraid your brother would recognize you. Yet you were worried enough about his condition that you called Angie Villanova, asked that she refer Kevin to me."

Drops of rain pushed by the wind dotted her cheeks, her lashes. Her beauty hurt my heart.

"The name Casey," I went on, as though it mattered anymore. "It's from Karen Carlyle Wingfield. Your mother's maiden name is your middle name. So you used the first letters of each. Plus, like most people who assume a new identity, you picked a last name with the same first letter as your own. W, for Walters. Makes it easier to remember."

Though our shoulders were touching, sitting next to each other, I could feel us growing apart, moment by moment. A space, widening.

"Then I remembered Paula Stark. That robbery suspect you said you had to release for lack of evidence. You had gotten *her* to call the police from Arizona, claiming to be you. You gave her a script. All the things to say. No wonder she sounded drunk on the phone. She'd had to screw up her courage to get through the performance."

I took a breath. "That's why when she broke down at one point, and said she couldn't do it, you seemed so alarmed in Sinclair's office. I watched your face. I thought it was concern for Karen's plight. Instead, it was fear that Paula was going to blow it."

I couldn't tell if she was listening. Gazing out at the violent night.

"By pretending to be Karen Wingfield, Paula spoke *for* you. At last, the truth about your father's incest could be revealed. To the cops. To the world."

I stared at her until she looked back. Her eyes were empty.

"When did you decide to use Paula Stark? After Kevin was murdered?"

She took the handkerchief from me and began wiping the blood from her forehead.

"I ran away from Banford soon after my father left. I hated my foster parents, how they treated me. The poor, troubled Wingfield girl. Total slut. Did it with her own brother. Ruined her father's life. So I ran...and kept running. Changed my name, my look."

"Kevin told me he'd heard you'd gotten married."

"Lasted a couple years. A ranch kid out west. I got pregnant and he freaked. Times were hard. Believe me, it took everything I had to turn that detective away when he found me. Holding out my father's offer of reconciliation, and all that money. But I didn't want any part of my father. *Or* his money."

"Did you have the child? As Paula said on the phone?"

She smiled. "No. That was more Paula's life. I wove some of her personal story into mine to throw up a smoke-screen.

Besides, I figured the more similar to her own life, the easier time she'd have telling it."

She fell silent.

"You didn't answer my question, Karen," I said at last. "What about *your* child?"

"Like I said, my so-called husband freaked. Then he left. I didn't have anywhere to turn. So I got an abortion. Some quack in Taos, New Mexico."

She rubbed her face with her hands. "I was young. Broke. It was the only thing I could do. But I guess he botched it. They tell me I'll never be able to have children. Probably just as well. With *my* genes."

I shifted on the floor next to her, reached out to touch her. She stopped me.

"Don't, Danny. Please."

She leaned back, closed her eyes. "But it turned out I was smart. And God knows I have the gift for attracting men. So I picked out a rich one in Denver and got him to send me to college. I graduated *cum laude* and applied to law school. But he didn't want a lawyer, he wanted a blonde babe to drink wine spritzers with and impress his old-fart married friends. So we split and I came east again."

"Were you ever in touch with Kevin?"

"No. I'd heard from some distant relative about his being in and out of mental hospitals. After I started practicing law here, I put out some feelers. But of course I had people looking for a Kevin Wingfield. I didn't know he'd changed *his* name, too. So I never found him."

I said nothing, watched as tears began to slide from her closed lids.

"Eventually, I made enough of a name for myself to land a job in the DA's office. I won't pretend I'm not ambitious, Danny. And I like getting the bad guys."

"I can imagine why." I paused. "Then came the night they brought Kevin in, after he'd been assaulted…"

Karen pushed back the tears in her eyes with her palms. As a child does. As Kevin did.

"I happened to be working that night, so I went down to the Box to join the interview. Then, when I looked through the glass and saw who it was...It's funny, after all those years, but I recognized him immediately. My baby brother Kev."

"But that's what I don't understand. Why didn't you go inside? Let him know who you were?"

"I don't know, Danny. I just...couldn't. After all that time, wondering about him, trying to find him. But suddenly I was so ashamed. I realized *he* must have been, too. He'd changed his name, like I had. We'd each chosen to go on with our separate lives. What right did I have to screw with that?"

Her eyes found mine. "Besides, what if seeing me again did something bad to him? I mean, psychologically. Kevin seemed so fragile...like he was barely keeping it together as it was. So I didn't go inside. Didn't let him see me. But I was so worried about him, I called Angie Villanova."

She sighed. "I felt so much better when I knew he was in treatment with you. I thought it would buy me some time to figure out what to do. Whether to tell him about me."

Her voice caught. "And then he was murdered. My little Kev...poor baby...poor baby..."

She broke into wrenching sobs, and I cradled her in my arms. Kissed her wet cheeks, the side of her neck.

"I understand now," I said quietly. "When Wingfield came forward after Kevin's death...the grieving father, throwing his weight around with the cops..."

Her face craned up, flushed with anger.

"Yes!...That's when I decided to take him down. I owed it to Kevin to expose our father's crimes. But I didn't want to come forward myself. All that publicity. The loss of the life I'd built for myself. I couldn't give him *that*, too."

"So that night I first met you, when you complained to Polk about their case against Paula Stark..."

She nodded. "I'd already decided to use her. Polk was right. We *did* have enough to charge her. But I spoke with Paula in private and...well...committed a felony."

"You offered to let her walk, in exchange for leaving the state and making the calls to the DA's office, pretending she was someone named Karen Wingfield."

"Paula's not stupid. She knew ten minutes into my pitch that *I* was Karen Wingfield. But she didn't care. She treated me as though we were sisters-in-arms, fucked by men and the system and life. Don't get me wrong, she was happy to skate on armed robbery. But she was almost as happy to help bring down my sick bastard of a father."

"Where is she now? Do you know?"

"That part's the truth. She's somewhere in Europe. I arranged for the flight myself. With no outstanding warrants, Paula Stark and her son can go anywhere they want. She told me her plan was to marry a Count."

"Poor Paula."

"I know. But I wish her well."

I felt her move under my embrace, so I let my arm fall away. She gave me a sad smile, tossed the bloodied handkerchief on the floor beside her.

"It's funny," she said calmly. "It took Kevin's death for me to finally learn about his life all these years. From his hospital files. The Sisters of Mercy. Clearview Hospital. The suicide attempts. I know it's lame to think so, but maybe at least now he's finally at peace."

Another silence grew between us.

Finally, I found the words. Asked the only question that seemed to matter to me right then.

"Karen...why didn't you tell me who you really were? From the start?"

"I *wanted* to...really. But I couldn't take the risk. If my father found out who I was too early in the investigation, he might've bolted before we could bring him in. As it is, he almost got away..."

She averted her eyes. "Anyway, that's what I told myself. But it's not the truth. I was really afraid that if you knew I was Kevin's sister, you'd pull away from me. You'd think it was wrong, or unethical or something..." She took a short breath. "I was afraid I'd lose you..."

I hesitated. "You could never...lose me..."

She looked up at me again. Then her lips were on mine, a kiss as tentative as a school girl's. Then, just as quickly, looking away again.

I tried to think. *Would* it have mattered if I'd known? Probably not. I'd been lost in her from the moment I saw her, against my every instinct. Regardless of doubt or reason. Like a madness I welcomed with open, lonely arms.

And whose loss I was already beginning to feel...

She sniffed, giving me a sidelong glance. The old Casey. "Any other questions, Inspector?"

"Just one. About coming here. When you called and told me about SkyLark Aviation, and that Sinclair and the Feds were just treading water—"

"I'm sorry, Danny. It was a shitty thing to do. But I was afraid my father was going to escape. That he wasn't going to pay for anything he'd done. To me. To those poor patients. But especially to Kevin."

She tapped my chest with a closed fist. "I guess I hoped you'd feel something similar. That you'd get on your goddam white horse and—"

She looked down. "I didn't know what I wanted you to do. Stall him. *Kill* him. But then I realized I'd sent you into danger, and drove as fast as I could here myself."

"Good thing, too. If you hadn't opened the door when you did..."

"Oh, Danny..." She leaned up and took my face in both hands. Kissed me again, deeply this time, our lips slick with tears and rain and blood.

Suddenly, I heard Trask stirring outside the room. I got gingerly to my feet, hoisting the Uzi, and whispered for Karen to stay down. Out in the hall, I found Trask barely conscious, bleeding from the head and neck.

I called into the lounge. "Hey, this guy's not going to make it if we don't get an ambulance here soon."

Karen stood in the doorway, wiping tears from her eyes. "I thought you said Garman went for the cops."

"Dammit, I should've stopped him. There may be more guys like Trask in the building. Or in the hangar."

As if on cue, the phone in the lounge started ringing again. Karen ran to the broken window, shards of glass crunching under her feet, and peered into the night.

"The jet's still on the tarmac, with the engines going. And I don't see any patrol units. Any lights."

I took another look at Trask, then joined Karen in the middle of the lounge. I handed her the Uzi.

"What are you doing?" She gazed dumbly at the gun.

"I'm going to find Bert before it's too late. Use that damn phone and call the cops. If Trask moves, shoot him. Understand?" She managed to nod.

As I headed out of the room, her voice stopped me at the door. "Danny…?"

We looked at each other.

"Yeah, I know," I said, and hurried off.

Chapter Sixty-six

I took the stairs two at a time, stopping at each floor and searching the darkened halls. The office doors were all locked. No sign of security, or anybody working late. Maybe Wingfield had cleared the place out before.

On the lobby floor, I found a well-lit kitchen, and the steward, Stevens, huddling behind a tiled counter.

"Are you okay?" I went over and crouched next to him.

"I heard shooting." His teeth chattered. "Gunfire. At first I thought it was the plane's engines, but—"

"Where is everybody?" I asked.

"Mr. Wingfield sent his staff home earlier, except for Mr. Trask and myself. I was just about to leave when I heard the shots."

I pulled him upright, just as the faint sound of a siren in the distance pulsed through the walls. Somebody must have spotted Wingfield's body on the tarmac.

Steven stared at me, wide-eyed. "Perhaps I should stay here, sir. In case Mr. Wingfield needs me."

"Trust me, he doesn't. Feel free to take the rest of the night off."

I turned and headed back out to the lobby. More sounds from outside. Voices. Airport security, maybe.

I was too worried about Garman to wait and find out. After a quick search, I found the door to the hangar. It swung open with a pneumatic whoosh.

The tunnel itself was low-ceilinged, lined with lights like a runway and filled with Muzak piped in from hidden speakers. My running footsteps echoed as if in a dream.

The set of double-doors at the other end opened into the hangar, a yawning structure with high, curved walls and rows of hanging ceiling lights, none of which were on. I could only make out their outlines in the cross-hatch of shadows overhead. What light there was came from small wall lamps placed at intervals around the hangar.

I made my way carefully through the dim, nearly empty space. Except for the two remaining Skylark jets angled away from me, their wheels locked.

My footsteps clicked on the concrete as I moved around the fuselage of the nearer jet. The cockpit was empty. Then a sudden rush of wind made me turn around.

At the far end of the hanger, the huge doors stood open, walls-on-wheels bolted to their tracks. Beyond, on the tarmac, I could see the jet Karen had mentioned, still idling. Lights flashing. Waiting to take off.

As I crept slowly across the floor, my thoughts kept returning to Casey—to Karen. Something she'd said was stirring in my mind. Some vague notion whose contours I couldn't yet see...

I heard a sound. A muffled cry—

My heart began to pound as I moved through the darkness, the emptiness. A feed-back loop of echoes and wind and the quick cadence of my own breathing.

Where the hell was Bert Garman?

Another dozen paces and I'd reached the second plane, sleek and silent, a dull sheen of plastic and glinting struts in the uncertain light. Its wings halved the space before me like knives suspended in air.

I ducked my head and slipped under the fuselage, coming up on the other side.

To nearly stumble over Bert Garman.

I jumped back, righting myself. He lay panting on the cold asphalt, one elbow down, trying to push himself up.

"Bert!" I helped him up.

"Danny." He gasped and began flexing the fingers of his right hand, more shamefaced than injured.

"What happened?"

"I guess I tripped."

He blinked in the dimness. "Look, I know I shouldn't have run off on you, but I went to call the cops. I can't find a phone. Everything's locked. Then I heard something and ran in here—"

He glanced around. "Dark as hell, isn't it? I keep stumbling over stuff, and…"

I just looked into his pale, watery eyes. And knew.

"*You* were at Clearview Hospital, weren't you, Bert?"

"What?"

"When Casey mentioned it upstairs, it reminded me. You were on staff there. You told me yourself, remember? You came from there to Ten Oaks."

"Yeah? So…?"

"You *knew* Kevin, didn't you? When he was a patient there. You were both there at the same time. Funny, during all this, you never mentioned that fact…"

Bert Garman shook his head sadly, then turned away. When he turned back, he held a gun.

"Aw, hell," I said.

"Yeah."

Chapter Sixty-seven

Garman waved the gun.

"Know what this is?" he asked lightly.

I shrugged. "A .22? Maybe a .38. I don't know that much about guns."

He beamed. "That's not what I meant. See, Danny, this is the gun that killed Brooks Riley."

"You mean—"

He took a couple steps back, out of my reach. No fool.

"My wife Elaine. My soon-to-be-*ex*-wife. She thinks she's so smart. Like I wouldn't find out about her and Riley. Like I'd stand for being cuckolded by that bitch. After all the shit she's put me through."

I had it now. The pieces clicked together in my mind.

"*You* killed Brooks," I said, "just before the patient riot. When you left your office for my files. You told Polk and me you'd just need a minute…"

"I was right. That's all it took."

Never taking my eyes from his gun, I reached to grip the wing strut beside me. I needed the feel of its cold solidity to ground me. Order my thoughts.

"You went down to Brooks' office, shot him, and brought the files back to your office. *Easy*. Then the alarm bell sounded. Per your arrangement with Lucy."

"Yep. See, you had the steps down right, but figured the wrong person. Elaine."

"But Lucy admitted to the cops it was Elaine who—"

"Christ, Danny. I *told* her to finger Elaine if the cops pressed her. *I'm* the one keeping her supplied with nose candy. Her main man, she calls me. Trust me, that's all she gives a shit about."

"While you get to see your wife charged with murder."

"Sweet, eh?"

He shouldn't have smiled. But he did, dropping his guard for only a moment.

Which was all I needed.

I pivoted off from the wing strut, kicking out at him with my left foot. Literally airborne for a second. I didn't connect—knew I wouldn't—but it changed the equation. Startled, he staggered back, gun jerking in his hand, firing. Into the rafters.

I hit the pavement hard and rolled to my left, under the jet's fuselage.

"Goddam you, Danny!" He righted himself. Fuming.

I stayed low, moving along the length of the jet's body, keeping it between me and Garman.

"Now where the fuck did you go?" Garman's voice echoed off the high ceiling.

I made my way to the jet's tail, crouched beneath the crosswings. Behind me, one of the hanging lamps threw an oval of pale light. I saw Garman's shadow creeping slowly on the other side of the aircraft.

At the same time, my mind raced, knitting the story together. What really happened at Clearview. Garman had had an affair with Loretta Pruitt, one of his patients. Maybe he wanted to break it off, maybe she did. But Kevin happened to be on the roof and saw the whole thing.

Garman was getting closer, on his side of the jet. My best bet was to keep him talking. Distracted.

"Kevin saw you strangle Loretta Pruitt, didn't he, Bert? That night on the roof."

His laugh was bitter. "So that's how we're gonna play it, eh, Danny? Cat-and-mouse. Okay, I'll play. Except I'm the one with the gun."

A shot boomed, loud as cannon-fire. I ducked just in time, as a slug tore into the jet's tail above my head.

"Truth is, Loretta was a total pain, but a maniac in bed. Nothing like a woman with low self-esteem, I always say. But I wanted to end it, so she threatened to talk. Destroy my career. Naturally I couldn't allow that."

His shadow froze where he stood, a silhouette with a gun in its hand. He was trying to orient himself.

I backed away from the jet, out of the light. Felt my way behind me in the dark with my hands.

I kept my voice even. "But she'd already told Kevin. They'd become friends. Maybe she even told him she was meeting you that night. So he followed her."

"Who cares? All I know is, I squeezed the bitch till she was dead and tossed her off the roof. Then I looked behind me and there's Kevin Merrick, staring at me…"

An irritated grunt. "Where the hell *are* you, Danny boy? This is getting—"

But I saw it coming. I rolled to the floor as Garman leapt from behind the jet's tail and fired. The bullet whizzed over my head and shattered a wall lamp, spraying glass. The pool of light winked out.

"Shit, Danny, now we're *both* in the dark."

Gulping air, I crouched and edged toward a bank of thick wooden work benches along a far wall. I had to keep pressing him, throw off his concentration.

"So Kevin sees you kill Loretta, you threaten him—"

"I didn't have to." I tracked Garman's footsteps as he advanced. "He *knew*. Ran down the stairs and disappeared. I searched half the night for him. Then all hell breaks loose the next morning. Cops everywhere. No way to get him alone, know what I mean?"

The footsteps stopped. The scrape of shoe on concrete as he swiveled, looking for me. "Funny thing. He *could've* told the cops what he saw right then. But he didn't."

"I'm not surprised."

And I wasn't. Kevin was probably traumatized by seeing Loretta killed. He'd spent a lifetime keeping secret the things that had been done to *him*. Or maybe he thought the cops wouldn't believe him. God knows what his mental state was during the questioning. I doubt he came off as a credible witness.

More importantly, Garman was a therapist at Clearview. A powerful authority figure, like his father. He probably figured Garman could get away with anything. Again, like his father.

"Kevin was too terrified to talk. That's why he took off. He knew his life was in danger."

"*His* life? What about mine?"

He fired again, and I winced as the bullet whistled past my ear. His anger was making him reckless.

"It drove me crazy knowing he was out there somewhere. That he might still talk. So I looked for him. Checked other hospitals. Everywhere. But he'd vanished."

He was on the hunt again, this time for me, moving, shifting, stalking. Like he'd stalked Kevin.

The sharp edge of a heavy work bench pressed against my spine as I leaned back, hugging the shadows. I was running out of options. Risking the sudden movement, I dropped to the floor and crawled behind one of the thick wooden legs. And, hopefully, out of sight.

"Then you took over at Ten Oaks. Which meant you led the peer supervision group. One day, years after Loretta's death, I present a patient for discussion. A kid named Kevin Merrick..."

Anger choked his words. "Can you imagine how it felt, hearing you describe him? Realizing that he'd surfaced at last."

"And was beginning to open up..."

"Right. He might tell you about Loretta's murder. You'd urge him to go to the cops. Even if he didn't, *you'd* know about it. And God knows where *that* would lead, confidentiality or not."

He was right about that.

Plus, I thought, Ten Oaks was just about to be acquired by UniHealth, which would make Garman a wealthy man. But Kevin Merrick could end all that.

"So Kevin had to go," I said. Moving again, pulling myself along the floor with elbows and knees under the row of work benches.

"No other choice, Danny boy. Then, when you presented his case, how he'd begun looking and dressing like you...I saw a way to kill Kevin but make it look—"

"Like *I* was the target," I finished for him. "That the killer had mistaken Kevin for me."

Garman changed position, an indistinct outline in a shaft of light from the opposite wall lamp. The gun barrel glinted dully.

He was talking easily now. Trying to draw me out. Get me in his sights.

"I didn't enjoy killing him, by the way. A bloody mess. I wanted it to look savage, crazy. That's why I thought the kitchen skewer was a nice touch."

"So was planting it in my office. Using the key that fell out of Kevin's pocket. So it would look like the killer was still out there, tracking me."

I'd crawled the length of the work benches, and was back near the tail fin of the jet. That's when I saw it, off to my right. Even from this new angle, it was nearly invisible in the dim light. A service ladder, aluminum, leaning against the fuselage on the other side of the jet.

I ducked low and crept silently toward it.

But still I had to finish it. Had to know it all.

"Same thing the night Richie Ellner died." I reached the ladder, started climbing. Raised my voice to dull the sound of my feet on the rungs. "The manikin, impaled with the second skewer."

"Cool, eh?" Garman chuckled. "See, I have it ready in the trunk of my car. Richie takes his little dive into eternity, I duck out in all the commotion, break into *your* car and put it behind the wheel. Your crazed killer strikes again!"

I stepped off the highest rung and onto the top of the fuselage. The surface was polished, slick. I quickly knelt, for better balance, both palms gripping the bowed width. I figured I'd also be harder to be see.

Taking a breath, I began sliding carefully along the top. Garman was on the floor on the other side of the jet, maybe a dozen feet forward and to my left.

Now the silence between us grew ominous.

I risked leaning out over the side and saw him, his face taut, alert. As though listening for my breathing. To find me, sense me in the darkness.

But suddenly all I could think about was Kevin. My patient. My responsibility. His sad, lifeless eyes looking up at me as I cradled him. His blood pooling beneath us in that cold, empty garage.

And Bert Garman. My friend and colleague. Who'd played me for a fool since this whole nightmare began—

And who whirled suddenly, eyes searching above him. Scanning along the top of the jet.

He knew where I was. His gun came up. He was taking aim—

With a gutteral cry, I sprang up and charged down the length of the fuselage, hurtling myself through the air at Garman, arms outstretched. He looked up, mouth agape, trying to register what was happening.

Too late. I was on him.

We hit the floor with bone-rattling impact. His gun went flying. He tried to scramble away, but I grabbed fistfuls of his shirt and collar, hauled him to his feet. Put everything I had into a hard right to the jaw.

His eyes rolled up in his head, but I didn't stop. *Couldn't.* As though suddenly possessed, in the grip of something deep, primal, out of mind. I hit him again.

My years of training in the ring, of technique and discipline, dissolved into nothing. My father's harsh lessons about holding back, staying in control—gone.

All I saw was a kind of pulsing scarlet before my eyes. All I felt was a nameless rage.

As I pounded his face and body. Felt the crack of bone, the pulp of bruised flesh beneath my knuckles.

Until, gasping, stunned at my own actions, I flung him to the floor. Moaning, Garman scuttled, crab-like, away from me. Spitting blood.

I looked down at my throbbing, reddened hands. What the hell had just happened? I swayed on my feet. My temples pounded, my ears rang. As though punch-drunk.

Maybe I was. Because I didn't see until too late that Garman had rolled over on his side. There was something in his hand. Metallic. He'd found his gun.

I took a half-step toward him, but my luck had run out. He fired, and I felt a searing pain slice across my side. My legs gave out from under me.

I hit the floor hard, hand going to my ribs. Blood oozed from between my fingers.

Garman, coughing blood and spit, face splotched with bruises, got shakily to his feet. It was taking his every ounce of strength to stay upright.

Breathing hard from the effort, he steadied his grip on the gun. Slitted eyes burning with malice.

"You shoulda killed me when you had the chance." Each word forced out between split, swollen lips. "You sure wanted to. But you don't got what it takes. Never will."

He raised the gun and aimed it at my head.

"Good-bye, Danny boy."

Suddenly, a harsh voice boomed.

"Freeze, Garman! Police!"

Sgt. Harry Polk was two-handing his regulation firearm and pointing it at Garman.

"I mean it, ass-wipe. Drop the fucking gun."

Garman's eyes flickered before he turned on one foot, gun sweeping the air, in Polk's direction.

Polk crouched and fired. Garman screamed as the bullet buried itself in his thigh and he collapsed to the floor, his gun skittering away.

Wincing, I managed to stand up as Polk came over, still holding his automatic on Garman's writhing body.

"He's a bleeder," Polk noted passively.

Eyes never leaving his suspect, he bent and scooped up Garman's gun. "The rest of him don't look too good, either. *Some*body got a little carried away, eh, Doc?"

I didn't give an answer. Didn't have one. At least not one I wanted to look at right then.

Instead, I wearily threw my jacket on the floor next to Garman. "Here. Wrap your leg in that before you bleed to death."

Garman gasped. "Fuck you."

Polk turned to me. "Ya know, for a shrink, you got lousy taste in friends."

"Not necessarily. I got *you*, right? Speaking of which, what are you *doing* here?"

"Hell, I've been followin' you for two days in an unmarked sedan. Only I missed the exit on the parkway, and got caught in traffic goin' the other way."

"How'd you know where I was?"

"I didn't. I was makin' myself nuts driving all around the airport, lookin'. Then Casey Walters calls me in my car, tells me to get my ass over here to Skylark."

He grinned. "Look, none of my business, but are you two hooked up or what? 'Cause *she* was the one who asked me to follow you in the first place. In case the killer tried somethin'. I figured, sure, why not? Then she'd owe me."

I clapped him on the shoulder. "Jesus, Harry. Looks like you saved my life."

Polk grimaced. "I lost my head."

He gestured at my blood-stained shirt. "Speakin' of your sorry-ass life, how bad *is* that?"

"It's nothing. He just grazed me."

"Let's see what a medic has to say. You can ride in the ambulance with your buddy Garman here." Again, that wolfish grin. "Won't that be fun?"

Garman wasn't going anywhere, but Polk cuffed him anyway before calling for an ambulance. Meanwhile, I'd already headed out of the hangar and back into the lobby.

In the distance, through the glass doors, I spotted Stevens talking to some security guys. Behind them was an airport vehicle, lights flashing. And a body on the ground with a sheet over it.

I took the elevator up to the top floor. The lounge was cold as a meat locker. Icy wind blew freely through its shattered windows. I found Trask, covered in his own blood, lying on the carpet.

And no one else.

I knelt and felt for his pulse. He was unconscious but still alive.

Slowly, I stood up again. Felt the bite of the wind. Heard the snap of strewn glass as I walked in a kind of circle around the room.

For no reason, really. As though it were something I ought to do. As another, final truth sunk in.

Casey—Karen—was gone.

And I knew, the way you sometimes know these things, that I'd never see her again.

Chapter Sixty-eight

Noah Frye was in the hospital rec room, playing some be-bop riffs on an ancient upright. His neck bandages were scarcely visible under his shirt collar.

"Hey, I hear you're getting out of here tomorrow." I pulled a folding chair up to the piano bench.

Around us, other patients played cards, watched TV, or complained about their ills to bored family members.

Noah's voice was a quiet rasp. "And I hear *you* just might escape a whole shit-load of litigation. Dr. Nancy came by with the news. Wingfield's lawyers have shrunk back into the netherworlds from which they spawned. Praise be."

"Not exactly. Though Harvey Blalock tells me they'll have enough on their plates for years to come without having to maintain a dozen lawsuits against me."

"Especially since the killer was after *Kevin* all along. Had nothin' to do with him lookin' like you."

"Where are you getting all this?"

"The self-same Nancy Mendors. She's got a *huge* jones for you, in case you didn't know." He winked. "But don't tell her I told ya. She's got me on enough meds already."

I stood up. "You going to be all right, Noah?"

"Other than an annoying throat-clearing tic, I think I've come through just fine." As if to demonstrate, he cleared his throat. "How about you? How's *your* war wound?"

I gingerly touched the bandage under my shirt. "I'll live. I'm going back to work tomorrow. See if my patients remember who I am."

"You woulda been better off takin' my advice and spendin' the past two weeks on a desert island."

"Next time, I'll listen."

I'd started off when a sharp seventh chord made me turn back again, to find Noah's sweet, familiar smile.

"Danny. The thing about life is, you don't always have to know everything. You just gotta know enough."

I left the rec room to the rhythmic strains of *Take the A Train.*

The hills stood cold and wet against thick, shoulderpad clouds forming a backdrop. The storm had left some minor rain damage in its wake, as well as slick cobblestone streets and rivulets of runoff. From my porch, I could see city maintenance trucks crawling dutifully through the old, low-roofed neighborhoods, belching exhaust.

There was a message on my office VoiceMail from Sylvia Lange. She was giddy as a teenager.

"Did you hear the news, Doc? 'Cause we're celebrating in Bucks County tonight!" Amid peals of laughter.

Before I could call her back, my home number rang. It was Sam Weiss.

"Listen," he said, "don't forget our deal. The rise and fall of Miles Wingfield is my next book, and I'm gonna need you big-time. Maybe even cut you in for a piece, since you're so famous now and everything. Though I hear you turned down Larry King *and* Katie Couric. Shit, Danny, I may have to do an intervention."

"I appreciate your concern. But all I want to do is get back to work. *And* find a good chiropractor."

"Forget that. Let me give you the number of the Happy Hands Massage Spa. Ask for Beverly."

"Look, Sam…"

"Hey, I almost forgot why I called. I need a quote from you for my story tomorrow about the Handyman movie."

"What about it? Now they're making it a musical?"

"They're not making it at *all*. The studio got spooked by all the bad press. Making a cult figure out of a serial killer, that kinda stuff. They're claiming the production fell apart due to 'creative differences,' but that's just Hollywood spin. I think they were afraid their 100-million-dollar picture would tank."

So *that* explained Sylvia's exuberant phone message.

"Well, I can't say I'm sorry."

"Me, neither. Score one for the good guys," he said cheerily, and hung up.

◇◇◇

I watched the sun dip behind the Point, sending silver lights darting along the Allegheny's darkening surface, then showered and dressed.

I had a dinner meeting scheduled tonight with Angie Villanova and the assistant chief. My guess was, they wanted to take advantage of the current publicity value of having me as a consultant while making sure my future actions stayed more within departmental guidelines.

Given recent events, I couldn't say I blamed them.

I glanced at my watch. Time to go. I bent at my living room window, making sure the plywood repair would hold for another night until the glass could be replaced. On the phone earlier today, Angie had insisted I have an alarm installed at the house. I told her I'd think about it.

I'd turned to the door when something made me look back into the room. At the small, rolltop desk on which sat my answering machine.

The message light was blinking. A call must have come in while I was in the shower.

I thought about checking it later. Instead, I went over and pushed the button.

It was Karen's voice. Plaintive, but steady. Sure.

"Danny, I couldn't just leave it like this, without saying good-bye. Without saying again how sorry I am for ...well, for the way things turned out. I have to disappear again. My real name will inevitably come out in the course of the investigation. As well as my arrangement with Paula Stark. I'm an officer of the court, and I've committed a felony. Tampering with evidence, for starters. Hampering prosecution. At least a half-dozen more. So the career I've worked so hard for is over anyway."

I heard the smile in her voice. "But I'm pretty good at re-inventing myself, as you know. And I'm already far, far away."

I sank into a chair, staring at the machine's blinking light. Imagining her on the other end of the line.

"You would've figured me out eventually, Danny. I know it. Hell, my own therapist back at college nailed it. Classic symptoms of an abused child. Borderline traits. Rapid mood swings. Like Kevin, eh? I remember reading that in your treatment notes. Except that in *my* case, I was light on the suicide attempts, heavy on the adventurous sex. My therapist said I 'sexualized my relationships.' Something like that. You know how you guys talk. He said the only connections I felt safe to make were erotic ones. Where *I'd* be in control..."

Something in her tone changed. Softened.

"Not that it ever feels that way to me. Most times, it just feels like I'm falling. Falling and falling. Never hitting bottom, but never getting to stop, either. You ever feel like that, Danny? Probably not. Not Mr. Stand-Up Guy."

A pause. "Well, maybe just the part about never getting to stop. I bet you feel like that all the time."

Her voice sank to a whisper. "I *did* love you, Danny. *Do* love you. And I hope...well, no. Better not go there." A longer pause. "Good-bye, Danny. Remember me."

‹ › ‹ › ‹ ›

I drove toward the lights of the city without even feeling the wheel in my hands, or hearing the drone of the all-news station on the radio. I just kept my eyes focused on the cars in front of me, the road ahead.

Until the meaning of the announcer's words suddenly penetrated the fog. It was unbelievable. Ironic, too, given what I'd learned from Sam Weiss only a few hours earlier.

Troy David Dowd, the Handyman, had been successful in his latest appeal. Once again, his planned execution had been stayed by a higher court. The announcer cut to a reporter on the scene, who had to shout questions at Dowd's attorney over the raucous protests of a surrounding mob.

Suddenly, I didn't feel like hearing the answers. Didn't much care. I shut off the radio.

So. Dowd's evil still lived in the world, at least for the moment. Miles Wingfield's didn't. Maybe some kind of balance had been struck. Maybe that's the best we can get.

As I wove through night-time traffic, I thought about Karen, and wondered what her life would bring. And Noah Frye, whose sanity depended on the right combination of pills and the goodwill of his friends. I wondered too about Harry Polk, getting drunk in some bar somewhere, nursing memories of his failed marriage. Even Harvey Blalock. Though I wasn't going to be needing his legal services, I had the feeling he and I might become good friends.

Finally, I thought about Kevin. Little boy lost, in Lowrey's words. Or else finally at peace, in the words of his sister. Depended on how you looked at it.

The night loomed thick and black and heavy over the horizon, and I drove into it with my eyes open.

In the end, I thought, it just came down to justice and compassion. Whether you're a cop or a shrink. The helper or the helped.

Justice and compassion. Everything else is just... talk.

To receive a free catalog of Poisoned Pen Press titles, please contact us in one of the following ways:

Phone: 1-800-421-3976
Facsimile: 1-480-949-1707
Email: info@poisonedpenpress.com
Website: www.poisonedpenpress.com

Poisoned Pen Press
6962 E. First Ave. Ste. 103
Scottsdale, AZ 85251

CPSIA information can be obtained
at www.ICGtesting.com
Printed in the USA
LVOW12s0608160817
545221LV00001B/76/P